CHARLES BEADLE was a world traveler who was born at sea in 1881. When he was eighteen years old he expatriated from England and spent a dozen years exploring South Africa, Rhodesia, Zambia, Uganda, the Congo, Mozambique, Borneo, and Morocco. In his mid-twenties he organized an expedition to Fez and traveled there disguised as a dancing girl to interview the sultan of Morocco. In the 1910s he lived in Montmartre, where he befriended his neighbor Beatrice Hastings, the mistress of Modigliani and translator of Max Jacob. Modigliani later portrayed Beadle in a drawing titled *Le Pèlerin* ("The Pilgrim"), which may have been a reference to Beadle's first banned book, *A Passionate Pilgrimage*. During World War I he traveled to the United States, where he published stories in *Adventure* and in the *International*, a cultural journal edited by Aleister Crowley. He returned to the City of Light in the fall of 1919, where he lived throughout most of the 1920s, eventually moving to the French Riviera.

In 1938 Jack Kahane's Obelisk Press published Beadle's last novel, *Dark Refuge*: an unrecognized modern masterpiece that quickly fell into obscurity. It contains thinly disguised portraits of Modigliani, Max Jacob, Beatrice Hastings, Léopold Zborowski, and various other figures who haunted the Parisian demimonde of this period. Beadle's brazen portrayal of drug fueled pansexual orgies prevented the chronicle from being distributed in the Anglo-Saxon world despite its literary merit and lyrical beauty.

In 1941 Faber and Faber published *Artist Quarter*, a nonfiction work pseudonymously coauthored by Beadle with Douglas Goldring, which is still considered to be the urtext of Modigliani biography.

Although the time and place of his death remained a mystery until 2025, we now know that Beadle spent his final years in Nice, where he died on 27 January 1957.

ROB COUTEAU is a Brooklyn-born author and visual artist. His publications have been praised in *Evergreen Review*, *Publishers Weekly*, *New Art Examiner*, *Midwest Book Review*, and *Witty Partition*. In 1985 he won the North American Essay Award, sponsored by the American Humanist Association. His work has been cited in books such as *Ghetto Images in Twentieth-Century American Literature* by Tyrone Simpson, *Gabriel Garcia Marquez's 'Love in the Time of Cholera'* by Thomas Fahy, *Conversations with Ray Bradbury* edited by Steven Aggelis, and David Cohen's *Forgotten Millions*, a book about the homeless. His interviews include conversations with Pulitzer Prize-winning author Justin Kaplan, *Last Exit to Brooklyn* novelist Hubert Selby, Simon & Schuster editor Michael Korda, LSD discoverer Albert Hofmann, Picasso's model and muse Sylvette David, sci-fi author Ray Bradbury, film star and bibliophile Neil Pearson, and historian Philip Willan, author *Puppetmasters: The Political Use of Terrorism in Italy*. Couteau has appeared as a guest on Bob Barrett's *The Best of Our Knowledge* (WAMC), Len Osanic's *Black Op Radio*, and on Monocle 24 in Europe. In 2023 he published *Intimate Souvenirs*, a memoir featuring an Introduction by Robert Roper, author of *Nabokov in America: On the Road to Lolita* and *Now the Drum of War: Walt Whitman and His Brothers in the Civil War*. Since 2020 he has devoted himself to republishing annotated texts of important but forgotten authors such as Stanley Marks, Charles Beadle, and Francis Carco.

JOHN LOCKE has been fascinated by the pulp magazine era and its fiction, particularly in the 1920s and 1930s, for many decades. In the 1990s he started collecting information on the era, which led to writing historical treatments about the publishers, editors, and most of all the authors. Many of his findings have been published in his Off-Trail Publications books. Charles Beadle featured in two collections of Africa adventure fiction (*The City of Baal*, 2007; *The Land of Ophir*, 2012). In 2018, Locke jumped up to book-length histories with *The Thing's Incredible! The Secret Origins of Weird Tales*. He's currently completing a book about writers behaving badly in the 1920s.

A Whiteman's Burden

Charles Beadle

Introduction by John Locke

Edited with Annotations and
an Afterword by Rob Couteau

DOMINANTSTAR

Contents

Portrait of Charles Beadle, courtesy of Beadle's great-niece Patricia and her daughter Liz. An inscription on the back identifies it as a Christmas gift from "your loving son." Circa 1899.

Gulfs of Misunderstanding in *A Whiteman's Burden*: An Introduction by John Locke

Well, let's tackle the biggest issue first. Why is "whiteman" in Charles Beadle's 1912 novel one word? Kipling's famous poem, "The White Man's Burden," employs the canonical form of two. However, in that era, "whiteman," "blackman," and even "redman," were standard racial descriptors. Whether Beadle intended to invoke something more than the vernacular remains an open question.

Of course, the bigger questions are what Kipling meant by "white man's burden" and, particularly, what did Beadle intend in appropriating the phrase?

The poem, published in 1899, during the Spanish-American War, which won the United States its first overseas territory, the Philippines, presents the European colonial tradition as an altruistic enterprise, which the United States should emulate. The "white man's" superior civilization should be imparted to colonized peoples to elevate them above their unenlightened state. The "burden" was both the duty to follow this philosophy and the cost of doing so. In one couplet, Kipling exhorts colonialists to "bid the sickness cease."

Beadle's novel, as Rob Couteau notes, appears to take place circa 1904-06, the approximate time when Beadle visited Uganda and the Congo, and the time when the sleeping sickness was taking its dreadful toll on the people of the region, a major theme of the novel. In the story, the sickness has devastated native Africans but is now working its way through the colonial population, previously considered near-immune. "Bidding the sickness cease," that is, the duty portion of the burden, would become the main theme of Beadle's 1923 novel *The Lost Cure*, also set amidst the crisis, whereas *A Whiteman's Burden* details the cost.

My first reaction to Beadle's Africa adventure stories—published in American fiction magazines like *Adventure*, beginning in 1918—was that he scored high marks in authentic atmosphere and intriguing plots, despite a hastiness of style. The source of many of his plots was the strange relations between the European colonialists and the native Africans. A gulf of misunderstanding resided uncomfortably between the two parties, making their relations strained and unpredictable.

In my analysis, this condition was a product of geography and history. Europeans and sub-Saharan Africans had evolved in isolation from one another for thousands of years. European mariners, believing the Sahara went on forever, were slow to venture far enough south to discover the lush land beyond, whereas Africans struggled with survival on the planet's largest equatorial land mass, an environment made barely hospitable due to heat, farming challenges, wildlife, and especially insects. When at last, in the late fifteenth century, mariners traveled below the Sahara, two alien cultures came into contact. Slowly but surely, to bridge the difference, the "white man's burden" took root in Africa.

Still, by Beadle's time, the white man's achievements in "civilizing" the continent were limited. Europeans had infiltrated, even plundered, Africa, but only Europeanized Africans in limited degrees. In Beadle's adventure tales, conflicts across the gulf of misunderstanding are accentuated—in that genre, it makes for more exciting stories. In *A Whiteman's Burden*, a literary work, a more nuanced view emerges. The alien cultures are indeed mingling. For instance, some Africans have been persuaded to substitute Christianity for their own tribal superstitions. Biologically, relations across the racial divide create "mulattos," i.e., mixed-race offspring, a critical theme. Overall, European-administered multiethnic societies have taken shape.

Indeed, the examination of gulfs, diverse points of view, mingling, and the results thereof, are the predominant theme of the novel. Europeans discuss African behavior among themselves, struggling to understand it; and Africans seek to explain the sleeping sickness through the actions of Europeans, highlighted by the affair of Yama Yama, Matalisi, and Samwili, who vow revenge.

Another gulf, a common theme in much literature, exists between men and women. The novel measures this gulf through its two couples. Fedden, the British administrator, exemplifies the "white man's burden"; he's dedicated to duty. Whereas his wife Maude wakes up to find herself in a hostile environment with a husband she doesn't love or understand, and who doesn't understand her. It seems their only salvation is in separation. Whereas Fedden is an institutionalist, carrying the flag of empire, his antagonist Burke is a freelancer, living off the bounty of the colonized lands. He and his mulatto paramour Sula, express the burden, paradoxically, through the taboo crossing of racial lines. Civilizing means sharing philosophies, not genes.

Burke is probably another refraction of Beadle himself. In his most autobiographical novel, *A Passionate Pilgrimage* (1915, reprinted by Dominantstar), the events of the story track Beadle's own experience. He left England for South Africa at the turn of the century, then ventured north from there; the protagonist of *A Passionate Pilgrimage* does likewise. More precisely, this protagonist, Jim, fled to South Africa in response to a romantic failure in England. In parallel, Burke, in *A Whiteman's Burden*, had come from South Africa six months earlier, where he was another refugee from romance in England, a fiancée who had reneged. Burke is also an iconoclast who "cared for no man's opinion and little for his own," as we imagine Beadle the artist, who favors literature above empire, to have been. We've tracked Beadle's many travels; as to whether a bad romance exiled him to Africa, that possibility has yet to be confirmed.

There remains one significant gulf depicted in the novel, one inherent to the fiction of Africa, whether literary or genre: namely, and most forcefully, the separation between Man and Nature. In Europe, civilization removed Man from Nature, protecting him in homes and castles. In Africa, the European finds scant escape. The heat, the mosquitoes, the rain, are omnipresent. Beadle emphasizes the conflict by setting the plot into motion at the start of the rainy season. Indeed, the second half of the narrative is drenched with rainfall. We get a sense of civilization disintegrating before the relentless onslaught of the elements, as if humankind is being reclaimed.

Nature, oblivious to points of view, is neither an identity nor an understanding. Or is it? Beadle finds a way to express nature's otherness of perspective through the thoughts of Kichui, Sula's pet leopard, as he's unleashed into the bungalow. (Rob Couteau quotes this passage at length in his afterword.)

On the other side of the divide, Man contemplates the mysteries of the sleeping sickness through its manifold elements: where does it come from? how does it spread? who is immune? how can it be treated? (*The Lost Cure* addresses the ultimate question of eradication.) At the time of *A Whiteman's Burden*, some of these questions have been answered, steps made across the gulf. They know the sickness is spread by the tsetse fly. Through a microscope, they can see the parasite in a blood sample. It has become painfully obvious—like the relentlessness of the rain—that no one is immune. Their best treatment, arsenic, is, alas, just a slower form of poisoning.

To distill the tapestry of their lives into literary form, to dramatize the matrix of gulfs dividing them, Beadle lets the rain confine his characters to their bungalows where they're forced to experience each other's maladies and misunderstandings while contemplating their inexorable return to earth.

Fever of the heart and brain;
Sorrow, pestilence, and pain,
Moans of anguish, maniac laughter,
All the evils that hereafter
Shall afflict and vex mankind:
All into the air have risen
From the chambers of their prison;
Only Hope remains behind.
   – Longfellow, "The Masque of Pandora."

DEDICATED TO COLONEL SIR DAVID BRUCE,* C.B., F.R.S.
AND TO
ALL THOSE WHO HAVE WORKED AND
SUFFERED IN THE LAND
OF THE TSETSE

---

* Editor's note: In 1903, the causative parasite of the African sleeping sickness (Trypanosoma brucei) and vector (the tsetse fly, or Glossina morsitans) were identified by the Scottish microbiologist Major-General Sir David Bruce (1855 – 1931).

A WHITEMAN'S BURDEN

CHAPTER I

Dawn. In the east the stars fainted into the pale rose flush heralding the approach of day.

From the deck of the launch *Mackinnon* the denser shadows of the sheltering islands grew slowly to delicate tracery of treetops against the sky. The perky little funnel sticking up through the center of the awning, which ran fore and aft, poured forth a stream of smoke; at the base the newly awakened furnace, fed by a lusty native stoker, glowed ruddy in the breaking gloom. The diminutive poop was converted into a sleeping apartment by canvas walls, wherein shrouded figures were stretched in sleep, some in luxury upon camp beds, others upon the hard deck: forward under the open awning were the dark forms of natives in all postures of sleep, on native mats upon the deck, and upon piles of assorted luggage.

On the break of the poop stood a thickset khaki-clad figure in incongruous Wellington boots, a pair of small twinkling eyes peering out from under grey-touched shaggy eyebrows across the oily surface of the lake. Pulling meditatively at a small moustache the man popped his weather-burned face clear of the awning to glance out at the sky, grunted with satisfaction and spoke in a sharp undertone to the stoker; then pulling over the starting lever he took charge of the steering wheel as the little engines sighed and spluttered. The *Mackinnon*, awakened and throbbing with fresh life, crept out of the shelter of the islands into the open water. One of the sleepers, stirred by the first revolution of the screw, sat up in his blankets and looked about him. His action awoke another man, who inquired:

"Whatsh matter?"

"Underway again."

"Ugh!" grunted the other, and turning over upon the hard bed curled up again.

Fedden, discarding his blankets and stretching lazily, stood up in pajamas and stepped over his neighbors towards the taffrail.

"Morning, Harvey!" he said.

"Good morning, Fedden! You're up early, eh?" returned the helmsman, revealing smoke-stained stumps of teeth in a genial smile.

"Yes, that bed's too hard," replied Fedden gravely, brushing up his drooping yellow moustaches.

The other man laughed.

"Oh!" said he, "you've had too much comfort at home I can see, eh? Always spoils you fellows; that's why I never go home!

"The comers of Fedden's mouth tightened by way of a smile at this amiable fiction, for Harvey, a Maltese of twenty years' continuous residence in Uganda, loved to pose as a son of the old country.

"Yes," replied Fedden. "D'you know, I'm really glad to be back, particularly to see the sun again. I almost forgot what it was like over in London."

"Ha! Ha! Ha!" roared Harvey, who appreciated this as an excellent joke. "You are funny, eh?" he added, blinking his small eyes. "How's the wife? How does she like it, eh?"

"Oh, well enough, thanks. Of course, highly delighted at present. Thinks it heaven on earth, but – well, I don't know – I hear that Mrs. Britten has gone home?"

"Yes, couldn't stand it; but then – well" – slowly – " she was Mrs. Britten, eh?" shrugging his shoulders as if in explanation.

It was now broad daylight and the golden flush had stormed half the arc of the heavens. Fedden glanced astern. A thickly wooded islet seemed to burst into flames as the sun leapt above the treetops. The southern horizon was a dead level of water and sky, save to the southwest, where a small cluster of palm tops appeared to be suspended in vapor above the water level; to the north a wooded archipelago, new points, bays and channels were flying by in succession. Trees seemed to be wading out into the lake; some with all but their tops submerged holding up a despairing hand as if for succor. The wash of the launch rippled astern among the dense reeds and roots, rising and falling in gentle sucking sighs.

Forward of the funnel the deck was soon alive with dusky forms; the women busy round a lighted brazier, cooking food, the men chatting and basking in the warm rays of the morning sun. Midway between the native quarters and the poop a Goanese and his swarthy wife squatted upon a pile of blankets, illustrating the niceties of the color scale.

On the poop the whites were in the throes of a scanty toilet. Black servants supplied each in turn with a bucket of water, soap, and a towel. The water was renewed by the simple process of dipping the bucket over the side. Soon the canvas walls were rolled up, the blankets bundled away, and a camp table set up. The sliding lid of the companion over the tiny cabin was drawn back to allow the ladies of the party to emerge, having performed a very unsatisfactory toilet with the aid of a cracked mirror hung beneath the tiny porthole. Everything on board was diminutive and gave the sensation of living in the land of the Lilliputians.

A blue linen sunbonnet over a wealth of bright auburn hair framing a piquant freckled face appeared above the deck level. The owner paused to gaze entranced at the flying dream islands.

Fedden came forward to assist his wife.

"Good morning, dear," he said, taking her hand. "Come along, let Miss Griller come up."

"Oh, I'm so sorry," exclaimed Maude, hastening to comply. "Oh, but it is lovely," she added, pausing again to watch a new treasure.

"Yes, dear," assented Fedden unenthusiastically.

Miss Griller, a sallow-faced woman of thirty, with her straw hair drawn back tightly into a workmanlike sunbonnet, was a missionary returning to her work from the coast, where she had escorted a sick colleague. She was a serious-minded resident, missing the beauty of extravagant nature, seeing but the horrors of disease and the blackness of the heathen's mind.

Soon the European party were assembled at a breakfast of broiled lake fish. Beside Fedden and his wife sat three Roman Catholic priests. Two – one Belgian and one Frenchman – were White Fathers of the French Roman Catholic Mission, dark faced and thin; the third, a rubicund Father of the Mill Hill Roman Catholic Mission, noted for joviality and marvelous for his abounding health. Next to them sat Miss Griller and a knight of the rueful countenance in the shape of an ordained member of the Church Missionary Society.[1] Then in sharp contrast was the whimsical face of an adventurous young man who had drifted into Uganda to seek what fortune he might. He was in animated conversation with a Danish lay worker of the

---

[1] In Beadle's tale, the historically competing Catholic and Protestant missionaries are represented by Father Anthony, a jovial Roman Catholic "White Father," and his dour-faced Anglican rival, Reverend Blackber. "The acceleration of both Protestant and Catholic missionizing in the late 1880s meant that many on the Lake Victoria littoral lived within a day's journey of a Christian mission or community of converts. Two groups – the Catholic Society of the Missionaries of Africa (White Fathers) and the Anglican Church Missionary Society (CMS) – were of particular relevance to the Sseses. [The Ssese Islands archipelago in Lake Nalubaale, Uganda.] Amid the religious and civil wars of the late 1880s and early 1890s, the White Fathers founded missions first at Bugoma, on the westernmost point of Bugala Island near the Buddu shore, and then at Bumangi in the island's center. The Sseses, like most of Buganda, were a contested field of evangelization, and after years of religious unrest and occasional confrontation, British authorities intervened to 'divide' the islands into Protestant and Catholic spheres in 1891, much to the chagrin of the White Fathers." Mari Kathryn Webel, *The Politics of Disease Control: Sleeping Sickness in Eastern Africa, 1890-1920* (Athens, Ohio: Ohio University Press, 2019), p. 50.

English Mission, who with lugubrious accuracy doled out local information. Another young face, that of a collector returning after furlough, with Harvey, the genial collector, magistrate, and navigator, completed the party.

The White Fathers confined their remarks to each other. Fedden talked shop to Harvey and his colleague. Maude chatted gaily to the rubicund Father, interrupted by intervals of flirtation with the adventurer young man, who had evoked a greater torrent of information from his neighbor than he could digest.

Maude was enjoying herself hugely. After a rather hurried marriage, for which her husband had been compelled to request a month's extra leave, she had been hurled out of the comparative monotony of English life into a seething maelstrom of moving life and scenes. It was all very wonderful, beautiful, and fascinating. Her husband was very reserved and undemonstrative, but that had been of little consequence in the thousand and one novelties that had filled her life. As yet she had not had time to form a firm opinion of him. She did not imagine that she was in love with him; in fact, she had long ago dismissed the idea of love as puerile sentimentality. Everything had been a whirl of sightseeing and pleasure. There had been one or two shocks, but of such a trivial nature that they barely rippled the serene surface of her pleasure. For instance, when at a station on the Uganda railway two huge Masai bucks, clad in earrings, bangles, and yellow ochre, staring at her in genial curiosity, had laughed and playfully made a movement as if to catch her. She had screamed and clung to her husband who, smiling grimly, had cursed them in their own tongue.

With the mounting of the sun the morning breeze had sprung up, and now white caps chasing each other's tails sported on the surface of the lake, making the launch wriggle and roll to the discomfort of her human freight. The islands to the north had given place to picturesque tongues of the wooded mainland, revealing in the depths of their mouths masses of dense reeds and swamp. Now and again the undulating tops of a banana plantation could be seen in a break of the forest.

Maude, considerably sobered by the untoward motion, was lounging in a chair, chatting spasmodically to the genial Harvey.

"When shall we arrive?" inquired Maude, for the third or fourth time.

"'Bout half an hour," returned Harvey, pointing. "There's Entebbe just beyond the next point, eh."

"Have you been long out here?" queried Maude.

"Long time," assented Harvey.

"Did you know my father?" pursued Maude. "He was out here, you know – died here or in the Congo."

"Your father, eh?" said Harvey. "What name, eh?"

"Veddes."

"Veddes, eh? Oh yes, I knew him well, said Harvey, smiling. "He was a great friend of Mwanga, eh?"

"Who was Mwanga?"

"Mwanga, eh? Mwanga was the late king. We sent him away and put his young son on the throne, eh?"[2]

"Mr. Harvey," said Maude, after a pause, leaning over towards him, "did you know my father – well?"

"Your father, eh? Yes, I saw – met him – several times. Very good man your father, eh?"

"But, Mr. Harvey, tell me, do you know how and where he died?"

Harvey appeared uncomfortable.

"Died, eh?" he said at length. "Oh – just died – you know – up country."

"Yes, but where and how?" insisted Maude.

____

[2] Mwanga II of Buganda was deposed *in absentia* on 9 August 1897.

Harvey cleared his throat and scratched his moustache uneasily.

"Well, Mrs. Fedden, you know, he died – he was killed, eh?"

"Yes, where?"

"Up on the Congo border, eh?"

"And how?"

Harvey glanced over at Fedden as if searching for help.

"By savages, ma'am; killed by savages, eh?"

"You are quite sure?" persisted Maude suspiciously. "Mind, I shall find out if – some day –"

"Yes, ma'am, of course, Mrs. Fedden. There's the Murdock Channel to Jinja," he added, pointing a stumpy brown finger towards a village on a small hilltop nestling like a brown jewel in a setting of banana fronds.

"What a perfectly lovely spot," exclaimed Maude. "It looks so cool and comfy: and what a lovely view over the lake!"

"Yes, very lovely, eh?" assented Harvey.

"But I can't see any people there," added Maude, in a disappointed tone. "Nor any cows and things."

"No, eh?" returned Harvey. "You see we've made them all, or nearly all, shift inland, eh?"

"Why?"

"Sleeping sickness."

"Oh!" exclaimed Maude, sitting up. "But – but does it come out here? I mean can anybody get it on the boat?"

"No: the fly hangs around the lake shores – over there – all around the swamp and jungle and on the islands, eh?"

"Are you sure? Do many die?"

"Sure, eh? Yes, quite sure. Yes, a good many die, eh? Over there" – pointing to the south – "are the Sesse Islands – look, you can just see the tops of the trees on the horizon, eh? One time there were a hundred thousand people there; now there are not ten thousand – eh?"

"O-oh!" exclaimed Maude nervously, paling slightly. "But," she added, after a pause, "it only attacks natives, doesn't it? I mean, white people never get it?"

"Never get it, eh?" replied Harvey, his small eyes twinkling. "Yes, white people can get it, eh? Two missionaries and one of our fellows died of it."

Maude's lips trembled for a moment; she got up with a nervous movement and went to her husband.

"Herbert!" she exclaimed, clinging to his arm, "you never told me!"

"Told you what, dear?" he asked.

"Why, Mr. Harvey has been telling me about the sleeping sickness – and and" – piteously – "I thought everything was *so* lovely!"

"Clumsy fool!"muttered Fedden under his breath, and aloud: "There's no need to be alarmed, Maude. I told you of it long ago."

"Yes, yes, but I didn't imagine it was like this," she explained vaguely.

"Like what, dear?"

"Like this – all over the place – over there," pointing a tragic finger. "And I didn't know white people could get it. Oh, Herbert!"

"Harvey's a fool – you mustn't be frightened, dear. There's only been about two cases of whites known."

"Mr. Harvey said three."

"Well, three at the most. Why, Harvey's lived here for twenty years and I've been here ten, and we haven't got it. Look at all the whites in Entebbe and the missionaries all over the country, they don't get it. Only the niggers are likely to get it who live down in the swamps."

"Ye-es, but – but if the fly bites you – you are dead, aren't you?"

"Oh, dear no. You see, Maude, the fly carries the germ from one person to another. A hundred flies may bite you, but if they haven't bitten an infected person within a certain number of days you do not get infected. The doctors have discovered that it is only about two percent – if that – who carry the germ."

"But suppose the fiftieth one, or whatever it is, bites me?"

"But it won't, dearest. There's hardly any chance of a fly biting you at all. I'm not going to let you run about in the swamps catching butterflies. Come now, dear, be brave, as you said you would. Go and have a chat with Miss Griller."

"But Mr. Harvey said –"

"Harvey!" exclaimed Fedden. "Come here for a moment! Look here, you've been frightening my wife about the sleeping sickness. My dear" – to Maude – "Harvey has his wife and sister-in-law here; isn't that so, Harvey?"

Harvey grinned amiably, apparently considering it all an excellent joke.

"I didn't know you were married," exclaimed Maude.

"Yes," assented Harvey. "My wife is in Entebbe – for years, eh? and my sister-in-law – and all in very good health, eh?"

"I am glad," said Maude, reassured. "But I was frightened. You see, Herbert," she continued, "I forgot all about – what you told me, and it does seem horrible. All this lovely country and birds and things, yet underneath – ugh!"

Twenty minutes afterwards they were abreast of the last point, and within a half mile of Entebbe. From the deck of the steamer the old capital of Uganda appeared as if conjured up by the wand of an artistic fairy. The diminutive peninsula ended in a grass-crowned hump, on the slopes of which the town was built. The red-tiled roofs of bungalows were tiny splashes of bright color in the brilliant sun amid the cool dark greens and shadows of the tropical foliage. At the foot a small wooden jetty crept timidly out of the swamp grass into deeper water; to the left the broad expanse of lake ended in the mystery of the heavy forest of the mainland; on the right the cultivated order of the experimental botanical gardens set below Government House merged into the grandeur of the primeval forest, broken by the brown grass roofs and homely smoke of a Baganda village, the whole fading into the soft tints of swamp and jungle at the neck of the peninsula.

As Fedden and his wife watched the white-clad Fathers and officials waiting on the jetty amid a crowd of natives she suddenly said:

"But, Herbert, supposing you were to get it?"

"I won't," said he simply, and turned away to give some orders to his servants.

CHAPTER II

On the slope of a rugged spur on the top of the Congo watershed two tents were pitched at the end of a line of rude grass huts forming the rough street of a native village, and next to the chief's house, a square hut, larger than the rest and boasting of mud walls, in front of which stood two papaya trees desolate and forlorn. The tall, rank grass, almost the thickness of young bamboo, rioted below the village down the precipitous slope; above, it dwindled into barren crags upon the crest. Several native footpaths ran out to crudely cultivated land down the valley and to other villages.

In a bare space of ground, some dozen yards wide, between the two lines of huts, were smoking embers of green wood, half a dozen small fowls, pecking in a desultory fashion among smoke-blackened calabashes, three emaciated goats and an odd mongrel dog or two. In the doorway of the huts, mere holes in the grass sides, lounged native women clad in ballet skirts of rush grass, wearing quantities of heavy iron bangles on their limbs, like metal leggings from knee to ankle, elbow to wrist. Around their necks were iron triangles, lips and tongue decorated with copper rings, the latter jingling musically and twinkling in the mouth as they chattered. Some, with hideously pendulous bosoms, were the mothers of the yellow infants crowing and sprawling about; others, pear-breasted and supple-limbed, maidens.

At a distance of a few feet from each and every hut was a similar diminutive structure some eighteen inches high. These were for the accommodation of the Evil Spirit, on the principle that if suitable shelter were not provided the devil would perforce be encouraged to entertain himself at the expense of the inmates, with disastrous consequences. Their primitive minds, with considerable logic, did not consider it necessary to propitiate the good spirit on the ground that immediately it ceased to be good it became evil and was therefore provided for under that category.

In one doorway sat a wizened man whittling a stock of fresh arrows from bamboo grass stems. Mighty squalls of anguish came from behind another hut, where a mother was engaged in digging out the jiggers from the sole of the foot of an infant with the blunt point of a soft metal native knife, whilst another woman, possibly the aunt, held the child still by the simple process of sitting upon him.

These small insects, which burrow into the tender part of the foot or under the nails, where they lay and hatch their eggs, had, through neglect, riddled the child's feet; and so the primitive mother industriously dug away for her son's good, finishing off the operation by brushing the shrinking, swollen foot with a rough corn cob.

At the back of the Europeans' camp, amid the grass, rose the curling smoke of the porter's fires, who were housed in temporary huts formed by hacking a clear circle of three or four feet, tying together the tops of the surrounding eight-foot grass and piling the waste upon this rough framework: inside three or four men curled up together like so many rabbits for mutual warmth. Immediately behind the tents a native, sumptuously clad in a cast-off suit of khaki, sprawled on his belly, watching another man busy over a stewpot.

In the front of the larger tent, lounging in a collapsible canvas armchair, was a dark-hued young girl, her long, wavy black hair far below her shoulders. A deep-red chequered cloth wound round her waist fell just below her knees, and a roughly sewn, short-sleeved calico jacket enveloped shapely shoulders, yielding a suggestive outline or firm bosom. At her feet, stretched out like a lazy cat, was a half-grown leopard cub asleep.

From her chair at the entrance to the dingy tent she could have viewed the magnificent effect of a sunset, the gleaming rays setting fire to the rugged hills in the northeast and tinting the somber, shadowy mists of the ocean of the Ituri forest, in the depression to the southeast, with crimson and gold. But the long-lashed eyes of Sula were fixed intently upon the valley immediately below.

There came one of those strange pauses when all nature seems to hush in awe of the majesty of the dying sun. Babies ceased squalling; dogs, goats, fowls, and men were gripped in the brooding silence of vast solitudes. The smoke from the village curled up noiselessly, no sound of bird nor beast. A flight of parrots appeared like silent specters against the sunset. Then the noise of the old man's knife broke out with alarming distinctness: the laugh of one of the porters seemed like the crash of an orchestra.

Presently the girl's keen eyesight, inherited from her native forebears, detected the top of a slouch hat peep for a moment in the sea of grass below. She called a warning to the man by the fire to hasten, and rising, disappeared within the tent. The leopard cub, aroused by her movement, lifted his head and blinked lazily, seeming to consider for a moment; then, rising to his feet in that effortless manner of wild creatures, shambled into the tent after the girl.

At length the sound of excited chatter brought a reassuring sense, and a tall, sunburned man emerged from the wall of grass with the effect of one suddenly popping through a blank wall. He swung towards the camp, followed by his native gun bearer and a line of jabbering villagers, armed with spears, bows, and arrows.

His shirt was open at the neck in a V-shape, revealing fiery red neck and chest; his trousers, encased in leggings, were covered in green slime and hundreds of grass spearheads; the large blue eyes twinkled in a sweat-grimed face as he strode towards the tent, reeking of abounding vitality as he shouted:

"Heh! Wangi-i! whiskey soda. Bath – Upesi! – Hello! tiddley winks!" he added as the tent flaps opened and Sula darted out.

He caught her by the waist with two hands and lifted her breast-high, laughing.

"Thought I was lost, eh, Sula?" he said, setting her down. "Had to spend a night in a damned tree, that's all. Got two fine bulls though."

"Sula glad!" exclaimed she, hanging on to his bare forearm. "Sula glad; Sula tort Lolly no come back. Sula glad!"

Laurie Burke sprawled back in the chair, giving the leopard cub who had followed her a terrific smack in the ribs. The cub, nearly knocked off its balance, came playfully charging at him.

"Hey! ye devil you," he exclaimed, seizing it deftly by the throat and flinging it backwards.

"Hey, Wangii!" shouted Sula, "viskey soda – upesi!" (quick). She turned to a group of Bambiba bearing four fine elephant tusks, and rapidly gave them instructions in a patois of dialects. As she stood issuing orders and commanding with a quaint imperiousness, her lithe, spare figure was outlined against the golden aura of the sunset.

Laurie lounged in the chair with a glass of whiskey in one hand whilst he did battle with the cub with the other, laughing boisterously.

"Eh, Sula! "he called out as he paused to watch her amusedly, "ye're a devil, Sula!"

"Sula glad – Sula glad!" she flung at him between a lengthy harangue at the stupidity of the natives in not immediately understanding her.

At length Sula, having secured the trunk and feet for their own delectation, made the grinning, shouting Bambiba deliver up a fair portion of the huge slabs of elephant meat to the porters. She dismissed the noisy horde to their village and came back to Laurie as he sat pretending to strangle the leopard cub amidst growls and whimpers of delight.

As she advanced he looked up at her with genial admiration in his eyes. Her skin-sandaled feet padding the earth and the lithe swing of her hips and supple body suggested a kinship to her playmate, the leopard cub. She half crouched for a moment before him, with eyes laughing and gleaming, snowy teeth; then, with a feline toss of her head, the mass of black hair rippling, she voiced a joyous "Yo-ow!"

Laurie laughed. Hurriedly putting down the glass he let go the cub in time to catch her as she leapt on to his knees. She bent down, grabbing him fiercely by the hair, and bit his ear, shaking her head and growling liquidly like a terrier worrying a bone. The next moment, with an agile leap to the ground, she disappeared within the tent, trilling with laughter.

"Ye're a devil, Sula," shouted Laurie after her, smiling as he smacked the quarters of the cub slinking after its mistress.

"Sula glad!" came her voice from within, followed by another ripple of laughter.

"Some women and cubs," said Laurie, nodding at his glass of whiskey, alternately caressing a torn finger and his smarting ear, "measure their love by the depth of their bite!"

Finishing off the whiskey at a gulp he rose, and stretched brawny arms in the pale rose of the short twilight, laughing a deep chested, chuckling laugh, which he seemed to roll over and over again, loath to leave it for the sheer joy of the thing.

He made for the tent in two strides as a mocking chuckle taunted him. But Sula had slipped out through the rear of the tent, followed by the spotted shadow.

The faint pallor died out in the east and the stars began to twinkle. The lights of the line of village fires grew ruddy, thick curling smoke of the greenwood enveloping and revealing the silhouette figures of the villagers preparing to dance a celebration or the feast of elephant meat. The distant mass of hills, clear-cut against the perfect night, emphasized the gloomy mystery of the distant forest depths. Upon a range of hills to the south a grass fire was burning; the wavy lines of flame presented the appearance of some fiery army advancing in serried ranks, one above the other, to the storming of the stars. Now and again the harsh cry of some night bird, the distant yowl of wild beast or the sharp yap of jackals broke above the hum of native voices and the insistent chorus of insect life amid the grass.

From within the tent came the sound of a mighty splashing, grunting and hissing as of a groom: outside Sula sat curled in a chair, dreaming with half-lidded eyes, her clear, chiseled profile silhouetted against a candle lantern upon the small camp table; the cub sprawled at her feet.

As Sula smiled dreamily the cub pricked up his ears at the sound of bustle and a torrent of swear words – "damned stud" being the only articulate ones – issuing from the tent behind them. A hard, breathing, choking sound, a few more stifled oaths, then a boisterous laugh, and:

"Eh, Sula! chakula tayari?" (dinner ready?)

Sula sat up in her chair and sharply admonished the cook, a dim form hovering over the smoky fire, to hurry.

In a few moments Laurie emerged from the tent, a stalwart figure in conventional evening dress and opera hat, looking as if he had been caught up by a whimsical jinni from the steps of a club in Pall Mall and dumped down here. A close inspection might have revealed the fact that the collar was somewhat soiled and the shirtfront slightly spotted, but laundries were as yet rather scarce in this part of the world. He stood in the circle of candlelight engaged in rolling a cigarette, with tobacco dust culled from the corners of his dinner jacket pocket, in a piece of torn newspaper. Sula sat up purring with delight; the cub sniffed doubtfully and growled in his throat. The clumsy cigarette rolled, Laurie lit it with extravagant sighs of satisfaction, and shooting his cuffs, struck an attitude.

"Damme, Sula!" he exclaimed, blowing smoke and holding the cigarette in a mincing, elegant fashion; "deuce of a dawg, damme, what?"

Sula gurgled with laughter and walked slowly round him in misguided admiration for these atrocities of civilization. This she did as a sort of ritual on every occasion upon which he appeared in this moribund glory, usually twice a month, partly "for fun" and partly for the serious reason that it helped to prevent one slacking off in the matter of cleanliness and dress so common to lonely exiles. He was her god and these the sacramental vestments.

"Lord! what this brings up," he exclaimed. "Here, cabby! Come along, Sula" – catching her by the arm – "jump in; we'll dine at Prince's tonight!"

Sula's face had grown dark with anger and envy as he stopped to roar with laughter. She resented the mention of places and memories she could not know.

"Come, little woman," he said, smiling and stroking her hair; but she pushed his hand away petulantly, jerking back her disheveled locks. He caught her to him and kissed her forcibly, she squealing and struggling the while.

They sat opposite each other at the camp table, an incongruous pair, eating their simple fare of boiled elephant trunk followed by sweet banana fritters from Kavalli's village over the hills. The chant and shuffle of the villagers beginning their dance mingled with the laughter and yells of the porter's camp in full debauch of meat feasting in the starlit night.

From their dinner table the forms of the savages appeared like fantastic gnomes materializing and dematerializing in the wafts of curling smoke. The monotonous, high-voiced chant of ten syllables in even tones, ending perpetually in a sudden bass grunt, seemed to have a sinister note, as if foretelling horrors of debauch to come.

For a while, after the table had been carried bodily away to the kitchen fire, Laurie sat back in his chair, smoking, with Sula curled on his knee, the cub at their feet growling and snarling enjoyment over a piece of raw flesh or bone. Such had been their custom always. Sometimes his thoughts wandered to the old country, at others debating local prospects of trade. Sula remained silent, purring to herself like a contented pussycat happy in the presence and touch of her lord. By fortunate circumstances – for Laurie and his kindred – the boundary of the Congo and Uganda was in dispute, resulting in the fact that a wide strip of territory, beginning a few miles to the east of this village, was more or less neutral ground: this narrow belt was the happy hunting ground of a few adventurous spirits who, nominally trading for ivory and rubber, actually shot their own elephants, claiming, if caught by the Belgian authorities, that they were under British jurisdiction and – vice versa. But elephant was more plentiful on the fringes of the Ituri forest, so that Laurie more often than not poached over the border, slipping back again into the neutral territory immediately he had made his bag, and passing the tusks as trade ivory. The Belgian officials at Irumu and Masindi were well aware of these little maneuvers, and sought to make an example: not perhaps so virulent as in the case of Sula's father who, having been lured into the station, was arrested after dinner, charged with gun running and hanged as high as Haman.[3]

In the present instance Laurie was in high good humor, having secured six fine long tusks, and intended striking camp upon the morrow for Toro, the first British post across the border. Twice before he had narrowly escaped being caught

---

[3] Haman, a Persian minister in the book of Esther, who is hung after plotting a foiled massacre of the Jews.

red-handed, but the danger only added zest to the game. If he were captured they would have to send him to Boma for trial; but he knew well enough that few prisoners ever survived the long overland journey through the mighty forests; such a lot of trouble and red tape was saved by the death of a prisoner – say from fever.

The monotonous chant of the dancers ceased for a moment until the high-pitched falsetto of a soloist and the crashing chorus at the end of each verse or line betokened a new stage in the dance. Laurie looked across: the men were now herded together on one side of the line of fires, the women in a bunch on the other.

"Come along, Sula," said Laurie, rising and setting her on her feet; "we'll have a look at 'em."

She shouted to a servant to bring the chairs, and together they walked towards the village, she holding and swinging his hand, *wandeling;*[4] he with opera hat at a rakish angle at the back of his head. She shivered slightly with cold, for the nights were chilly on the top of these bare hills. He noticed and called to Avunga for coats. They sat in separate chairs, she muffled up in a spare coat, Laurie with one leg crossed, his shirtfront gleaming in the ghostly firelight – like a couple of conventional stallites,[5] Sula on her way to a fancy dress ball.

The grass fire away on the distant hills had reached the summit and seemed a jagged, wavy line of flickering tongues about to devour the cold bright stars low down on the horizon. In the lazy curl of the smoke from the newly fed green fires the bucks of the village capered and leapt, throwing back their shoulders, legs well forward, stooping and shuffling, a primitive form of the cakewalk; whilst across the fires the womankind shambled and shrilled in ear-piercing chorus.

---

[4] Wandeling: A Dutch word, meaning to stroll or walk.
[5] A rarely used term referring to a spectator who occupies a theater stall.

The men were nude, save for a cat- or goat-skin flapping from the waist;. the women's dwarfed ballet skirts undulated like a Genée[6] as the fitful glow threw ruddy gleams on their bronze bodies and points of light from the jangling metal bangles.

Out of the ruck sprang a young man, frizzy haired, nearly foaming with excitement, an enormous ivory bracelet gleaming a light yellow. A series of terrific leaps in the air, yelling like a fiend the while, a forward rush and back, disappearing for a moment in the acrid smoke to emerge specter-like, and, with a running jump, he landed in the middle of a fire, scattering embers broadcast like an orthodox devil popping up from hell. Then, with a screech, he bounded on to the women's side where, like a hawk swooping on a pigeon, he seized, amid a crescendo yell from his companions, a young girl in his embrace, hugged her, dropped her, and sped back to his comrades, clearing the fire with a tremendous jump. Another man sprang forward – and so the game went on across the line of smoking fires.

On the first occasion the scene had brought to Laurie's mind a glimpse of his nursery days when he had gleefully sung in chorus with the kiddies:

> "Here we go gathering nuts and may,
> Nuts and may, nuts and may.
>
> And who shall we send to fetch her away
> On a cold and frosty morning?"

Towards nine o'clock the crest of the hill at the back of the village blackened against a growing pallor, swallowing the stars and presenting a few spear-headed grass tops, swelled out of

---

[6] A reference to Dame Adeline Genée (1878 – 1970), the celebrated Danish-British ballet dancer.

perspective, sharp against the silvery crescent of the moon peering down upon the revels of these savage children. As the lower lobe seemed to bound a few inches from the earth, like a captive balloon, a man loped past the tents bellowing, in a broken-winded voice:

"Bulamatadi! Bulamata-di!"

In an instant the screaming and shouting chorus ceased; a dozen or more took up the word in a subdued cry, and the newcomer, a wild-looking creature, with a bow and a sheath of arrows slung over his shoulder, was surrounded by a clamoring throng.

Laurie sprang to his feet with a loud oath, and strode through the crowd, scattering the excited villagers like chaff. The stranger started back with a cry of alarm upon catching sight of this strangely clad whiteman; but Sula, in a few jumbled words of patois, reassured him. Laurie tried him in Kiswahili, the only native language he knew fluently, but as the man stared open-mouthed he stood impatiently silent whilst Sula, her large eyes sparkling in the misty moonlight and her small hands flitting up and down like bats, interrogated him in her quaintly arrogant manner. A clamor of voices from the reeking mass around her brought out a fierce, declamatory order for silence. At length she turned eager eyes to Laurie:

"Dis man bla' fool," she exclaimed indignantly. "He say sumting Bulamatadi (Belgians) live there," pointing an eloquent hand down the valley to the west, and then to the south.

"Hell!" ejaculated Laurie. "Kweli (sure), Sula?"

"He say," repeated Sula, and turning to her informant bombarded him with a hurricane of fresh questions.

"Yes, he say," said Sula; "he say armies Bulamatadi – askari (native soldiers) plenty."

"Hell!" exclaimed Laurie again; "two parties, eh? From Masindi and Irumi! They mean to catch me this time!" He began to laugh his rolling chuckle and moved away towards the camp.

"Can't get out by Kavalli's," he said to Sula.

"No, no," agreed Sula energetically. "Lolly go Butiti, plenty road Butiti –"

"Good, Sula," pulling up. "The very thing. We've got about eight hours' start – for they won't move till daybreak. Come along – Avunga! Mombii! Haya! Haya!"

Sula darted ahead, calling shrilly to the headman, the cub gamboling around her under the impression that this was a new game.

CHAPTER III

Fedden, unintentionally, had committed bigamy, although he did not and would never recognize the fact. He was like many an artist – wedded to his work. Such men ought never to marry. It was as though Nature intended his type to be a human drone – but with an essential difference, physically. He took his work seriously and earnestly, administering his district with a firm hand. He did not entertain any false sentimental views of the natives, but treated them as children to be severely dealt with when naughty, and to be encouraged and helped upon occasion. Extremely reticent by temperament the long years of solitude had built an impenetrable wall between himself and everybody else. Suffering at times from loneliness he forgot that it is epicene in many phases of life and persuaded himself that a congenial wife would make him happy and wholly contented. Simple-minded and blunt he was the least qualified of men to choose a wife successfully. When the first bloom of the honeymoon was beginning to wear off he had already discovered that he did not understand her. Vaguely he had imagined that she would immediately comprehend and sympathize with all his ambitions and his work – which was the only subject which interested him – by virtue, apparently, of the fact that she was his wife.

But he had been driven back into his shell perplexed and unhappy upon discovering that she was frankly bored to death. Now he felt injured; although he tried to persuade himself that she would alter when they were alone together upon the station, and she could live in the atmosphere of his work.

Maude, on the other hand, save for the fright she had experienced, was more or less contented. Her husband was as stupid and slow as she had imagined him to be, so in that she was not disappointed: most men, save one, and he – well, the ashes of the past are the leavening coke of today.

The Feddens were staying with Harvey and his wife, a buxom, dark-haired Portuguese, who by reason of her nationality withstood the ravages of the climate in contrast to her northern sisters.

After three days in Entebbe, Maude had almost forgotten the existence of sleeping sickness in the whirl of fresh interests. It was all a delightful picnic from the moment when she had entered a rickshaw on the jetty and been pulled and pushed by three natives in smart print uniforms up the road, an avenue of gigantic trees, past sweet little bungalows covered in flowery creepers nestling in gardens of enormous roses enclosed within symmetrical hedges of bright flowers, to the Harveys' house set on the crest of the first rise overlooking the southern aspect of the lake, cool in the daily breeze. After a warm welcome from Mrs. Harvey and her sister, a charming, dark-eyed girl, a dainty lunch awaited them served by deft, soft-footed brown servants in spotless white.

"Perfectly devy!" voted Maude, smoking a cigarette in the seclusion of her quaint mosquito-curtained bed in which one felt like a caged bird. Tennis in the cool of the afternoon with dozens of young men clamoring for partnership. Some of these, Maude noticed, were sallow and bashful like her husband. Afterwards she learned that these men were from outside stations: the others, in faultless tennis clothes and immaculate starched linen by night, were headquarter officials. A bath after tennis, clean linen, and a long chair on the commodious verandah where they sat and chatted in the cool, watching the golden pageantry of the sunset lighting up the sky in gorgeous Turneresque effects and playing tinted lights of mystery on the waters of the lake, growing placid as the breeze died away.

A round of duty visits on the next day, commencing with a call upon Government House, where Her Excellency received them in a Paris gown and dispensed tea and cakes as if in a London drawing room. A fine wire netting, enclosing the wide verandah of the house built up on piles, attracted Maude's attention as they were going up the steps, at the bottom of which placed two Sikh sentries. A spasm of anxious doubt crossed her face until reassured by her husband that the wire was only a luxury to keep out the ordinary fly by day and mosquitoes by night.

Fedden, anxious to get back to his work, had intended to start for Mbale on the third day, but somewhat grudgingly he consented to stay a week, at the instance of His Excellency, on behalf of Maude.

The next few days were spent in rickshaw visits to Kampala. Kampala is the generic name for the seven hills which have constituted the native capital of Uganda from time immemorial. As each king died he was buried upon his hill. The successor took up his royal residence upon the next. Kampala hill is the site of the old fort. Then they went on to Namirembe, where the gabled thatched roof of the Protestant Cathedral, built upon the summit of the hill, is outlined against the sky with extraordinary effect. On the next hill is the stronghold of the French Roman Catholics; another holds the Mill Hill Fathers; whilst yet another farther away is the seat of the Mohammedan invasion; and almost in the center lies Mengo, the hill of the present child king, Daudi Chwa, surrounded with jealous creeds fighting for his soul – which was then in the triumphant hands of the Protestants. The story of the struggle over his father, the deposed King Mwanga, has a bloody niche to itself in the turbulent history of the country.

Maude was more interested and amused by sights and sounds than by disjointed versions of the history of the country supplied by her husband in his solemn, lecturing manner. A hillside and valley of waving fronds looked like an Atlantic billow; here and there blue smoke curling up indicated native houses hidden by these vast plantations of bananas. In the villages, with their conical huts, were giggling brown women dressed in a red-brown bark-cloth sheet wrapped round under the armpits; funny little yellow children rolled about in the ditch or the doorways, their abnormally distended tummies, wobbly big woolly heads and whites of inquisitive brown eyes giving a fantastic golliwog appearance.

On the king's hill, travelling up the broad native road, some twenty yards in width, between lines of neatly plaited rush matting fence six or eight feet high, the square thatched roofs peeping over the top, Maude met solemn-looking natives with white embroidered pillbox caps dressed in what appeared to be voluminous white nightgowns. These were subchiefs and native officials, she was told, and rocked with laughter at the quaint dignity of their demeanor. No common people, but men of weighty affairs, they seemed to be saying. A crowd of demure lads clad in white came in procession down the hill, very superior and complacent.

"Mission young men doing a sort of Church parade."

Farther along the road was a similar group of youths, one of whom wore a European coat and felt hat. As the rickshaw came abreast he politely raised his hat, revealing a mop of straight hair, and said "Good morning!" Maude, leaning forward in surprise, noticed that he had a fairer complexion than any one of his companions, and an aquiline nose.

"How strange," she remarked to her husband: "that child has quite European features!"

"Yes," he said, the corners of his mouth tightening; "he has."

"Are they all taught English?" she persisted.

"Oh no; only Johnny Vlimbi."

"Johnny! why Johnny?"

"That is his father's name, dear."

"John! John? Why, is his father Mr. – Oh!" She sat back thoughtfully. After a minute she turned to glance round at the lad, who was standing apart, smiling amiably after them.

"Do all –" she began and paused.

"Yes, dear?"

"Nothing," she finished and, glancing suspiciously at her husband, settled back in her seat to stare at a few peasants clad only in the humble loincloth, five of them wearing metal crucifixes upon their glistening brown chests. By the side of the road in the fringe of a banana plantation was a small thatched shed of rushes, in which a gowned man industriously worked a commonplace sewing machine. In another similar hut a craftsman hammered tree bark with a corrugated wooden mallet into the native bark cloth. Farther on were several more little sheds by the roadside, each a shop selling cotton gowns, meat, sugar, and native foodstuffs wrapped in fresh banana leaves. On the top of the next hill they came to the bazaar, nearly all of which was owned and run by Indians or Goanese, their sleek or blowsy proprietors squatting within ready for business.

Fedden and his wife lunched with the collector of the district, who lived in a long bungalow set in a garden gone mad; roses, convolvulus, flags, tulips, pinks, hyacinths, native flowers, lemon, papaya, and cedar trees rioted in every direction, a wild, crazy tangle of luxuriant beauty.

By the time Maude's rickshaw was being pushed up the hill into Entebbe by panting, perspiring natives, still joyous and laughing, after a five-mile run from the last relay point in the twenty-mile switchback road between eight-foot walls of long grass, she felt tired with the heat and excitement.

As they breasted the hill the thought suddenly came to her that she owed all these delights and novelties to the grave-eyed man sitting beside her; in a spasm of gratitude she turned to him and, to his embarrassment, kissed his hand, exclaiming:

"Oh, you are a dear, lovely old thing! I really do love you!"

The action offended his grave sense of the fitness of things, and the adjective "old" hurt his vanity. Any man of thirty-two does *not* like to be called old; and Fedden was apt to take things too literally.

"I am not old, dear," he protested seriously.

"Of course you're not, you silly old – I mean, darling thing, you!" she retorted laughing. "Oh!" she added, glancing at his solemn eyes, "you are too – too –"

She failed to find the right word.

"Here's the Club," he said. "I'm sure you want some tea."

He called to the "boy" between the shafts who, swerving to the side, set them down before a small bungalow devoid of garden, opening on to the road.

Whenever a dozen Britishers meet in any part of the world the first thing that occurs to them to do is to form a club. This tiny bungalow, just large enough to form a card room and a small bar, was the local embryo. Plainly and neatly furnished with cane chairs and green baize card tables, it formed a rendezvous for bridge enthusiasts over whiskey-and-sodas at night. A small bookcase in a subdued corner held the Club library, formed of a miscellaneous assortment of books contributed by the limited membership. Here Maude grimaced over stewed tea – few native cooks can be persuaded *not* to stew tea – whilst Fedden absorbed the usual peg.[7]

"Funny little place!" cooed Maude, to the silent indignation of a few outstation members present at that hour. The young bloods were busy at tennis, hockey, or cricket below the township.

Maude, feeling refreshed and cooler, decided she would walk, and strolled out into the sun. Opposite she noticed the roof of a long, barnlike bungalow behind a high hedge on the other side

---

[7] Peg (British): drink.

of the road ditch crossed by small wooden bridges. From the entrance she could see a corrugated shed containing a number of rickshaws; she wandered along the road in search of something more interesting, whilst her husband dallied in the Club, talking uninteresting shop. Just beyond the rickshaw garage her eye caught an opening in the hedge leading up the hill, on the slope of which she noticed a series of kennel-like structures upon poles, and, at the foot of one, a sad-looking monkey.

"Oh, the darling!" she exclaimed, and immediately proceeded to investigate.

On either side of the little avenue within the hedge were plain whitewashed buildings with a wide verandah around each, and beyond various native outbuildings.

As Maude approached, another member of the community poked his head out of a neighboring box and chattered excitably, but the smaller object of her curiosity evinced no emotion whatever, continuing to stare in a bored and meditative manner at the ground.

"Oh, you funny little chap!" said Maude, prodding his tail with her parasol.

The monkey took no notice, until receiving a second poke he slowly turned his head to stare stupidly in the direction of the attack, after which he resumed his meditations.

"Oh, you lazy thing!" exclaimed Maude, "you look as if you were half asleep. Cheep! cheep! Wake up, do!"

She scratched the ground in front of the monkey, who merely blinked his eyes slowly.

"Oh!" murmured Maude disgustedly, "I've never seen such a stupid thing. Hullo!" she added, glancing up at the other, whose bright eyes were peeping at her round the edge of his tiny door. "Hullo! You seem more lively!"

The monkey grimaced at her and scratched vigorously. She wandered on to the next compartment and looked inside. An extremely emaciated monkey was lying asleep upon the straw.

"Good gracious!" exclaimed Maude. "This one's *quite* asleep! What an extraordinary lot of monkeys! Hey! Hullo! Wake up!" But this one did not even blink its eyes. "Oh, how thin and ill he looks, poor dear!" she commiserated, observing the sharp shoulder blades sticking through the skin like the ridgepoles of a tent.

She started as a voice said at her elbow:

"Yes, I'm afraid he is very ill."

She turned and recognized a young doctor whom she had met at the Harveys, a tall, dark-mustached man.

"Sorry if I startled you, Mrs. Fedden," he continued. "Rather a sad sight, isn't it?"

"But I don't understand," said Maude. "They all look so sleepy!"

"Exactly," said the young doctor, smiling grimly; "they've all got sleeping sickness. This –"

"O-oh!" exclaimed Maude, involuntarily stepping a few paces away from the patient. "But do monkeys get it as well?"

"That I can't exactly say; you see, this is the experimental hospital – out here. We inoculate them with the germ."

"Oh, how cruel! And will they all die? How *wicked* of you!"

"Not at all, Mrs. Fedden. You see," he went on in self-defense, "we know so little about it that we must use every chance to discover a remedy against it. We have to experiment somehow, so we infect these brutes and try various antitoxins – remedies, you know – upon them; but we haven't discovered any cure yet, unfortunately. Arsenic is the best up to the present; but it's no good in the long run. We have a lot of rats and birds over there in different stages of the malady. This chap," indicating the sleeping one, "is in the last stage. He'll be dead in a few days or a week or two. Just sleeps away."

"Oh, don't," exclaimed Maude, shuddering. "Horrible!"

"That one capering about up there," continued the doctor heedlessly, "has only just been inoculated, so he's quite lively still; besides, he's got a lot of arsenic in him, and that bucks him up. The other fellow's about halfway lethargic, loses interest – even in nuts –"

"Oh, don't!" exclaimed Maude, stopping her ears. "It makes me feel sick."

They turned at the crunch of feet upon gravel and saw Fedden hastening up with a look of distress on his face.

"Oh, my dear," he exclaimed to Maude, "I wish you wouldn't wander about by yourself! I didn't want you to see this. It will be sure to frighten you. Evening, Mac!" he added.

"Oh, it's horrible – horrible!" exclaimed Maude, slightly pale. "I feel sick. Take me away!"

And as she went down the avenue on her husband's arm the brilliant sky seemed dark and somber.

CHAPTER IV

The villagers, having elicited all information available from their neighbor – a runaway from another village raided by the Bulamatadi – abandoned the dance; and after a short and excited dispute with their chief – a tall, pockmarked man with heavy ivory bangles – were engaged in a wild scramble to gather together their bits of household gods and their skinny goats preparatory to a night flight into the hills, the fear of the hated Bulamatadi (or more particularly of their native police, who had anything but gentle and considerate habits) overcoming the fear of evil spirits, which were supposed to invest the mountains in the night.

Around the porters' fires the men, intoxicated with meat gorging, sprawled about, those able still stuffing singed lumps of red flesh, chanting and howling; others, overcome, slept stertorously like pythons fed to repletion. Upon this scene descended Laurie and Sula like a night tornado. The headman, bloodshot of eyes and lethargic, was disturbed by a violent kick in the ribs. He sat up blinking at Laurie, nodding stupidly at the ominous word *Bulamatadi*. One man, whose faculties were more awake, leapt to his feet with a stifled yelp at the very name, and in blind fear bolted into the grass like a frightened rabbit.

Laurie took off his opera hat, folding it up as he rated the man, whose eyes followed the process in round-eyed amazement. Laurie, noticing it, laughed, and let it fly open with a click in the other's face. He seemed galvanized into life, and with a guttural cluck of horror turned to run away. Laurie caught him by the arm, shaking him about.

"Come here, you fool," he said, laughing. He proceeded to take advantage of the man's awakened senses, giving emphatic instructions whilst the other watched the bewitched hat with distrust out of the tail of his eye. By dint of a few judicious kicks, laughter, and reprimands, he aroused the meat-sodden crowd to a state of active fear of the arrival of the Bulamatadi, and leaving the headman to gather together the loads, departed to don his weather-beaten khaki.

Sula, in the meantime, had blackguarded the personal "boys" into some show of activity in tying up camp equipment into their accustomed bales. By the time that Laurie emerged the tent ropes were loosened, and a sleepy-headed gang, more fuddled than usual, through fright of the Belgians and the terrors of the night, muddled through the stages of breaking camp. The dying embers of the fires glowed dully in the light of the rising moon, which dimly revealed a deserted village, save for two old hags squatting at a hut door watching, with uncomprehending stare, the bustle of the whiteman's camp.

By midnight Laurie – still bullying and chaffing the men into a good humor – contrived to get the caravan started on the indistinct footpath running round the edge of the hill crest, and winding through the tall grass of a slight depression towards another ridge rising gloomy and mysterious in the indigo shadows. It was no small effort to get these men to face even a moonlight trip through the bush; he had half feared that either they would turn sulkily obstinate and refuse to budge, or that they would passively resist by lying perdu in the grass.

He stood with Sula on the crest watching the line of loads, visible here and there above the grass tops, winding past in snaky fashion until the last man had actually left camp.

Then on in the rear with Sula, supple and shadowy, gliding along in front of him, flashing the whites of eyes amidst the gloom of her hair as she flung a look and a remark or warned him of a hole or obstruction in the narrow path invisible in the grass; the cough or grumble of a porter, an exclamation of annoyance, above the steady shuffling patter of feet; the rhythmic breathing and the rustling whisper of the green tops brushing the bales and boxes; the flutter of wings and protesting cries of birds disturbed; a distant raucous scream of a parrot surprised by some nocturnal enemy. Once in the bottom of the depression a fierce snort, a sound of galloping hoofs and swish of grass as a startled buffalo dashed away, fortunately in an opposite direction, sent a hesitating pause and a quivering mutter of panic through the line of carriers, reassured by Laurie's voice bellowing encouragement from the rear.

On again once more. The outline of a single tree on the crest of grass upland grew blacker in silhouette against the luminous sapphire of the moonlit horizon. Presently a small square object rose dark beside the tree, followed by a spidery arm and shoulders. The object paused and suddenly disappeared, followed by others performing the same operation. At length Laurie and Sula arrived to find the caravan spread in a sprawling circle around the tree, resting. Laurie glanced at his wristwatch; they had been marching just over an hour and a half; not a bad stretch. After lighting his pipe, sitting on a bale, he arose and walked a little way to the supreme crest of the hill and stood gazing towards the east.

The country descended in a gentle slope of grass and scattered bushes; then, falling abruptly, gave way at some distance to broken bush country, declining gradually to the flat Semliki river plain, odd snaky bits of which glinted far beneath. Away to the southeast a silvery sheen glittered on the placid waters of Lake Albert; to the northeast the ragged masses of Gamballagalla, a hint of snow-capped peaks frosty and pale in the moon rays.

On the horizon between these large efforts of nature the dim outline of the Uganda plateau loomed faintly. From Laurie's position on the top of the Congo watershed in the Balegga hills the vast corridor cleft between the two countries seemed like a glimpse of a stupendous Olympian cart rut through the middle of Africa, leaving as pools after the rain the mighty chain of lakes, Albert, Albert Edward, Kivu, Tanganyika, crushing up on either side the excrescences of Gamballagalla*[8] and the Congo hills. For a while he sat in the moonlight forgetting to smoke, lost in contemplation of the colossal design of nature, drinking in the philosophy and awed worship which she implants in those who dwell in the shadow of her more titanic moods. The splendor and majesty seem to weigh upon the human soul, tending to crush out all conceit, even the idea of a personal God in the obvious sense of the insignificance of man and all his puny works. Laurie sat perfectly still, pipe half held to his mouth, apparently hypnotized by the sight, feeling, with a melancholy emotion, the feebleness and impotence of human things, the native laughter and joyousness subdued by the contemplation of the relentless solidity and vastness of space and design. The presence of the resting porters, lazily sprawling behind, were forgotten: he felt as if he were the last antlike human left crawling laboriously and painfully across material infinity.

A bang against his legs recalled him with something of a shock to find the cub sniffing at his feet; and Sula, hand across eyes, staring out across space, mutely, for need of words to interpret her thoughts, worshipping at the same shrine.

"Sula!" he called softly. As she turned towards him, smiling, her absent eyes melted to close range and he felt a shaft of mutual sympathy and understanding pass between them. She moved across with a sinuous movement and looked up at him. The thought came to him that here in these eyes was all that his soul pined for, but – she, too, was dumb. He felt himself struggling to express in her idiom an emotion which he could scarce translate in his own mind; then, not knowing why, he kissed her reverently on the forehead. Her eyes, usually suggesting an untamed tiger cat, were wonderfully soft, and in

---

[8] Beadle adds a one-word footnote: "Ruwenzori." The Ruwenzori mountain range forms a natural border between Uganda and the Congo.

some mysterious way she seemed to understand the reason of that strange kiss. She showed no surprise, as Laurie vaguely expected her to do, but as gently brushed his cheek with her lips. They looked at each other in a vague, bewildered manner and then his solemnity broke and, laughing with his characteristic chuckle, he turned away to smack the cub's ribs, crying:

"Haya! Sula! time we got along! We'll be glad to get to Butiti's, eh, Sula?"

"Sula glad! Sula glad!" she responded; and, as light as a Pavlova,[9] danced down towards the carriers, shouting to them: "Haya! Haya!" the cub, as ever, gamboling at her heels.

Away to the west black clouds of a rainstorm, the first of the season, were banking up; as Laurie paused to look a vivid streak of lightning ripped open the dense envelope, striking a distant rugged hillside. The country in the foreground, rolling billows of bare and rugged hills, looked as inhospitable as the cold green seas of the Atlantic in winter.

By 8 a.m. they were winding in and out through parklike country, broken and cut up by centuries of water action. Here on a level coming abruptly upon a washout, descending the precipitous sides into a green-swarded amphitheatre beneath, in the center of which a clump of earth, like a section of cake, bush topped, appeared in the moonlit glamour as some fantastic cathedral of spires and towers. Once more up the other side to descend again into a sloping bed of a mountain watercourse.

The moon, now high up in the western heavens, was fitfully obscured by lazy strips of gauzy clouds. At length, after the third rest, they entered the legitimate flats through shorter

---

[9] Anna Pavlova (1881 – 1931): Russian prima ballerina of the Imperial Russian Ballet and of Sergei Diaghilev's Ballets Russes, who created the role of "The Dying Swan." The first ballerina to make a world tour.

green grass, clumps of euphorbia and cactus. The carriers – although tired – quickened their pace in the knowledge of the proximity of their destination.

Sula, wiry limbed, still glided in her effortless manner, the cub shambling at her heels, ahead of Laurie, who strode along with the mechanical swing of the accustomed walker. Presently there was a slight commotion, a mutter of voices, and the caravan came to a halt like a goods train, each man stopping with a jerk against his neighbor in turn down the line. The sound of loads bumping on the ground sent Laurie at a run through the grass to the lead, which he discovered to be halted at the beginning of a cultivated garden, or rather fallow, for a glance showed him that all was overgrown with young weeds and grass, the stumps of felled trees, characteristic of native gardens, standing just above the level of the vegetation riot like solemn, warning fingers.

In the center stood a dilapidated thatched structure on poles, used by the rustic guard appointed to scare away marauding buck and birds from the young crops, with a despondent, mournful appearance of desertion. These shambas,[10] he knew, must adjoin the village of Butiti, an ancient Sudanese who was a relic of the days of Emin Pasha's[11] old guard; he had settled here and become titular chief of the district. The look and feel of those deserted gardens gave Laurie a sense of uneasiness, and the same emotion was evidently responsible for the sudden halt of the leaders of the caravan, who were now standing together like a flock of frightened sheep, whispering together.

Laurie strode on over the tangle towards them, asking in a loud voice the meaning of the delay. The bush around seemed to whisper the echo of his voice with sinister emphasis. A bird flew out of an adjacent tree with a whirring flutter of wings,

---

[10] An African term for a piece of cultivated ground; a garden or plantation.
[11] Emin Pasha (né Eduard Schnitzer; 1840 – 1892): Ottoman physician.

cawing dismally; a passing cloud obscured the moon. Laurie wriggled his shoulders as if endeavoring to free himself of a cloak, and spoke again sharply. Several men muttered sulkily, the headman pointed an eloquent hand at the tangled gardens.

"Kuna nin? " Laurie demanded once more.

Again an uneasy movement and muttered remarks.

"Are you all frightened of an old garden?" inquired Laurie. "Butiti's just close. What's the matter with you, you fools? Haya, haya! Pick up your loads – follow me!"

They stood sulkily immovable until Laurie picked up a bale and energetically heaved it on to the head of one of them. The man automatically raised his hands to balance it on his bare skull, grumbling at the absence of the head pad, a circlet of twisted grass, which Laurie adjusted for him under the load. A few of his companions began to follow suit. Laurie continued on towards the village with Sula, who had waited near him, unusually silent. He glanced at her as he moved away, noting the wide-opened eyes.

"What's the matter, Sula?" he asked.

 Sula shook her head slowly.

"Sula not know: Sula flightened," she replied, speaking in a whisper, her eyes darting searching looks on either side.

"'Why Sula frightened?" he inquired, pausing to glance back at the men who were resuming their burdens.

Again she slowly shook her head.

"Sula glad Lolly here," she whispered, herding closer to him. She bent down to caress the cub, who was shrinking against Laurie's legs.

"Damme!" muttered Laurie half to himself, shaking his shoulders free of an incubus. "Damme, I'm getting scared myself! This is sheer damn nonsense. They've only abandoned this patch for a fresh one, as they do every year or so. Haya! Haya!" he shouted to the caravan still hanging back reluctantly.

"Haya! Haya!" whispered the bush back at him.

Involuntarily he wheeled sharply, as if expecting to see somebody.

"Come along Sula!"

They plunged onward again as the moon shone clear.

For a quarter of a mile they wound along the track by the edge of the cleared land, pausing now and again to listen for sounds of the caravan en route. Upon rounding a curve in the fringe of bush they saw the ragged faint pallor of daybreak. At the first shadow of the plantation Laurie pulled up again to listen. Silence, save for an occasional rustle of some small animal in the grass, the buzz of a mosquito, or a squeaking twitter of birds in the depths of the plantation. Then a man's subdued voice way back down the trail, distinct on the silent air.

"It's all right: they're coming," Laurie remarked to Sula. She nodded her head.

"What *is* the matter, Sula?" he said, half querulously, conscious that she was unusually parsimonious of speech.

"Sula flightened," she whispered again, catching at his hand.

"What the devil of?" he inquired, and as she did not answer, turned and strode on.

The lower fronds of the bananas, he noticed, were unkempt and ragged, bunches of fruit unpicked were decayed and rotten, eloquent of neglect. The hard light of day had not yet penetrated the grove; the faint moon cast shadows ghostly. He pulled up abruptly once, at the sight of a *whiteman* in ducks standing under a banana plant watching him: he blinked and looked again in amazement. Yes, he could almost see the features.

"Hello-a!" he called, Sula watching him with saucer eyes.

"'llo-o!" echoed the banana grove in a faint whisper. The figure seemed to melt into a moonlit patch.

"Damn!" He swore viciously, glanced at Sula, who was clinging to him tenaciously, and back to the site of the vision. There was nothing there but the eerie shadows and the filmy patch of moon ray. A small black object flitted across, probably a rat.

"Damme!" he swore again. "I'm fey!" and strode on muttering to himself. "But what should suggest a whiteman? Why a *white* man?"

Suddenly, jumping, as it were, out of the plantation, appeared the inverted V of hut tops against the glorious dawn: a few more paces and the rough palisading of tree branches around the village. Then, after a subdued choking sound, a rooster's challenge cut the silent air triumphant and clear, carrying with it a sense of normal affairs. The vague sense of uneasiness which had seized Laurie seemed dispelled by this assurance that all was well with the world. His step quickened as he approached the entrance, but his spirits fell again as his observant eye failed to detect the usual wreath of blue smoke rising. He halted in the gate, a mere gap in the stockade, and took rapid stock of the interior.

To the right was the usual square hut, with clumsy verandah posts, of the chief Butiti; upon the other side half a dozen beehive huts; at the far end a weather-beaten tent, the ropes loose, the canvas sagging; in the center a ragged shelter used as a gossip house or reception room for strangers, underneath which the ashes of dead fires. As they stood watching, the cock, somewhere behind the huts, crowed dismally again, and the mangy cur ran out, yelped feebly, and shuffled back. Kichui, crouching against Sula's legs, snarled. As Laurie made a movement to enter, Sula clung to him protesting.

"Lolly! Lolly, no go: no good, Lolly!"

"Don't," said Laurie roughly. He drew his revolver – in case of emergency – and shaking her off, strode in to the village. Sula shrank back outside the hedge, hugging Kichui close to her, staring after Laurie through a gap with frightened eyes.

He made straight for the guesthouse and felt the ashes with his hand. Two heaps were stone cold, the other had live embers.

"Someone here lately, anyhow," he muttered, and walked into the chief's house. At first, in the darkness, he could distinguish nothing: then some calabashes, a bunch of rotting bananas, a jumble of spears, a broken native pipe and a rusty ancient musket grew out of the gloom in one corner of the bare, mud-walled room. A hideous stench assailed his nostrils as he turned towards the other and darker end. He saw the outline of a native bed with some dark form upon it. Laurie felt for, and struck a match, holding it aloft. In the flickering light the outline of a human body showed dimly under a blanket.

He stepped forward a pace, holding out the spluttering match. A face, black cavities for eyes grinned at the roof, the skin wrinkled and purple brown; the neck and shoulders were bone beneath a coverlet of skin alive with vermin. One emaciated arm, protruding from the bedside, was covered with ivory bangles, which gleamed as the match flared up, and went out. Laurie, recognizing the remains of Butiti by these bracelets, stumbled out of the hut, sick with the unbearable effluvium.

The eastern sky was now alive with the pageant of sunrise; great shafts of liquid gold shot across an ocean of purple, fading into seas and lakes of russet and pale amber mounting across the heavens, melting into fiery glory at the source.

For a moment Laurie stood in the warm sun rays searching for an explanation. He heard Sula's plaintive voice calling: "Lolly! Lolly!" then the cock crowed again. Glancing in its direction he cursed the bird savagely and made for the tent. A lilt of the flap door revealed the corpse of what had been a whiteman; the terribly emaciated form, clad in dirty ducks, a weak, half-grown beard sprouting on the blue-and-purple skin, was lying on a camp bed. Around it were the paraphernalia of camp: a rifle slung on the tent pole, boxes in a heap, a whiskey case as table, with a tin cup and a guttered candle.

Laurie turned away with a shudder and walked in the sun to the middle of the village, racking his brains for the solution of the problem. The cock crowed again with irritating clarity. He turned and cursed it violently, still automatically clutching his revolver in this village of the dead. Stooping at the door of one round hut he peered in and quickly withdrew his head with a shudder of horror. As he paused, uncertain for a moment, the whine of the cur from the next hut attracted his attention. He bent again to look within and saw a figure squatting just inside the door. It was a woman, old and emaciated to a degree; her rheumy eyes were deep sunk in their sockets, the wrinkled skin literally hanging upon the supporting bones, her withered breasts drawn and scaly. The eyelids blinked slowly as Laurie spoke to her.

"What's the matter?" he demanded.

She nodded slowly, wearily.

"Kuna nin?" he inquired again.

After a long pause the parchment lips moved slowly; she whispered something.

He bent closer to her, repeating the question. Once more the subdued choking chuckle, and the rooster crowed with unabating vigor.

Laurie muttered angrily and strained his ears to catch the slow, sibilant hiss of her whisper, faint, like the first mutter of a kettle on the hob. [*Hob (British): cooktop.]

"Sosolossi" – (sleeping sickness).

CHAPTER V

In the shade of the mud walls of a half-built hut lounging upon a grass mat was a local chief, Yama Yama; he was a lusty, stout man of middle age clad in the white robes, a trifle discolored, of the Baganda, with a tuft of woolly beard upon his chin, which he scratched in a meditative manner. Near to him Matalisi was lying, a muscular young petty chief, with small, cunning, sharp eyes and a sulky expression. Squatting around the walls were a number of other natives; some in dirtier robes, others in native loincloths. Near to the door sat a copper-skinned man in a comparatively clean white gown; his head lolled listlessly to one side, leaving the white pillbox cap, and jowl decorated with isolated patches of woolly moss, in a shaft of sunlight. A darker hued, small man near him, with typical Negroid features, wore a black bead rosary around his neck, from which was suspended a crucifix. Another man, at the far end, sprawled upon his elbow, asleep or dozing, his shaven skull peeping beneath a greasy, ragged turban.

The hot afternoon sun blazed at an angle through the framework of the unthatched roof, throwing patchwork shadows halfway down the far wall; through the door the brilliant light leapt up from the sandy clearing between the huts. Before one of these a native woman, her fly-blown-eyed child wrapped on her back in a greasy robe, diligently ground corn between rough, flat stones. Several diminutive chickens, fatigued with the heat, rested in the shade of the hut beside her. Having exhausted the faint interest in local news, the men had relapsed into the typical semisomnolent state of the native. The chief raised his head sleepily at the shuffle of bare feet without. A shadow darkened the threshold and a peasant man entered, straining his eyes to pierce the gloom of the hut. He saluted the chief, who nodded lazily.

"What is the news?"

"Good," said the stranger, subsiding on the ground. "Bwana Fedden sends a message that Yama Yama shall visit him at the Boma."

"U'm," grunted Yama Yama.

"He hath returned but now from Ulayi (Europe)," the messenger went on; "and hath brought a white wife."

A flutter of interest stirred his audience.

"And what like is she?" queried Matalisi, sitting up.

"Long hair, the color of a stormy sunset, after the manner of white women, and eyes like the midday sky."

Matalisi clucked approval and inquired:

"And is she fat like the wife of the Bwana Kubwa?"

"Nay; neither is she like the women of the missionaries, but plump like a partridge at harvest time."

"E-eh!" chorused the crowd.

A yellow-faced Baganda whispered to his neighbor; they both laughed lasciviously, showing white strong teeth beneath the dull-red blubber lips.

"Where are they now?" inquired Samwili Maliko, from the lintel of the door.

"They passed by the village of Luba a moon since; heard ye not? Now they dwell at the Boma, Mbale; the Bwana B'ink'y still stays with them; but they say he returns to Jinja upon the new moon."

"Why doth he linger?" demanded Yama Yama.

"Nay, how should I know?"

"Perhaps he stayeth by reason of the sickness," suggested a mild voice.

"Nay, nay, what whiteman shall have it?" protested a peasant.

"True," said another; "for is it not their gift, the curse of the whiteman?"

"So they say, the people of the south; but it doth not eat us up," said Yama Yama. "That," he added with a deep-chested laugh, "is only for ye dogs of the whitemen, the Waganda."

"True, the whitemen brought it," affirmed a Baganda, "but it is at thy gates, O Yama Yama. Think ye that they will let ye escape?"

"Nay," exclaimed Musisi, bending forward excitedly so that his crucifix glittered in the sunlight. "Nay, the whites have not brought it, for my Katoliki father says –"

"Bah!" interrupted Muhammad, who wore the turban, "thy father is a son of Satan. But ye are right, for it is a curse of Allah on ye unbelievers."

"Yes," chimed in another man; "for hath not a whiteman contracted the sickness? How would a man drink of his own poison?"

"That is as naught," shouted Mahommed; "all whitemen are mad!"

He grinned vastly, and scratched his shaven poll, well pleased with the laughter his sally had evoked.

"Yillah! it is true," he added. "Hath not the prophet so said?"

"The prophet was ever a liar!" announced the bearer of the crucifix.

"Nay, nay, thou Katoliki pig!" exclaimed the other, violently gesturing, pouring out a torrent of abusive epithets.

"'Tis true, the prophet is a liar!" shouted Samwili in the pillbox cap, supporting Musisi for the nonce.

For a while the two allies bore down the son of Mahommed in a torrent of invective until he cunningly sought to divide the partnership.

"You – you pig of a Katoliki!" he screamed. "What are you? Does not thy brother" – pointing an accusing finger at Samwili – "say that thou and thy prophets are liars, too!"

"Aye, aye," cried Musisi, turning upon Samwili, remembering past grievances. "You filthy Protestant, you –"

"What have you to say, you son of a cannibal? You dog," retorted Samwili, streaming obscene execration.

And so they fell to wrangling, as, alas, they had been taught to do. Whilst Mahommed exhausted his vocabulary upon both with impunity, Yama Yama and his pagan colleagues sat mute, watching them.

At length, in a pause for breath, a voice remarked:

"All your gods are liars!" whereupon the three champions of religion united in an attack upon the heathen.

"Bah!" said Yama Yama, when opportunity offered, "you are all cowards! You are all afraid of the whitemen!"

"Nay, nay," screamed Mahommed, foremost in indignant denial. "We Mohammedans have ever beaten the whitemen who dared to come within our country. Have we not beaten them in the Sudan? killed them and taken their women? Wait! wait! we *men* will drive them out of the land, as it is written in the Koran. Mahommed is with us!"

"Liar!" yelled Samwili, turning upon him. "Are *we* not the chosen of Isa Masiya, hath not the Book said that we are the chosen people who shall reconquer the earth? The Omusumesa (missionaries) tell us so; it is true."

"No, no," protested Musisi, the crucifix dangling on the rosary as he raised a protesting hand. "We – *we* are the chosen of the Great Spirit; you will all go to hell – that is true. We are the chosen people; all other people –"

"E-eh?" sneered Mahommed, "you are afraid of the whiteman; you are women, not men. No *man* hath only *one* wife; a *man* should have many wives, as we have. Is that not true, O Yama Yama?"

"Aye," assented Yama Yama, grinning; "a *man* should have many wives. Muhamadi was the wiser man. But why do ye two quarrel?" – to Samwili and Musisi – "are ye not of the same prophet?"

"No, no," commenced Samwili. "Our evangelist says –"

"He is a liar," protested Musisi. "Our Maruti says –"

"He says one thing and the other says another," interrupted Mahommed with a sudden burst of logic; "therefore are they both liars! Ours is the only true faith."

"Was Muhamadi black or white?" queried Yama Yama.

"Black! Of course he was! Are not his chosen people black?"

"Liar!" screamed Musisi.

"What color was Isa Masiya," pursued Yama Yama.

"Blackman!"

"Whiteman!"

"Liars!"

"Black! Black!" persisted Samwili.

"A whiteman!"exclaimed Musisi angrily. "My 'father' says he was white and your Omusumesa says he was white. I heard him say so!"

"Tss-ah!" ejaculated Samwili derisively. "You don't believe all that *they* tell you! Of course they *say* that because they are white."

"No, no," protested Musisi violently. "He was white, I know. I know, for" – triumphantly – "have I not seen pictures of him in the book of the Omusumesa? He had a white face and brown beard. I know!"

"Fool!" shouted Samwili. "Dost not know that the whiteman can make the picture any color he likes? Doth not the Omusumesa say that all men, black and white, are equal in the sight of the Great Spirit? Would any man but a fool speak thus, unless he knew that the other is greater than he?"

"Of course; your Omusumesa says that," interrupted Mahommed scornfully, "because they are liars *and* fools. They want to take *your* country and *your* women! What else do they leave *their* country for, the unbelieving pigs! But the country shall belong to the Faithful. Great is Allah!"

"Isa Masiya was a whiteman," insisted Musisi doggedly.

"Ye are all liars and thieves!" exclaimed Yama Yama with a great laugh. Muhamadi, Protestanti, Katoliki, ye all want to take my country, as Mtesa (King of Uganda) did of old; but *he* was a man. He fought. You all come sniveling, for ye are all cowards."

"True, true," screamed a man with a cicatrized face and filed teeth, squatting beside the chief.

"Cannibal! Eater of human flesh!" sneered a chorus.

"And if I am," cried the man, who was a member of a cannibal tribe from the Congo, "and if I am, so are ye!"

"Liar! Liar!"

"Nay, nay; I am not a liar! What is that which your" – gesticulating at Musisi and Samwili – "Omusumesa call Okusekimu Okutukura?"

"True, true!" exclaimed Yama Yama, leaning forward excitedly. "He speaks true, the cannibal! Do not thy Omusumesa say it is the blood and body of Isa Masiya? Why should not a man eat his brother if he may eat his master?"

"But," protested Samwili, "it is really only bread and wine –"

"Then are thy teachers proved liars!" exclaimed Mahommed.

"Liars! Liars!" chorused the pagans.

Musisi remained silent, chewing the cud of this new idea.

"They are liars even as I have said," retorted Samwili hotly; "but their God is the true God, and *we* are the chosen people. They seek to claim equality; for all whitemen are cowards."

"No, no," said Musisi feebly. "The whiteman strikes hard."

"Coward!" screamed Samwili. "They strike you hard, but no whiteman ever struck *me*. It is they who are frightened of us, else why do they not conquer us? Bah, whitemen –"

"Thy crowing is like a cockerel upon a dung heap," sneered Matalisi, "who flieth at the approach of a woman!"

"Liar!" yelled Samwili. "Of no whiteman am I frightened. I would kill a whiteman as my woman kills a chicken –"

"Tss-ah!" said Matalisi scornfully, "more boasts of the cockerel! I would give ten head of fat cattle to have a whiteman killed."

"Good, good!" chorused the crowd. "Are they not the harbingers of sickness and death? Down with them!"

"E-eh!"exclaimed Yama Yama, "these are coward curs. I would add fifty head. But – tch! –cowards all. Now I myself –"

"Liar!"screamed Samwili, springing to his feet. "What is a whiteman? I will kill thy whiteman for thee since thou art afraid. The cattle are mine. We are the chosen people; the time is come. Now will–"

He ceased abruptly, arrested by the clip- clop of boots outside. In the sudden hush they all turned to see a European in khaki and felt hat advancing toward the hut. Samwili sank back upon his haunches again as the white stood on the threshold peering within.

"Jambo, Bwana;" said Yama Yama amiably.

"Jambo!" returned Laurie, whose figure seemed to fill the door.

"Habari gani?" pursued Yama Yama politely.

"Yema!" said Laurie, taking stock of the assembly. "Which is Yama Yama?"

"Mimi, Bwana."

"Njoo!" (come here) continued Laurie, turning away from the door. The cannibal man giggled nervously: a sulky look spread over Yama Yama's face.

Laurie's big figure filled the doorway again.

"Njoo! Sikia?" (d'you hear)? he demanded peremptorily.

An ingratiating smile stole across Yama Yama's thick lips as he shambled to his feet with some show of alacrity, and followed Laurie out into the hot sun.

"Pig of an unbeliever!" said Mahommed sotto voce.

"Son of a –" muttered Samwili.

"Who is be?" whispered Matalisi.

"A stranger," returned Samwili.

"Kill *him*, Allah hath sent him," urged Mahommed.

"Aye, there's your chance to win the cattle," sneered another.

"No, no; wait till he is out of the village," cautioned Matalisi, who had no wish to be an accomplice in the murder.

"Aye," whispered Samwili; "I will wait till then."

Laurie's voice floated in from outside, giving instructions to Yama Yama to send food and chickens to his camp. Yama Yama's deferential, "Indio, Bwana (Yes, master), Indio, Bwana!" in staccato accompaniment.

Samwili's sulky face lightened as he bent towards Matalisi, whispering rapidly. The other laughed and nodded approval, whereat Samwili scrambled to his feet and emerged from the hut. He started back in alarm at the sight of a half-grown leopard, but paused in amazement as he noted that the beast was held by a collar and chain, led by a powerfully built man whose limbs were covered in iron and copper bangles, jingling as he moved.

Kichui was lying in the sun whilst Sula patted and caressed him. After a moment of staring at Sula, whom Samwili took to be a white woman on account of her hair, he walked up to Laurie, who was turning away from Yama Yama.

"Goo' morning Bwana!"

Laurie, arrested by the unexpected English, turned to look at him.

"Me spik Englees," announced Samwili with a conciliatory smile.

"Oh, do you?" exclaimed Laurie, who held a prejudice against English-speaking natives. "Well, go to the devil!"

"Me bring you chickens, sah?" called Samwili after him, smiling amiably.

CHAPTER VI

Laurie rejoined Sula, and together they struck off from the village through acres of native gardens in rich loamy soil. This portion of Busoga, upon the borders of the Victoria Nyanza, was thickly populated, rich in bananas and maize.

After about four miles of flat country, passing villages innumerable, from which the women set up the shrill tremolo scream (smacking the lips with the fingers) denoting the approach of strangers, they came to a rocky ridge. On the top, by the side of another village, Laurie noticed a barnlike building with a wooden cross upon the apex of the roof, a pastoral church. From the far slope, as the path swerved round parallel with the ridge, the blue waters of the lake burst through the treetops from far beneath, the land dropping in a series of plateau steps to the lake level. From every side over the parklike clumps of bush and trees rose filmy spirals of blue smoke, the occasional yapping of village dogs, the cries of children; now and again a green glimpse of banana fronds, far less numerous here than in Uganda, a few papaya trees and patches of cornland studded with tree stumps.

As they reached the next short plateau through a rough defile amid bushes and rocks the smiling lake seemed to leap up at them. A bunch of reed-encircled islands, spangled with clumps of trees, appeared to drop back into the water from the shimmering heat void. As they walked round the head of a small bay numerous other diminutive islands appeared, the strips of blue water seeming like long fingers studded with emerald rings. Quite close inshore, near the fringe of reeds which wrapped the beach, were three high-prowed canoes full of men, the water glistening like diamonds as the distant paddles splashed. Down yet another short escarpment, losing the lake in the wooded copse, picking it up again upon a broader plateau of rich soil amid tall cedar and olive trees, here and there fallow patches of gardens.

The native path suddenly gave way to a broad track through an avenue of young eucalyptus trees, on either side of which stretched symmetrical rows of young plants; at the end were a bunch of native huts, around which fat babies and lean chickens disported; and standing apart, with a curious air of haughty aloofness, a long, low, thatched bungalow, a wide, trunk-posted verandah running around it.

At the sound of the crunch of Laurie's boots a native in spotless white, holding a knife in one hand, a newly killed chicken, all bloody feathers, in the other, appeared at the door of a small square kitchen hut, amid a reek of blue smoke.

"Jambo, Bwana!" said he.

"Jambo!" nodded Laurie, pausing to inquire: "where is the master?"

But the cook was gazing open mouthed at Kichui, sniffing and licking his chops in the direction of the blood drips.

Laurie repeated the question sharply.

"In the front of the house, Bwana!" returned the cook at last, disappearing into the swirl of smoke.

The bungalow was built upon the verge of the plateau; the ground dropped sheer away, in tangled trees and boulders, from the foot of the front verandah, down some sixty feet to the level of the lake shore beneath. In a lounge chair by the door, commanding a magnificent view of the lake and the curve of the diminutive bay, sprawled a whiteman in dirty blue shirt and greasy khaki slacks, mopping his brow with a sheetlike handkerchief, breathing hard. A felt hat lay on the floor beside him, amid a group of five panting mongrel terriers in various attitudes of doggy exhaustion and heat.

The sound of boots ringing hard upon the sun-dried bricks brought the pack to their feet with shrill barks and yowls. Their master turned his bullet, cropped red head and opened wide his red-lashed small eyes at Laurie's boisterous greeting:

"Hullo, Natts!"

"Burke!" exclaimed Natts, wriggling out of the depths of the chair. "Where've you sprung from? – Shut up, Tinker! lie down, you! Didimalla!" to the dogs, lifting one out of his way with the toe of his boot.

"Oh, I've come over to give this side a show," said Laurie, shaking hands energetically. "Got a bad fright but – tell you later."

"Sit down, have a drink. I'll get a chair. Shut up, Tinker! – Hallo!" he exclaimed, pausing abruptly as he caught sight of Sula standing demurely behind Laurie.

"Oh!" said Laurie, smiling as he turned. "Let me introduce Mr. Natts – Sula."

"E-eh!" murmured Natts, his small eyes twinkling.

Sula, with a toss of her head, sending her wavy curls rippling, held out a slim hand in a quaintly mincing manner, and said simply, by way of greeting: "Sula glad!"

Natts took the proffered hand clumsily, without a word, and Sula, quickly noting his embarrassed manner, laughed softly, a silvery chuckle.

"Glad to meet you, m'm," said Natts, at length jerking out his words. "E-eh!" he interposed again, staring at her in undisguised admiration; then, with a mumbled, "Get a chair," dived inside.

Sula turned to Laurie, who had stood an amused spectator.

"Funny man!" she whispered naively, whereat Laurie chuckled, stroking her hair.

Natts appeared again, dragging two chairs after him and shouting to his servants. Sula, meanwhile, with an air of queenly right, sank into the lounge chair, curling her small sandaled feet beneath her red-tartaned skirtlike robe.

"Well," said Laurie to Natts as they sat down, "how's things? You look very comfy here!"

"Eh?" said Natts, bending towards him. "Speak up, I'm deaf."

"What's the matter?" bawled Laurie.

"Don't 'zactly know," returned Natts. "Got up deaf from my last bout of fever. Rotten hole this!"

"Damned pretty place," exclaimed Laurie, sweeping his eye across the bay. "Much fever? What sort? Tick[12] or just common or garden?"

"Tick, I think," whispered Natts. "Quinine had no effect. Been walking too much; ankles sore and swollen, feet rotten and a sort of nettle rash, but I'm all right now."

"Queer!" exclaimed Laurie, peering into the tanned, yellow face. "My ankles are bad, too, but I've been quite fit right along. You look rotten, Natts, you ought to clear for Europe."

"No," muttered Natts, pursing his lips. "No Europe for me. Want another five year 'fore I'm ready to clear out o' here for good."

"What're you doing this time?"

"Timber – good market below – Nairobi. 'Member Bartlett? 'Fore your time, eh? Well, he and I bought this place from old Luba. He's dead now – blackwater – Bartlett I mean. – Get out o'it, Tinker. – Whiskey or tea? – good! Lady have tea?"

"Tea, Sula?" queried Laurie.

"Sula glad! Sula glad!" said she, nodding vigorously, for she loved tea inordinately – with half sugar and milk.

"What're you over here?" inquired Natts, charging his glass afresh with whiskey.

"Going up Rudolf way," returned Laurie. "Game played out over the Semliki."

"Bulamatadi too hot?"

---

[12] African tick bite fever. A common malady in sub-Saharan Africa caused by the bacterium Rickettsia africae and transmitted by tick bites.

"M'm, yes; but – to tell the truth, sleeping sickness decided me to get."

"Hell!" ejaculated Natts, sitting up in his chair. "Started over there, too?"

"Yes, crept up Semliki from Lake Albert, I suppose. Coming down from Balegga Hills to old Butiti's. Remember what a fat, healthy mob they used to be there?"

Natts nodded. Laurie recounted his experiences.

"Poor Stops," interposed Natts. "One of the finest shots and hardest drinkers I ever met – for a young man."

"Yes," assented Laurie. "Horrible business writing to his people though, poor devil. But, damme if I can understand the spook part of it."

Natts shook his head and helped himself to more whiskey.

"One often meets a man who had an aunt who knew someone who saw a ghost," said Laurie meditatively; "but – well life is ten percent concrete facts and ninety percent unsolvable problems. Telepathy's the –"

"Eh?" inquired Natts.

"Telepathy's –"

"What's that?"

"Oh, nothing – well, then – I came back to look for the caravan," he continued. "Loads all in the grass – not a beggar there. Had a hell of a picnic: had to walk round the hills to Kavalli's. They were all right up there in the hills. I had to give a bolt of bafta apiece to get 'em to fetch the ivory on next day. Gad! d'you know, Natts, I'm not easily scared, but the march from Butiti's to the Semliki gave me cold shivers for days. It was like walking through a charnel house, village after village deserted with their dead, miles of deserted gardens – like a Biblical plague. – Devil of a lot of fly there!"

"Pesky lot o' fly round here, too," interposed Natts.

"Any cases?"

"Not that I know. Gosh, though, it'll come round the lake sure's death. Buddu is rotten with it."

"Ugh, I don't like it," said Laurie, a graver note than usual in his voice. "Got bitten dozens of times, so I might have it now for all I know. Ugh!" He finished his drink at a gulp. "What's the matter with the white-eyed tyke?" he inquired after a pause. "He looks bad, poor little chap. Come here, sonny! – and his coat's all staring."

"Dunno," said Natts indifferently.

Laurie, patting the dog, examined him.

"Poor old man, what's the matter? Why, you're a skeleton and you're half asleep. Wake – Good God, Natts!" he exclaimed, "I believe the dog's got the sickness."

"Oh, he's been like that for a long while. Have another?" pushing the bottle along the floor.

"Yes, I suppose so," said Laurie, helping himself. "Alcohol ought to kill germs. Damme! Whiskey in: fly out!"

"Eh?" whispered Natts, straining his ear.

"Oh! feeble jokes are like prudes – not worth kissing twice."

Natts looked up from his fourth whiskey perplexedly.

"What's that?"

"Something that doesn't grow in this part of the world – thank Heaven!"said Laurie, chuckling to himself.

"Don't know what you're talkin' about," grumbled Natts.

"Only trying to play five-finger exercises – with stiff fingers on a dumb piano," he added sotto voce.

"M'm! – Stayin' long?" inquired Natts. "Got spare camp bed –"

"Thanks!" said Laurie, "but I'll stick to the tent – out behind there. Getting on to Mbale tomorrow. Good three days' march, isn't it?"

But Natts, busy with the whiskey bottle, did not hear. Laurie watched him quizzically, shrugged his shoulders and lit a fresh cigar, sweet fruit of civilization.

They sat wrapped in the mantles of their several personalities, as those who dwell in the waste places of the earth are wont to do. The blue of the lake waters changed imperceptibly to various hued tints of violet and green as the sun sank towards the diminutive headland in deep shadows. Sula lifted her thick eyelashes and listened intently.

"Wapagazi come!" she announced with a musical jingle of ivory bangles as she moved.

The faint shrilling scream of native women heralding the approach of strangers floated on the still air, and presently the men's voices shouting a chorus at intervals: "Weballi! Weballi!" – followed by deep-chested "oughs!" then the high, piping voice of the soloist between the bass refrain.

The two whites, with Sula, went round to the back of the bungalow, where crouched Kichui asleep, with his attendant. Squatting beside him, engaged in making friends, was Samwili. As neither Laurie nor Natts took any notice of him, he remained silent.

By the setting of the sun Laurie's camp was pitched. After his usual splash he went over to the bungalow, leaving Sula to her toilet – which she never neglected when possible – to rejoin Natts for dinner. He found him sitting on the verandah in the dark, staring at the horizon where the dark body of the lake slashed the star-strewn heavens in half. Laurie paused in the door, killing a scout of the mosquito battalions upon his nose.

"Come inside, Natts," he said; "and shut out these damned skeeters."

"Have a drink," said Natts' voice in the gloom. A tinkle of teeth against glass followed.

"With my dinner," said Laurie. "Come along in – it's waiting."

Natts gathered himself together and came into the room hugging a black bottle, followed by the pack of terriers.

"You do yourself well," remarked Laurie at the end of dinner to Natts, who had eaten nothing.

"Eh?" said Natts, putting down his glass.

Laurie repeated the statement, adding:

"Lake fish, I suppose? Chickens, mutton, and banana fritters! Damme, I can't get my cook to dish up five-course dinners!"

Natts gazed at him as ii struggling to comprehend. At length he muttered:

"No fish here nor mutton! Leastways I never get any."

"Well, where's this sumptuous repast sprung from?"

"Dunno," returned Natts indifferently, plugging his pipe with a blackened forefinger. "Have a drink?"

"Sula know, Lolly," said she. "Klistian nigger Samwili, he bring."

"Samwili, Sula?" inquired Laurie.

"Samwili. Lolly 'member Klistian nigger speak 'Nglees?"

"Oh, that damned English-speaking beast. What's he doing here? – D'you know the man, Natts?"

"What man?" said Natts, who had now reached a stage wherein he only heard sentences bawled at him. He shook his head in answer, vaguely comprehending as he grabbed the whiskey bottle once more. Laurie looked at him, frowned annoyance, and shouted the question again with details. But light refused to penetrate the fuddled mind of Natts, and Laurie gave it up in disgust.

"Heathen nigger," remarked Sula, who had been watching Natts with bright, inquisitive eyes, "plenty good, little bad; Klistian nigger plenty bad, little good; whiteman often like nigger."

Having delivered herself of this little epigram culled from varied remarks of Laurie's and the evidence of her own eyes, she gazed at him, pleading for approbation.

"Quite right, Sula," he said, chuckling and glancing at Natts, who sat mute, staring with filmed eyes at the black bottle.

"Look here, little girl, you run away now. I want to have a chat" – he grinned at the obvious futility – "with Natts here."

Sula laughed and departed. Laurie got up and sat himself closer to Natts.

"Natts!" he shouted in that worthy's ear, shaking his shoulder vigorously, who turned and blinked at him owlishly. "Natts! What's the matter with you? Pull yourself together, man!"

Natts mumbled inarticulately and reached out a brown, clawlike hand for the bottle. Laurie swiftly placed it out of reach.

"That's enough," he said sharply. "You'd best taper off."

Natts scowled and snarled at him, exhibiting yellow fangs. The whole expression of the man had changed from the person whom Laurie found upon the verandah in the afternoon sun.

"Natts!" shouted Laurie again, shaking him vigorously, whilst the other continued to snarl feebly. "Pull yourself together. Here!" he seized a sauce bottle and poured a two-finger peg into a spare glass. "Here! Drink this, damn you!"

Natts protested feebly but drank it after a pause. The hot seasoning caught him by the throat. He coughed and choked, bringing tears to the eyes, which cleared and grew a shade brighter as if washed.

"Now eat something," commanded Laurie, jerking a plate of tepid meat under the patient's nose. Natts shuddered, threatened to vomit and turned away. Laurie, watching him keenly, shrugged his shoulders and said: "Feel better?"

Natts shook his head despondently and clawed at his moist mouth.

"Look here, old man," urged Laurie in a milder tone, "why don't you pull yourself together, eh?"

A glimmer of awakened intelligence flittered through the other's eyes. He blinked as if endeavoring to dispel the blinding mists and said at length:

"What's the good? There's nothing else to do."

Laurie knew the attitude of mind too well.

"That's rot, man. Will you take my advice and clear home for a spell? Look here, if you will I'll stay over and come back as far as Jinja with you."

But Natts wagged his head mournfully, and made a furtive reach for the whiskey bottle.

"Now drop it, Natts," exclaimed Laurie, placing the bottle out of reach behind him. "The country's got into your blood," (he little guessed how literal his words were) "I know: and when it's like that it's time to clear out. Do as I say, there's a good chap! Promise to and I'll fix up everything for you. Remember your people would like to see you again."

The eyes brightened once more for an instant, then the head wagged again maudlin, despondently.

"They're dead," he whispered thickly; "haven't heard of 'em for twenty years."

"Well, you'll find 'em all right if you'll only go home. Come, let me fix it up for you."

"No," obstinately. "Want 'nother thousand. – Got three. – Want 'nother settle down f' life."

"Nonsense, man; trip'll do you good."

"No." The head wagged owlishly again.

"Rubbish!" exclaimed Laurie, and for an hour or more he sat arguing, persuading, pleading, whilst this Swiss sample of a successful wreck made feeble, futile efforts to get at the whiskey again, becoming more owlish and stupid as the effects of the counter-irritant evaporated.

The one-sided conversation was brought to a close by the patient overbalancing in an attempt to reach for the bottle behind Laurie and collapsing on the floor, upon Tinker, who fled with a shrill yelp, raising an indignant chorus from his fellows. Laurie raised up the little man and dumped him back in the chair, where he sunk inert.

"Hopeless!" muttered Laurie, pursing his lips as he surveyed the grubby-haired face and red-rimmed eyes: then, picking him up like some great baby, he carried him into the bedroom, partitioned off from the square of the bungalow by a reed fence.

His feet stumbled over a quantity of "dead marines "as he approached the camp bed with his burden. The dogs, following the inanimate form of their master with one accord, led by Tinker, leapt upon and took possession of the bed.

"Vootsak! get out of it!" shouted Laurie. They obediently vacated the bed to allow Laurie to dump Natts upon it, but only to resume their position immediately, lying indiscriminately around and upon their master.

Laurie stood back and chuckled.

"Dog fancier," said he whimsically; "a dead drunk entirely surrounded by dogs! Get out of it, Tinker!" he added, taking the dog by the scruff of the neck from off his master's chest. "You'll give him bad dreams, you fool!"

Tinker merely wagged his tail and leapt back again.

The patient, suddenly awakened from his stupor by the dog's feet in his stomach, clutched at Laurie's coat as the latter turned away.

"Gimme a drink! Christ, gimme a drink!" whispered the hoarse voice.

"Go to sleep," urged Laurie. "You'll have a drink in the morning. I'm not going to knock you off altogether."

"I'm dying. Gimme a drink!"clamored the other, crawling on to the edge of the bed.

"Well, lie down, then," said Laurie, pushing him back; "and I'll get you *one* – no more, mind."

He paused with his hand upon the bottle.

"I'll give the beggar a sleeping draught with it," he muttered to himself, and went out for his medicine chest in the tent.

Hardly had his white-clad form melted into the night than a yellow-brown face, fringed with woolly patches, appeared in the opposite doorway, followed by its owner's body, a broad-bladed stabbing spear in the right hand. The eyes were bloodshot and the thick lips twitched convulsively as the figure stole on naked feet into the lighted room. The eyes lit upon the tumbler of raw spirit awaiting Laurie's return. A yellow palm on a skinny wrist snatched it up greedily. Samwili gasped with satisfaction as the liquor warmed his throat and the eyes sparkled wickedly. A crash from the inner room, combined with a moan, a tinkle of bottles tumbling about the floor and protesting whimpers from the dogs, made him jump violently. He paused for a moment trembling, whites of eyes rolling in an access of fright. The shuffle of limbs being dragged along the ground, heavy breathing, the clink of bottles cannoning, and the bleary, bloodshot eyes of Natts appeared in the bedroom doorway. Crawling upon all fours, he paused upon the threshold, and lifting his head stared stupidly, hungrily at the whiskey bottle upon the table, appearing like some grotesque, red-haired baboon.

Silently Samwili moved a step backwards as Natts continued his crawl, unconscious of the other's presence. Samwili's eyes were attracted by a rent in the worn khaki jacket between the shoulder blades, showing a glimpse of blue shirt beneath. Yama Yama's laugh rang in his ears; the thick lips gibbered and the eyes rolled as he lifted the short-bladed spear, taking aim for the ragged slash of blue. But at that moment the sharp rap of a boot heel upon the verandah floor sounded, followed by growls from the dogs on the bed inside. With a sidelong glance of fear Samwili turned to run. The movement, and a shrill bark from Tinker, made Natts turn his head in time to see a misty, ghostly figure flit through the door. Laurie entered the back door to find Natts huddled on the floor gazing stupidly into the night, whilst Tinker, with three assistants, gave tongue upon the verandah.

"Good Lord!" exclaimed Laurie, picking Natts up and dumping him into a chair; "What on earth are you trying to do? Ah!" – as he noted the missing glass of whiskey – "been at it again? Why couldn't you wait till I came back, you idiot? Where's the glass? D'you hear?" he shouted into the other's ear, "where's the glass of whiskey I poured out for you?"

Natts, whose bleared eyes were still fixed on the door, pointed a shaking hand in that direction.

"What's the matter?" inquired Laurie.

"Nigger went out there," stuttered Natts.

"What nigger? With the whiskey?" exclaimed Laurie, and stepping to the door peered out. "Shut up, Tinker – be quiet!" he commanded to the dogs, who still stood in a line on the verandah edge barking at the night. "Nonsense, Natts," he continued; "there's no one there. You've drunk it, I know; but what have you done with the glass?"

He searched under the table and about the floor; but Natts shook his head and pointed again to the door.

"No, no," said he more soberly "I – I turned my head and saw a nigger standing over me with a spear. He bolted. He was going to murder me. I know it."

"Murder you?" echoed Laurie, looking at him; then he smiled to himself. "Come, come, get to bed! – you've got d.t.'s already," he added sotto voce. "Come along, Natts."

He took Natts by the shoulders and carried him to the bed again, where he lay, looking with scared eyes at the doorway, cuddling Tinker with one arm. Laurie poured out another whiskey, added a sleeping draught and gave it to the patient, who drank greedily.

"Now be quiet," adjured Laurie as Natts made an effort to get up; "and I'll take off your boots. – There, shut up, man! You dreamt it. Go to sleep!"

Laurie left him staring at the ceiling, drew the curtain across the partition doorway, and stood for a moment gazing at the table.

"Damned strange," he remarked to himself; "that glass has certainly disappeared. Perhaps he did see some nigger thief making off with it. That's what disturbed the dogs. Murder him, rot!"

He turned out the lamp, closed the door, and went off to bed.

***

Next morning, as the soft dawn light filtered through the ill-fitting doors, made of the sides of packing cases, Natts stood at the table in the dining room mixing a "corpse reviver" whilst Tinker and company stretched and yawned themselves awake.

Natts, a little bleary and pouched under the eyes, appeared a different individual from the bloated, fuddled creature who had been carried to bed. Although commencing first thing in the morning to drink himself stupid by bedtime, yet he always arose in a fairly fit and alert condition. As he replaced the glass with a sigh of satisfaction Laurie opened the door and entered, ready attired for the road.

"Morning, Natts," said Laurie. "Feeling better?"

"Good morning,' replied Natts, ignoring the inquiry. "Off today? Have a drink?"

"Yes, I told you so last night," said Laurie, helping himself. "Now look here, Natts" – and sitting at the table he tried anew to persuade him to take a trip home, but Natts remained as obdurate sober as he had been drunk, a little more lucid, but just as obstinate, showing signs of offence at any inference that he was not perfectly sound in mind and body.

"Well, all right if you won't. I suppose it's no use, but just say the word and I'll stop the caravan now and come into Jinja with you. No? Ah well, you're a damn fool; but still I suppose a fool and his folly are as hard to separate as a bug and a blanket. Hullo, Tinker, what's the matter?"

He rose and opened the door, letting out the dogs with joyous yelps, flooding the room with rose light. He stood on the verandah awhile, smoking a cigar and staring across the lake which was merging from the glaucous tint of early dawn to the rippling hues of molten gold and violet of the rising sun, the mists hanging around the shore and islands dissolving at the touch of warm day.

Natts elbowed past him, the grimy, drawn lines of his wizened, unshaven face showing clearly in the daylight.

"Gotter get down and stir them lazy devils up," he remarked. "Gettin' wus and wus every day. Sorter restless and indifferent," he rambled on, pausing on the edge of the steps to plug his pipe. "Goodbye," he jerked out and disappeared down the escarpment.

"Goodbye, you old fool!" shouted Laurie, smiling. He paused for a moment, watching the tails of Tinker and company flipping in succession over the edge.

"Obstinate old idiot!" he remarked to the empty air and went off to join Sula for the road.

CHAPTER VII

On the verge of a marshy plain extending to the northeast shore of the Victoria Nyanza and widening northwards into a vast series of shallow lakes and swamps, all choked with dense papyrus sudd, stood Fort Mbale, perched on a mound like a piece of chalk upon a billiard table. Immediately at the back frowned a high, steep hill like a section of cake, the perpendicular sides ragged and bare, scored with small waterways cut by innumerable streams emerging from the thickly wooded top. At a few miles to the east of this point the ground commenced to swell gradually, growing steeper and more rugged, into the ten thousand feet summit of Mount Elgon, the distant mass, usually mist wreathed, appearing as an African Fujiyama. The smaller hill was shaped like a hog's back, and the Government fort, a square between three long thatched buildings, enclosed within palisading and protected by a broad ditch or moat, rode upon the hinder end of the rump. A flagstaff stood in front of the long bungalow, facing the bare square and opposite the gate, the store and offices on either side. At a short distance to the west of the fort were the native police quarters, two lines of round huts; at some distance below these the bazaar, which consisted of one street of corrugated iron shanties on a gentle slope, owned and run by Indians; beyond was the native marketplace, a clear space around a large tree.

The residential bungalow consisted of four rooms, formed by the simple process of chopping off the length of the building with three partitions; those on either side were bedrooms, the ends of which, at the back, were subdivided into small compartments, thus providing each with an attendant bathroom; the sitting- and dining-rooms were in the center; all opened on to a verandah on both sides through large French window frames covered with mosquito wire netting instead of glass.

One hot, steamy day Maude was seated on the front verandah reading a novel between dozes. A slight bout of malaria had already stolen her fresh complexion; yet, clad in white lawn,[13] her pale face, framed in an auburn halo, looked very pretty and attractive. A fly, with characteristic persistence, buzzed around her head. For the twentieth time it made an abortive attempt to settle upon Maude's nose, to be driven off by an exceedingly irritable gesture of the bejeweled white hand.

The book sank into her lap once more as she dropped her head back on to the cushions with a sigh and frown of annoyance. The barking coughs of the native sergeant-major drilling a police squad floated across the square in the hot, shimmering air. By the verandah of the offices on the right a dozen or more nude natives squatted patiently; from inside came the murmur of voices. Maude lay for a while disconsolately fanning herself. The rattle of china within the room attracted her attention.

"Malima!" she called.

A bronze giant, with the aquiline nose of the Bahima race, clad in a calico uniform, came out.

"Bwana – he – coming – oh, what is it? Bwana jangu, eh? (Master, come here)."

Malima smiled amiably and started off towards the office with the obvious intention of calling his master.

"Oh, no, no," exclaimed Maude. "Come back, you idiot! Bwana jangu? Can't you understand?"

Malima smiled vaguely.

"Bwana jangu? You fool, you. Bwana – when – he – come?"

---

[13] Lawn: a fine, sheer linen or cotton fabric of plain weave, which is thinner than cambric.

Another exhibition of gleaming teeth, amid a bewildered expression.

"Oh," ejaculated Maude, stamping one foot, "go away, do! I've never seen such a fool. Go away," pointing one tragic finger.

"Don't stand there grinning at me!"

Malima disappeared within. Maude fanned herself vigorously.

"Phew! it's so hot and he's such a fool! Oh, *why* did I ever come into such a beast of a country?"

There was a stir amongst the waiting crowd of greasy natives. Fedden emerged, putting on his helmet as he strode into the brilliant sunlight. He looked a little more yellow than before, the eyes more worried, the moustache more melancholy.

"It is a long way past one," complained Maude fretfully as he stepped into the verandah; "and – and Malima *is* a fool. He can't even understand his own language!"

It was characteristic of him that there appeared nothing humorous in this assertion.

"You must learn some more words, dear," he said gravely. "Aren't you coming to lunch?"

"Oh, I don't want any lunch," declared Maude petulantly.

"Oh yes, dear, do have some lunch; you must, you know," he said without enthusiasm. "Come along in!"

He stepped inside without waiting for her. Presently she followed him in and sat down before a smartly set lunch of cold chicken and salad, cool and inviting. He helped her quietly and commenced to eat, still obviously wrapped in his official work.

She pecked at the food in silence for a while, pushed the plate away and fanned herself furiously.

"Heavens! One might as well have a tête-à-tête with a mummy!" she exclaimed at last.

"How, dear?" he exclaimed absent-mindedly.

"How, dear?" she mocked. "You come in and sit like – like a heaven knows what – without a word."

"Well, what shall I say?"

"How do I know? Haven't you two ideas? Can't you see I'm bored to tears? What am I to do all day? Nobody to talk to – nothing to do – Oh – I'm fed up!"

"My dear!" exclaimed Fedden, who was of the type to be shocked by slang upon his wife's lips.

"Yes, fed up,"[14] she retorted energetically. "It's the only phrase that expresses what I mean. What do you suppose I can do with myself? I can't read and sleep *all* the time. You go off at seven and come back for an hour, looking like a dyspeptic owl; away again till four, and after that you potter about with a filthy crowd of men, women, and children covered with horrible diseases – ugh! Then when you are with me you do nothing but think about nasty dirty niggers, or sit messing about with papers and things. Oh, it's horrible; it's bad enough to live in a beastly land of flies, and – wriggly horrors, and Heaven only knows how many awful fevers and things!"

"Well, why don't you do something?" inquired Fedden patiently. "You know how I want you to take an interest in my work? You could be such a help, dear! There's the dispensary, you might –"

"Oh! don't," cried Maude, shuddering. "You make me feel ill – loathsome, disease-eaten wretches, ugh!"

"Well, if you don't like that you could help me so in that administration scheme for –"

"Oh, don't, Herbert; you know I don't understand these beastly things. Oh, phew – it's too hot to talk!"

---

[14] *Fed up* was first employed as a "slang" term circa 1900; so the expression was barely a dozen years old in October 1912, when *A Whiteman's Burden* was published in London by Stephen Swift and Company.

She arose and flopped into a hammock chair, sighing and "phewing" with hot disgust of all things. Fedden finished his lunch in silence, afterwards sitting beside her for coffee. Whilst the "boy" brought in the coffee tray they both smoked cigarettes in silence. Suddenly her mood changed, and jumping up, she pecked him a kiss on his cheek and exclaimed:

"There, Herb, we'll be good, won't we?"

She stood back and giggled as he frowned annoyance at the contracted "Herb," which she well knew he detested.

"Come along – no, stop there, Herbert, and I'll play to you. How I wish I had somebody alive to play with!" she added, sotto voce, as she disappeared into the next room.

He leaned back in his chair, smoking, and listened to her playing on the piano which he had had brought, on the back of many porters, and at great expense, from Entebbe. She had a fine, delicate touch which was quite lost upon him. He liked music, although he did not understand it. He had once been caught describing it as a "nice noise," but had not repeated the phrase.

As the hands of a little cuckoo clock on the wall pointed to 2 p.m. – she had long since strangled his cherished cuckoo – he arose to return to the office with greater punctuality than any city man. Maude continued to play for half an hour or more until, saturated with the result of such exertions in this moist climate, she returned to a hammock on the back verandah to read and doze into a peevish mood once more.

Such was their life. The wife of an exile in a savage, tropical country is born, not made. She must be a genius: self-contained, interested in ethnology and suffering primitive mankind, the masculine type of woman who would seek sport as a relaxation. Fedden was the ideal type of man: serious-minded, patient, with no brilliant intellectual edges to chafe his soul. The position as an uncrowned king of many thousands, whose wish and advice was practically law, flattered his vanity; although he, lacking any inclination to self-analysis, was wholly unconscious of it. He took his work too seriously and was wholly wrapped up in it. Nothing else, save an occasional shooting expedition for recreation, interested him. Work was all-sufficing, absorbing; and he was apt to resent any one approaching it without due solemnity. Ten years' devotion to an ideal, a mission, had permeated his very being. Twice before he had spent his biennial leave, like the postman, in the company of a brother official instead of the orthodox trip to Europe. Upon medical advice he had reluctantly consented to visit the land of his birth to be misunderstood, bored, and miserable, pining for his beloved station. Then he had met Miss Veddes, an orphan, whose father had died in Uganda. Fedden, of course, was familiar with the name. This was the first – and last – bond of common interest between them.

Any man, after ten years among savages, is apt to look upon an ordinary English girl as an angelic being; and Maude, endowed with looks above the average, seemed the materialization of his ideal. As a matter of fact, he had never had any definite ideal; but he thought he had, which amounted to the same thing in the long run. Maude, who lived – or vegetated, as she expressed it – with an elderly, indulgent aunt, having infamously jilted one man, was suffering from a bad attack of pique, with the result that she played with Fedden much as a cat sharpens its claws on the bark of a tree. He – lacking any sense of humor, and not understanding the modern game of battledore and shuttlecock[15] with hearts – took her seriously, considered the half-contemptuous toleration which she had given to his dissertations upon native administration – the only topic upon which he could be induced to open his mouth – as evidence of her interest in his lifework. Then, before

---

[15] Battledore and shuttlecock: a game of ancient Asian origin that evolved into badminton.

she quite realized what had happened, they were married. She had attempted to handle an unknown quantity and, like a child snapping threads of cotton, had got hold of a piece of steel wire, with the result that she had cut her fingers badly.

They had been some five months at Mbale, one whole month of which had occupied Maude in attaining complete disillusionment. The journey from Jinja had been a more or less delightful picnic. Maude, carried all day in a machila, had thought it an ideal method of travelling, although the mosquitoes, jiggers, and flies had somewhat marred the trip. The second day out some insect had bitten her wrists, raising angry red pimples. She had hastened, pale with fright, to her husband, who had replied, after a solemn investigation:

"Oh, they're only Mbwa (dog) fly, dear. They only bite; don't do any harm. No; don't try to crush them, else you'll drive them into your flesh; they're as hard as crystal. Just catch them and take off their head with your fingernail. What, dear? – Oh, nonsense."

Nobody but her dour-visaged husband with whom to flirt, she had begun already to miss the presence of other Europeans.

One day, while being paddled in a cranky[16] canoe across a narrow, snaky waterway cut through the dense papyrus sudd of an evil-smelling swamp – one of many intersecting the road – she experienced a sensation like a red-hot needle being thrust into her flesh through her blouse, and a big, grey- looking fly skirled[17] away. She winced and cried out at the momentary pain. Fedden appeared a trifle graver as he admitted that it was a tsetse fly.

"But there's no fear dear," he added; "they're not infected in this district." Yet the horror of that memory lingered in her mind.

---

[16] Cranky (of a boat): easily tipped.
[17] Skirl: a shrill, wailing sound:

Upon arrival at Mbale, fatigued by the hot sun, the bungalow had appeared a veritable haven of cool rest and comfort. For nearly a week the station held novel interests to her; from the verandah the sunsets on the flat horizon were a gorgeous panoply to be admired; the furniture to be rearranged; linen to be overhauled; man-dressed curtains to be reset; the cooking to be attacked – to the gesticulating indignation of the native chef – and relinquished in despair.

Then as her husband resumed his duties, leaving Maude to her own devices, the dead monotony of the life began to eat into her soul. All the evening she would sit at the piano, almost afraid to stop playing in fear of the buzzing silence that seemed to weigh upon her. For an hour after dinner they would sit on the verandah, in a mosquito-proof cage, her husband content to smoke silently, immersed in his own interests, she growing more and more restless until she felt she could scream. Day after day the sun rose in brazen glory at the same hour – only the difference of a few minutes all the year round. The boy would bring in the coffee, they would bathe and have breakfast, after which her husband disappeared all day, with the exception of the lunch interval. Sometimes they would take a constitutional together down the hill at the back of the fort, visit the kitchen garden on the flat, potter about with the miniature irrigation, and wander round to the main road through the bazaar and home.

What to do with herself she did not know. Household work was distasteful to her; and, moreover, was carried out by the large staff of native servants. For a while music, books, and embroidery, until she grew to hate the very cover of a book, and colored reels of wool brought out beads of perspiration. For hours she would potter about, picking up a book to discard it, attempt to study a native dictionary to get bored to tears, and finally work herself up into a moist frenzy of irritable boredom. No matter what she said or did her grave-eyed husband continued with his work imperturbably. She tried to interest herself in the sick parade; but the ghastly sights and mutilations filled her with physical nausea. Sometimes she would become frantic; at others sink into a state of inert lassitude. Stray mosquitoes bit her face, and she suffered agonies of offended vanity with one eye swollen out of recognition. Then one morning she felt abnormally flushed and thirsty, with a racking headache. Fedden produced a short glass stick and insisted upon thrusting it into her mouth, which tickled her throat and made her want to vomit.

"Just a touch of fever, dear," said he, complacently examining the clinical thermometer.

She felt irritated and ill beyond endurance, and finally collapsed in a shower of tears: nothing seemed to be able to move him: it was like trying to carve one's initials upon a granite slab with a penknife. In nearly every case the first attack of malaria is severe. Maude had to retire to bed, be swaddled in blankets and swallow tabloids of phenacetin, whilst a runner left for the nearest mission station. On the second day, whilst Maude was still delirious, the grim Miss Griller arrived, very plain and capable. Fedden, who had nursed Maude with unremitting care, returned to his duties. Upon recovering her normal senses, Maude's first emotion was one of gratitude for the presence of Miss Griller, but within the space of a few hours she had developed a violent dislike for her nurse, whose voice sounded as hard and starved as her soul must have been, and whose views upon the state of the native's moral well-being obsessed her to the exclusion of more human and interesting topics. For hours she would sit, gaunt and prim, beside the sickbed whilst Maude lay racked between the desire to talk to someone and a terror of Miss Griller's well-meant homilies.

Even Fedden's placidity was shaken by her incessantly expressed opinions upon the native question; she doubtless considered it a Heaven-sent opportunity to teach an official how to understand the native mind. The gospel of love and kindness she preached to excess, which Fedden resented as reflecting upon his sense of justice, striving to hold, as he certainly did, fairly even scales in the matter of reward and punishment. Miss Griller was an enthusiast; but enthusiasts drink their ideals neat, which naturally quickly affects the head. Maude inconsequently felt a pang of envy and a thrill of wicked delight to see her husband stung into a hot-tempered retort over an accusation of cruelty to natives in flogging them. That he was evidently annoyed with himself he showed by coldly declining to discuss or listen to her for the future: whereat Miss Griller went about her duties with prayers to soften his heart, dour, indignant eyes, and punished Maude to prove her own sense of equity.

One of the household servants was a renegade Christian. She presented him with a copy of the Bible, in Luganda, to reconvert him – and succeeded, so he said – and his colleagues; lectured Maude upon her wickedness in neglecting to hold service at least twice a week; sniffed at her protests and succeeded in whipping Fedden into the dry retort that their souls were outside his jurisdiction – sniffs from Miss Griller and subdued giggles from the sickbed. For another fortnight Miss Griller conceived it her duty to minister to the wants of the sick, although, after a week, Maude assured her, fervently, that she had sufficiently recovered to fend for herself, and could not consent to keep her from the native flock.

At length Miss Griller departed in her machila and life sank to the normal routine.

Fedden's office hours were supposed to end at 1 p.m. on Saturday as in any orthodox office in the old country. Upon one such blazing hot morning Maude sat awaiting his arrival for lunch, fidgeting in her chair, dolefully dreaming of the teas of other days in dear Rockchurch, beautiful in the unattainable distance. Somewhere in the kitchen quarters someone was singing a hymn refrain woefully out of tune, a relic of Miss Griller. Maude frowned annoyance, and unable to bear it longer, went to the back verandah and shouted: "Sirika!" (be quiet) – the one word, from constant repetition, of which she was quite sure. The voice ceased abruptly amid subdued laughter, and she returned languidly to her chair, yawning.

At length Fedden appeared, abstracted and worried looking as usual. Save for a few desultory remarks from Maude lunch was eaten in silence, making her wonder vaguely why on earth they ever troubled to wait for each other at meals; afterwards she poured him out some coffee and made a second effort at conversation.

"Well, how's the case going on, Herbert?" she inquired listlessly.

His duties usually consisted of a monotonous series of petty cases punctuated with an odd murder or cattle theft, so that she knew that the question was safe.

"Eh, dear? Oh, slowly, slowly. They're all such liars that it is very hard to sift the truth from the mass of lies."

"Still the police theft one?" she inquired, with some show of interest.

This was a case of a native policeman accused of stealing a bunch of firewood from a peasant woman over which, from the conflicting evidence of professional witnesses and others who suffered from a chronic inability to tell the truth in any circumstances, three days of a highly paid official's service had already been wasted. But Fedden was of the hyperconscientious type; he scrupulously inquired into every detail.

"Yes," he said wearily, rubbing his eyes, "I'm afraid that it'll take another day or two yet. They've brought a petty chief into it now. He swore yesterday that he was not there; now he swears that he saw the policeman strike the woman, and the woman admits that the scar on her forehead, which she swore yesterday was given her by the policeman, was caused by –"

But Maude's feeble interest had died. She had heard so often these wearisome details of petty cases.

"Are you coming for the usual?" she inquired listlessly.

"It's too early," he protested in mild surprise; "and far too hot."

"It's just as hot lying about in here. Besides, I must go somewhere, do something or – or shriek. Oh – are you coming?"

"I can't, my dear; there's the sick parade I must attend to, and the sun is too powerful. Wait till five –"

"Oh bother the sun!"

"Wait till –"

"Oh, I can't," returned Maude petulantly from the door. "I must go – now."

"Very good, my dear," assented Fedden. "I'll walk down the bazaar afterwards and meet you. I want to see –"

He paused as Maude disappeared into her room, sighed patiently, and walked out into the sunlit square.

Maude emerged ready for her solitary walk in a man's terai hat pinned on her red hair and strolled despondently down the hill towards the kitchen garden. She paused once to turn about and stare resentfully at the rooftops of the fort outlined against the burning turquoise of the sky.

"Oh, how I hate you," she cried aloud, and continued her way moodily until she reached the garden, where an Indian coolie was at work. She stood awhile watching the man, an irritable frown wrinkling her face. In common with most people who spend a major portion of their existence alone she had developed the trick of talking aloud to herself.

"I loathe you, too," she muttered, glaring at the inoffensive Indian and the country at large. "Nothing but black monkeys, flies, and every creeping horror and – Oh, if I'd only known! If only something would happen!"

She pottered discontentedly about the garden for a while, anathematizing the rows of dull cabbages – grown into small trees in this tropical climate; kicked away, with one small foot, a mud dam controlling the miniature irrigation reservoir and giggled delightedly at the declamatory distress of the Indian gardener, bewailing the consequent swamping of a newly sown bed. She turned away after this episode, feeling better tempered, and followed the well-worn footpath round the hill which led into the main road from Mbale to the Nile. Through this broad track, cleared of grass and bush, the old native path ran, winding from side to side like the convolutions of a snake, solely used by the native who, with characteristic obstinacy, preferred its twists and turns to the possibility of marching in a fairly straight line. Down this track Maude turned with the unwilling gait of one walking for the mere sake of exercise.

The sun blazed pitilessly, throwing short, hard-edged shadows of the odd trees and the wall of grass of the roadside, which wound away to the north to avoid a swamp. A bunch of nude Kavirondo suddenly popped out of the grass, following some bypath bisecting the road. They stood in the dappled shadow of a large tree, arrested by the unusual sight of a white woman, and watched her pass with amiable laughing faces, jabbering to each other. Maude, used to the curiosity she evoked, continued her way, scarcely conscious of their presence, having, by this time, lost the newcomer's nervousness and nearly attained the resident's indifference, merely regarding them as one at home does sheep in a field or the dogs in the street. The Kavirondo followed her with their eyes until a bend in the track hid her, and then continued on their way, apparently vastly amused, cracking jokes characteristic of the savage mind – and for that matter common to the civilized male in herds.

After some twenty minutes Maude began to tire of her lonely constitutional, and was about to return, when her eye caught a glimpse of a man in European clothes at the end of the straight. She stood for a moment wondering who he might be. Possibly a Goanese trader who affected European dress, or perhaps the Rev. Blackber from Kibwezi? But this man was too tall for either. He swung along the path with a rapid stride, followed by two natives, one in the white gown of a Baganda. Maude became self-conscious, wondering what one ought to do upon meeting a complete stranger in the middle of Africa – and if he were a Frenchman or German without English how awkward it would be! Whilst she hesitated he drew near. He had seen her and was staring curiously as he approached.

She was suddenly aware that the swing of those shoulders and the general carriage was familiar. He lowered his head a trifle, the flap of his felt hat throwing his face into shadow. As she stood irresolute he was close upon her. She felt her heart give a great leap and her face pale as she met the smiling blue eyes. She gasped with the shock of unexpected recognition, and wonder grew in his eyes, arresting his hand in midair. For a moment they paused, staring at each other, while the two natives halted, watching them curiously.

"Good God!" he ejaculated, the first to speak.

"Laurie!"she stuttered.

"Yes, Laurie right enough," he said, his mouth drooping into a cynical smile. "And Maude, of all people on earth!"

"Why – why –" she commenced.

"Exactly," he replied dryly, recovering self-possession. "Why – that's what I'd like to know! But won't you shake hands? – for the benefit of the spectators," he added.

"Of course I will," she exclaimed, a genuine note of eagerness in her voice.

They shook hands silently; she nervous, with tremulous lips, he coldly smiling with satiric corners of the mouth.

"Come!" he said, after an awkward pause. "Walk along. I suppose the fort is your home. And we'll straighten things out."

"Good Heavens!" she exclaimed. "Fancy meeting *you* here!"

"Yes," said he, smiling. "Rather unexpected, eh? The fancies of today are not always the facts of tomorrow though, are they?"

"I *am* glad to see you!"she exclaimed impulsively, failing to notice the gibe.

"Are you?" he said, raising his eyebrows as he turned to walk beside her.

She flushed and glanced up at him.

"Er – have you been out here long?" he inquired lamely.

"Only six months. I thought you were in South Africa?"

"I was," he said. "But I'm here now."

"Oh," said she; and then as another thought struck her she burst out: "Oh, but my husband –"

"Ah, yes, your husband," he said, with the shadow of a sneer.

"Don't," she exclaimed, looking away. "Can't – won't you forgive me? I – I made a mistake."

"And I made a mistake," he added bitterly. "Made a very bad mistake. But being a woman I suppose you have the right to play with a man's life as it suits you, and then be quite annoyed because the stupid victim has the bad taste to remember."

"You brute!" she murmured, and commenced to sob quietly.

"Forgive me!" he exclaimed, scared into repentance by the sight of a woman's all-conquering tears. "I – you see it hurts rather."

"I – I can't stand it," she whispered, turning a tearstained, tragic face to him. "I – I'm so miserable. Forgive me!"

"Yes, yes," he said hurriedly. "I'm a brute. Don't have a scene, for Heaven's sake!"

"You will forgive me, Laurie?" she persisted, drying her eyes.

"Yes. All right, I promise to. But here's a whiteman coming."

She glanced up to see her husband advancing.

"Yes, my husband. Remember, I've only just met you."

"But why?" protested Laurie.

"For Heaven's sake do as I tell you," she whispered hurriedly. "Oh, Herbert," she exclaimed to Fedden, who looked inquiringly at Laurie, "this is a Mr. Burke; I met him coming along. Mr. Burke – my husband."

Laurie took the other's measure in a quick glance: Fedden eyed him gravely in his preoccupied manner.

"Glad to meet you," said Laurie, smiling as he extended his hand. "Most unexpected delight to meet your wife. Diana in the wilderness," he added, glancing at Maude, who stood watching the two men nervously.

"Howd'youdo?" replied Fedden, in a stiff, official manner. "I've heard of you by name."

For a moment Laurie appeared perplexed.

"Oh, yes, from Toro – of course," quickly. "Give a dog a bad name, eh?"

CHAPTER VIII

They walked to the fort together. Maude remained silent, leaving Laurie to talk lightly and answer Fedden's cross-examination of his business intentions. Laurie had earned a certain notoriety in official circles, and Fedden, ever jealous of the sanctity of his own province, immediately desired to "choke off" this undesirable poacher person. Of this fact Laurie was well aware. He immediately proceeded to subject him to the treatment he meted out to all official persons: a satiric deference which they usually took seriously, mixed with a light banter, as if scouting the notion of any illicit trading, while at the same time he laughed openly. Europeans, other than officials or missionaries were few and far between, and in all previous cases – with the exception of a distinguished civilian explorer, to whom Fedden was compelled to kowtow – were of a lower social grade and therefore did not require to be entertained. The official is a race apart: the divine paradox of a servant and master of the public. Therefore Fedden's natural inclination was to freeze, which operation he somehow felt rather difficult.

"Er – about camp," he remarked, as they climbed the hill past the Indian bazaar. "The camp is just below the marketplace. I'll _"

"Ah, yes," replied Laurie amiably. "Never use old camps myself – too full of jiggers and ticks. Your quarters are just on the rise, aren't they? I'll pitch my camp just beyond for the present. Water down below, eh? Thanks; awfully good of you."

Fedden had not suggested anything of the sort, Laurie merely deducing that the Government fort would be near the best position, and within easy reach of water. Maude, watching her husband's face, smiled: Laurie always had had "a way with him."

"Charming position you have, Mrs. – er – Fedden? Sorry: never can remember – fresh names."

"You must be dying for a cup of tea, Mr. Burke," suggested Maude; "and of course you'll dine with us tonight. Do make him, Herbert?"

"It's awfully good of you," declared Laurie to Fedden. "I should really enjoy it."

"Yes, do," said Fedden tonelessly, breaking his long silence.

As a matter of fact Laurie had fully intended to dine with Fedden and his wife when he had left his caravan behind in the early morning – although he had had no notion that he would have the mixed pleasure of the company of his old sweetheart.

As they sat on the verandah taking tea the onus of conversation fell upon Laurie, who had the happy faculty of chatting and thinking of two different subjects with facility. Maude, answering queries at random, was busy feasting her eyes upon her old lover and attempting to decide what attitude she would adopt. She was unfeignedly glad to see him; in the first place because he was something to flirt with, and secondly because there was a distinct element of danger in the situation. She had given as much of her heart to him as her undeveloped temperament permitted; the jilting process had only been attained at considerable cost and determination; and after all her scheming and callous conduct she had missed the great prize, who had fallen to the wiles of a symmetrical limbed member of a Frivolity chorus, conducing to the thought that the ordinary girl would secure just as many titled scalps as the chorus young lady were she permitted to exhibit her native charms in the open market with equal freedom.

It was undoubtedly something of a panacea to Maude's wounded vanity to discover that this man had really and truly buried himself in the heart of Africa for love of her – and stopped there; so many victims of unrequited love merely turned it into an excuse for a hunting trip, arriving back in town bronzed and irritatingly cheerful. The more she gazed at him, and consequently brought up visions of the past, the more she thought how eminently desirable he was. This line of thought logically increased her resentment against her husband. She glanced at him with a little pout of disdain, which the observant eyes of Laurie noted and acknowledged with a cynical twist of the lips.

Fedden, wrapped as usual in his everlasting debate on official subjects, seemed a very morose and unsociable man to Laurie who, divining that they could not possibly be happy together, was racking his brains to remember to what title or wealth the man was heir, for he could not conceive the mercenary little woman opposite him marrying Fedden for any other motive. Laurie discovered to his own annoyance that his affection for her had not diminished in the slightest, or had certainly reawakened with equal intensity and vigor. He immediately decided from signs and symptoms displayed that she fully intended an attempt to subjugate him again. But the challenge already in her eyes he studiously ignored, and determined that he would never let her see that she still retained the old grip over him, thinking bitterly of the perfidy of women in general.

By the time that tea was over Maude knew by intuition that Laurie was not indifferent to her and decided that she could bring him to heel again without the odious necessity of using her husband as a stalking horse. She did not seek to know or care what the result might be; she had been bored and unutterably miserable for so long. Now she felt thrills of anticipation at the opportunity of thoroughly enjoying herself. Laurie, observing this attitude, mentally stiffened and determined to show a cast-iron front.

Pale violet shadows enveloped the verandah ere Laurie bethought him of the dilatory caravan.

"I'll take a walk to meet my men, and show them the camp site," he suggested to Fedden, and meeting Maude's watchful eyes, smiled sardonically as the thought of Sula flashed into his mind.

Fedden nodded his head gravely and stood up.

"It's out at the back on the crest, isn't it?" inquired Laurie, and without waiting for an answer, turned to Maude, still sitting in her chair.

"Well, au revoir, Mrs. Fedden! Dinner at eight, you said?"

"Yes, but I want a walk," she said, getting to her feet. "I'll come with you. I shan't be long, Herbert."

"Oh, but I couldn't think of troubling you," objected Laurie, who did not feel equal to a tête-à-tête.

"Yes, do let me come," cooed Maude, looking him straight in the eyes.

"I'm sorry; but I have to walk some distance," said Laurie, meeting the attack coolly.

"No, no, my dear," remarked Fedden; "better not go. You're quite tired in this heat."

Laurie, raising his hat, turned away with the memory of an angry flash in her eyes; and smiled ironically to himself as he strode across the square.

The sun, low down on the horizon, threw great shafts, violet and purple, across the arc of the sky, tinting with ruddy gold a mass of cloud hanging over and around the summit of Mount Elgon in the east. The traders in the bazaar were busy closing the rickety shutters and doors of their corrugated-iron shops. Some of the sleek, swarthy owners were grouped discussing local trade, or squatting in contemplative isolation after the manner of the Buddha. Here and there a lithe-limbed child played in a doorway, the long black locks confusing the sex. Now and again the gleam of sloe eyes, the bright tint of shawls and the jingle of silver bangles denoted the womenfolk hovering in the background. The marketplace below the bazaar was deserted save for the dilapidated tents of a Goanese trader who, squatting in the door, shouted: "Goo' evenin', mister," to

Laurie, in the peculiar singsong voice of the Babu and his kindred.

Away over the flats hung a steamy mist, denser to the north near the broad belts of papyrus swamps and lakes into which the sun dipped, producing strange color schemes and light effects. As the last rays lit up the wooded crown of the bald-faced hill behind the station in a silver halo[,] a trumpet call rang out in stuttering notes from the native police camp.

Laurie turned away from his point of vantage commanding a view of the road without having seen any signs of the expected caravan. At about five miles from Mbale there was one of the numerous papyrus-choked waterways, stretching from Lake Choga[18] like the tentacles of an octopus, to be crossed by means of a single canoe only capable of carrying three loads at a time, which Laurie concluded was the cause of the delay.

By the time that he had crossed the wooden bridge into the fort the night had swallowed the mass of distant Elgon, and the seas of color had dwindled to flaming pyres over the grave of the sun. The mosquito-wired door and windows of the bungalow were closed. A lamp was burning in the dining room with an attendant aerial battalion of moths hovering about it. The soft, yellow light gleaming on the table cutlery was soothing and abnormally inviting to a camp-worn man. In a chair in the shadows sat Maude, leaning forward, supporting her head in two shapely bare arms as if listening or lost in thought, her face just in the circle of lamplight.

As Laurie, treading lightly, paused a little to one side of the window, her profile showed clear against the deep shadows of the room, a few stray locks of hair gleaming ruddy, the mellow, half-shades softening the contour of her neck and bosom. A native servant entered as he stood watching, breaking a spell

---

[18] Lake Choga: a large shallow lake in central Uganda, north of Lake Victoria, now known as Lake Kyoga (pronounced "choga").

that held him unwillingly. A quick frown of annoyance fled across her face as she rose and disappeared into the gloom. He heard Fedden's voice calling "Maude," and to his anger found himself cherishing a sudden violent hatred and loathing of this man, her husband. The fit was momentary, and, smiling cynically, he stepped forward with unnecessary noise, and rapped with his knuckles on the doorframe, calling "Hodi! Hodi!" the customary self-announcement of the country.

"Who's there?" inquired Fedden from within in Kiswahili.

"Burke. I say, my safari hasn't –"

He stopped as Maude appeared in the room in a close fitting evening gown.

"Oh, Laur –" she clapped her hands over her mouth, laughed and went on – "Mr. Burke, do come in! Can't you find your caravan? How tiresome!"

Stepping full into the circle of light as Laurie closed the door after him, she raised her arms to fiddle with the lamp. She paused in the middle to glance over her shoulder at Laurie. He was observing her, so she turned up the wick until it flared, and exclaimed in distress:

"Oh, *do* help me – Mr. Burke! The lamp's flaming! Look!"

Laurie looked and smiled, but made no move. Having adjusted the wick without assistance, she turned and faced him.

"Why didn't you help me?" she demanded in a low voice, feigning annoyance.

He smiled enigmatically and sat down.

"May I have some soap and water?" he inquired placidly.

She hesitated for a moment.

"Certainly, Mr. Burke," she said, in the unnecessarily loud tone that a woman adopts upon such an occasion. "Herbert! Mr. Burke's caravan hasn't arrived. He –"

"I can't hear, my dear," came Fedden's muffled voice.

"All right; I'm coming!" she called, and flinging a disdainful glance over her shoulder at Laurie, she picked up her skirts and vanished.

"The devil a woman was he!" quoth Laurie, and leaning back in his chair laughed his rolling chuckle.

For a while Laurie was left to listen to the faint drone of mosquitoes and the occasional whizzing burr of a flying beetle blindly charging the wire-gauzed door in vain attempts to reach the light. From the far bedroom he could hear Maude's light treble and protesting monosyllables from Fedden, who obviously did not welcome the entrance of a stranger upon the domestic hearth, merely, be it noted, from a desire for solitude.

At length the couple emerged. Maude dismissed Laurie in charge of a servant to her husband's room, where, to his amazement, he found a suit of Fedden's ducks laid out for him. As he commenced to bathe he heard the tinkle of the piano. Music was one of the adjuncts of civilization that he had missed most in his sojourn in the wilds; and the familiar sound of the instrument raised memories that he had rather left undisturbed.

Maude, opening with a scrap from the latest musical comedy she had heard in London, perversely glided into a version of the "Old Folks at Home," and variations, quite contrary to her usual repertoire. Laurie, pausing in the act of a vigorous towel scrub, listened for a moment and then swore, "Damn the woman!" for the commonest sentimental tune heard in the environment of the frontier has a dire effect upon the most hardened adventurer, even if he be a musical classicist.

Then she, perhaps fully aware of this primitive weakness, and desirous to be lenient, played Mendelssohn's "Spring Song" with verve, as if endeavoring to convey to the intelligent listener the joyful abandon at having found her lost love. But Laurie failed to interpret this subtle message, if intended, merely thankfully drinking in the bubbling joy of the masterpiece, capering and prancing about the room as he struggled with Fedden's trousers, many sizes too small for him.

When he at length entered the sitting room, clad in his travel stained khaki jacket, with white trousers displaying a maximum length of sock, he found Fedden huddled – the man never appeared comfortable – in a chair behind his wife, who was turning over music leaves in the rose glow of a shaded lamp upon the piano. She glanced at him as he sought a seat and remarked:

"Oh, Mr. Burke, my husband has sent an askari to await your caravan and show them the camp."

His conventional thanks were drowned by the crash of an opening chord, sending a shivering thrill of recognition through him. It was the prelude to Tosti's "Goodbye," which Maude had so often sung to him in far-off Rockchurch. It had been his favorite. As Maude's full soprano rose and fell the light died out of Laurie's eyes and his mouth tightened in pain. In the interval of the verses she threw a rapid glance at him, but he was staring into space, being strangled by memory. In the second verse she put all the passionate feeling into her voice of which she was capable. As her last note died away in the warm, still air, she half turned to look at him. In the silence the high, piping solo of a stray mosquito in the room sounded against the faint chorus of its fellows out on the verandah. Laurie became conscious that she was watching him with lash-veiled eyes. He glanced across at her husband. Fedden was prosaically scribbling on a writing pad. Laurie looked back at Maude, looked straight into her eyes, and knew that she knew that she was deliberately torturing him, and was gloating over the fact.

"You're fond of music, aren't you, Mr. Burke?" she inquired brightly.

"Yes," he answered, a trifle thickly.

She smiled triumphantly.

"How do you like this song?"

The necessity of speaking roused him: he pulled himself together.

"Ah, that is not a fair question," he protested. "One cannot praise the earth in the presence of the sun, for what would the earth be without the sun?"

She raised her eyebrows as if in surprise at this unexpected rally.

"True," she retorted, "but the rays of the sun don't seem to warm the moon, do they?"

"No," said Laurie smiling "You see the moon has been burned out long ago, is dead and cold – so the astronomers say."

"Ah yes, but I don't believe everything they may tell us – they're only men – after all."

"Even men have been known to tell the truth, much as you may doubt it: in fact, men usually handled the truth naked until Mother Grundy – a woman, you see – made lies to dress it in."

"Hence the proverb that women are born liars and men only acquire –"

"Chakula tayari," interrupted the voice of a white-clad native servant.

During dinner Laurie endeavored to draw Fedden out, but with signal failure, for Fedden – anything but a conversationalist – was too immersed in chewing the cud of official affairs to do other than reply in monosyllables. Always a miser in words, except in that brief period of his honeymoon, he would have much preferred to dine in silence and retire to his office afterwards. After the rather trying ordeal of forcing conversation upon a man who doggedly refused to respond, and fencing with Maude, Laurie was glad when they moved to the other room for coffee. He made another attempt to escape on the plea of searching for the dilatory caravan, but Maude scouted the idea of their arriving at all, begging him – on behalf of her husband – to make use of the spare bedroom furnished by Fedden for the reception of brother officials. Laurie refused, but consented to have coffee. Fedden, who lived methodically in all things, only smoked after meals, and having exhausted the supply, went across to the store to fetch another box of cigarettes. Maude, who had seated herself at the piano, idly strumming, swung round on his departure and looked quizzically at Laurie, who, fuming inwardly at this unexpected tête-à-tête, was searching in his pockets for a cigar which he knew was not there. For a moment she did not speak: he dropped his eyes.

"Oh, Laurie, you *are* a humbug!" she said, laughing nervously.

"Am I?" said he. "I'm afraid I don't follow you."

"Don't be idiotic!" she exclaimed petulantly. "You know as well as I do that you're dying to know how this" – she nodded in the direction of her husband – "happened. Oh, Laurie, I am sorry! What a mistake I made!"

She got up and sat down beside him.

"Laurie, will you forgive me?" she asked, with genuine emotion in her voice, leaning forward towards him.

"There's nothing to forgive," he assured her hurriedly, glancing towards the door. "Besides, it's too late now."

"Yes, it's too late now," she repeated, trying to meet his eyes, but he avoided her.

"Look!" she said gently; "there's a moth crawling up your shoulder." She leaned forward, plucking the insect, real or imaginary, from him. Her hair brushed his face as she did so. She felt him tremble.

"There!" She laughed softly. "The moth of – memory, shall we say? creeping back and I plucked it away!"

"Don't," he said hoarsely.

She sat back. They were silent for a moment. Fedden's voice calling a servant sounded. Laurie looked towards the door as if for help.

"Laurie, I was cruel to you!" said Maude.

"You are far more cruel to me now," he retorted. "Heavens, if I had only guessed that you were here!"

"I am glad you didn't," she said. "You wouldn't have come. Laurie, I'd do anything to undo the past."

"God Himself cannot do that," said he; "so why not forget it?"

"Can you forget it?" she asked, leaning over towards him again. "Don't lie to me, Laurie. Can you forget?"

"You cannot accuse *me* of having lied," he retorted bitterly.

"Oh, why are you so cruel?" she persisted.

"You are cruel, not I. I did not come here knowingly."

"Laurie! Look at me!"

"I will not," he said. "You are unfair. You know I'm weak in these surroundings – music – sybaritic luxuries – and that sort of thing and –"

He paused, glanced at her and quickly dropped his eyes.

"And what?" she demanded sharply.

"Well, damnation," he said fiercely, "hunting me! You're clever, Maude," he went on savagely; "you always were clever – as I knew you, but –"

"I'm a huntress, eh?"

"Well, yes. You caught me once, pawed me like a cat with a sparrow and threw me aside. I can't and won't stand another mauling. You haven't got a heart, otherwise I wish you'd get caught and mauled."

"I was a fool," she said quietly.

"No, I was a fool! – yet – yes, you were a fool. But it's the everlasting hunt. A man hunts happiness and a woman hunts the hunter – and always pulls him down, so the quarry escapes both."

A patter of feet sounded on the verandah and a light gleamed outside the door, which neither noticed.

"I only want you to know that my cruelty to you has ruined my life as well!"

She spoke slowly, caught his eyes and held them.

"Lolly!"

Maude sat back in her chair hurriedly.

The door burst open. Sula ran in, her face agleam with pleasure, swinging a hurricane lamp in her hand.

"Lolly!" she exclaimed. "Sula glad! Sula –"

She ceased abruptly as her eyes fell upon Maude leaning forward, staring with startled eyes at the intruder. Sula's eyes narrowed; her lithe body stiffened like a cat suddenly confronted with a terrier. Laurie ejaculated, "Good Lord!" and stood up. For a moment the mosquitoes let in by Sula hummed joyfully. A step on the verandah and Fedden entered, pausing in amazement on the threshold.

The two women eyed each other: intuition told them their relative positions. Laurie glanced at Fedden. They spoke simultaneously, breaking the tense spell.

"Sula –" commenced Laurie.

"Who is this?" inquired Fedden slowly. Sula, without taking her eyes off Maude, moved to Laurie and clutched his arm with a curiously possessive, confiding air. Maude swept Sula with a look, and rising to her feet, moved aside. She turned to Laurie, her eyes blazing with anger.

"Yes, who is this?" she sneered.

The tone of contempt stung Laurie into complete self-possession. He smiled cynically, and moved with Sula towards the door, saying coldly:

"I think under the circumstances that we had better leave, Sula." He turned at the door and bowed formally to Maude and her husband. "I thank you for your hospitality," said he. "Good evening!"

Sula, still clinging to his arm, went out with him, her head turned, watching Maude till the last. As the door closed and they were swallowed up by the darkness Maude, who had stood in the center of the room glaring at Sula, turned upon her silent and amazed husband.

"What do you mean by allowing me to be insulted like this?" she demanded angrily. "You knew this and allowed that man to come here. You –"

"You forget, my dear," he answered placidly, "that *you* invited him. I did not."

"I did nothing of the sort – beyond common courtesy. You *knew* that creature was coming."

"I did not, my dear – besides," he added slowly, "I do not know who she is yet."

"Don't know who she is!" retorted Maude angrily. "Have you any need to ask?"

"But, my dear," he protested, "one might guess; but until –"

"You – *you* make excuses – defend him! The custom of the country, I suppose," she sneered. "Oh, you brute, how dare you bring me here? I might have known –"

She suddenly turned and fled to their room, leaving him perplexed with her, angry with Laurie in his grave, placid way. He stood for a few minutes turning the matter over in his mind. The sound of startled sobs made him hasten to find her lying at full length on the bed. She raised a tearstained, disordered face, and angrily cried:

"Let me alone! For Heaven's sake go away!"

He hesitated for a moment and then went, gravely disturbed and annoyed at the unaccountable actions of women.

CHAPTER IX

Convention to a man of deep emotions is as the curb rein to a mettlesome horse; and when a savage spur prick of a blighted love idyll is added either animal, if he can get the bit between his teeth, will surely bolt. Laurie had bolted and shown his teeth at his late rider. Convention. Fortunately he had shown some consideration for others in clearing out of England. In South Africa, and later in Uganda, he had flung his own will and pleasure in the face of convention, making a god unto himself, doing whatever seemed good to him, adopting the principle that if others did not approve they could do the other thing, as he cared for no man's opinion and little for his own. He had met Sula living with her mulatto mother upon a shamba bequeathed her by her father, a whiteman, who had apparently, like himself, gone fantee.[19] She had been partly educated by missionaries, but had early developed some of her father's rebel spirit and returned to her mother, a consistent pagan. They were a pathetic pair, living in solitude, barred association with whites by reason of their native blood, and scorning the black.

Sula's wild beauty fired Laurie's blood, and she fell in love with Laurie. Laurie took her away, with her mother's delighted consent. The mulatto woman had found a white mate, so it was but natural that she should welcome a whiteman for her daughter. The ceremony of marriage had no meaning to her other than the formalities of a sale. In accordance with his principle of candid and open conduct he refused to adopt the usual discretion customary to the country in such matters. He

---

[19] Fantee (chiefly British): wild, unrestrained, primitive; an anxious or excited state. To "go native" or to adopt the habits etc. of native people. E.g., "He was perpetually 'going Fantee' among natives, which, of course, no man with any sense believes in." Rudyard Kipling, "Miss Youghal's Sais," *Plain Tales from the Hills*.

persisted in treating Sula as a lawfully wedded white wife, to the righteous indignation of the residents who, for the greater part, kept their brown amours well in the background.

Naturally, after this unorthodox mésalliance, Laurie was ostracized, to which he replied that their room was preferable to their company, adding, with a cynical laugh, that light o' love[20] was better than light love. He became notorious as an abandoned character from one end of the Protectorate to the other and even beyond. A few of the kindly disposed matrons shook their heads sadly, whilst one bold virgin, soured by broken ideals, shocked official tea circles by observing with a sneer that "at all events he was in very good company!" which caused not a few young married women to look extremely uncomfortable, mindful of facts which everybody knew. Still, one open sin is quite unforgivable, whilst many unostentatious indiscretions are – well, quite another matter.

Laurie's unexpected meeting with the primary cause of his blighted life had created a chaotic influx of new ideas and emotions in the back of his mind, hitherto held in abeyance by the necessity of conversing rationally. After a futile attempt to soothe Sula, who divined that this strange woman had, or had had, some big influence with the man she loved and feared accordingly, he spent the major portion of the night in marching up and down in front of the tent, smoking innumerable cigars, engaged in thrashing the matter out. Sula, who for the first time felt the talons of jealousy tearing into her very being, was in a state bordering on distraction, alternately sobbing and cursing the cause of her trouble.

Laurie, after considerable effort, succeeded in subduing and sorting the various emotions which besieged his mind. Normal men and women are divided, roughly, into three distinct

---

[20] A person who is inconstant and fickle in love. Also, a prostitute or a sexually promiscuous woman.

classes: wanton polygamous and polyandrous; bigamous; and monogamous.

Laurie belonged to the second, in which a man may love two women at one and the same time; to the one love pure, to the other passion pure. Naturally, although it is seldom the case, love and passion may be directed towards or absorbed by one object only. Had Laurie married Maude then all would have been well, for she could have responded to both sides of his nature. His feeling towards Sula was paternal when it was not passionate, but she, necessarily, could never fill the void of mental understanding and fellowship. But what was the use of dallying over the impossible? Maude was married and Sula – well, Sula had many claims upon him which he did not intend to shirk. His passion for Sula was deep and genuine; but then passion is plural, love individual. However, although the even tenor of his mental attitude, bitter enough beyond the sphere of Sula's influence, was rudely shaken and all the old twinges of might-have-beens were awakened, he determined to grin and bear it as best he might and, to assist that course, to leave the neighborhood as soon as possible.

As he grew calmer his sense of humor was restored; inconsequently remembering from whom the clothes he wore were borrowed he chuckled sardonically.

Maude, too, had spent a sleepless night, sharing the agony of Sula, although she persuaded herself that it was the insult that had wounded her pride, and inconsistently enough blamed her husband. A woman is seldom insulted; it is either that her vanity is hurt, her jealousy aroused, or she is playing to the gallery. Fedden, after solemnly meditating upon the utter impossibility of understanding women and making a futile effort to find the cause, retired to bed merely vexed with his wife and annoyed at the interruption to his official routine.

By the time that Maude got up next morning Fedden had departed to the office. A cup of tea and an egg, over which she nearly wept with peevish vexation at the stupidity of the servant in failing to understand her, sufficed for her breakfast, after which she retired to the shady side of the house, irritable, miserably desiring to wreak vengeance for her troubles upon someone – Sula for preference. She decided to go down to Laurie's camp and tell him what she thought of him, or, to be exact, what she imagined for the moment she thought of him. However, she abandoned the idea as incompatible with her dignity – and, besides, she was rather afraid of muzzled thoughts at the back of her mind. As she sat fidgeting and unhappy Laurie passed the far gate of the fort on his way to the bazaar. The sight of the familiar swing of his shoulders brought a leap of the pulse which made her hate herself; the next moment brought an aftermath of vain regrets and bitter thoughts.

Intruding upon the privacy of her misery came Samwili around the farther side of the bungalow, from the kitchen quarters. He had arrived with Laurie's caravan, having kept very much in the background during the march, and had spent the early hours of the morning pumping the garden coolie. He advanced upon Maude with the object of using his newly acquired knowledge to the best advantage. Fedden had had all his servants for a number of years, and would not have considered Samwili's valuable services for a moment, particularly as he was a convert, holding, in common with most long residents in the country, that a converted native was merely an adept at collecting all the whiteman's vices and forgetting his pagan virtues. This Samwili knew well: his cunning had taught him a safer plan. Accordingly, sweeping off a dilapidated hat, which he affected under the incorrect impression that it added to his dignity, he grinned amiably and said:

"Goo' mornin', Missus!"

Maude, who had been vaguely wondering what he might want, started upon hearing the unexpected English.

"You want boy, Missus? – goo' servant spik Englees?" he went on obsequiously.

She stared at him curiously.

"Where do you come from?" she inquired.

"Klistian genelman," he stated. "I work for Mistaire Cromb. Here" – producing a greasy envelope – "you read my k'racter, Missus."

Maude read the papers. The first was a lengthy epistle setting forth the virtues of the bearer, Samwili Maliko, adding that he was a good Christian and ate of the Sacrament regularly. At the last statement she glanced up at Samwili. The thought that this creature, a brother Christian, partook of Holy Communion in common with herself – only when she had been at home by the way – gave her a mild shock of disgust. The second paper was short and to the point, "The bearer Samwili has worked for me for two months – too long. He is fairly honest as far as I know, but a fool, (signed) 'T. O'Brien."

Maude repressed a smile and inquired: "Can you read English?"

"Yes, Missus. I read Englees, quick. Papers velly good."

Maude smiled broadly this time and added sotto voce: "And a liar, too!"

"Who is this man, Mr. O'Brien?" she asked.

"Mistaire O'Brien work – work –" he paused at a loss for the word, scratching his woolly head after the manner of the yokel. "He work all same Gov'rnment," he finished.

"What, in Entebbe, or where?"

"No," said Samwili, "he not Gov'rnment – not miss'un'ry – all same Gov'rnment." Then, as if with a flash of inspiration: "He drink an' keep woman all same Gov'rnment!"

For a moment Maude hardly knew whether to laugh or frown. The unconscious irony hurt deeply as well as amused her.

"Oh!" she said at length and turned the subject. "You know how to wait at table?"

"Yes Missus!"

"How much do you want?"

"Twenty rupees," demanded Samwili greedily.

"Ten rupees," she offered, in accordance with the recognized method of barter.

"No, Missus. I allays get twenty rupees. Mistaire O'Brien give me twenty-five. I velly good boy."

"I'm sure Mr. O'Brien didn't do anything of the sort. I'll give you twelve."

"Orlright, Missus," agreed Samwili, after a long pause, eyeing Maude appraisingly.

"Very good. Now go to Malima and tell him I've engaged you."

"Orlright, Missus," he answered affably.

"I work now?"

"Or course."

"I go get my things," he said, and slouched away thinking of the row there would be when the present staff knew, for they were all of a different tribe to Samwili.

Maude, left to her own reflections, fell into torment again between the desire to see and speak with Laurie and the futility of mending her fate.

Laurie, returning later in the morning from the bazaar, saw the cool white of her dress upon the verandah as he entered the fort gate. The sight of him raised an indignant storm in her mind as she thought he would dare to approach. But he swiftly turned off into the office, angry with the surge of emotion which her presence evoked. As he could not avoid interviewing Fedden upon official business, he felt it advisable to apologize to him for the unfortunate contretemps of the previous evening, surmising, from his knowledge of women, that Fedden must have experienced a *mauvais quart d'heure*[21] for his sins. From the impersonal side Laurie felt sympathy for Fedden as a man who had most obviously made an unhappy marriage.

Grouped around the verandah edge in the broiling hot sun was the usual stoical crowd of native witnesses; plaintiffs of some petty cases, emissaries from outlying villages with complaints or reports for the Bwana MKubwa, all humbly sitting at the feet of justice in the shape of a whiteman who, from their point of view, dropped out of the sky to rule them with an iron hand. On the threshold of the room, from which came a singsong intonation in Kiswahili, stood a native police sergeant as janitor. He smartly saluted Laurie as he stepped round the motley squatting throng, odoriferous in the heat, and peered within.

Fedden was seated at the far end of the room at a deal table littered with writing materials, a volume of the Indian Penal Code, and other law tomes and reference books; at another small table crouched the Goanese clerk; opposite him a native prisoner stood in a very self-conscious manner between two police guards, bursting out ever and again in wild contradiction of a nude Kavirondo chief, the plaintiff, who committed perjury every five minutes under the bullying cross-examination of the court interpreter, posing hand upon hip by the table of authority. Fedden, grave-faced and patient, was leaning slightly forward, watching each speaker's face, deliberately and conscientiously searching for the needle of truth in a very large haystack of lies – his common round and daily task. The interpreter stopped abruptly in the middle of a long

---

[21] *Mauvais quart d'heure*: literally, "a bad quarter of an hour," conveying the sense of a brief but difficult period that will soon be over. Akin to a "rough patch" or "moment of hardship."

gesticulating harangue at the prisoner as Laurie appeared in the doorway. Fedden glanced up, nodded slowly and inquired:

"You wish to see me – officially?"

At Laurie's assent he hesitated for a moment, glancing doubtfully at the prisoner, looked at his watch, and rising, adjourned the case till after tiffin.[22] Laurie stepped inside to allow the prisoner and guard to march out. Fedden, standing up in his embarrassed manner, offered Laurie a seat, and dismissed the Goanese clerk, who had sat huddled at his table chewing the end of a pen and watching the stranger like a curious monkey.

"Yes, Sah," he exclaimed obsequiously, galvanized into action at the sound of Fedden's voice. "I will depart," and forthwith shuffled away.

For a moment or two neither spoke, Laurie covertly watching the other's awkwardness with an inward smile.

"Officially," commenced Laurie," I want permission to trade in this district."

"Yes, yes," said the other formally. "I cannot stop you – I mean – that is, the country is open – as far as the Turkana boundary: you are aware that the country beyond is closed – not considered safe for Europeans. So of course you must not go over the border."

"Of course not," said Laurie, with a smile.

The Government jurisdiction, beyond a few miles to the north of the station, was merely nominal: and Fedden knew from Laurie's reputation that he could not prevent him from going where he chose without some actual offence proved against him. Had Laurie been a Greek or half-caste trader, then other means might have been employed to retard or get rid of an undesirable, but this man had means to set wires jangling unpleasantly at the home end. A fifty-pound game license,

---

[22] Tiffin (chiefly British): a light midday meal: luncheon.

entitling the possessor to shoot two bull elephants, amongst other game enumerated, was granted with some demur on Fedden's part, who also knew well enough that Laurie did not intend to keep to the specified number, merely requiring the license as a tangible excuse for his cordite battery. After other small official details had been discussed Laurie moved as if to go, and said:

"Oh, by the way, I fear I owe you an apology for the unfortunate contretemps which occurred last night. I am really sorry but – er – as you know, it was quite unforeseen. Perhaps you will convey to your wife my sincere apologies?"

"I have already explained matters to her," returned Fedden coldly.

"I am afraid the offence seemed aggravated," pursued Laurie, speaking stiltedly in his endeavor not to appear flippant, "by your hospitality and the – er – kind reception and entertainment accorded by your charming wife. Many, I assure you, would envy you your fortune in life."

"I do not think there is any need to discuss the matter further," said Fedden in his official manner. "In fact," he added, stung by the memory of Maude's bitter attack upon him, "I think that my wife is to blame in having so hastily offered hospitality to an utter stranger."

"A stranger? Ah yes," said Laurie, and laughed.

"In view of your reputation," continued Fedden coldly, "I think that you might exercise more discretion – er – in your private life."

Laurie raised his eyebrows, looked straight at the other and laughed insolently.

"I see," he said, smiling cynically; "the present indiscretion is greater than many past indiscretions and – er – little weaknesses. Well – carpe diem, you know. Good morning."

Laurie turned on his heel and went out into the glare of the sun, glancing towards the bungalow, where his eyes caught the white of a dress. "Damn the fellow," he muttered to himself as he walked out of the fort gate. "I really meant to be polite – I hate fools."

And Fedden, sitting at his table within, gnawed his moustache with anger when the gibe reached home – for at any rate the plurality insinuated was unjust.

CHAPTER X

The blazing sun reached overhead, reducing a man's shadow to the round blob in which he stood. At the door of Laurie's Wimbledon tent, pitched below the fort, Sula was playing and talking to Kichui, who was now almost fully grown and a dangerous pet. He spent most of his time chained to a stake in the ground, where he would lie out like a huge cat basking in the heat, taken at evenings for a constitutional by the powerful Bambiba man, his keeper. Sula, in some subtle way, still retained her power over the beast. In his most irritable moods, when the hereditary desire for the freedom of the hills tormented him, he would not allow anybody except Sula to approach; even then he would growl wickedly and curl his lips whilst she patted and caressed him fearlessly. Kichui had been asleep all the morning, and so perhaps felt good-humored, for he showed signs of the kittenish playfulness of his cub days. Dropping his flat head to the ground sideways, he would shoot out a steel-tendoned paw with distended talons, playfully trying to pat Sula's arm, seeming to laugh with his wicked yellow eyes the while.

Every now and again Sula would cease playing, and carefully withdrawing out of reach of the paws sit motionless, gazing towards the station, anxious for Laurie's return; worrying in her simple, jealous mind lest he had gone back to the charms of the woman she was sure was her rival. Her eyes were bloodshot with weeping. Little pathetic lines furrowing her mouth were the outward symbol of the upheaval of her childish soul. She knew and rejoiced that they would be on the march upon the morrow, but the talons of jealousy tearing her made each hour seem a week, and fraught with terrible possibilities.

Behind and a little apart stood the kitchen tent, and in the hot shade of the single canvas roof sprawled Samwili, cogitating upon the success of his plans, lazily watching the cook tinkering about a smoky fire. After the abortive attempt upon Natts he had decided to follow Laurie with the hope of accomplishing his murderous intent. During the journey no opportunity had offered. Samwili's mind, now obstinately set, brooded upon a plan to attain his end. Upon arrival at Mbale he had overheard some of Fedden's servants joking among themselves at the strange antics and gestures of Maude in her vain attempts to speak their language. This had given him the idea of seeking employment, and by such means obtaining easy access to the house, with the object of murdering either or both, if possible, as they slept in the early morning. Ever since an Ethiopian Evangelist had sown the seed of political and religious superiority of the downtrodden blackman, Samwili had cherished a desire to strike a blow for the cause, quickened into action by the gibes of Matalisi and Yama Yama. He conceived, with the wild ardor of the fanatic, that the killing of even one of their oppressors was a laudable endeavor towards freedom. Little brooding upon the subject obsessed his primitive mind until he became a monomaniac, but one step removed from running amok upon the first European he encountered.

Somewhere in the tangled labyrinth of Samwili's mind a darker shadow of fear lurked – fear of the consequences, a superstitious dread that his sinister plans would become revealed to the whiteman: that almost supernatural being of death-dealing tubes and canoes driven by fiery devils. This fear he strove to ignore by calling up the scathing sneers of Yama Yama and Matalisi, as a stronger juju[23] to defeat the rebel. He was busy now congratulating himself upon his exceeding cunning, and rehearsing, over and over again, like an endless

---

[23] Juju: a fetish, charm, or amulet of West African peoples.

cinematograph[24] film, the scene of the deed and his triumphant escape. Standing over the sleeping whiteman and his red-haired wife, he saw himself raise the short stabbing spear, two swift blows and he would glide out of the door to return in company with another servant to discover, with great show of horror, the sweltering corpses of his master and mistress. Then the scene shifted to the company of Yama Yama and the scoffers where he – Samwili – bravely recounted the deed of prowess and received their adulation and envy. He showed the whites of his eyes; and his dead-red blubber lips curled, revealing white teeth, as he squirmed with the righteous joy of a holy deed in anticipation.

Then rising up and gathering his small bundle of blankets he cast a lascivious look at Sula as he passed her on his way to the kitchen.

Meanwhile Fedden had returned to the bungalow for lunch, still meditating upon his encounter with Laurie, feeling sore and hurt, sullenly resenting the fact that he had ever brought a wife to disturb the tenor of his life. However, he could not undo the past, and considered it his duty to bear the extra burden he had taken upon his shoulders. With customary reticence he did not speak of the interview to Maude, whom he discovered with a book upon her lap staring at space with a peevish eye. He washed his hands and returned to the table. They both avoided each other's eyes, Maude making necessary remarks in a toneless voice, to which he answered in monosyllables, becoming more and more uncomfortable as he felt the heavy atmosphere of a storm. Maude, who had left her food untasted and was staring despondently out of the door into the glare of the sunshine, remarked listlessly, without troubling to look at him:

---

[24] Cinematograph (chiefly British): a movie camera, projector, theater, or show.

"Oh, I forgot. I've found a man who can speak English, so I engaged him."

"Indeed, my dear?" said Fedden, raising his eyebrows. "But don't you remember that I object to having any strange servant here?"

"Oh, yes, I know," retorted Maude irritably. "But I can't go on like this. I must have somebody who can understand when I speak to him."

"Well, I object," said Fedden evenly. "Where has he come from?"

Maude told him impatiently.

"I can't give my consent," said Fedden. "I've told you repeatedly that I will not have men I don't know about me. I have had these servants for years. Besides, you don't understand these matters, my dear. If you insist, I will get you an English-speaking servant from Entebbe; someone whom –"

"Well, why haven't you done so before? You know that I've been nearly driven out of my mind with these fools and their silly language. I insist upon having this man until your model creature arrives. At any rate he's better than nothing, and he can't do any harm."

"I'm sorry, my dear, but I cannot agree. You should have asked before!"

"I did ask before," exclaimed Maude angrily; "and you were pleased to chide me like some school miss, and tell me to learn the language."

"I'm sorry," repeated Fedden, rising from the table. "But I cannot do this even to please you –"

"Please me, indeed!" she cried. "Pray, what have you ever done to please me? Besides, I've engaged the man; you can't make a fool of your wife before everybody."

"You should have thought of that before you engaged him," retorted Fedden, taking a cup of coffee from the servant.

"I'm not a child!" exclaimed Maude. "No, no!" to the servant. "I don't want any coffee!"

"I'm sorry," repeated Fedden monotonously, stirring his coffee; "but that man cannot stay here."

Maude bit her lip with vexation and turned away.

At that moment the cause of the disagreement appeared on the verandah.

"Goo' mornin', missus," said Samwili obsequiously. "Dis man, Malima, he say –"

"Is this the man?" inquired Fedden.

As Maude nodded, too angry to trust her tongue, Fedden spoke to him in the vernacular, bidding him begone.

"But missus, she say –" began Samwili.

Fedden got up and went to the door. Samwili cringed as he approached, watching him like a spaniel expecting a beating. Fedden called sharply to the police sergeant on duty at the office, instructing him to see Samwili off the Government premises. Samwili departed, protesting in English and throwing a vengeful glance at the cause of his discomfiture. As Fedden reentered the room with the cup of coffee in his hand, Maude confronted him, tears of angry humiliation welling in her eyes.

"It amounts to this, Herbert," she commenced, her voice quivering with suppressed emotion, "this cannot go on any longer. There are limits of indignity and insult. I cannot – I won't stand it –" She choked with emotion.

"I'm sorry," he began awkwardly.

"Sorry!" she echoed, finding her voice. "Sorry! You're an automaton – not a man. You're always saying 'I'm sorry'" – she mocked him savagely – "like a gramophone. You ought never to have married anyone. You ought to have had –" She hesitated for a moment and then rushed from the room to throw herself on the bed in a paroxysm of tears.

He placed the coffee cup mechanically on the table, picked up his helmet, and walked slowly across to the office. He found a runner newly arrived with a letter, informing him that Brinkley, the Commissioner of the district, was on the road to inspect the station.

Behind the fort at Laurie's camp there was the bustle of preparation for departure on the morrow, for Laurie found that the proximity of Maude was becoming almost unendurable. He felt the grip upon himself weakening; the temptation to seek and speak with her required all his strength of will to resist, realizing with the force of awakened love that she was his only and true mate. He stood in the broiling sunshine superintending the arrival and packing of bales for the donkey caravan which he had purchased to relieve the difficulty of finding and keeping porters. Sula harried the men with laughter and threats into double work in her frantic eagerness to be gone. Ever and anon she would catch Laurie's sunburned arm, laughing into his face, crying joyfully: "Sula glad! Sula berry glad!" and pause in the midst of a run between boxes and the tent to stare anxiously towards the fort as if affrighted that "she" might come and take her beloved away. And Laurie, too, would occasionally discover himself gazing at the same center of interest, half hoping, half dreading, the glint of a white skirt.

But Maude, red-eyed with passionate weeping, forced herself, with savage determination, to commence writing letters to England preparatory to her departure, struggling the while with an ever-increasing desire to send for or to speak with Laurie once more. A sudden wild thought came to her to go down and plead with him, make him run away with her to Europe or anywhere where they could forget the past and be happy. The writing materials were scattered as she leapt to her feet, her eyes aflame with the idea. But she sank back again as she realized the impossibility of the scheme, and sadly fell to moody contemplation. She did not seek to ignore the fact that she was jealous of Sula and hated her, excusing Laurie on the reasonable ground that had it not been for her action in the past he would have been hers only; also Maude was not a prude, looking the facts of life and of men's lives straight in the face. Her resentment against her husband had nothing or little to do with what she surmised had happened in the past; although she illogically flung such innuendoes at him in her passionate outbursts, illustrating the fact that loss of control from temper – or wine – does not always bring out the truth – particularly from a woman.

Maude did not for a moment imagine that Laurie could be in love or have any deep regard for Sula; her love for him warped her judgment, for had his case been an impersonal one she would have pointed out the fact that the girl was very beautiful, and that men are very apt to be held in thrall by passion alone. The more she thought of him the keener grew the desire to see and speak with him once more, until, like a moth drawn unwillingly to the candle flame, she rose up, put on her hat with the harmless intention – so she tried to convince herself – of a walk in the direction of the bazaar. But she discovered her feet carrying her, apparently of their own volition, out of the back verandah and down the hill. She made a faint attempt to resist the impulse. The sight of Laurie's camp drew her into a compromise; she would walk past the camp down towards the kitchen garden.

As she reached the path turning off to the camp a tremor of hesitation seized her. She could see Laurie sitting on a box, drinking a cup of tea and smoking. By his side sat Sula, whose keen eyes had detected her. With an effort Maude continued on to the garden, covertly watching. She knew that Laurie must see her, and hoped that he would understand and meet her halfway. A final rapid glance over her shoulder, which she could not resist before the crest of the hill shut out the camp, showed her that Laurie had disappeared, leaving Sula crouched on a bale, staring intently in her direction. Maude walked on doggedly to the garden, her heart in a flutter, half expecting

Laurie to appear against the skyline every moment. But he did not come, and she returned, furious with herself, intensely hating him – for the time.

During the evening she received Fedden with icy politeness; fidgeted about, played the piano spasmodically, leaving it to jump up and stare out of the back verandah, where she could see the lights of Laurie's camp. She went to bed early, to lie awake till near the dawn. When Malima came in with the early morning coffee she was lying disheveled and half clad, sleeping heavily, beneath the gauzy mosquito curtains. He put the coffee on the table at her side and stood looking at her whilst his eyes glazed filmy, his hands twitching convulsively. She stirred slightly and sighed, which seemed to startle the big black figure, for he turned away and stole to the door. When at length she did awake, heavy lidded and tired, it was some little time before the weight of her misery settled down upon her again. Fedden had long gone to the office. She breakfasted feverishly alone, suddenly abandoning an egg to seek her hat, and, with her little mouth firmly set and her eyes dangerously bright, she marched straight out to Laurie's camp – to find the warm ashes of deserted fires and the trodden grass squares of his tent site.

CHAPTER XI

About eleven on a morning, four days later, Yama Yama and Matalisi were squatted in the mottled shade of a big tree by the side of the main road near to the latter's village. At a distance of fifty yards was the Government rest house, a long thatched roof supported upon poles rising from a low reed fence; the whole, resembling an elongated porch of a country church, was enclosed in a large compound dotted with young papaya trees, capable of accommodating the native retinue of the European traveler. The road beyond sloped broad and yellow between the cool green of large trees down towards a palm-log bridge across the usual swamp, the even feathery tops of the papyrus sudd yellow-white in the brazen sun.

The two men sat like graven images, after the manner of the Negro, staring into space with the expression of extreme wisdom common to the ruminating ox. The slow slap of feet upon earth broke the hot, buzzing silence. They turned their heads slowly as into view appeared a tired brown figure, wrapped native fashion in a very dirty white blanket. He carried on the right shoulder a bundle, levered by a stick across the other shoulder held in the left hand. The face, fringed with detached tufts of black wool, was absolutely expressionless, as the native is when on the march, plodding mechanically along. Matalisi looked heavily at Yama Yama, whose grey-tinged woolly beard, wobbled and contorted, showing a gleam of white teeth. He muttered something to the other, and croaked out:

"Eh! Wangi-i!"

Samwili, who had passed without noticing them, pulled up and looked round. The vacuity of his face lit up with a startled expression, which faded into an amiable grin as he advanced and squatted before them, his bundle by his side.

"Where hast thou been?" inquired Matalisi, after the orthodox greeting.

Samwili told them that he had been to Mbale upon urgent business connected with the death of one of the wives of his father. Matalisi grunted and Yama Yama grinned.

"Where goest thou now?" said Matalisi.

"I return to my village," answered Samwili sheepishly.

"Are the white tyrants there then?" sneered Matalisi.

"Good!" quoth Yama Yama, with a great laugh. "My cattle will still be herded by my children."

Samwili rolled the whites of his eyes as he retorted: "Nay, thy cattle are mine."

"How so?" exclaimed Yama Yama, plucking at his beard.

"We have not heard the good news yet," said Matalisi sarcastically.

"Nay, nay," cried Samwili, gesturing excitedly; "but ye will!"

Leaning forward he began to relate an exaggerated version of his attempt upon Natts, attributing the failure to the unexpected entrance of Laurie, with whom he had had a fierce hand-to-hand struggle, only being overwhelmed by the assistance of Natts and three cowardly dogs of servants. He graphically described how he had tossed them about like straw in the wind. Then the thought had come to him that it would be a more valorous action to kill an official, an active tyrant, and so he had journeyed to Mbale, where again, according to his account, the treachery of the renegade servants had alarmed the whiteman, who had had guards to accompany him night and day. He had been waiting an opportunity when an imperative summons had reached him to attend to domestic affairs, but after – ah, after –!

Yama Yama and Matalisi received the story with noncommittal grunts. As Samwili finished with a portentous scowl silence reigned for a moment.

"Hah!" said Matalisi at length; "a lion gets little by waiting."

Yama Yama emitted a series of deep-chested grunts by way of a chuckle as Samwili protested valiantly.

"Mahommed hath newly arrived," pursued Matalisi. "He hath smelt for the blood thou didst promise him, but he sayeth that water runs in thy veins."

"Eh!" exclaimed Yama Yama, who had been staring down the road; "here cometh a prophet of Isa Masiya. There is food for thy blade."

"No, no," said Samwili; "he was my teacher. Liar and perjurer though he be, yet I may not kill him."

"Huh!" sneered Matalisi scornfully. "Then we will find thy chosen one for thee. A whiteman of the Serkali" (Government) "arrives at Kibwezi tonight; he will sleep here tomorrow night. Is thy blade still blunt?" he laughed derisively.

Samwili's brown face went a greeny-grey with wrath at the taunt.

"By the womb of my mother," he swore, "will I take his cowardly life tonight! Hear me, O Yama Yama, I have sworn it!"

"I hear thee, O son of many fools!" said Yama Yama. Matalisi laughed.

Samwili rose, grabbing his bundle, and sulkily bade them farewell, adding:

"Remember, O Yama Yama, thy cattle are mine – and thine too," to Matalisi.

"The cockerel on the dung heap croweth valiantly," said Yama Yama to Matalisi as Samwili went off.

"E-eh!" responded Matalisi; "our cattle will bring us many calves. The Waganda were ever sons of whores."

Samwili was stirred to the depths of his being with dull wrath, the whites of his eyes blood injected with passion. He plodded on towards the bridge where stood the Rev. Blackber talking to a passing peasant. The little parson, clad in well-worn khaki and helmet, recognized him with a hearty salutation uttered in a thin, weak voice. Samwili responded and extended a yellow-brown paw, to be clasped by the white as an equal and a brother.

The Rev. Blackber had the extreme virtue of not being a hypocrite: he acted as far as he knew how to the letter of his teaching – towards the natives if not to his fellow whites; for with a curious method of reasoning he held that the native mind, being in the dark in matters spiritual, was equally blind, and hence venial, in matters material, whereas there was no excuse for the white who had the light both ways. He had commenced life as a draper's assistant in Camden Town, and being blessed – or cursed – with a pious turn of mind, had received a call to the Church, finding his fate as a missionary amongst the heathen, which vocation he had taken up sincerely, striving to save their souls in the orthodox manner. Although he taught the equality of black and white, yet, subconsciously, he considered himself eminently superior to any black skin, although he would never recognize the fact. To the other Europeans in the country his attitude was divided. Other denominations and religions were woefully in error, both in thought and deed, a curse and a misfortune; the officials and traders were also wickedness incarnate, openly held up as bad examples to the blacks whom they were set to rule. Had he and his kidney had their will all the Europeans, and missionaries of other sects, would be banished from the country, lest their presence contaminated the black converts. Yet withal he meant well. He stood smiling and blinking through spectacles at Samwili, whom he cherished as one of his most promising and intelligent pupils, a zealous, pallid little man, straw haired and weak of chin.

Samwili dutifully answered queries regarding the health and welfare of other converts and relations, rejoicing smugly over the conversion of his uncle, an old pagan who had withstood the Church's blandishments for years. As they chatted Samwili was vaguely uneasy to be off, but the pastor was unwilling to part with this shining example. Presently half a dozen porters filed along the rickety bridge with the parson's impedimenta; and down the road from a village, hidden among the trees, came a gang of young men, running and laughing to greet him. As they grouped about him shouting salutations, amid much handshaking, Samwili attempted to continue his march, but Blackber feigned surprise and chaffed him for his hurry. As Samwili sheepishly admitted that he had no need of haste, an idea began to dawn in his brain: he remembered that Kibwezi, where the hated official was due to encamp, was but two hours' march; he could get there and back in the night without difficulty. Samwili consented to stay, and moreover announced his intention of sleeping there the night in order to see more of his beloved preceptor, in whose camp he spent the afternoon.

Towards sunset the Rev. Blackber called together the members of his flock, some twenty in number, and kneeling in the open, held prayers. Samwili led the responses and sung hymns lustily. A few Roman Catholics, denoted by their crucifixes, and the heathen, stood apart, watching in stolid silence. Among the latter Samwili caught a glimpse of the grinning faces of Yama Yama and Matalisi; but he ignored them, and sang so loud that Blackber afterwards complimented him upon his exceeding zeal.

After the evening meal of boiled banana in leaves and fruit, which the parson ate with the natives – for his fare was as frugal as his mind – Samwili pleaded that he might share his tent, as the porters' shelter was already overcrowded and the nights were chill. As a privileged individual his plea was magnanimously granted.

So Samwili unrolled his mat and curled himself up in his blanket at the farther end of the parson's small tent. Blackber was slightly troubled with insomnia through excessive malaria. About ten o'clock he was disturbed by a curious scratching sound and wobbling of the tent ropes. He called to Samwili. A prodigious snore and the croaking of bull frogs answered him. Some little time later he awoke from a brief doze and called to Samwili once more. Receiving no answer he struck a match. Samwili had disappeared.

CHAPTER XII

Two days later Maude awakened at dawn, to lie impatiently thirsting for her morning coffee, staring retrospectively at the warm light stealing through the mosquito-wired windows, tinting the white lace curtains and creeping gently towards her until the white net around her bed was suffused with violet and silver from the rising sun. The whole of the previous day had been passed in miserable solitude, picturing Laurie upon the march – with Sula. At every suggestion of her, Maude felt her heart contract until she was physically ill with jealous nausea. It seemed as if the minutes were vomiting more miles between them, intensifying her longing for him. She could have cried aloud at the pain of it, each thought avenging her injustice to him a thousandfold, and her injustice to her husband. That she would not see Laurie again she never doubted. At times, when she remembered that she would soon be leagues of ocean away, the anguish became nigh unbearable. She thought wildly at times of rushing after him – running, running, until she dropped of exhaustion. She felt that all emotion was being crushed out of her, that her heart was in death agonies; and then she would find herself coldly entertaining a morbid suggestion of the arsenic in her husband's dispensary.

Fedden greeted her at meals and during the evening in his placid manner, apparently indifferent to her approaching departure or her present attitude, for which she actively hated him. She was isolated with the troubles of her own making: no relief; no one to sympathize. She had never realized how miserable she had been until the coming of Laurie; the contrast between what might have been and what was appeared as black against white, the limit of extremes. Sometimes the loneliness grew so intense that she felt she could have even forgiven her husband if he would only show a little sympathy, a little water of understanding in her dry desert of misery and remorse. She would have to endure another week of this torture before the start could be made for the coast via Entebbe. She wondered dispassionately, speculatively, whether she would be able to endure it. She plucked at the lace counterpane petulantly as her ears caught the sound of native voices from the kitchen. She glanced at her watch on a stand upon a table beside her bed. Quarter-past six! The boy was not due till half-past; he was usually punctual, a virtue instilled by years of Fedden's training. Maude could endure it no longer; she parted the curtains and leapt out of bed, her hair in a ruddy shower over her blue-ribbon-befrilled bosom, lighting in the shaft of sunlight into molten copper nimbus.

"Malim-a!" she called. "Malima!" and hearing a reply on the verandah scuttled back to bed, like a diaphanous coryphée.[25]

A bass "Hodi!"and a knock sounded on the door as Malima entered with the tea upon a tray. "Thank Heaven!" murmured Maude, huddled up in the sheet, stretching out a shapely white hand through the curtains. She took the cup and sipped it. Malima stood like a draped bronze statue, holding the tray.

"What's the matter with you?" said Maude irritably. "Put it down there – there, you fool!" she added impatiently, pointing to the table, disarraying the clothes at her neck in the gesture. Malima put down the tray in a mechanical manner; his eyes were still upon her as he sidled crab fashion to the door. Maude frowned annoyance as the door closed. "What on earth's the matter with the 'boy'?" she mused, as she drained her first cup and reached thirstily for the teapot. "I've never seen him look like that before. He must have been drinking," she concluded, and wandered back into the chaos of her mind.

---

[25] Coryphée: a ballerina who dances in a small group instead of in the corps de ballet or as a soloist.

The day passed drearily somehow. She gave up the futile attempt to read, finding herself perusing a paragraph half a dozen times without grasping the meaning. She sauntered out in the blazing sun and fell to contemplating the site of Laurie's encampment. She felt like a felon isolated in the remand cell – at the mercy of vain regrets, knowing that there was no escape from a heavy sentence.

She looked at her husband during lunch – or rather during his lunch, for food seemed to choke her; only an unquenchable thirst raged – in a new light, as if she bad never seen him before, and, in the bitterness of the knowledge that she was to blame, a gust of passion shook her against him – against his very existence; for if he – He glanced up and caught her expression. His eyebrows went up, and for the first time since the open rupture he referred to it.

"Why do you look at me like that?" he inquired slowly.

She blinked in an effort to subdue the strangling sensation of excessive emotion, and bowing her head in her hands burst into a storm of dry-eyed sobs.

He stood up and gazed at the throbbing corymbs of copper hair with an expression of cold concern. The sobs seemed to tear at the very root of her soul, hollow and dry as her love for him. He stepped towards her in his methodical, deliberate manner and patted her on the shoulder, a favorite trick which he had abandoned since the honeymoon days.

"My dear! My dear!" said he.

She shrank from his touch, blindly pushing him away with her hands as she burrowed deeper into the cushions. Fedden stood back and watched her body writhing in the grip of sorrow – remorse – he could not guess. Then he turned and walked away thoughtfully, tugging at his sad moustache, repeating parrot-wise to himself: "I cannot understand her – I cannot understand her."

The hot afternoon wore on to the accompaniment of the buzzing of flies. When tea was announced by Malima, Maude dragged herself from the bed, where she had lain in dumb misery, and mechanically commenced the brewing operations. As she glanced idly out of the window across the square she noticed a native police messenger, carrying a note in the cleft of a stick, cross the bridge into the fort, bearing signs of extreme fatigue in his rolling gait. The sergeant janitor took the letter from him as he collapsed in a heap by the verandah post, exciting the curiosity of the usual crowd squatted without the office. She glanced up again as she heard her husband's voice speaking in an unusually sharp tone, distinct in the still, hot air. The throng scattered as he appeared in the doorway and commenced to cross the square in the broiling sun without his helmet. A native policeman ran after him with it. He nodded and placed it on his head mechanically, and proceeded towards the bungalow, staring at an open letter held in his hand. As he approached her Maude noticed that his eyes looked heavier than usual, the moustaches seemed to droop more sadly. He came in and sat at the table without removing his hat, still staring at the paper as if he could not believe the contents. Maude handed him a cup of tea, her curiosity faintly aroused by his unwonted bearing.

"What's the matter, Herbert?" she inquired.

He looked up at her blankly for a moment. She suddenly noticed that his eyes were drawn with pain.

He placed the letter on the table and said slowly:

"The subcommissioner has been murdered."

"Murdered!" echoed Maude, and sat down staring at him. "Not murdered!"

"Yes, murdered!" he repeated slowly. "The missionary Blackber writes to that effect. He was found early yesterday morning, huddled in a chair by his writing table, stabbed through the heart from behind. Poor Brinkley!" He stared out of the doorway. "Poor Brinkley!" he added again, after a pause.

"Where? Who is the murderer?" queried Maude, pouring out tea.

"At Kibwezi – camped there on his way here," explained Fedden, picking up the letter again. "Blackber thinks that the murderer must have crawled under the flap of the tent, and escaped the same way. No; no more tea, dear. I must prepare immediately."

"Why? Where are you going?"

"To Kibwezi, to investigate – immediately. It is just within the boundary of my jurisdiction."

"But," said Maude, startled, "what am I to do?"

He paused on the way to the door to gaze at her doubtfully. He had forgotten her for the moment.

"I know!" exclaimed Maude, her face lighting up. "I'll come with you; then I can go on to Jinja and the coast."

His eyes drooped for a moment.

"Yes, you had better do so," he said, after a pause, and turning, walked away.

Maude stared after him for a moment, vaguely vexed because he did not raise any objection. "Good heavens!" she exclaimed, "they might murder him!" She flushed in dull shame at a thought that had leapt unbidden to her mind; then her face blanched, as in logical sequence came the idea of Laurie in danger. The pain of the suggestion was swamped in the wave of dull misery in the fact that he was out of her life forever. With an effort she subdued the inclination to give way once more, and turned away to commence packing. The voyage home and arrival in England in dull autumn weather at duller Rockchurch, impertinent questions, sneers, gossip of busybodies and conventional life, occupied her mind as she collected her things together in heaps; and the pain of it, the gnawing empty years to come, tied and bound to a name, the agony of the future, with Laurie's eyes hovering in the background – Laurie with Sula.

But, with tears welling in her eyes, she savagely thrust inoffensive garments into boxes and portmanteaux, resolutely determined to carry out her decision as the only solution of the problem.

With that inexplicable inconsistency common to most people on the eve of departure, this bungalow and the country, the life she had hated and spent so many miserable hours in, seemed suddenly possessed of an extraordinary fascination. The gloomy clouds of life in England glowered in the future; but she did not hesitate for a moment.

The fading light suggested a lamp. As she turned from a pile of lingerie scattered upon the bed, a footfall in the dining-room caught her ear.

"Malima!" she called; "Kiberiti" (matches). A musical jangle of ivory bracelets brought her about, to see a wild-eyed Sula standing in the doorway. The thought of the proximity of Laurie caught Maude by the throat.

"Lolly, he die!" gasped Sula.

"My God!" whispered Maude. She caught at the bedpost to save herself from falling.

"Where?" she demanded, with bloodless lips.

"Lolly, he die! he want you!" gasped Sula, tears streaming from her eyes, her breast heaving in the agony of forcing the hated words. "Lolly, he here. Come!"

She pointed a tragic finger towards the back of the bungalow, galvanizing Maude into action.

"Quick!" breathed Maude, starting towards Sula, who turned and reached the door as Fedden entered from the front. He stared in amazement at Sula, and then at his wife, as she hastily followed Sula.

"What –" he began.

"Lolly die!" repeated Sula over her shoulder, pausing on the threshold.

"Go on quick! Oh, go on!" gasped Maude wildly.

"Maude!" exclaimed Fedden. "Maude!"

But Maude was hastening in the gloom after Sula, who had glided round to the left with lithe, swinging strides.

"Where? Where?" panted Maude, holding up her skirts as she ran; but Sula, with flying hair, an ethereal figure in the half lights, did not pause until she reached the crest of the hill; then, with an inarticulate cry, she stopped and pointed below.

Maude reached her side, to see a crowd of natives winding along a path, bearing a machila in their midst. She divined that Laurie was there, and raced on after Sula, who was already halfway down the hillside. When Maude reached there the men were standing aside, whilst Sula bent over the hammock, peering intently. Maude's heart stopped for a second; she hardly recognized the pallid, wasted face of Laurie on the pillow. She fought hard to repress the desire to catch him in her arms.

"Laurie! Oh, Laurie!" she whispered.

Together the two women stood bending over the sick man, the white dress and copper hair of the one in sharp contrast to the deep red skirt and blue-black hair of the other.

"Lolly!" whispered Sula.

"Oh, Laurie!" whispered Maude.

His eyes opened, bright with burning fever. He stared at them without recognition.

"Water," he murmured feebly; and then added: "Maude! Maude!" looking about him as if searching for her, wringing a stifled sob from poor Sula's lips.

"Laurie! Oh, Laurie, I'm here, darling!" whispered Maude, grasping his hot hand, thinking that he knew her.

But he snatched his fingers away irritably, rolling his head deliriously, crying again: "Maude! Maude!"

"Oh God, Laurie!" she cried, as she realized that he could not recognize her.

"Allays he say that," whispered Sula pitifully; "allays cry for you."

And even in the moment of anxiety Maude felt a thrill of exaltation. Then suddenly realizing the futility of standing weeping over him in the roadside, she said to Sula quietly:

"Come, bring him to the house. Tell the men to go on."

The machila-bearers, in response to Sula's orders, moved on. The two women marched in silence on either side, anxiously watching the sick man, replacing an arm thrown deliriously over the side of the hammock, or jealously seeking to ease the restless head. The night closed in; the mosquitoes and distant bull frogs were commencing their nocturnal chorus as they reached the verandah. Maude, without a moment's hesitation, directed the men to carry Laurie inside.

Hearing the noise and commotion, Fedden came over from the office to see what had happened to his wife. He found Laurie being placed in bed in his room, Sula bending over him, smoothing him and settling the pillows, whilst Maude stood by the bedside with a glass to ease the fevered thirst. For a moment he stared in blank amazement, holding a sheet of paper he had absent-mindedly carried off with him in his hand.

"My dear," he commenced in protest, "what has happened? I –"

At the sound of his voice both women looked up. Maude handed the glass to Sula and rushed to her husband.

"Come here," she said, unceremoniously dragging him by the coat sleeve into the next room. "He's very, very ill. Go to him and tell me what is the matter, and what to do – quick!"

"But, my dear," commenced Fedden again.

"Herbert!" she cried angrily. "Go to him. Tell me what to do. Oh, he's dying! D'you hear? he's dying. You must go. Oh, quick!"

"But this woman –"

"Oh, never mind the woman. You shall go. You can't let him die. Come. Oh, Herbert, come!" she almost screamed in her wild anxiety. In a frenzy of distress she half led, half dragged him into the room.

He stared doubtfully at the figure in the bed, and then slowly walked over to examine him. Once by the bedside he seemed to do things mechanically. Calling for a clinical thermometer, which Maude flew to fetch, he thrust it in the patient's mouth and waited, whilst the women breathlessly watched him, Sula's great eyes wide and pleading. He withdrew the little glass tube, raising his eyebrows as he glanced at it closely.

"Hundred and six point two," he muttered, and looked at Laurie's wandering bright eyes doubtfully.

"What does that mean?" demanded Maude. "Oh, do hurry – what is the matter? Fever? What can I do? Speak!"

Sula's large eyes scanned his face, dumbly seeking to read his decision by the expression alone.

"Blackwater fever, my dear," replied Fedden at length. "Rather bad, too. I'll give him some calomel and as much champagne as he wants. That's the only hope – to keep his heart going." He turned from looking at the patient, raising his eyes to Sula.

"This person can nurse him, I suppose. Very awkward in the house, though. Still, he's very ill, and as we're going tomorrow –"

"But we can't go tomorrow!" exclaimed Maude. "Not now."

Fedden looked at her in surprise.

"But we must, my dear," he said, walking into the next room. "I'm bound to –"

"I don't care what you're bound to do," broke in Maude explosively. "I simply cannot leave him – to die. Oh, my God!"

"I am going tomorrow morning," repeated Fedden quietly; "and you are coming with me."

Maude stared at him for a moment, and then turned upon him angrily.

"You – you – you –" she stuttered with rage. "All you think about is your horrible official business. A man who is dying matters nothing to you. But *I* care – I care more than anything in the world! I don't care what you know," she cried wildly. "I am not coming. You can go – go anywhere. I don't care. I'm not coming. I shall nurse him. You must send tonight for a doctor, d'you hear? He must be saved. Oh, my God! my God! what shall I do?" she broke off hysterically. "I – I must be sane. I must try to be sane."

Her voice fell low, as if communing with herself, whilst Fedden stared in silent amazement.

"Don't look at me like a stuffed sheep!" she suddenly cried at him. "Sane, I said. You've nearly driven me mad. Yes, *you*, with red ink in your veins and red tape for sinews! You can't see anything under your nose!"

"Yes, my dear," said Fedden soothingly, "of course; but, you see, you can't stay here with him alone. You know what people –"

Maude stopped in the act of turning away, to gaze at him blankly. She commenced to laugh – dry, mirthless chuckles.

"Oh! ha! ha! ha! The shadow of Mother Grundy haunts even the Equator? The pap of convention is in your very blood! Men may die and women's hearts may break, but still bow down to the god of convention."

"My dear, think of me then," protested Fedden.

"My dear!" she mocked, "my dear – an apt expression of the breadth of your soul – my dear! Oh, go – go! I tell you that you may do what you like! I shall remain and nurse that man, whether you like it or whether you don't."

She turned with a contemptuous gesture and left him staring after her, dully collating the events of the evening, the sullen anger of an outraged sense of right stirring at the back of his mind.

CHAPTER XIII

In times of common danger or stress the most bitter foes, national, individual, or animal, will act in concert amicably. During that long moist night the two women, their natural hatred for each other drowned in the flood or anxiety for their common love, ministered and watched with Argus-eyed vigilance to his needs. Sula crouched by the bedside, motionless as a panther, subservient to Maude, to whom she looked for skill and knowledge, dependent solely upon her intuition, whilst Maude, drawn-eyed with terror, hovered silent footed, hope rising and sinking as the stimulants took effect or evaporated. "The patient's life mainly depends upon keeping up the heart action." The remark of a doctor in Entebbe flew to her mind, giving her, in fact, the one chance to save Laurie's life. From outside came the distant throaty chorus of the frogs, with the high humming plaint of the mosquitoes; now and again Fedden's footsteps in the next room or on the gravel of the square, still busy preparing for his call of duty.

Towards midnight he came to the door and peered in, grave eyed and troubled. Methodically proceeding with his official duties, he had at length come to the conclusion that his wife was distraught at the advent of serious illness; therefore, in a cold way, he felt for her a pang of sympathy, strangled at birth by the knowledge that she defied his authority. He stood on the threshold, gravely watching Sula crouched silent at one side of the bed, Maude kneeling at the other, holding a tumbler of champagne in readiness for the sick man, whose feverishly bright eyes held a gleam of sanity. Moved by an impulse of sympathy for the sick man he advanced softly to the bed to observe him.

Maude glanced up with a soft warning "Ssh!" after the manner, Fedden noticed in an odd, detached sense, of one addressing a stranger; Sula pleaded with her eyes. In Laurie's face he saw, with the experienced eye of one who had seen many such cases, the contracting of the pupils and the bloodless lips of exhaustion. He remained silent for a while, pulling at his sad yellow moustaches; then without a word he walked softly out of the room, to return within a few minutes with an open leather case in his hand. Maude noticed it, and rose with a questioning look.

"Strychnine," he said.

Taking one of the patient's bare arms he signed to Maude to hold it. Sula, leaning forward with anxious fear, not understanding what was about to be done, gasped sharply as the small needle punctured the flesh. A quick glance at Maude reassured her that this strange rite must be for Lolly's good, and she subsided to her place as Fedden returned the hypodermic syringe to its case. Maude glanced up at her husband as she quickly replaced the arm, bearing a small pink spot.

"Thank you!" she whispered, and the expression in her eyes made her husband feel that this was a woman he had never known.

His eyes saddened and he tugged at his moustaches in an effort to subdue a wave of emotion as he gazed at the coppery mass of hair bending solicitously over the sick man in whom his interest had suddenly died. After a moment he turned sorrowfully away, feeling dimly that he had done a great injury to his wife, which he could not fathom nor understand. He had meant to call Maude and firmly insist upon her accompanying him, but somehow the intention faded; he found himself with a dull ache, wondering what had happened to make him see her in a new and wholly inexplicable light. The depth of light that had shone in her eyes as she had whispered "Thank you!" haunted him; he felt that in having failed to win that expression for himself alone he had missed some great prize, so lofty and desirable that he could not even conceive the joy of it. He sat down slowly in a chair and fell to gazing at the scorched and dying moths struggling in the rim of the lamp, vaguely conscious that he was hurt as he had never been before, painfully seeking the cause.

The minutes slowly crept into hours, and still he sat staring moodily at the lamp; the trend of his thoughts wandering from the present to the past, revived to a small degree the resentment and condemnation towards his wife for her lack of interest in the grand motif of his life – his official work. He felt, although the thought did not take definite form, that she had wronged and deceived him in marrying him; he had thought her to be his ideal of an official companion – and as she had failed him so deplorably he had been aggrieved; but now the boot seemed to have got on the other leg in some mysterious manner. He had wronged her; but how? The answer he could not conceive. Then gradually the training of years asserted itself and his mind fell back into the rut of official duties. He glanced at his watch. It was past three o'clock. In another hour it would be time to prepare for the march. He sighed wearily, wishing in his heart that such troublesome things as wives had not come to disturb the even flow of official routine, and sat back in his chair to doze.

He awoke with a start, to see Maude standing over him. Her eyes were alight, tears streaming down her cheeks, unchecked and unashamed, as she smiled gloriously through them exclaiming, "Thank God!"

"My dear!" he said, sitting up.

"Oh, Herbert, thank God you've saved his life!" and then to his amazement she sank at his feet and burying her head on his knee sobbed as if her heart were breaking.

"My dear!" he expostulated once at a fresh outburst. He tried vaguely to fathom the cause of her grief. If the man were dead he could have understood a natural outburst of grief but –

The storm of her sobs gradually ceased; she lifted her face to meet his look of concerned bewilderment, smiling.

"He's better," she whispered. "He's sleeping – like a baby. Oh, Herbert, I am glad!"

"Yes, my dear," he said tonelessly.

"Herbert," she continued, carried away by a wave of gratitude. "I shall never be able to repay you for this. O God, I *am* grateful!"

"My dear!" he protested, raising his eyebrows.

"Herbert," she rose up and sat upon the arm of his chair. "Herbert, I've been a brute to you. No, don't," as he was about to reply. "No, don't. I know; but you don't. It hurts me to tell you – you have never understood me. I'm wicked. I –"

"Maude, my dear!" – he stirred uncomfortably in his chair – "I –"

"Herbert, I'm deceiving you!" she spoke rapidly, bending towards him. "I've deceived you. I'm wicked, and, my God! I've been punished. You are going tomorrow – this morning – in a few hours' time. You may never see me again. I –"

"Maude!"he sat bolt upright under the shock. "May never see you!" he repeated slowly. "What do –"

"Let me speak – while I may," she interrupted him. "I am the cause of all the trouble – of my own misery. No, no, let me speak. I – I knew Laurie before. I was going to marry him – engaged to him – at home. And I – I jilted him. It was my own fault. I didn't know what love was – that I was capable of it. I was ambitious. I wanted – never mind what. You came along, and – and – oh, why shouldn't I tell the truth? I was wicked, I *never* loved you! I married you. I don't know why myself – out of pique because I hated myself – and him. There never was anything in common between us. I – yes, I knew, if you didn't; and I married you. You don't understand women – you never will, but I have suffered the most. Yes, yes, I know that you have suffered too, but nothing like I have. God! *after* I married you I awoke – awoke to the fact that I loved him. But it was too late – and he had gone – gone to South Africa. I tried – tried so hard to forget and settle down with you, but it was no use – no use. I was slowly going mad; and then he came. My God, if you could only realize what that meant to me! No, no, you can't. You are not a woman – you could never – never understand. And then – you know the rest. I've finished. That is all. I had to tell you because – because you – *you* have saved his life."

She turned her head as she ceased speaking, to glance anxiously towards the door of the sickroom; he continued his troubled stare out into the night.

"You still love him?"

He asked the question in the same tone as he might have inquired the time.

"Yes," she said simply, rising and sweeping a mound of dead moths on the table.

"Then you *have* wronged me deeply," he said, wondering why he had felt that he had wronged her.

"Yes, I have wronged you – and him – and myself. O God, what a mess I've made of life!"

He looked at her afresh, as if to reassure himself of the reality, and passed his hand across his eyes wearily.

"I don't know," he murmured

"Don't know what?" she said, half turning towards him, a slight note of irritation in her voice – perhaps because he did not upbraid her.

"I don't know what to say – or do," he said at length.

She looked at him curiously.

"Aren't you angry?" she inquired.

"Angry! Angry? What is the use of being angry? What are we to do?"

"I'm not a hypocrite," she said, apparently answering an unspoken thought. "At least not now. – I – I can't ask you to forgive me; I can't forgive myself."

"What are we going to do?" he repeated dully.

She turned from him, commencing to beat a devil's tattoo on the table, ceasing as she glanced again towards the sickroom. She looked at him again: he was still staring heavy-eyed out into the night. His silence irritated her. Why didn't he do or say something? He was always sullenly silent – a silence that seemed the reproach of a dumb animal. She had never stung him into a retort or show of temper – only Miss Griller, in her attack upon his official duty, had succeeded in arousing him – and even now the most extreme provocation a man and a husband could receive failed to dispel his verbal lethargy.

"Well?"

"I'm thinking, my dear," he said quietly, without looking at her.

"Thinking!" she exclaimed. "Heavens!" and turning left him.

As she entered the sickroom, the impatient scorn of her husband in her heart was driven out by a sharp stab of jealousy, for crouching by the bedside she saw Sula in the act of gently kissing Laurie's unconscious fingers protruding beyond the covering sheet. Sula's eyes followed covertly as Maude walked to the bedside and watched the even breathing of the sick man with tender eyes. As Maude sat wearily in the chair she shot a vengeful glance at Sula. Their eyes met like the crossing of the blades of two adversaries. The truce, by reason of their common anxiety, was withdrawn. For a while Maude struggled against the overpowering desire to sleep after her night's vigil and excitement. At last, as the first pale tints of dawn stole through the windows, she succumbed in her chair. But not Sula, who still crouched like a bright-eyed sphinx.

***

The sound of scurrying feet in the square, and then, as the police trumpet rang out, Fedden appeared in the door. He hardly noticed Sula, his eyes resting speculatively upon the sleeping form of his wife in the chair. Sula watched him, judging from his garb that he was going on the march somewhere, and wondered. Fedden went off, his footfalls dying away across the square. The distant crowing of cocks and Laurie's regular breathing were the only sounds for a while, till Malima's footsteps on the verandah bringing coffee; then a cluck of surprise as he entered Maude's empty room. Sula glided swiftly to the door. He showed the whites of his eyes as she met him. For a moment he seemed half inclined to disobey her whispered commands, but an angry flash in her eyes made him change his mind. He left the coffee with her and went away, muttering in astonishment.

Sula softly put the coffee on the table, and making sure that Maude still slept, drank it herself. She resumed her vigil by Laurie's bedside; now and again her glance would wander from Laurie to Maude. She was torn between the desire to awaken Laurie gently, with the object of stealing just five minutes of him from the other woman, and the intuitive knowledge that he should not be disturbed. As the sunlight filled the room her wish was granted. Laurie opened his eyes and stared stupidly at the ceiling for a moment; then he stirred feebly, and turning his head, saw Sula's great anxious eyes watching him, pleading for recognition.

He smiled and murmured, "Sula!"

Her eyes caressed him as she whispered, "Lolly!"

"Where am I, Sula?" he muttered, his eyes wandering perplexedly round the walls.

"Sula bring Lolly Bibi Fedden," she explained reluctantly.

"I see," he murmured reflectively, and Sula's heart grew icy as she noticed a new light come into his eyes as they looked towards the door inquiringly.

"Yes, she here, Lolly," whispered Sula at length between her set teeth.

His eyes turned eagerly, not noticing the pain in Sula's voice. "Where?"

She nodded silently across the bed. Laurie feebly turned his head as Maude awoke.

"Maude!" he whispered.

"Laurie!" she cried softly, and bending towards him eagerly kissed him on the forehead.

Then Sula felt her heart break, and, collapsing in a heap, buried her head in the loose end of the sheet, sobbing bitterly.

Laurie, distressed at the thought of pain to her, tried to rise, only to sink back with a groan of exhaustion, which enraged the jealous, protective instincts of Maude, and made her turn upon the weeping offender with wrathful eyes.

"Be quiet! Be quiet!" she cried in an angry whisper, and was round the bed standing over the prostrate Sula bidding her begone. As Sula took no notice other than to sob more pitifully, Maude seized her by the arm, wrenching her, in a frenzy of passion, from the bed. The wicked flash of Sula's eyes made her pause in the act of a second attack.

"Maude! Maude!" whispered Laurie from the bed.

"Yes, yes," answered Maude, darting towards him.

"Leave her alone," he gasped. "Let her come to me!"

Maude flushed with anger and stood aside to glare at the form of Sula huddled in the center of the room, her head buried in her arms, gasping with deep-chested sobs.

"Sula!" whispered Laurie faintly. "Sula!"

She heard him instantly, and crawling humbly along the floor came to him, clutching the hand he extended to her breast, fiercely kissing his arm.

CHAPTER XIV

Again on a day Matalisi sat with Yama Yama in the guesthouse of the latter's village. The eyes of Yama Yama were sunken in the sockets; the vastness of his paunch was drawn and wasted. A few yards away sprawled three children of about ten years old, silently gazing at the elders with a half curious, half-indifferent expression. Two pairs of eyes were hollow and heavy lidded; their owners' frames were grotesque skeletons grotesque by reason of the abnormally distended stomachs of native children in contrast with the ribs and bones staring through their hanging covers. The mother of one, with pendulous withered breasts, slept in the doorway of an adjacent hut, the stone grain-mortar idle in front of her. The sun blazed overhead, the flies buzzed around the children's eyes with apparent impunity, whilst Matalisi talked volubly to Yama Yama, who, seemingly bored to death, nodded sleepily between yawns. Matalisi, one of the first to hear the news of the murder of Brinkley, which had flown through the countryside within a few hours of the discovery, had hastened to overtake Yama Yama, who had started for his village at daybreak next morning.

The actual fact of the accomplishment of their plot, made on Matalisi's part half in earnest, half in jest, had awakened in him a sudden and appalling fear of the whiteman's vengeance. The thought that Samwili would appear to claim the cattle brought a vision of the Government police swooping upon him there and arresting them all as accomplices; the possibility of retribution brought out all the latent superstitious belief in the miraculous power of the whiteman. The fact that the whites must know all their secret plotting grew to a certainty in the mind of Matalisi. With interminable loquacity he recounted the possibilities of discovery and punishment to Yama Yama, who seemed unaccountably indifferent to whatever happened. Once, after an emphatic recital of the probable consequences, Matalisi paused to stare anxiously at the other, who was gazing in a sadly reflective manner into space. The eyes were heavy lidded. Matalisi bent forward and shook him gently. Yama Yama looked up in vague protest, smiled vacantly, and seemed to recover slightly.

"Thou hast the whiteman's curse!" exclaimed Matalisi.

Yama Yama shook his head slowly.

"No, no," said he, "I am but tired; leave me to sleep."

As he spoke the sound of a new voice saluting somebody in the village floated across the hot air, arousing Matalisi to a frenzied whisper:

"It is as I said. Here comes the dog to claim his cattle and bring destruction on our heads."

Yama Yama woke up a little more and peered out across the open sunlit village.

"True," he muttered, and laughed feebly in his beard – a hazy, weak echo of his usual guffaw.

"Quick," whispered Matalisi; "what shall we do? Listen! dead men tell no tales. We will act together. Do as I bid ye!"

"Greeting, my masters!" came Samwili's voice from outside.

Matalisi returned the salutation; Yama Yama merely grunted lazily. Samwili squatted down beside them, glancing covertly from one to the other. He saw that they had heard the news of his prowess, and smirked with proud satisfaction. For a moment or two neither spoke; then said Samwili, grinning:

"Thou hast heard the good news? I have come for the cattle."

Matalisi shot a glance at Yama Yama's expressionless face.

"It is good," he said gravely. "The cattle are thine: they await thee in the pastures beyond Avimi's village."

Samwili showed no surprise, although he had expected some difficulty in obtaining his material prize.

"Let us go and count them," Matalisi continued, preparing to rise.

But Samwili had no intention of forgoing the joy of the recital of his prowess. He drew the short stabbing spear upon which he had slung his bundle and pointed, silently grinning, to the blade where, in the shoulders, lay a dark brown stain of clotted blood. His eyes gleamed malevolently as he began to speak.

"Look, my brothers," he said, gesturing; "the sword of the righteous bit deep and hard. Listen!"

Matalisi subsided upon his haunches again, conquered by the curiosity to know how the deed had been accomplished.

"On the night when ye gave me the good news," proceeded Samwili, "did I meet as ye know, the missionary, my father, and as he spake with me I saw light. We prayed together, he and I and those of the faith; and when night fell I craved permission to sleep within his tent." He smiled evilly at the remembrance of his cunning. "Then, when he was well asleep, did I leave the tent silently as a shadow, and travelling fast reached Kibwezi's ere the moon rose." He glanced triumphantly at Yama Yama, who was watching him with tired interest.

"Then, my fathers, did I crawl as a snake through the fence of the compound, and coming to the back of the tent saw that a light burned within. In front paced the fool of an askari, proud as a hedgehog, with his rifle and bayonet. – Eh! my soul coveted it! – Then, peeping beneath the flap of the tent, I saw the accursed son of shame sitting writing at his table, even though it was nigh unto morning. For a moment my liver turned to water, but thy words and the cause of my going strengthened me, and my heart swelled as a lion's! E-eh! Slowly I crept within the tent under the flap, slowly I crawled by the bedside, until, rising softly, I stood behind the tyrant's back. E-eh! Then, my brothers, holding the blade" – he mimicked the action, spear in hand, so realistically that Matalisi dodged nervously – "thus did I strike for the cause." He paused at the end of the thrust to glare and broke into a low, chuckling laugh. "The pig," he continued contemptuously, "just grunted and died. E-eh! but the thrust was good, for I saw the red blood follow the blade as I plucked it out. E-eh! Not a sound more as the blood flowed down" – he licked his thick lips in ecstasy, his eyes bright with the echo of the excitement. "E-eh! It was good!"

He ceased, rolling the whites of his eyes at the twain.

"And then?" inquired Matalisi, interested.

"Then," resumed Samwili triumphantly, "I returned as I came. And behold at the coming of the sun I slept peacefully in the tent of the missionary – *who saw me awake!*"

He chuckled sardonically. Yama Yama grunted approval; Matalisi for a moment said nothing, giving himself time to recover from the excitement of the recital.

"Come!" he said again, preparing to rise.

"He is but the first of many," interrupted Samwili. "Now that the lion hath arisen" – he spoke proudly, as of a leader of men – "will the jackals follow. *We* shall be avenged. *We* are the chosen of God. Now is the appointed time to rise and sweep the accursed white usurpers into the sea. – What ails him?" He broke off suddenly, staring at Yama Yama on the verge of sleep as he sat resting against a supporting roof pole.

"He is afflicted by the whiteman's curse," said Matalisi, "as are all who dwell under their accursed shadow."

"Even as I said!" quoth Samwili triumphantly. "Ye and all who bow to the whiteman shall be eaten up by their magic. Follow me, and I will lead you to your own. Look! Look!" He pointed excitedly to the children and women, as if he had not noticed them before. "There are the fruits of the white rule, even as I said. Will ye not listen? I am chosen to tell you. Such is spoken of in the book of Isa Masiya whom these white dogs stole from us. I –"

"Come thou!" interrupted Matalisi, whose enthusiasm for the downfall of the whites had been completely expunged by his fear of retribution. "Come thou, and claim thy cattle. – O Yama Yama!" Once more he shook Yama Yama out of the insidious coma and quietened a fresh outburst on Samwili's part.

"Come, we go to the village of Avimi, to give Samwili his just reward," said Matalisi, as Yama Yama rubbed sleep out of his eyes.

"But –" commenced Yama Yama.

"Remember, fool!" exclaimed Matalisi, rising. "Come!"

Yama Yama, looking somnolently indifferent, clambered heavily to his feet.

"Walk on ahead of us," commanded Matalisi of Samwili. "I would speak with Yama Yama."

And Samwili, wondering vaguely, did as he was bid, whilst Matalisi, shaking his companion vigorously, whispered fiercely in his ear as they walked into the blazing sun:

"Listen, fool, and remember what we agreed! Our lives – *my* life depends on it. If the accursed Serkali take him they will take us too."

The intensity of his voice and demeanor seemed to awaken Yama Yama a little, for he nodded slowly and grunted:

"Yes, yes, we are agreed"; and then, after a pause, looking owlishly at Matalisi, he inquired, "What did we agree?"

"Fool!" said Matalisi. "Have I not told thee a score of times?" He pulled up as they came to the footpath through the bush, and looked about him as if seeking a new and live accomplice. "We agreed," he commenced, and suddenly seeming to conclude that it was a hopeless task to make the other's dulled intelligence grasp an idea, concluded: "Do as I bid ye; for your life – our lives depend on it!"

"On what?" persisted Yama Yama stupidly.

"No matter. Do as I bid ye. Come, follow me," and he moved ahead towards Samwili, who stood under a tree awaiting them.

"Yama Yama would say that ye have not proved the deed," said Matalisi to Samwili, glancing behind to see that his fellow chief was following.

"E-eh!" ejaculated Samwili, who had been astonished that they had not raised an objection before. "True, but ask ye of this good blade," he commenced, holding up the weapon in the dappled shade of the big tree.

"No matter," said Matalisi. "I have convinced him that it is as ye say. We will to the cattle now."

"But –" commenced Samwili, reassured, but disinclined to be cheated out of another harangue upon his prowess.

"Nay, nay," said Matalisi; "it is settled. The sun grows high …. Come!" and he led on down the path.

Samwili, as befitted him, waited for Yama Yama, who, after a pause which seemed necessary before the suggestion to proceed filtered through the dulled senses and took action, shuffled on down the path in the wake of Matalisi. In Indian file they marched on in silence, leaving the tilled land behind, across the clumps of bush and open grassland, for upwards of an hour. As they neared a small sea of gently waving banana fronds, walking between very high rank grass, Samwili, in the rear, suddenly sprang from the path with an exclamation of pain, clapping a hand to the back of his neck. A grey thing, like a horsefly, flew away. Samwili, cursing to himself and rubbing the wounded spot, regained the path to find Matalisi in conversation with a peasant. It was Musisi, who immediately proceeded to retail the news of the murder, adding adverse comments upon the murderer, the metal crucifix swinging on his bare chest flashing points of sunlight as he gesticulated. Matalisi listened gravely, as if he had not heard before; Samwili experienced a violent inclination to announce himself as the proud author of the deed. However, he repressed the desire and fell to quaking, lest Matalisi or Yama Yama should denounce him with a view to securing his arrest and consequently saving their cattle. But neither made any sign, Yama Yama standing stolidly by with the tranced expression of a sleepwalker.

Musisi had apparently completely forgotten the conversation in which the murder had been plotted, for he greeted Samwili in the usual manner, and treated him to a wholly imaginative account of the crime, torturing that hero with an itching desire to call Musisi a liar and correct him regarding the actual details. At length Musisi passed on up a path at right angles to the travelers, to an outlying field to which he was bound. Matalisi led on without comment, and together the three vanished in an Indian file into the shadows of the banana plantation.

***

At about an hour later Musisi came padding down the same path on his way back. He was chewing the cud of the murder news, which, from his simple-minded point of view, he considered a terrible offence against the good white God, personified in the shape of the White Fathers, and in a lesser degree the white officials. They, he had been taught and could see, benefited him and his kind by freedom from the persecution of native chiefs. They were a power for good, therefore to be believed in and propitiated. The suggestion that a crime by one of his brothers might be avenged by the enraged whites upon all and sundry – a logical process in the native mind – disturbed him and added to his indignation. For days this fear had increased, until he grew to dread any absence from his village lest he might return to find it burned about his ears. There was more than one precedent for such action on the part of the whites, which he and all his brothers never forgot for a moment.

In his trouble he sought his White Father, and by him was reassured. But still doubts clamored at his heart. He was a faithful believer in the Church, as taught to him, and in the mercy and intelligence of his white rulers, yet the pagan idea that might is right caused a pessimistic outlook at the hint of danger. He argued vaguely that justice tempered with mercy was good in theory, but that, in practice, things very often went the other way; and although well grounded in the virtue of innocent martyrdom, he felt that he, in particular, was not built for such lofty aspirations. Musisi was typical of his class, Catholic, Protestant, and pagan. To the pagans, lacking the comfort of a weak faith in immunity from injustice, the terrors of vengeance loomed larger in their minds.

As Musisi entered the shadow of the bananas, his mind ruminating upon these matters, and struck off from the beaten path on a short cut to his village, he noticed the figures of two men in the deeper recesses of the plantation.

He swung round towards them, and, on nearer approach, saw that they were digging at something with a short spear. He hastened towards them, eager to satisfy his awakened curiosity. They heard him, and one looked up. It was Matalisi. Something in his demeanor made Musisi pause some yards from them.

"What do you want?" demanded Matalisi, while Yama Yama paused and looked on.

"Nothing," said Musisi timidly.

"We're digging some sweet potatoes," went on Matalisi; "do not tell Avimi, or he will make us pay for them."

This statement rather appealed to Musisi's predatory instincts; he advanced a step.

"Come here – come and help us," invited Matalisi, and taking the impromptu spade from Yama Yama's hand advanced towards Musisi.

"I do not need any potatoes," stammered Musisi, affrighted.

"Yes, they are good and sweet," said Matalisi, pointing with the spear as he continued to advance. "Come, and you shall have a share. You –"

But Musisi suddenly wheeled round and raced away through the plantation, as if in fear of his life.

CHAPTER XV

The Rev. Blackber was encamped at Kibwezi's village awaiting the arrival of Fedden. The little man had been inexpressibly shocked at the news of Brinkley's foul murder. After he had hurried to the scene, he had experienced more than an effort in persuading himself to make an examination, for although fond of preaching the doctrine of the futility of death, he entertained a lively horror of that grim messenger in actuality. Towards the evening of the same day he had interred the remains with the full rites of the Church, for the tropics have but little respect for the dignity of human obsequies. He had, morbidly, but subconsciously, reveled in this opportunity to exercise his profound office for the first time upon a whiteman. At a few yards from the Kibwezi rest house a small hillock, surmounted by a rough wooden cross, by the roadside under the shade of a Mubula tree marked the grave of another untrumpeted hero fallen in his country's service.

On the morning of the fifth day the little parson sat in the verandah of the rest house nervously debating the pros and cons of the situation. He secretly suspected the local headman, Kibwezi, or one of his men, prejudiced towards them because of their paganism, and attributing the motive to the prevalent heathen notion that the plague of sleeping sickness, stealthily stretching out a tentacle from the southwest, was a curse brought by the whitemen.

On awakening in the morning after the night of the crime, he had found Samwili rolled in his blankets, asleep. An obvious excuse for the man's temporary absence during the night suggested itself, and no suspicion stirred in the parson's mind at the inexplicable disappearance of Samwili since the arrival of the news. From a peasant he had heard that Samwili had been seen walking in the direction of the village of Matalisi, which conduced to the thought that Samwili was, in all probability, following up or searching for some clue to the assassin. When the fourth day had passed and Samwili had not put in an appearance, Blackber began to entertain some uneasiness for the man's safety, arguing to himself that perhaps in his zealous indignation Samwili had jeopardized his life at the hands of the pagan plotters. No other travelers between the villages could give any further information regarding the missing man.

The previous afternoon Blackber had devoted to a lengthy cross-examination of the chief Kibwezi, and from the grey-wooled old man's scared demeanor, easily led into wild contradiction by panic, had come to the hasty conclusion that his surmises were correct. Although speaking Luganda fairly fluently, and of long residence among the natives, he seemed incapable, as so many Europeans are, of grasping the demoralizing effect of leading questions, particularly effective in dealing with bucolic minds.

"You and your people, in your pagan ignorance," he had said to Kibwezi, "believe that the sickness is brought by the whiteman?"

"Yes, yes," assented the old man, ready to agree to anything in order to conciliate the whiteman.

"If the whitemen were removed the sickness would depart?"

"Yes, that is so."

"But you would not allow your people to commit such a wickedness?"

"No, no," in a panic of fear lest he be accused.

"But your people, who walk in darkness, may have done this deed?"

"That is so," stammered Kibwezi, in a fresh panic that he might be held responsible.

"But *you* do not know?"

"No, no; I do not know."

"You have lied to me?"

"Yes, yes; I have lied," affirmed Kibwezi automatically, wondering to which lie the whiteman referred.

"The sickness is the wrath of the Great Spirit on the wickedness of you and your people who refuse to accept His word," stormed the little man.

"Yes, yes, we know it," assented Kibwezi.

"Do ye not know that the wages of sin is death?"

"No, no," mumbled Kibwezi, eager to please.

And so the futile examination went on, Kibwezi, driven by sheer fright, willing to admit that he habitually spent weekends in Brighton if the whiteman suggested it.

Now, as the earnest little man sat sadly debating the chaotic result of these amateur detective efforts, he found consolation in the hope that ere long the conversion of these pagans would render such deeds impossible, although inclined to the opinion that the officials were but reaping the wages of sin through these wretched instruments. Struck by a sudden thought he got up, and calling to two of his native lay teachers, made his way to Kibwezi's village. Kibwezi he found squatting at the door of his hut, talking with the elders of the village, two of them emaciated and hollow-eyed victims of the "whiteman's curse." Kibwezi, dismissing his companions, greeted Blackber with a quick glance of apprehension. Then Blackber, squatting in the shade against the hut wall, supported by his laymen on either side of Kibwezi, the wings as it were of an army cutting off the enemy's retreat, proceeded to storm the citadel of the pagan's nonbelief. Within the hour Kibwezi was nominally converted, for he, suspecting some ulterior motive, eagerly assented to everything suggested by his tormentors, with the one exception that he was concerned in the murder conspiracy.

At the close, when the unwilling proselyte was assenting to the demands of his eager preceptors to submit to the orthodox baptism in the faith, a uniformed Government messenger arrived with the news that Bwana Fedden was about to arrive.

Blackber rose immediately and hurried to the rest house, feeling a glow of enthusiasm in the belief that he had secured the soul of Kibwezi from utter damnation at the eleventh hour – for he was now convinced that Kibwezi was the assassin or the instigator. Blackber poured into Fedden's ears the tale of events and his own convictions, with a mixture of pious horror and self-approbation. Fedden listened gravely to the recital, thanked him for his professional services, took not the smallest notice of his suspicions and conclusions, and, to the little man's indignation, politely reprimanded him for interfering with matters which did not concern him – afterwards fully justified by the news that Kibwezi had disappeared.

Fedden retired to his quarters and proceeded with his official business of the investigation, leaving the Rev. Blackber to sulk with offended vanity, sore at the escape of a promised convert.

However, the police, surrounding the village, soon had every able-bodied man under guard, and by evening had discovered the absconding chief hiding in the bush. Next morning Fedden opened his impromptu court. Kibwezi, in a pitiable state of fright, was gently cross-examined by Fedden, who, quickly divining that the old man had been scared out of his senses by injudicious questions, soothed and reassured him. The result was that, after some difficulty in persuading the witness to speak the truth, an alibi was proved by one of the old man's wives. At the conclusion of the day Fedden felt satisfied that the murderer was not present; nevertheless, he detained Kibwezi and a few others as witnesses for the prosecution.

Fedden dismissed the court with a sigh of relief, and taking up his helmet prepared for a solitary constitutional along the open road. The Rev. Blackber, sitting in the door of his tent, a pathetic, lonely figure, drew a wrinkle of annoyance on Fedden's forehead, for he resented the proximity of this man, whose personality he disliked, and whose profession amongst the tribes he privately considered an unmitigated nuisance.

Stick in hand he turned out of the gate of the compound, gloomily lost in an eternal debate with himself upon official problems.

The dying sun cast a glare of light under the low boughs of the Mubula tree, lighting up the rough-hewn cross at the head of the new-made grave. He turned aside, standing bareheaded beside it, staring moodily.

"Poor Brinkley!" he muttered as a requiem. "Poor Brinkley!"

He looked up sharply at the sound of rustling grass. Out of the shadow of the tree rose the cassocked figure of Father Anthony, his rubicund face grave and concerned.

"Good evening, Mr. Fedden," he said, holding out a plump hand in a slightly embarrassed manner.

"Good evening, Father!" returned Fedden, gravely shaking hands. "This is a sad business."

"Yes," said Father Anthony. "I am encamped over by Kivuma's – we have a mission house there as you know. I was on my way to see you. I turned aside to pay my respects to our dead friend – God rest his soul! A better man never lived, Mr. Fedden; he was an earthly father to these children."

"Poor Brinkley!" said Fedden, whose simple expression concealed a genuine grief. "It's many years since such an outrage occurred in this country."

"Yes," agreed the other; "quite six or seven since poor Brackley and Hampton – and the site of the murder of Bishop Hannington is just over there at Luba's. But they all died in a good cause. *Requiem aeternam dona eis, Domine!*"[26]

"*Deo volente!*"[27] said Fedden, feeling compelled to answer in kind. "Come, Father, let's return to my camp. You will dine with me?"

---

[26] A prayer that beseeches God to hasten the transit of souls from purgatory to heaven.

[27] "God willing."

The presence of the Rev. Blackber he had for the moment forgotten; although the meeting of two champions of rival creeds was not conducive to social harmony, yet he could neither withdraw the invitation nor snub the other man.

As they walked up the road Fedden resumed his helmet, and Father Anthony permitted his eyes to twinkle once more. The sound of voices singing a hymn tune rose on the evening air. Turning in at the gate they beheld the Rev. Blackber leading a small party of converts at evening prayer. Fedden glanced at the Father, half expecting an expression of annoyance; but his companion's mouth was noiselessly accompanying the hymn, nodding his head to the rhythm. Father Anthony looked at him and smiled.

"I hope he won't think I'm poaching!" he said, with an amused twinkle.

Fedden seemed to think the remark flippant.

"I was afraid you would be annoyed," he said gravely.

"Annoyed!" The round face of the Father was wrinkled in laughter. "Why?"

"Oh – er – I don't know – I thought – you see he –"

Fedden felt embarrassed. The Father chuckled, rubbing his smooth jowl.

"What an idea – for a layman! No. Why should I be annoyed? – There are many roads to heaven; but of course I think mine is the best," he added, with a sly twinkle.

Fedden could not respond to this idea. He led the way to the tent without remark. The Father seemed intensely amused as he washed in the camp basin.

"By the way," said Fedden, "I am inviting the Rev. Blackber to dinner. I – er – hope that you will find no objection. I ought to have told you before."

Again the Father chuckled consumedly.

"No, no," he said, "why should I object? I don't think I've had the pleasure before, although I think we've often gazed upon one another from afar. Now," he said seriously, subsiding into the only chair at the request of his host, who sat upon the bed; "now, if you are of a mind I will unburden myself. Well – how harmoniously those voices blend, don't they? Quite good singers some of these Protestants," he interjected, with a twinkle – "Well, may I ask first if you have come to any conclusion as to the identity of the assassin?"

"No," said Fedden, "I haven't. This fool – I mean" – the Father's lips twitched – "the Rev. Blackber jumped to the conclusion that Kibwezi was the man, and frightened the old man out of his senses; but I am convinced that he is quite innocent. Whether he knows anything about it is another matter."

Fedden suddenly wondered why he was confiding his official work to Father Anthony, contrary to custom and rule.

"Well," returned the other, "I think that you will never catch him."

"Oh, but," protested Fedden, as if slighted. "I assure you that the resources at our disposal –"

A plump hand was upheld.

"Nevertheless I'm afraid that he's beyond your jurisdiction."

"If he's fled to Uganda or Buvuma," began Fedden.

"No, no; you don't take my meaning. He's dead."

"Dead?"

"Yes. Wait; I will explain. As you will know, the secrets of the Confessional are inviolable, but in this case I have permission to disclose to you anything that I consider in the interests of justice. I have, in fact, brought the man with me, so that if you wish he will repeat his statement. In brief, it amounts to the fact that a convert of ours named Musisi was present at a conversation in which some petty chiefs offered a hundred head of cattle to any one who would kill a whiteman, the result, I believe, of the prevalent idea amongst the tribes that the sleeping sickness has been brought by the whites. A man named Samwili Maliko, a pseudo-Christian – not of our faith, thank Heaven – and imbued with the doctrines of the Ethiopian Church, swore that he would accomplish the deed. Then it appears that the day after the crime Musisi met these two petty chiefs and the man Samwili walking in the direction of a village. Musisi seems to have forgotten the incident of the instigation at the time, for he says that he told them of the news of the murder. He passed on, and upon his return saw two people digging in the depths of the plantation. He approached and discovered Yama Yama and Matalisi. Matalisi's manner, it seems, was strange. He told Musisi that they were digging sweet potatoes, and advanced upon him with a spear. Musisi became frightened and ran away. That is all there is to do with the case; but I think that it will throw a useful light on the situation. I can vouch for Musisi. He is a very simpleminded man, and quite incapable of using sufficient imagination to invent such a circumstantial lie."

Fedden tugged at his drooping moustache thoughtfully as the Father related the evidence.

"Thank you," he said. "I think that it will solve the problem – providing, of course, that it is as true as you surmise. It certainly bears the stamp of extreme probability. Samwili," he repeated. "I remember the name; but there are so many Samwilis. Does he speak a little English, d'you happen to know?"

"I really couldn't say," returned Father Anthony. "Musisi would probably know – and Mr. Blackber over there will be sure to know him. Samwili, I understand, is a convert of his."

"I'll ask him when he comes over; but don't say anything about it at present. He's sure to be hurt and indignant if he thinks we suspect a protégé of his."

"Naturally," murmured the Father.

"Er – will you have a whiskey peg?"

"Certainly," assented Father Anthony, smiling and rubbing his hands. "My throat's quite dry, I promise you."

As they sat under the verandah flap of the tent, with whiskey, a sparklet bottle,[28] and glasses on the camp table, the Rev. Blackber appeared in answer to Fedden's invitation. He approached diffidently, prepared to greet the Father with ill-concealed hostility. Fedden introduced them.

"Very glad indeed to meet you, sir!" exclaimed the Father genially, and, rising, held out his hand in a manner that forbade a refusal.

"Pleased to meet you," murmured Blackber stiffly.

The Father smiled as he wrung the other's limp hand.

"Will you join us?" suggested Fedden.

"Thank you, no," replied Blackber, in a reproving manner. "I am not a believer in strong drink."

Fedden frowned, thinking the remark in bad taste. Father Anthony smiled across at the little man.

"That's where you make a great mistake," he remarked. "A little wine to make the heart glad – to say nothing of the stomach in these climes."

Blackber did not reply, looking uncomfortable. Fedden, fearing an oasis of awkward silence, broke in with:

"Do you know a man named Samwili Maliko, Mr. Blackber?"

"Yes," he replied, with a surprised look. "A very worthy man; and I'm glad to say a member of our congregation." A particularly unctuous tone crept in whenever he spoke of his profession. "Strangely enough he has disappeared the last few days. Let me see, I think that it was on Tuesday last he was at morning prayers with me, and was seen on the road to the village of Matalisi – so I am told; since then I cannot get any news of him; in fact, I fear that some harm has come to him."

---

[28] Sparklet syphons were marketed for producing carbonated drinks at home.

Father Anthony exchanged glances with Fedden.

"But why do you inquire?"

"Oh, nothing of importance," said Fedden. "He was mentioned in evidence this afternoon. Have you had any further news from Mulazi?"

"Yes," said Blackber, "I had a very sad letter indeed from John Maimba, the evangelist. He says that twenty of his congregation are suffering from this dread disease, and that nearly all the surrounding villages are greatly stricken, and that a panic has set in, causing numbers to flee the district."

"Yes, that's the saddest part," interpolated Father Anthony. "Many of those who seek a haven from the plague are already inoculated, and consequently carry on the disease by infecting the fly in fresh districts."

"It's a very distressing calamity to the country," said Fedden.

"Ah, yes, a calamity indeed," assented the Father, playing with the crucifix upon his chest. "I sadly fear that the whole country will be in the grip before long. The whole of the south of the Lake is in the shadow, and now it is rapidly spreading inland from the northern shore; and I hear from Father Anselm that they have had several cases up the Nile."

"Yes," corroborated Fedden. "Pornick at Mruli reports cases as well. It is having a very serious effect upon the native mind. Not unnaturally they blame us, and the notion is fomenting in the minds of the malcontents. There is considerable sedition rife amongst the Wasoga. Have you heard much from among your people, Father?"

"No," said the Father, pursing his lips; "and I'm afraid that I'm not likely to, for I'm so well aware that my people are carefully avoided by any conspirators."

"*I* think that there is very little in that idea," said Blackber. "On the contrary, I am quite confident that I should know from *my* people if anything of the sort was stirring amongst the masses. Fortunately nearly all the chiefs of any importance are Protestants."

The last remark was evidently intended as a mild jibe at Father Anthony, for, as the majority of the Catholic converts were among the peasant class, the Protestants made a contrary boast – from the young King of Uganda, Daudi Chwa,[29] and his Regent, downwards to subchiefs. But the Father did not rise to the bait, smiling indulgently as he said:

"I'm afraid I cannot agree with you, Mr. Blackber. Perhaps my knowledge of human nature may be larger than yours, but anyhow, you must not forget, from a native point of view, that any convert – no matter to what particular creed – is regarded by the pagan as a sort of renegade to the side of the whiteman. Unfortunately I am compelled to admit that many conversions are – well, not so much a question of belief as merely a political move. That is one of our greatest sorrows and one of the hardest evils to guard against."

"I am afraid that I cannot agree with you, Father Anthony," said the little parson, bridling. "At any rate it is not so with *us*."

"Ah, Mr. Blackber, I'm afraid that your enthusiasm blinds your perception. What do you think, Mr. Fedden? Oh," he added, laughing at Fedden's obvious embarrassment at the prospect of stepping into the ecclesiastical fray, "I mean on the subject of the native unrest?"

"I think that it's extremely difficult to get the truth and to measure the extent and force of it," replied Fedden thoughtfully. "There is always an undercurrent of disaffection, which is naturally fanned by circumstances like the present; but the problem is whether it is likely to burst into flame?"

---

[29] King of Buganda from 1897 until his death in 1939 (aka Ssekabaka Daudi Chwa II). He became king at the age of one after his father, Kabaka Mwanga II, was forced into exile, following a rebellion against British colonial forces. The child king was governed by regents until he came of age and assumed full royal responsibilities in 1914.

CHAPTER XVI

One afternoon Laurie, stretched in a hammock chair on the back verandah of the fort bungalow, was staring heavy eyed across the flats at the dull white of the bald-browed kopje[30] shrouded in the mist of a heavy downpour, the first of the short wet season. A little to his left were the tops of the tents in which Sula was supposed to dwell alone. He felt uneasy. A fluctuating desire to move about drove him to wander disconsolately into the bungalow and back on to the verandah, suppressing a vague wish to saunter out in the rain across the fort and on to the camp, with no particular object in view save to satisfy the incessant craving of restlessness. At Maude's persistent commands and his own physical weakness he had subsided in the chair, to twitch and fidget, as if unseen fingers were ever plucking at his nerve strings. As he became convalescent he determined to determine the equivocal position in which fate had thrown him.

The incessant warfare carried on between the two women hurt and irritated him. Ever since his first conscious return from delirium Sula and Maude had continued hostilities in a thousand and one incidents. Maude would remain to nurse the invalid, barring Sula from the room, outside which the latter would crouch patiently, like a cat at a mousehole. At the sound of her name on his lips she would enter softly, casting a vengeful glance of triumph at the disconsolate Maude. At first Maude had insisted upon taking her sleep in a chair beside the sickbed, at which Sula, who never seemed to sleep, would creep softly in until she awoke. At Laurie's request Maude at length consented to go to her room to sleep properly. Immediately she had reluctantly departed Sula would glide to her place; then

---

[30] Kopje: a small usually rocky hill, especially on the African veld.

Maude, feigning rest for ten minutes, would return upon some excuse, to discover Sula. Laurie, if awake, would chide Maude for breaking her much-needed rest, and to her angry discomfiture insist upon Sula remaining. Once, finding Laurie dozing and Sula nestled by the side of the bed, she had ordered her from the room. Sula had silently refused to obey Maude's imperious gesture, with eloquent eyes. Then Maude, in jealous anger, had attempted to drag her from the bed. Trembling with rage as the hand gripped her shoulder, Sula had bitten Maude savagely in the arm. Maude squeaked with fright and pain, which had awakened Laurie.

So this insidious enmity had continued. Maude, usually sane and reasonable, had lost all perspective. Later she would hate and despise herself for creeping stealthily to the window and peeping out to see that Laurie was alone. The perpetual strain upon her nerves darkened her eyes and drew lines upon her face. Sula had grown abnormally silent. She would crouch for hours beside Laurie, or as near as she could get, with her large sloe eyes as watchful as a cat, gleaming malevolently at the sight of Maude, glowing with dumb affection as they rested on Laurie. Every morning she would inquire of Laurie how he felt, and ever receiving an assurance of better health would ejaculate: "Sula glad, Lolly. Oh, Sula much glad!" and relapse into silence for the rest of the day.

As Laurie stared out into the rain mist Sula appeared over the rise. Enveloped in one of his mackintoshes over her head, hood fashion, falling to her bare ankles gleaming wet above the sandals, she padded quickly across the open with her characteristic gliding motion. Laurie fell to comparing her grace of movement with Maude, who had the art of walking to a greater extent than any European girl he had ever known. But the lithe, easy sway of Sula's hips and the effortless motion of her limbs were unapproached by any women save perhaps Italian or Spanish peasant girls. Sula ran lightly up the steps, discarding the dripping ulster[31] at the top, and sank beside him, smiling her contentment to be near him.

Laurie had intended to say something to her, but he had forgotten what it was by the time she reached him. Of late he had been strangely disinclined to speak: it seemed too much trouble to search for words to express an idea. Indeed, consecutive thought had become such an effort that he had postponed and evaded any discussion with Maude.

Scarcely had Sula settled herself than a light footstep sounded within. Maude came out on to the verandah. She frowned at Sula and drew up a chair on the other side of Laurie.

"Feeling better?" she inquired. "Let me rearrange those pillows, Laurie. They don't look comfortable."

"No, no," said Laurie irritably. "Let me alone. I'm all right."

Maude pouted as she sat back in her chair.

"Don't you care for that novel?" she asked. "Let me get you another one?"

"No, no," said Laurie, fingering the discarded book nervously. "I don't feel like reading. I don't feel like anything," he added with a touch of petulance.

"Poor Laurie!" cooed Maude soothingly.

"Don't!" he exclaimed with a frown, and added with a weak smile: "Sympathy to the sick is like salt to an open wound – beneficial, but smarts damnably!"

Sula, watching the twain, winced at the exchange of sympathy. She laid a hand on Laurie's arm, like a dog pleading for a share of attention. He interlaced his fingers in her hair, whereat Maude frowned as she said:

"Good; that sounds more like the old Laurie!"

"Does it?" he said. "The ghost of the past –" He paused and passed a hand across his eyes. "What was I going to say? D'you

---

[31] Ulster: a long loose overcoat of Irish origin, made of heavy material such as frieze.

know my memory has all gone to pieces? – In fits. – I can't think for ten seconds consecutively. – There, it makes me feel tired to get that out."

The rain had ceased as they talked. The sun shone brilliantly again, intensifying the damp mists which hung around the kopje and the flats. Away over the lake to the south another dark mass of storm clouds hovered.

Laurie moved his feet restlessly and leaning forward, rubbed his ankles.

"Still puffed slightly," he said in answer to Maude; "and ache abominably. Been like this ever since I started from Kampala. Can't understand it – unless –"

"Unless what?" queried Maude.

"Unless – oh nothing," he said, lying back in his chair with a sigh.

Maude watched him anxiously, glanced at Sula and back to him.

"*Je desirez vous tête-à-tête avec moi,*" she said haltingly, for Sula's benefit, who glanced up suspiciously at the sound of the unfamiliar tongue.

He smiled weakly at the stumbling French, and after a pause turned to Sula and said, stroking her hair:

"Sula go over to the camp and come back at teatime."

She flashed an angry look at Maude and obeyed, her eyes welling with tears.

"Well?" he said as Maude drew her chair closer.

"My husband will be back tomorrow."

"Well?"

"Laurie! Laurie! Won't you understand? We – I quarreled with him – for you: And told him – that we had met before – everything."

"I could never understand," he said, after a pause, "why you didn't tell him at first. What must he think of me?"

"Think of you!" she echoed. "What does he think of *me*? I did it for your sake, Laurie. You were ill – dying. That – that woman brought you to me – here. Herbert was leaving, and I had arranged to go with him and on to Jinja and home. D'you understand? I couldn't go on any longer, so I was going to flee – flee from you, Laurie; but – but fate sent you back to me."

She paused, watching him eagerly.

"Oh, Laurie, what is the use of pretending now? *He* saved your life – for me. And I was so glad – so grateful that I told him – everything."

He smiled faintly, staring out across country.

"What are you laughing at?" she demanded angrily. "My God, Laurie! you may laugh now, but *I* cannot. I made a mistake. I was brutal and deserved all I got; but – but I didn't know then. Oh, Laurie, Laurie, you make it hard for me!"

She paused. He remained silent.

"God, you are cruel, Laurie – cruel! Tell me" – she leaned forward – "did I make *you* suffer much – when you went away? I know you did, but tell me?"

He frowned as if in protest. "Yes," he said slowly.

"Well, multiply your sufferings a hundredfold, and you'll have an idea of what *I've* suffered. "Women suffer more than men, Laurie – yes, mentally as well as physically."

He made a protesting, hopeless gesture. She watched him with eager expectancy, changing to anxiety.

"Laurie, dear, why won't you help me?" she pleaded.

He closed his eyes with an expression of pain. She seized his hand and spoke hurriedly.

"Laurie, this is no time for conventional beating about the bush, but you make it hard for me, dear. After all, convention dies hard in a woman. Laurie, I want you. My husband will never divorce me – he's not that kind; but it's not too late. Will you go home and I'll go too; and then – oh, Laurie! – then we can go somewhere – anywhere where we can be together and be happy. Life is so short, Laurie. Don't shame me! I can't help it. I want you more than I want life, Laurie. He won't mind – I mean be never understood nor ever will understand me, and – and he'll be far happier here with his beloved work, Laurie. I shall leave him whether you consent or not. I cannot go on living – this life – with him. – Laurie!"

She had dropped on her knees beside him, clutching distractedly at his arms, striving to pierce the mask of his face.

"Laurie! Speak, dear! for God's sake answer me!"

He looked at her steadily, sadly.

"For the last time – and only since – since then – I tell you, Maude, that I loved you – and still love you as a man can only love once in a lifetime."

"Laurie!" she breathed, and half rose towards him.

"Wait, dearest; it can never be. Not because I'm so scrupulously moral – conventionally moral, I mean; that would not prevent me taking you. You wronged me deeply – once – but you could tread upon me and I should still love you. You wronged him and he wronged you; *but* he did not knowingly, poor devil! It's just an ordinary tale of mistakes – common enough. Mistakes breed faster than rabbits. What was I going to say?" He passed his hand across his eyes perplexedly. "I'm in a bad mood. I can't keep my thoughts together. – But no, Maude," he continued after a pause; "it can never be. I've tried to explain, but I'm so hazy. I'll be better later. My brain seems to clear sometimes. I remember that I wanted to tell you all this when – the last time – this morning – when – Oh, what am I talking about?"

His face twitched spasmodically in an angry effort to control his mind. Maude watched him with anxious suspense.

"Damn!" he exclaimed, after a mental struggle; "it's hellish! hellish! Wait! Let me finish."

Maude half rose to her feet in alarm.

"Oh yes, I know. Oh, Maude, Maude"- he bent over her, speaking normally – "I wish you could understand – know everything; but I cannot – cannot tell you. I would give my soul to take you off for good – always together. If there are such things as affinities – and I believe there are – you were – are mine, but with sardonic humor it is decreed that we shall only speak twice in the course of life."

"But, Laurie – tell me what you mean by –"

"I cannot dear, I simply – cannot. I've thought it all out in – in lucid intervals –"

"In lucid intervals!" echoed Maude. "Laurie, what *do* you mean?"

"A phrase, dear; that's all. Merely a phrase. I've thought it all out, and it can end only in one way."

"Laurie!"

"In – in – I can't say it; but one day you will know. I would sacrifice everything for your sake – if it were not for – for this horror. But as it is – I shall do as I've decided."

"Won't – won't you tell me?"

Maude's eyes streamed tears as she looked up into his face imploringly.

"I cannot, dear. God help me! I cannot."

He sighed heavily as she dropped her head on to his knee, crying silently. His hand caressed her coppery hair for a minute or two whilst he fought with emotion. Then he spoke thickly.

"Maude! Maude! Look at me, dear."

She held up her face, wet with tears.

"My God!" he muttered as he looked at her; "it is hard – bitterly hard. Kiss me, dear – for the last time."

Her arm flew around his neck, her lips clung to his with a salty kiss. Suddenly withdrawing her head she looked into his eyes and face, stroking his hair with one disengaged hand.

"Oh, dearest, *my* dearest," she murmured, "why, why must this be? Oh, Laurie, best beloved –"

The tears blinded her eyes and choked her voice; she clung passionately to his lips once more.

At the sound of a half-articulate scream their heads flew apart. Sula, her eyes wide and nostrils distended, stood by the door. Her lips were twisted with pain. She trembled violently from head to foot, a stray shaft of sunlight shimmering on her black hair. The look in her eyes was that of a mortally stricken deer. From her heaving bosom, at which her small hands clutched convulsively, came a short wailing groan of anguish. As they watched she gave a stabbing gasp and, turning, fled down the steps and across the open with the agile speed of an antelope.

Without a moment's hesitation Laurie divined her intention.

"Quick!" he said to Maude, who had risen to her feet. "Quick!"

"What d'you mean?" said she, looking at him in surprise.

But he had left the verandah and was running towards the camp. For a moment or two Maude hesitated between anxiety for him and anger at the way in which Sula had torn him from her arms. Then, as Sula's head disappeared below the crest of the hill, Maude gathered up her skirts and hurried after Laurie. As she scurried across the open she found herself wishing that he would be too late to save Sula. The thought that her rival meant to make an end of herself filled her with a pang of unholy hope. However, she arrived at the tent, panting and out of breath, to discover Laurie leaning against the tent pole, breathing hard and very pale. He was holding a revolver by the muzzle in a limp hand. On the bed lay the huddled form of Sula, squealing with passionate rage.

"Laurie! Laurie!" gasped Maude, still holding her skirts and clinging with the other hand to the tent flap.

A hectic spot grew in either cheek as he looked at her.

"For God's sake, go away, Maude!" he said.

"But, Laurie, you'll overstrain –" she commenced.

"Maude, will you do as I tell you?" he said angrily. "Have you no mercy? Go! I'll come to you presently."

Maude turned away reluctantly, twisting her lips in the effort to control her chagrin.

As the tent flap fell back Laurie flung the revolver into a corner and stepping to the bed attempted to gather the shuddering little figure into his arms. Sula repulsed him violently; he persisted, speaking soothingly; she darted a look of wicked hate at him, writhing to free herself, and bit his arm savagely. Laurie laughed faintly and forced her head back, compelling her maddened eyes to look at him.

"Sula!" he whispered. "Sula!"

The anger died out of her eyes. As he loosened his hold she flung herself on to his neck, sobbing unrestrainedly.

CHAPTER XVII

The red-blue rays of the warm morning sun tinted the glaucous waters of the bay with violet and silver, lighting the wooded promontory to the east in a ruddy blaze. The mists of dawn lifted slowly from the small reed-encircled islands. The first whispers of the perennial day breeze murmured in the treetops and gently flecked the placid surface of the lake. On the beach beneath the lower plateau on which stood Natts' grass-thatched bungalow the waters idly sucked in and about the dense reed-girt shore, lapping lazily at the bottom of two large native canoes drawn up within the thatched awning of the primitive landing stage. The mosquitoes began to retire for the day, leaving the world in the hands of the sun-awakened flies, lizards, and birds. Now and again a ubiquitous tsetse fly hovered about the native hoes, choppers, and cooking pots lying deserted by a dilapidated hut near to the landing stage. The harmonious voice of nature was unbroken by any human note; everywhere the birds and the beasts held happy carnival. A lizard with a flash of scarlet and vivid green disappeared upon an exploring expedition into a blackened cooking pot. A large fat rat busily breakfasted on sodden grains of corn in the shadow of the hut.

From Natts' house, hidden from the beach by the dense timber on the short flat and the steep escarpment, the customary blue curl of smoke was absent; the only sign of human life was a distant wisp of smoke away over by the far headland, hazy and intermittent in the bright sunlight. Up on the plateau behind the bungalow the group of native huts appeared eloquent of desertion. Half a dozen hens scratched and clucked about the refuse heaps; the rooster in charge crowed occasionally in a half-hearted manner.

No sign of men stirring for the day's work. The doors and windows of the bungalow were still closed. Under the eaves of the verandah the hornets had built numerous hanging nests. In the early freshness of the morning the whole place seemed unnatural, as if under a spell in the first stages of a hundred years' sleep cast by some malicious fairy.

Slowly the sun mounted in brazen glory. About eight o'clock there appeared a sign of human life – a fumbling of the latch within the bungalow, a subdued yelping as the door opened. Three of the terriers rushed out, two with joyous, shrill barks, the other more soberly, preceding Natts, who came slowly, yawning and stretching, on to the verandah. His small eyes, as they blinked in the rush of light, were scarlet rimmed and black lined, the cheeks sunken, fringed by a week-old beard. He paused, rubbing his forehead as if to stimulate his brain. Another terrier came slowly out, his coat staring, eyes lackluster and feeble. He sat down at Natts' feet as if exhausted with that small exertion. The man continued to rub his head at intervals and to stare stupidly at the silent kitchen and native quarters. The dog brushed his leg with a warm nose, as if demanding attention. Natts bent down and stroked him, looking at the animal sadly.

"Poor beast!" he said. "Poor beast!"

As he stooped over the dog a shaft of sunlight lit up his face, emphasizing the dark lines. The neck and chin, at one time scraggy and lean, suggesting an old tortoise, were now puffed, obliterating the line of jaw altogether. As he continued to pat and stroke the beast the two joyous ones returned from a constitutional scamper and noisily demanded a share of attention, followed by the other sad one, indifferent and bored.

"No, no," Natts admonished the others. "You've no call – yet. Poor beast!" he continued, caressing the first dog; "me and you – poor beast – and poor Tinker!"

He stood up suddenly and pinched his throat, muttering: "There might be – there might be!" He went back into the bungalow, from whence came the sound of the clink of bottles. Presently he emerged holding up a whiskey bottle against the light, turning it this way and that in pathetic attempt to discover some liquor. He broke into a torrent of language, and savagely flung the empty bottle at the group of fowls. The rooster leapt into the air with a squeak and a flutter of wings as the missile flew underneath him, and, with his shrill-clucking wives, fled to safety. The craving for spirits, which, owing to the nonarrival of carriers from Entebbe he had been without for three days, seemed to infuriate him. He continued to swear fluently, kicking a dog out of the way in blind fury. The absence of the men suddenly occurred to him as unusual. They had for a long while past been growing sulky and lazy; many had run away, others far too ill to work.

Natts strode down to the cookhouse, screaming hoarsely for his headman and the cook alternately. The idea of eating occurred to him. For years he had never eaten breakfast, but the suggestion, although he did not feel the need of food, served as fuel for his rage. Usually a very placid man, of late he had been subject to sudden fits of craving for wild excitement, appeased by flying into an ungovernable rage; then afterwards came lassitude and indifference. He had not been down to the scene of work – tree-felling – for some weeks. It became too much trouble to move from the bungalow, except to rush around the immediate neighborhood in mad anger.

As he approached the kitchen in the blaze of brilliant sunlight he appeared a stooping, shuffling figure of a very old man, the thin bloodless lips gibbering obscene oaths, the small eyes bloodshot and glassy. The two terriers gamboled around, gleefully chasing the chickens, as he kicked open the door made of packing cases knocked together. A cloud of flies emerged as he stumbled into the gloom, cursing and calling on the cook by name. Receiving no answer he shuffled out again and made for the headman's hut, the first of the line. A whine came from within as he battered the rickety door open. A roynish[32] native dog, a rheumy-eyed skeleton, crept out. He kicked at it savagely, cursing afresh as he missed it.

Natts disappeared into the gloom, still frothing curses, leaving the cur to exchange dismal confidences with the two lively terriers. For a while Natts stood blinking in the gloom, spluttering maledictions and commands. As his eyes focused to the shadows he gradually became aware of the figure of a human upon a heap of ragged blankets in a corner of the hut. He shambled over and roughly pulled it by the shoulder. The covering blanket fell away, revealing the brown withered breasts of a woman. She grunted. Natts swore violently and shook her. The eyes opened slowly, gazed at him without intelligence, and closed in sleep again. Half a dozen times Natts shook and shouted at her, inquiring for her man, but could not elicit any answer save a tired groan and prodigious sighs.

At length he stumbled out of the hut, his passion rapidly abating. In turn he visited several huts, but only found the cold corpse of a young child, horribly emaciated, in the furthermost.

As he returned, holding his eyes against the fierce glare of the sun, he paused at the cookhouse, reentered and sat down heavily by the door, rubbing his eyes and whimpering fretfully to himself. The two dogs roused him, and, after a scrimmage with the pariah, who had retired again to the hut, sat themselves down, tongues lolling in the shade, near him. The reaction had set in; within a quarter or an hour Natts, leaning against the lintel, slumbered gently, the flies foraging about him undisturbed.

For a long while the stillness remained unbroken save for occasional liquid snaps at irritating flies by the two canine

---

[32] Mangy; scabby.

watchers in the cool shade of the door. Once they rose and, after sniffing inquiringly at their recumbent master, went off in search of water, which they discovered in the shape of dirty soapsuds in an iron basin on the floor of Natt's bedroom. Having quenched their thirst they investigated the shrunken, wasted form of their quondam leader, poor Tinker, who was lying neglected, a lethargic and stupid skeleton of a dog, under a broken table amidst a litter of empty whiskey bottles. After an attempt to rouse their playmate, conducted with that subtle suggestion of sympathy combined with awe common to the canine world, they slunk back, tails well tucked away, to their post at the doorway of the hut.

The insects buzzed, and the sun grew hotter. The lizards disported themselves with impunity. The other two dogs crawled dismally and sad eyed to their two companions, dumbly and pathetically asking what the matter was? The fowls gave up their scratching for slugs and worms, and sought a cool shade for a matutinal siesta. Natts still slept on; his head, fallen upon his chest, half throttled the troubled breathing. Saliva trickled from the nerveless lips.

***

As the shadows were foreshortened there come the sound of footsteps – boots upon earth – bringing the two terriers to their feet, voicing glad growls: glad because something normal seemed about to happen. Down the track through the avenue of trees came the behelmeted figures of Fedden in khaki and Father Anthony in a white soutane, followed by a line of the police escort.

"Natts appears to have left already," said Fedden, halting at the top of the line of huts.

"I hope so," remarked the Father, looking about him. "Dreadful! I thought we might see signs of normal life here – at all events."

Fedden, proceeding on towards the house, paused at the sight of two dogs, feebly wagging their tails at the door of the kitchen. The other couple, after a friendly sniff at their sick comrades, drew Fedden's attention by yelps to the gloom of the interior. Father Anthony, patting the dumb sufferers, heard Fedden's startled exclamation. In a moment the whitemen, surrounded by a group of curious native police, were bending over the slumbering figure of Natts. Fedden shook him gently by the shoulder. His eyes opened at the second attempt, and blinked stupidly.

"Lemme 'lone!" he muttered sulkily, uncomprehending, and sank into sleep again.

Fedden looked at Father Anthony and shook his head anxiously.

"Bad case. I'm afraid there's no doubt of it," he whispered. "Look at the sunken features and swollen glands. Poor devil!"

"Terrible – very terrible," said the Father. "We must try to arouse him."

"Yes," said Fedden, and gave instructions to his police to carry Natts to the bungalow.

Natts protested sullenly as they lifted him up, blinking stupidly in the sunlight.

"Another man is in there, Bwana," announced the black sergeant.

Whilst the Father followed Natts into the bungalow Fedden reentered the kitchen, to find the cook lying in a comatose state upon a grass bed. He was, as far as could be judged, in a further stage of the disease than his master. Sorrowfully Fedden returned to the bungalow, leaving orders for the police to search the rest of the huts.

Natts he found in a chair. Father Anthony was perched upon an adjacent table endeavoring to awaken the patient's dormant faculties.

"I think," remarked the Father, "that a little stimulant would help him. He's been accustomed to a good deal of drink, hasn't he? The floor," he added, with a sad smile, pointing to the litter of empty bottles, "tells an eloquent story."

Natts had a stiff peg of brandy, which revived him slightly. He became conscious of his visitors' identity and talked rationally, telling them that for weeks and months, he did not know which, waves of lethargy had been enveloping him, in which he neither knew nor cared what had happened. Sometimes a restless fit would seize him, when he would wander about the bush, craving to go somewhere, anywhere. His men must have bolted; he remembered that he had not seen any of them for some while, but had no idea of time; it might have been a fortnight ago or yesterday,

"There's something matter with me head!" he concluded. "I feel sick, but I can't think what it is I want to do."

"When did you eat last?" inquired the Father.

"I dunno," responded Natts indifferently.

"Try to think," urged the Father, looking speculatively at an assortment of empty meat tins on the table and floor, green verdigris and putrefaction thick upon them.

"Oh, don't worry me!" whimpered Natts sulkily. "Lemme sleep."

Fedden offered him some more brandy, at which the small eyes brightened a degree. Natts drank it eagerly.

"Do you know what is the matter with you?" inquired Fedden, as Natts revived a little, a tint of faint color coming to his yellow neck.

"Eh? I suppose so," said Natts indifferently.

"Why haven't you gone to hospital?" pursued Fedden.

"Hospital? I dunno – what's the good?"

"Do you feel that you'd like some food?" suggested Father Anthony.

"I dunno – no – don't think so," said Natts, apparently indifferent to anything; his old passion for liquor seemed the only desire still awake in him.

"I think," said Fedden later, after a consultation with the Father, "that the only thing we can do is to send him into Entebbe. Of course he ought to have gone there months ago. But what's the use – as he says? They can do nothing – nothing – except pump him full of arsenic. I might give him some now, by the way. It may relieve the poor wretch."

"Terrible – terrible indeed!" said the Father sadly, glancing at the subject, a lethargic bundle in a chair. "I don't know what to advise – except that. More terrible than any plague of the Old Testament!"

"I intended to order all the villagers to migrate from the accursed lake shore, but there are none left – except the dead and dying. It's impossible to bring them all. Come, Father, we'd best have food."

"Aye," concurred the Father, pursing his lips. "Aye, keep life in the quick – as long as we may."

It was a despondent, gloomy meal. The Father was the only one to eat normally. Fedden ate a little, whilst Natts, after much persuasion and more brandy, swallowed three mouthfuls and fell asleep as they watched him chewing the fourth. The sight sickened Fedden into positive aversion to food. They awoke the patient again. But Natts whimpered: "Lemme 'lone," sullenly refusing to do anything, and so plaintively reiterating his plea that at last they sorrowfully left him to doze in peace.

Fedden, unable to leave his duty to take the patient in to Entebbe, and fearing to leave him to unskillful native care on the journey, asked the Father to undertake the melancholy office. He complied willingly; so it was arranged that both parties should start upon the morrow.

After lunch Fedden called for his medicine chest and persuaded Natts to commence a course of arsenic. Although he well knew that it was useless, yet it might serve to keep the stealthy disease in abeyance until the patient reached medical care.

It was a slow and painful afternoon for the two hale men. The last two days of the march from Kibwezi's had appeared like a nightmare: village after village, once populous, full of brown women and golliwog[33] children, had given place to silent, deserted habitations of the dead and dying. Skeletons – scarcely animate – greeted them; the stench of the unburied met their nostrils; yet the sun shone as brilliantly as ever, the birds chattered, lizards played hide-and-seek, oblivious to the plague upon man and beast. Often the grey-winged terror flitted across their path in the sunlight; neither could avoid being bitten. In the ranks of the police escort a thread of panic was percurrent.

In the back blocks of each whiteman's brain there was an uneasy suggestion, a fluctuating inclination to flee from this threatening horror, rising at times to an almost irresistible desire to cry out under the strain of subduing the clamor of panic. Now and again they saw a hint of a questioning look in each other's eyes; when either was bitten he ever endeavored to conceal the fact, angry at finding himself contriving to draw cold consolation from the fact that only two percent of flies were calculated to be infected with the trypanosome. Then at the end of the day's march had appeared Natts, a fellow white, hideous in the grip of the horror, bringing home to them the awful knowledge of what each might expect. Although these thoughts ate at their mental vitals, neither, in sight of each other or of their native companions, showed any trace.

---

[33] Golliwog: a type of black rag doll with exaggerated features and colorful clothing that was formerly popular as a children's toy in Britain and Australia.

Natts, in a semisomnolent condition, was lying curled up in a chair; Father Anthony sat near by, watching him with anxious sympathy. Fedden at a camp table on the verandah was immersed in blue official papers before his dispatch case, writing a lengthy report to headquarters. Five more bodies, discovered by the police in their search, were buried in the plantation by Fedden's orders, although only the military training and strict discipline compelled the panic-gripped men to carry out their grim task.

Father Anthony's eyes, as they gazed out across the blue expanse of the lake, had lost the whimsical twinkle. His ruddy, stout face was full of human sympathy and sorrow. Their utter impotency and the dismal prospect wrung his heart; and as the gruesome horror of the ever-victorious disease, sweeping relentlessly onwards over the country, was driven home by the sights of the past three days, a shadow of doubt in the mercy of God flickered for a moment in his innermost heart. Although he sternly extinguished it, a deep and abiding grief for his weakness, even in these most severe circumstances, remained. The more he thought, the more hopeless appeared the situation. When he had heard of the awful ravages in the Sesse Islands and Buddu from his colleagues and other sources, he had prayed in thankfulness that his district had been spared; but *now* he realized the terrible portent of the pestilence at close quarters. Yet comprehending to the full, he did not waver for one moment in the course of the duty which bade him, after handing over Natts at Jinja, to return to the hopeless fight against the sleeping plague.

Fedden was stricken to the quick by the insidious attack upon his children – for in his heart he felt himself a father to the natives – and ever chewed the cud of possible remedies or preventive measures. The apparent futility of coping against the disease ate into his soul, but never for a moment did any idea of abandoning his work or seeking a place of safety find entertainment in his mind. Consistently he had refused to think or to debate with himself over Maude's affairs, fearing the danger of weakening his attention to official matters if he allowed domestic affairs to gain preeminence. Nevertheless he experienced a pang of alarm at the unexpected extent of the ravages of the sickness spreading to the vicinity of the fort. But he dismissed the idea as unlikely. As he paused to search for words – for he found as much difficulty in expressing himself in writing as he did in speech – his eyes were caught by the blue stretch of the bay. He became unusually conscious of the beauty of the scene, the cool dark greens of the bush against the violet-tinted blue lake. It struck him as something new, never before appreciated; and the gloom of impending pestilence and death seemed to be removed to immaterial distance. Surely under so fair a sky there could not lurk such ghastly horrors. As he wondered dimly, unable to translate the thought into mental speech, one of the askaris appeared before him. He nodded abstractedly in answer to the man's salute, and heard him saying:

"Bwana, we have found five more dead people, and eleven nearly dead – five children, four women, and two men – in the village at the back."

The man's recital brought back the interminable tragedy with renewed force. Fedden saw again the endless line of charnel-house villages; he blinked and stared at the shimmering horizon, as if expecting to wake up. The man had paused and went on again diffidently.

"Bwana! Two of the men say that the sickness hath taken hold of them. The blood of the others is turning to water –" He paused and added with a rush, his voice rising to a falsetto squeak, as if unable to restrain his feeling; "Bwana, even my heart hath sickened within me! The land is accursed!"

Fedden brought his mind from abstraction and said quietly:

"Good, Matovuma, we leave upon the morrow." The man's face lit up. "Five men and a corporal, together with twenty carriers, leave for Jinja with the sick whiteman."

The man saluted excitedly and strode away.

"Poor devils!" murmured Fedden to himself as he resumed his writing.

Father Anthony, his rubicund face solemn, presently came on to the verandah as the servant brought tea. The Father stood gloomily staring out across the bay, twiddling his crucifix perplexedly. He paused as Fedden's pen ceased scratching, and said, nodding his head towards the door:

"He seems much better now. Quite normal. Do you know much about the symptoms? I suppose there's no doubt –"

"I'm afraid not," said Fedden slowly, caressing his moustaches. "It's probably the arsenic taking effect. I've only seen one case of a white before, but Mackenzie, in charge of the Entebbe hospital, told me a good deal. Starts, I believe, with a slight fever; then a rash – scarcely visible in a native – and swollen glands in the groin and neck; did you notice his neck? As it progresses the victim becomes lethargic, varying with fits of excitement, which gradually decrease, whilst the flesh fades away, until – well, we've seen what it ends in. My God, it's terrible – terrible!"

"Tch-tch," murmured the Father. "Does Mackenzie hold out no hope of a cure?"

Fedden shook his head, slowly stirring his tea.

"No; he says that, as yet, they know so little about it. The origin is unknown even. Started somewhere in the Congo. The trypanosome is carried away by the tsetse fly, and when arriving in its proboscis is conveyed to the next subject of a bite."

"Sainted Mother!" exclaimed the Father; "the tsetse is all over Africa! Why – why –"

He paused, and Fedden nodded silently.

"Yes, no one seems to realize that yet. The duration – Mac says" – he continued, "depends upon how long it takes to reach the spinal marrow. May take a few weeks or a few years –"

"Ugh!" muttered the Father, shaking his head, uncomfortably conscious of the number of bites he had experienced.

The corners of Fedden's mouth tightened in a ghost of a grim smile.

"Yes," he said, interpreting the other's thought; "still, only two percent , you know."

"Mother of Jesus!" exclaimed Father Anthony in an access of emotion. "We may – every mother's son of us – be full of it! – What effect has arsenic?" he added equably.

"Merely as a powerful tonic – seems to hold the disease in abeyance for a while. They've tried everything they can think of. Who's that?"

A police "boy" stood at the corner of the verandah, pointing with one hand, saying: "A whiteman is coming! "

Fedden and Father Anthony walked round the verandah together and saw the weary, hot figure of the Rev. Blackber hastening down the path. As he approached they saw that he appeared excited and very anxious. He shouted as he came up: "The rebellion! the rebellion!"

The Father and Fedden exchanged glances, and waited in silence until the little man arrived.

"What rebellion?" inquired Fedden. "The rebellion," gasped Blackber, who was in a very flustered condition.

"Wait a moment till you're rested, Mr. Blackber," suggested the Father.

"No, no," exclaimed the little man. "It's serious – I never could have believed – some of my own people," he jerked out as they walked round to the front verandah; "and many of yours, Father Anthony."

"Sit down!" said Fedden.

Pale, perspiring, Blackber sat down, mopping his face with a handkerchief.

"Phew!"

"Well?" said Fedden.

"Oh, terrible – horrible – unbelievable!" exclaimed the little man between dabs.

"What is?" inquired Father Anthony, with a suspicion of a twinkle.

"The rebellion! I came on – to warn you – as fast as – I could."

"What rebellion?" said Fedden quietly.

"Why – why –" spluttered Blackber.

"That Matalisi has been urging them to kill the whites because they brought the sickness – after all my teaching. Oh, dear, dear! And – and – they've massacred one of my evangelists: John – John – what's his name?"

"Never mind his name, now," said Fedden.

"And they've sworn to kill us all. Oh, dreadful – unbelievable! They're out on the warpath – drums going – and they've burned Kibwezichurch – between Kibwezi to the left. No one will attempt to go for help to Jinja."

"Are you certain?" queried Fedden.

"Oh, quite – quite. Some of my people with me – ask them," plaintively, "if you won't believe me."

"Where is this man, Matalisi?"

"He's with them – the rebels – at their head."

"Matalisi – that's the man, Father?"

Father Anthony nodded.

"Do you know if they're disturbed to the east, between Kibwezi and Mbale?"

"Yes, yes, they say so" said Blackber.

"But you don't know for certain?"

"No, no; only they're sure to –"

"You won't be able to go to Jinja, Father," said Fedden to him. "We'll have to retire on Mbale – for supplies and men. I'll send a man round by water to Jinja."

The Father nodded.

"I'll double the guard tonight," pursued Fedden; "although I don't think that they will attack us – here at any rate. S-sh! don't say anything," he added, as Natts appeared in the doorway.

Blackber stared at Natts, who was scratching his stubbly beard. His eyes had lost the heavy, glazed appearance, and were bright and clear.

"Have a cup of tea, Natts?" suggested Fedden.

Natts shook his head, searching the table with a quick, birdlike glance.

"What is it you want?" said Father Anthony.

"Whiskey," said Natts thickly.

Fedden, after glancing at the Father, who nodded, called to his servant to bring the liquor.

Natts poured out a large peg with a shaking hand and threw it down his throat, neat. He sat in an adjacent chair, sighed with satisfaction, scratched his neck, and smiled at the twain watching him.

"Who the hell's this?" he exclaimed, staring at Blackber.

"Oh, this is the Rev. Blackber," said Fedden. "Mr. Natts."

"Don't like parsons," said Natts uncompromisingly, and turned away as Blackber half rose in his formal way.

Natts' eyes wandered to the bottle again.

"That's good," he said, and getting up again walked to the steps of the verandah, changed his mind and came back, halting undecidedly at the doorway.

"Do you feel better, Natts?" inquired Father Anthony.

"Better? Ah, yes. Quite good, eh? Great God, d'you know I have not had one drink for – for weeks! Ah, I've been ill?" he wrinkled his brow perplexedly. "When did you come?" he said to Fedden. "My – I – can't remember –"

"Today."

"Today? Ah, I was in bed ill, yes? I – good God! all my men have run away – I remember; and – and Tinker is ill. Where is Tinker?"

"In your bedroom," said Father Anthony. "But he is very ill – dying, I'm afraid. He cannot move, poor beast!"

Natts had moved forward, then paused abruptly at the news of Tinker, which seemed to revive some dormant chord of memory.

"Mother of God!" he said, and glanced apprehensively from the Father to Fedden and back to the Father. "Tinker! why – why Tinker and I had – had the sickness. We – we were dying together; but I feel all right now. Ach!" He held his hand to his head. "I must be dreaming. My God!" he wheeled upon Fedden, and demanded fiercely: "*Have* I got it – and – and Tinker?"

Whilst Fedden hesitated, Father Anthony spoke.

"No, no, Natts, you're mistaken – quite mistaken."

"But have I been ill?" demanded Natts.

"Yes, yes," replied the Father soothingly; "but it was – the whiskey, Natts. You drank too much, you know."

Natts began to laugh, a hollow, thick chuckle.

"The whiskey – the whiskey – ach! is that all; and Tinker?"

"Oh, Tinker has worms; yes, Tinker is ill with worms."

But before the Father had finished his sentence Natts had disappeared within, to emerge with Tinker. He sat down with the dog in his arms. The poor beast was so emaciated that the staring[34] coat seemed hung upon an empty skeleton; the eyes were dulled with a whitish film, the head and limbs dangled like a doll.

"Tinker – you Tinker, wake up, you –" he used a string of obscene epithets caressingly. But Tinker was too far gone to

---

[34] Staring: To be conspicuous; to stand out.

even recognize him, lying inert and unresponsive. He shook the dog gently.

"Ach! you – you're drunk, you swine –" He paused and, lifting the head, peered into the filmed eyes. "What's the matter with you, Tinker? Great God!" he sat back abruptly. "Me and my dog," – he talked to the world at large – "me and my dog're dying together. Tinker get ill, then I get ill. My – my dog and me – we die. All the rest cursed swine" – another torrent of epithets – "they do not matter; but my dog and me – we are dying! You!" – he wheeled accusingly at the Father and Fedden – "you tell me I'm not ill. I am dying, I tell you. D'you think that I do not know? I have the sickness – also my dog – and we die" – his voice rose to a screech – "die, I tell you – me and my dog, you liars. – Tinker has worms!" he laughed harshly, shaking the dog, whose head and legs wobbled like a harlequin. "I am well – now. But it is the good whiskey. Give me whiskey – give Tinker whiskey. It is the only thing to keep life."

The other three watched him in pained silence. He suddenly got up and, putting the inert form of the dog in the chair, fell to pacing up and down the verandah, his face working with excitement as he gabbled half to himself and half at his fellow whites. A gape fly, on the way to its hanging nest on the verandah roof, fell foul of him and stung him on the bare neck. He did not seem to feel it. Halting at the edge overlooking the escarpment he shook his fist at the smiling bay, cursing the country and all that it contained, long and fluently.

"My dear sir – really –" expostulated Blackber feebly.

Father Anthony, not one whit shocked, went over to him and gently placing a hand upon his shoulder said: "Come, come, Natts; you're mistaken, you know. It isn't –"

Natts shook him off violently, and strode away towards the exit. Fedden half rose, thinking that the man was going to throw himself over the escarpment; Father Anthony called out quickly:

"Natts! Natts! Come and have a whiskey – it will do you good. Whiskey! It may keep him quiet, at all events," he added, sotto voce, to Fedden.

Natts wheeled back and came charging towards the three. He snatched the bottle out of Fedden's hand and half filled a tumbler with neat liquor, which he swallowed in two gulps.

"Dear, dear! you really ought to restrain yourself," mumbled Blackber. "Ruin – ruin –"

Natts sighed with satisfaction, wiping his lips with the back of his hand; then, catching sight of the dog in the chair, went over to him and, flopping upon his knees, kissed the black-and-white head, moaning: "Me and my dog – we die – me and my dog."

CHAPTER XVIII

The rainy season had set in. At Mbale the first ruddy flush of daybreak behind dank masses of clouds over Elgon was soon swallowed in a gathering storm which swept swiftly up from lakeward. Daylight at length filtered slowly through a grey reek of rain, pouring steadily down perpendicularly with the consistency and size of a billion bath taps turned on up above. The view from the fort was limited to a few hundred yards of grey falling water in the still, vaporous air. Down the sides of the hummock and from off every grass roof ran a thousand and one rivulets. The sentry on duty at the gate cowered beneath the eaves of the storehouses, his naked feet ankle-deep in water. Blue smoke percolated slowly through the grass roof of the kitchen, where the cook blew and coaxed the wet wood to boil the morning tea.

Over in the camp Sula was lying awake on the camp bed, listening dully to the roar of the rain on the tent and staring at the lines of water running down the inside of the inner canvas roof. The ground sheet was flooded, holding pools of water, and on top of a bed of boxes was Kichui, high and dry, fast asleep, chained to a stake in the ground. Sula, drawn eyed and miserable, had slept but little, lying for hours during the night staring at a narrow strip of starlight, nursing a sore and wounded heart. A persistent craving ate at her soul for Laurie. She knew that he was still sick, and divined that he would never recover. She did not know what the matter was, but knew that the old times, when she had him all to herself, would never return. Yet she felt that if Maude had not come back into his life all would have been well.

An impulse urged her to vengeance upon the destroyer of her happiness. For hours she would lie and moan with surpassing hate, imagining Maude in her power, divining means of satisfying her seething desire to wreak retribution upon her rival. Her mind was chaotic, forming ideas and thoughts rather through a series of imaginative pictures than mental words. She would wallow in this visionary cinematograph until she panted and gasped with rage, when suddenly the film would be obscured by a wave of dumb throttling misery, leaving her to moan with the anguish, impotent.

Then sometimes a flare of savage joy would leap at the thought that no one, not even Maude or Laurie himself, could take from her one unspeakable happiness. This dim consolation served, to some extent, as a brake upon her passionate jealousy. Yet the lingering thought of that joy in store sometimes seemed to urge her to give rein to the glowering desire for revenge, which since the episode of her attempted suicide had been fanned into almost uncontrollable ferocity.

Her whole being was centered in Laurie; nothing else counted. In the mazy depths of her soul his image, personality, blazed as a torch in an array of rushlights. And when he was extinguished by the suggestive hand of jealousy the resulting gloom and loneliness was excruciating torture. That he had lit another torch within the darkness of her soul, which would one day burn as brightly, was that one sweet consolation in her hour of blackest despair. Her mind was over in the bungalow with Laurie; the suggestion that Maude might be with him occurred for the thousandth time, sending a malevolent gleam to her large bright eyes, and a quiver of rage through her lithe little body.

Kichui awoke, stretched like a huge cat, and yawned a sleepy "yo-ow!" Whereat Sula, her attention drawn to her only confidant, leapt to her feet in one action and, bare feet in the puddles, hugged and caressed her pet, who blinked yellow-green eyes in affable contentment. To Kichui she was wont to whisper her secret desires, longings, and tales of anguish, to which Kichui, when in an evil temper, would sharply extend a talon-bared paw. Once Sula, as she dodged nimbly, had translated the act as a suggestive offer of aid. An idea for revenge had been born of the incident, which had sent Sula to bed aquiver with hellish joy of anticipation, hugged and nursed for long nights, revived and recaressed at every stab of jealousy received from Maude. The dread of Laurie's anger alone restrained her from action, tempered in moments of optimism by the joy of her sweet secret.

The thrum of the rain on the canvas had stopped. Leaving the leopard she pulled open the canvas door flaps and peered without: a grey wall of mist, through which the fort loomed dimly, magnified to half-again the normal size. But the rain had ceased. As she watched, the sun triumphantly broke through a rift in the clouds, showering irradiant diamonds upon the dripping world. Taking down a mackintosh hanging from the center pole, her sandals in her hand, she made a rush across to the bungalow.

As she paused upon the verandah step to put on her sandals, she saw Malima coming across from the kitchen with the morning tea. She hesitated a moment, noting that there was only one cup, feeling a pang of angry resentment that Laurie should not be served first. She slipped quietly in and opened Laurie's door gently, for fear of awaking him. But Laurie, barefoot in his pajamas, was pacing up and down the room, smoking a cigarette. As he turned, her vigilance noticed that he appeared slightly flushed, a bright glitter of excitement in his eyes. He started nervously at the sight of her, and frowned irritably.

"Lolly –" she began, and stopped halfway towards him, framed in the light of the open window. There was an unusual manner about him that disturbed her.

"Well, Sula –" he began, twiddling with the cigarette. He paused to stare at her, and moved to one side as if to get a better view.

"Sula!" He spoke sharply, unkindly. "Come here!"

As she advanced to him timidly, he spoke in the vernacular. She finished the distance in a flying leap, her eyes aflame with delight. He knew her secret! that was why his answer was strange. She had seized his arm crying:

"Sula glad! Lolly glad!"

But he turned from her roughly, ripping out an oath.

As she cried out in pain at his gesture of repulsion, a wild scream startled them. A second muffled cry sent Laurie hurrying out of the door, followed by Sula.

***

Meanwhile Maude had been awakened by the first rush of the downpour, and lay listening for any sound of Laurie in his room at the other end of the bungalow. She glanced at her watch through the mosquito net. Twenty minutes past six. With a pout of annoyance she fell back on her pillows, frowning at the dull roar of the rain, and fell to thinking of Laurie.

She had been both puzzled and annoyed by his manner and his speech. She could not fathom what motive made him declare that everything was over. The idea that he was bound by conventional scruples she dismissed as preposterous. Laurie, as she knew him, was too strong and independent a character to knuckle down to the dicta of the world. Besides, he had proved that by his life in Uganda with Sula. At the thought of Sula, Maude felt her jealous anger rising. If he could scorn public opinion because of Sula, why should he hesitate to pursue a similar course with one whom he really loved? Maude was quite convinced that Laurie did and always would love her. Had he not admitted it? His attitude to Sula Maude thought she fully understood. It was passion only – the impulse of sex, strong in every virile man. The comparison of herself to Sula wounded her vanity, but she recognized the fact that any woman's most serious rival in a man is passion. His veiled words and hints mystified and irritated her. Why couldn't he be frank? He had said he loved her and wanted her, and yet declared that all must be over between them, remarking in the same breath that no thought of her husband nor anyone could deter him from claiming her if it were not –

That she could not solve the problem maddened her. What could be the reason? Not Sula – those sort of people, she thought, can always be compensated with money. It is quite the customary thing. At the phrase she thought of the expression "sanctified by custom," and smiled dully in her pain, pondering vaguely where the line of sanctity began and ended. Then a revulsion of opinion set in. She imagined that Sula was the reason after all; that he had merely sought to stave her off gently – to avoid a scene, perhaps! She flushed with anger at the idea, which emotion was immediately swamped in a flood of passionate love for him. In her wildest moments she would have consented to any course of action which would give him to her, even, she admitted to herself in a frenzy of candor, to keeping Sula with him as well. Maude, like many women who can and do love deeply, would have agreed to any terms which would give them their chosen beloved. But naturally she fought., or had tried to fight, for the best terms possible.

Her husband did not enter much into her thoughts these days, except in the role of a cruel and unjust barrier to happiness. She knew that he would return soon, and dreaded the inevitable argument. She could not and would not give up hope of persuading Laurie to consent to some arrangement for the future. She was torn between the finality of his words and a passionate disinclination to give him up. Somehow she must cajole, persuade, force him into acquiescence. She was fighting for all that made life worth living. She had not realized till comparatively late that there was anything that was beyond all price, more desirable than comfort, reputation, jewels, and entertainment. She had been eating the dull, flaccid flesh of existence, and did not realize the surpassing sweetness until she had tasted one piece of the salt of life. Now she felt that she could not live without it.

She drummed irritably on the sheet, endeavoring to suppress the desire to go and see if Laurie were awake. The thought of what her husband would say and think, if he were ever to know she had even entertained such an idea, creased her brow again.

"Men are stupid hypocrites," she murmured to herself. "*They* may do anything, but their wives must be plaster saints, my dear! And even Laurie would pretend to be shocked if I went in to him like this. Oh!" She savagely plucked a bow of baby ribbon undone, and glanced out of the shuttered window at the streaks of leaden sky.

The quick patter of feet on the verandah and the whistling swish of a mackintosh brought her half out of bed. She paused to listen a moment, and flew to open the window. She was in time to see the black hair of Sula vanishing through the doorway. The rain had ceased and the sun shone brilliantly. Her mouth twitched angrily as she muttered, "Little beast!" and wrenched open the bedroom door in time to hear the far door shut.

At that moment a heavy footfall sounded, and the dining room door opened to admit Malima, bearing the morning tea. He stopped as he saw Maude framed in the doorway, bathed in a rush of sunlight from behind, which set fire to the masses of her hair and caressed the gauzy outlines of her figure. For a moment she hesitated, thinking only of Sula, and then flew back for a dressing gown. Careless and haphazard, she could not lay her hands on one for a moment, during which Malima entered. He closed the door with a motion of his hand, and stood just inside, holding the tray in one hand like a bronze statue, watching her hunting about for the missing dressing gown.

She glanced round at him hurriedly, and exclaimed impatiently:

"What on earth are you standing there for? Put the tray down, you idiot!" pointing to the table by the bedside.

Malima stalked across, with his eyes still upon her, devouring her, as she continued her search. He bumped into a chair, slopping the tea, which he lowered on to the table, still unable to remove his gaze, his lips parted. She found the dressing gown and hastily slid an arm through one sleeve. Halfway to the door she paused in a frantic attempt at the other sleeve, which happened to be inside out. She tore at it angrily, exclaiming: "Malima!"

He moved his lips in reply, but no sound came from them.

"Malima!"

He moved swiftly to her as she glanced round at him.

"Quick! Can't you see what I want? Pull this sleeve – this one, idiot! No, no." She looked round at him again as his hand touched her neck. His mouth was half open, his eyes were distended and narrowed at the pupils, a glassy shade over them. A sudden, appalling fear clutched at her heart ....

CHAPTER XIX

For the next three days the country was deluged with rain. A sulky grey drizzle enveloped everything, broken now and again by ominous black clouds, which seemed to break into solid sheets of water. In the midst of one of these vaporous tornadoes Fedden and his party arrived at the fort soaked to the skin, chilled to the bones with three days' marching through half-submerged swamps. Natts had lived upon arsenic and brandy, riding in a machila in a state of coma. On approaching the fort official affairs had been driven from Fedden's mind by grave concern as to the situation of his wife, his attitude towards her and Laurie.

As they entered the verandah Maude rose from a chair, book in hand, to greet her husband, who immediately became aware that something had happened. There was about her a subdued air, her heavily lined eyes gave an impression of startled alarm, as if expecting some unseen horror to leap out upon her. Fedden, slow at deduction, feared to listen to the suggestion which occurred to him. Laurie, lying in a hammock chair, saluted the party gravely, showing no surprise at the sight of Natts, who stood, drawn eyed, by the door, blinking in his continual effort to keep his mind awake.

Fedden formally introduced Blackber and Natts to Maude. Father Anthony sensed the atmosphere of gaucherie, and wondered. Everybody remained standing; the travelers in their soaked clothes dripping pools of water, whilst the rain soughed on the roof and the distant hum of the frogs seemed a lament. Fedden, glancing at Maude, tugged at his sad moustaches, and jerked out, with an obvious effort:

"Rebellion has broken out."

Laurie said, "Oh!" Maude did not appear to have heard, staring distantly at Father Anthony, the haunting look of fear still in her eyes.

"Yes, the people, sad to say, have revolted," said Father Anthony, feeling the necessity of saying something to break the tension. "A petty chief has goaded them to rebellion, blaming the white rule for the terrible sickness. Oh, Mrs. Fedden, it is really heartbreaking. I only fear –" He ceased, strangled by the oppressive atmosphere.

Laurie cleared his throat. Blackber's eyes were busy flitting from one to the other inquiringly. Maude still did not appear to hear, glancing apprehensively over her shoulder at an uneasy movement of Natts.

"Er – I – we must have our clothes changed, my dear," Fedden commenced again, still pawing at his moustaches. "The caravan will not be here till dusk. Father Anthony and the others had better use some of my spare things."

"Yes – of course," said Maude at last, in a low voice, moving towards the table. "Won't you sit down, Father, and Mr. Blackber? I'll see –"

She paused abruptly.

"Yes," said Fedden from the doorway of the bedroom. "Where's Malima? Malima!" he called. "Where are the servants, Maude?"

Her pale face blanched. She caught abruptly at her bosom, and subsided into a chair, gasping until a flood of relieving tears overwhelmed her. Every one except Laurie and Natts, who did not seem to comprehend anything, stared at her anxiously.

Laurie strode over to Fedden, and said in a low voice:

"I must speak to you privately. Come here!"

Fedden followed him amazedly, a terrible suspicion clamoring for recognition, but which was soon banished for another and more horrible certainty. In a few terse sentences Laurie told him.

"I handed him over to your police," he concluded. "If I may warn you – and this is no time for parleying – do not mention it to your wife. Her nerve is absolutely broken."

In the few moments Fedden's yellow-brown face had become ashen, his eyes dilated and drawn.

"My God!" was all he said, and sat down mechanically upon the bed, staring dully at the window.

Laurie turned his eyes away, and stood silently waiting. "Good God!" he heard Fedden mutter to himself. "Malima! For ten years – I – my God!"

"Come," said Laurie; "the others will wonder." Fedden stared at him uncomprehendingly. Laurie repeated, and added: "I will call the other men and get these people changed. Come!"

Fedden shook his head and, rising, stumbled to the door leading on to the back verandah. Laurie, understanding, did not attempt to restrain him. For fully half an hour Fedden remained leaning on the far verandah rail staring at the mist-laden country; then suddenly he straightened himself up, and, in his sodden clothes, walked heedlessly through the rain to the police camp. He dispatched the sentry who was standing under the eaves of the guardroom, for the native sergeant, whom he bade unlock an adjacent hut which served as a gaol. The sergeant obeyed with hurried alacrity, and receiving a curt dismissal rejoined his comrades, peeping from the door of the guard hut, to gossip upon the scandal afresh, and discuss the probability of the Bwana's wrath.

Fedden opened the door, stepped inside, and shut it again. As he stood waiting silently for his eyes to focus to the darkness of the interior, he heard a hoarse whimper and the rattle of chains. Presently, out of the gloom, he saw a huddled figure at the base of the center pole.

"Malima!" he said sternly, but softly.

A glimmer of the white of a terrified eye looked at him from the heap. The shackles rattled again as the form squirmed towards him to the limit of the chain. The man cried inarticulately, like the whine of a dog.

"Malima, stand up!"

The whine and rattle answered him, the eye disappearing.

"Stand up!" commanded Fedden imperatively.

Trembling violently, Malima hesitatingly commenced to crawl to his feet. In his fright the short length of the ankle fetters tripped him so that he fell down. Again Fedden ordered him to rise. Malima did so, standing short against the pole, his handcuffed arms held pleadingly in front of him. The tears were welling from his eyes, one of which was closed from a violent blow, like a child. The lips were still swollen and bloodstained. For a full two minutes Fedden surveyed the giant, who stood quite four inches above his own stature, in silence.

"Malima," he said at length, his voice thick with subdued passion and sorrow, "why did you do this thing?"

The man shivered and groaned inarticulately.

"Answer me!"

"Bwana!"

The voice was hoarse and imploring.

"Answer me!"

Malima shrank behind the pole to the limit of his shackles, which clanked ominously.

"Answer me!" demanded Fedden, a timbre of rising anger in his voice.

Malima dodged as if expecting a blow, and mumbled:

"Bwana! I do not know. The devil was within me."

"That is no answer. Have you not eaten of my bread for ten years, since you were a small boy? Answer me!"

Malima groaned assent.

"Why have you now eaten of the spittle of treachery?"

No answer save a rattle of fetters.

"Have I not been your father and your mother?"

A groan of assent.

"Are you a dog of the washenzi that you bite the hand that caressed you? Speak, for my sorrow is greater than my wrath."

"Oh, my father," Malima made answer, hoarse and stuttering, "I know not what evil entered my heart. My blood was made mad – my eyes were blinded by loveliness, so that I knew not what I did –"

Fedden winced, the intake of his breath through his set teeth hissing like a viper.

"For many moons had the scent of the flower hung in my nostrils, oft making me stagger and reel like a drunkard with beer. My strength for thee was like a rock in the stream, but if the torrent bear long enough upon the rock even it must give way. The torrent of my blood, in spate because of the loveliness, swept away the rock of my fidelity like a reed. Oh, my father, I have eaten of the spittle of treachery. My heart is as the dung of a carrion bird stinking in the nostrils of all men."

Fedden remained silent. The plea of the man that the temptation had been greater than he could bear appealed irresistibly to his sense of equity. In his heart he felt that he, and all Europeans who persisted in treating a native as a thing of wood or brass, an automaton, anything but as a human being, were really to blame. A savage, nearer to the animal, has stronger passions and control weaker than civilized races, yet the fact was ignored – because they were natives, a conquered people.

Nevertheless he knew that Malima must pay the full penalty of his crime, which was no crime, because of the prestige of the whitemen; because, understanding the faulty and primitive mind of the blacks, he knew the way in which any act of mercy, no matter how consistent with high equity, could and *would* be translated – only as evidence of weakness in their rulers, and as a direct incentive to crime. This man, no matter what the provocation, no matter in what extenuating circumstances, must be sacrificed, as in many cases in Europe, as a warning and a deterrent to his brothers. There was not only Fedden – and his wife – to be considered, but the honor and sanctity of hundreds of other white women living amid the same environment, in the present and the future. That they, in their ignorance and thoughtlessness, put needless temptation in the way could not be denied; but such sad fact could not be made an excuse, what would amount to criminal leniency, towards an individual case. The minority, as ever, must suffer for the benefit of the community.

Fedden scarcely knew why he had chosen to visit the man, save in his sorrow for one of the subject people whom he loved as a father does his children. At the sight of Malima the outraged natural man in Fedden had striven towards violent anger and revenge against one, and that an inferior, who had dared to attempt to pollute that which was his by every right of social and natural usage. But the appeal to his reason overcame personal inclinations.

Fedden could not find any answer, nor meet that dumb, pleading eye in the gloom of the hut. All anger died within him. Sorrow and a dull resentment against the universal injustice of the world remained with him. Without a word he turned away and walked out of the door. He stood for a moment or two, staring despondently, heedless of the driving rain, feeling physically ill with the hopelessness of all things: the horror of the sickness, the impasse with his wife, and now the necessity of sending this man to his death for a crime for which he felt he could not blame him any more than a child who, locked up with a pot of jam, eventually helped himself.

The native sergeant came up.

"Take off that man's fetters," Fedden ordered him; "give him blankets and put a guard on the door."

The sergeant saluted, and Fedden slowly made his way to the bungalow, sad and miserable, but not wavering for a moment in what he conceived to be his duty.

CHAPTER XX

Fedden had returned to the bungalow, with his teeth imitating castanets in the throes of violent ague; he paid for his improvident disregard of the climate by three days of malaria, during which he swallowed quinine in doses large enough to poison any man unaccustomed to the drug. From his sickbed, although burning with fever and half delirious, he continued to direct official affairs, fortifying the site of the township, and keeping the police force under arms. The natives in the vicinity of the fort expressed surprise at these precautions, professing loyalty to the Government and their intention of resisting any advance that the rebels to the west, towards whom they bore no goodwill, might make.

The rain had continued monotonously. These were weary and dull days for the inmates of the station. The bungalow had been turned into an impromptu hospital. Maude, still suffering from nervous shock, kept to her room; Natts dozed upon his camp bed in the dining room, or wandered about fretful and peevish in the intervals of excitement; Laurie, wrapped in fits of melancholia, would watch Natts with morbid interest, or fall to pacing restlessly up and down the verandah, at other times, regaining his normal state of mind, assisting Fedden in the routine of the fort. Father Anthony was the only man who retained any approach to cheerfulness. Even he was compelled to give way occasionally to moods of depression in the presence of the lugubrious face of Blackber, who seemed obsessed by the apostasy of his proselytes, the nerve-racking, feverish movements of Natts or Laurie, sometimes both together, and under the general impending horror of the sickness and rebellion.

Sula, hurt and offended by Laurie's brutal rebuff at the discovery of her secret, and embarrassed by the presence of so many strange whitemen, remained in her tent all day, sulky and miserable, pouring out her hatred of Maude, whom she blamed for Laurie's action, into the ears of Kichui, now becoming irritable and bad-tempered by his long confinement. At night, to appease the hunger in her soul for Laurie, she would steal across in the darkness and, concealed against the door of what she supposed to be his room (which was now Maude's, as Laurie slept in the dining room with the other men), remain for long hours in darkness and damp, consoled a little by the thought of his proximity.

On the fourth day she could bear her solitary existence no longer and, mad with disappointment that Laurie had not even troubled to send a message, crept over through the rain to the bungalow. Arriving on the back verandah she was confronted with the dismal countenance of the Rev. Blackber. He stared at her in amazement. Then, recollecting her identity, he resettled his glasses, sniffed superciliously, and proceeded with an ill-advised lecture in the vernacular. Sula, standing with one hand upon a verandah post, opened her large eyes in angry amazement, her chin rising, until, at a tactless quotation from Isaiah, a sudden flush of angry scorn and a fierce word flung between set teeth silenced him. He stepped backwards a pace, nervously. Sula, nearly mad with rage, swept past him with a gesture that made the little man feel smaller still. With nostrils distended, bosom heaving, she flung open the door of the room in which she had last seen Laurie, and marching straight in with a cry of "Lolly!" ran towards the bed.

A hurried movement and a startled scream brought her up in the middle of the room. Sitting up in the bed, her hair disheveled and wild of eye, sat Maude, staring at her. As Sula returned the stare, thoughts flashed through her mind. Where was Laurie? Had he gone? Was he dead? An icy hand clutched at her heart, blotting out the stream of indignant, angry questions which Maude flung at her. That Laurie was not there was all that mattered. Ignoring Maude, she flew to the door leading into the sitting room, at the other side of which sat Laurie, talking to Father Anthony. They both glanced up in surprise. In two bounds Sula was across the room and, heedless of Father Anthony, at Laurie's feet, sobbing a mixture of relief and pain. Laurie tried to lift her up, but she clung to his knees desperately. Father Anthony rose and, with a sympathetic smile at Laurie, strolled out on to the verandah, with a vast assumption of indifference.

"Lolly! Oh, Lolly!" gasped Sula, but Laurie's reply was damned by the simultaneous entrance of Blackber and Maude. Blackber halted on the threshold as if unwilling to intrude. Maude, who had not even paused to put up her hair, was excited, verging upon hysteria.

"How dare you bring that woman here?" she stormed. "She broke into my room and insulted me. I won't be insulted! I – I won't be laughed at. How dare that creature enter this house? Because my husband is ill you choose to insult me. I – won't have it: Mr. Blackber, how dare you see me insulted? I – I – oh –" she stamped upon the floor and subsided in a flood of hysterical tears.

Blackber stood with a scared, impotent expression. Father Anthony had returned, and going to Maude attempted to soothe her, whilst Laurie, with a weary, troubled look in his eyes, told Sula to follow him. Sula, still sobbing pitifully, obeyed. Blackber, shrinking up against the wall to let them pass on to the back verandah, paused irresolutely between the desire to remonstrate with Laurie, which, to be just, he conceived it his duty to do, and the fear of the lucid and emphatic advice which he knew such interference would draw forth.

The little man's attention, however, was drawn towards the sitting room, where Maude, overwrought, was determinedly endeavoring to have hysterics, which Father Anthony successfully discouraged by drastic, but simple and very effective, measures. Blackber rushed to expostulate against what appeared to him to be unduly harsh methods. But the Father, intent upon the business in hand, continued to shake the gasping subject into sane and healthy tears. Blackber fussed from side to side, murmuring appeals, like a toy terrier conducting a street fight. At length Maude, having been persuaded to take a mild restorative, retired to her room to sob herself to sleep, while Sula, having forgiven Laurie, returned to her tent to brood over the fact that she had spent hours of lonely and agonizing vigil beside Maude's room, which she interpreted as a premeditated and unforgivable insult.

On the tail of this emotional storm which had swept over the household, Fedden, who although deafened with quinine had taken up the reins of active official duties again, came in, haggard and as yellow as a guinea, with a letter in his hand. It was a message from Jinja, which had come via the lake, informing him that a company of the Sikh regiment had left for the relief of the besieged fort. During the afternoon a Goanese trader had arrived, who reported that he had made a detour around Kibwezi on hearing of the trouble, but had not met with any hostility, which seemed to infer that the rebellion was localized. The whole of the Wasoga, the man said, were panic-stricken by the sickness; those still able- bodied were fleeing to the north, out of what they supposed was the infected zone, in which were left deserted villages of dead and dying. Fedden realized that their very act of flight for safety was the principal cause of the spread of the disease, as in every case they infected fresh areas of the tsetse-fly belt; and he foresaw the futility of any preventive measures.

***

Night closed in under a mass of rain-laden clouds. From out of the mist-wreathed swamp of the plains came the dismal chorus of the myriad frogs; mosquitoes, enlivened by the humid atmosphere, sang joyously, hovering in dark battalions everywhere; around every article in the bungalow clung a dank rheum; the soaked roofs dripped in tearful monotony.

Dinner brought together the sick and sorry crowd of men. Maude remained in her room, suffering from nervous headache. Fedden dined upon beef tea and quinine; Natts upon arsenic and brandy; Blackber, dour of visage, complained woefully of newly developed rheumatism. Father Anthony, the only man to eat heartily, was still rubicund of countenance, but lacked the twinkle.

And over in the rain-soaked tent crouched little Sula, vengeful eyed and brooding, disdaining food, feasting upon her hatred and misery. Kichui, ill-tempered and spiteful, crouched in the other corner in unison with his mistress, flashing wicked yellow eyes in the gloom. He was in no mood for petting, even at Sula's hands; to her approaches he exhibited half a set of evil teeth, backed up by the angry swish of his tail and a suggestive baring of claws.

All the evening the twain remained nursing their respective resentments against the world of men; Sula huddled upon the bed, her hair in wild disorder over her staring, mad eyes, Kichui crouched, watching with veiled glances, venting his displeasure in the incessant flip of a wrathful tail against the canvas wall of the tent.

Towards midnight a rift in the clouds appeared, and ere long the stars shone brilliantly in a velvet heaven, save for the clustering reek around the mass of Elgon in the east. Sula, with feverish, bright eyes, trembling with hideous anticipation, peeped out of the tent flaps. A yellow light streamed out of Fedden's window across the verandah. A shadow passed in front of it as she watched, and the lamp was extinguished. Quietude and indigo shadows enfolded the bungalow. The distant yelping of a village pariah dog floated up above the chorus of the frogs and the humming plaint of the mosquitoes. A night bird screamed dismally away on the swampy plain. The air, warm and humid, clung caressingly to the flesh.

Sula allowed a small eternity to elapse; then, throwing open the tent door, approached Kichui in the faint light of the stars, her feet splashing in water heedlessly. Her ivory bangles jingled musically as she bent over the leopard, rattling his chain as she unfastened him. He snarled menacingly, and flashed luminous green eyes at her when she whispered sharply to him. She bent down and rubbed his head, murmuring soothingly, whilst he continued to snarl and thrash the canvas with his tail. Putting an arm round his neck she dragged him, heedless of his gurgling displeasure, to his forefeet, where, crouching beside him, arm still about his muscular neck, she began to stroke him caressingly, crooning the while. Slowly the beast seemed to answer to her charming, the snarl softened to a whimper, the angry thrash of the tail died to a gentle tattoo of the extreme tip.

Sula drew slowly away from him, watching the glimmer of the eyes in the darkness. Suddenly, as if realizing that she had mastered him, she fell upon his neck, kissing his head and hammering with her small fists at his loose, sinuous hide, which the brute appeared to enjoy. Pouring out a torrent of words in fierce whispers, she appealed, as if to a god, to let loose the furies of revenge, intermingled with savage instructions. Kichui, like an ancient Greek oracle, vouchsafed no sigh, but seemed to understand and exude acquiescence.

Erewhile, across the starlit space between the camp and the fort, stole the twain, a similarity in the effortless, gliding gait of the lithe girl and the shambling pad of the leopard. About them hovered a myriad cloud of mosquitoes, seeming to intone a monotonous anthem of vengeance in unison with the pulsing beat of Sula's heart, the jingle of her ivory bangles and the rattle of the leopard's chain a tremolo accompaniment. Making a slight detour to avoid the sleepy eyes of the black sentry posted at the western end of the fort, Sula and Kichui came to the verandah steps, and were swallowed in the gloom of the bungalow.

***

Kichui, pleased and refreshed by the walk in the open night, vaguely felt that at last his dim dreams of liberty were going to be realized. But when, at first, to his intense pleasure, the hand was released from his collar, he found himself entering alone into what seemed a new cage bearing a strong human smell, he paused to peer about him, snuffing suspiciously. The two soft hands of his mistress were placed upon his quarters, and with a sudden push the gate of the trap was shut behind him. He slunk back against the door for a moment or two, full of vague fears. The place was strange, the like of which he had never experienced. The cage seemed quite big, for he could see well enough in the darkness. There were a lot of squares along the walls, and from a white-shrouded thing (like the place in which his mistress slept) come a strong smell of mankind.

Suddenly he stiffened and snarled at the scent of dog. Then for a moment he was puzzled, for amid the various scents there was one which he knew, faint and old. He heard a movement outside and sniffed at the door, recognizing his mistress, who was whispering in a soft, persuasive tone. He turned and snuffed the air again. The dog scent was near, but not in the cage. Why had he been put here? His ears caught a peculiar sound coming from outside the room. It was a long-drawn rumbling, like a pleased growl, as his black master used to make when he slept. Kichui listened attentively. The sounds rose and fell monotonously. He padded stealthily in the direction, and smelt beneath the door: a very strong odor of humans mixed with dogs. The strangeness of his surroundings began to wear off. Curiosity began to stir. He returned to the door, from whence came the scent of his mistress, and, reassured, commenced a voyage of discovery. The first thing which attracted him was the human occupant. All humans were well-disposed towards him except when they shouted, and that meant trouble with a hard stick. He did not mind until they hurt him, and then he knew he would kill if he could reach them. But this was a female human smell, like, and yet quite distinct from, his mistress.

Kichui felt in quite an amiable frame of mind after he had got over his first vague misgivings. This was something new, and interested him, in contrast to the monotony of his usual life. The human was sleeping, he knew. He wanted to awaken her, hoping that she would pet him. He loved to be caressed and stroked when in that humor. He reached the bed and sniffed inquiringly at it. The human did not move. He could hear the regular breathing. Then his nostrils caught water scent. He felt thirsty. The trail led him to a white table, on the top of which was the water. Instinctively he raised himself until, with paws supporting on the edge, he bent his head and snuffed the water. It had a peculiar acrid smell, which he did not understand nor like. He lapped once daintily. The water tasted horribly bitter and greasy. Instinctively he sneezed disgust – "tss-sfft!" – as a cat does at anything distasteful. The regular breathing ceased. Turning his head he saw that the human was sitting up in bed staring at him.

The next instant a piercing scream so startled him that he knocked over the basin, which fell with a crash upon the floor, soaking him with water. Scared and angered by the continuous shrieks, he crouched against the wall as the sound of men's voices and the sharp barks of dogs reached his ears. The screams suddenly ceased as the door was burst open by a man holding a lantern in one hand; behind him were others, and between his legs darted two terriers, their hair bristling, barking shrilly, straight towards him.

Maddened by the sudden uproar Kichui crouched low, snarling. His first desire was to escape from his tormentors, for with the egoism of an animal he conceived that all this performance was done solely to bait him. There was only one way of escape – through the door in which the men stood. One dog was carried by the impetus of his rush farther than he possibly intended. Kichui made up his mind in a flash. In a leap he pinned the unfortunate terrier, breaking its back, and then, like a huge spotted ball impelled by a catapult, he flew straight at the men, with bared fangs and claws distended. He had no desire to hurt anybody; only the concentrated intention of gaining freedom.

Laurie, a few paces from the door, saw the beast rise in the air, shouted and dodged. Father Anthony, and Fedden behind him, half threw themselves to right and left, but the Rev. Blackber in the doorway could not see without his glasses, or was paralyzed with fright. Kichui landed full upon him, bowling him over like a ninepin, and ripping open his shoulder and chest in the passage. At the next leap he paused, tail thrashing, seeking for a way outside. The mosquito-wired window, which had been left open, caught his eye. Kichui, knowing not and wreaking naught of fine wire, went through it with a single bound, carrying the wooden framework with him, severely bruising his muzzle, and turning a somersault in the process. Amid an uproar of shouts and cries, lights flashing and men running, he lit upon his feet, took the palisading in a leap, which landed him into the moat, scrambled up the other side, and bounded rapidly away into the night – free.

***

In a sodden tent a lithe panting figure sobbed herself to sleep, racked with chagrin at the failure of her stratagem.

CHAPTER XXI

One morning, some five days later, Laurie and Father Anthony were seated on the front verandah. Inside upon a camp bed Natts was lying in his usual coma; across the room the thin, pale features of the Rev. Blackber peered out disconsolately from a mass of bandages. Maude was still confined to her bed, suffering from a bad nervous breakdown consequent upon the fright she had experienced at the escapade of Kichui. The sun had resumed his brazen sway, drawing a steamy blanket from the perspiring earth.

Father Anthony had been discussing the state of Natts and the curse of the sickness in general, describing with vivid detail the horrors of the stricken belt on the lake coast, the very country which Laurie had seen throbbing with native life. Laurie had listened drearily enough, frowning now and again as if some phrase or opinion hurt as a knife stab.

"And the remaining horror," concluded the good man – who had developed a morbid persistency upon the subject – "is that we may all have it; for I've been bitten by the fly more often than I care to think of. So has Fedden and – and –"

"So have I," finished Laurie, with a grim smile.

"But still," added the Father, as if determined to be cheerful – "still, fifty to one chances against it: fifty to one, or perhaps more."

"And I was always unlucky," said Laurie.

"Tchk! tchk!" murmured the Father deprecatingly.

"Well then, lucky at cards, unlucky in love! Life is love, and cards are death. I always had the devil's own luck at cards."

"Nonsense, "retorted the Father. "Now if you were in that poor fellow's position – tchk-tchk! Very sad – terrible!"

Laurie did not reply, and the Father relapsed into silence, staring gloomily at the shimmering air.

A couple of gape flies winged their way to a nest hanging in a neglected portion of the eaves. The murmur of voices floated over from Fedden's office. The intermittent querulous cry of Blackber inside – "Oh, dear! Oh, dear!" – at last brought Father Anthony to his feet, "phewing" and panting with the humid heat. Through the window he inquired of Blackber whether he could be of service.

"Oh, dear, oh dear!" complained the little man peevishly. "I don't know, I'm sure; I'm nearly suffocated with these bandages; and – and the wounds throb so painfully – and the flies. Oh, dear! I'm so hot."

"Like a sparklet?"[35] suggested the Father.

"No" – fretfully – "the water's lukewarm."

"Yes; but it'll moisten your mouth."

"Oh, dear, I suppose so. Thanks, I will then."

The Father went in and prepared the sparklet. Natts was awake, staring moodily at the other sick man.

"Well, Natts, feel better?" inquired the Father cheerfully.

"Eh? I dunno." He passed a gnarled hand across his eyes wearily. "I do wanter drink."

"You can have a soda if you like. Too hot for whiskey, my son."

"All right. What time is it?"

"Half-past eleven."

"Thought it was afternoon. Where's Tinker?"

"Tinker's inside – asleep," lied Father Anthony, for the dog had died.

"Is he?"

Natts seemed to lose interest almost before the words had expressed the thought, and with a sigh his eyes wandered into vacancy.

---

[35] A carbonated, aerated drink. See previous footnote on the Sparklet Syphon.

"Father! Fa-ther!" wailed a soft voice, as Blackber handed back the glass with his one uninjured hand.

"Yes, Mrs. Fedden, coming!" and the Father hastened into Maude's room.

At this period Maude, ever on the borderline of nervous hysteria, exhibited a frenzied dislike to everybody save the Father, whose genial face and sympathetic mind seemed an anodyne to her fears.

***

Laurie, alone on the verandah, sat staring out across the fort. By following Natts' treatment with arsenic – upon his own initiative – he had apparently succeeded in arresting the general atrophy. He found that at intervals he could gain some degree of command over his mental faculties.

When the significance of his symptoms had dawned upon him and he had recovered from the first shock of horror, he had merely felt a dull resentment against the decree of fate, alternating, according to his physical state, with a frenzied anger and resignation. As the disease gripped him closer the resigned indifference became deeper. Sometimes he would attempt to find a solution to Maude's difficulties, but with gradually lessening power of clear reason. The effect of the arsenic had been to clarify his mind, so that now he realized the relations of those about him, and, alas! the unrelieved tragedy of his own position. A mail runner had arrived with the Goanese, bringing Laurie a lawyer's letter intimating that, by the death of an uncle, he had inherited a substantial income. He was in a lethargic mood at the time, and it was not until three days afterwards that he perceived the grim irony.

With the flickering return of power of thought he had experienced a new sensation – in regard to Sula. The awakening of the paternal instinct amazed him. Sula suddenly appeared in a new light altogether. He had always intended to make provision for her financial future, but with the advent of this new possibility he felt that his arrangements were inadequate – even unjust. That a being bearing his blood in its veins should grow up to be treated with contumely, ostracized and handicapped from its commencement, angered him. He knew well the destiny of the usual half-caste; scorned by black and white alike. Sula was indeed a quadroon, but that would make little difference; even the social treatment of a full-blooded white born in other than the conventional state was unendurable. Any father sees in his child a portion of his own ego living again, and which will live when he be dead; and when the end of the passage is near that fact plucks with double strength at the heart strings.

Hence Laurie, in his unenviable position, might reasonably be expected to adopt more decisive measures than a man reviewing the situation in normal circumstances. Laurie suddenly determined that the child should at any rate have every chance in life. In an odd, detached way he felt that after all he was only being selfish, merciful to himself, as the infant would be part of his own being. He felt that it was a daring thing to do; had he been in any other position he might not have contemplated the experiment; but what did it matter? He asked himself. It was merely just. Provision could be made for Sula and the child to be placed in a wholly different environment, where she might be educated for the sake of his heir. The legacy would easily permit of such arrangements; money would cover a multitude of omissions.

His personal attitude towards his fate, as remarked, fluctuated with the state of his health, but on the whole was slightly inconsistent, inasmuch that before he had professed that he did not care if he were snuffed out like a candle flame in the draught. That was the point: a crushing catastrophe and oblivion, a definite end to a careless existence, with disappointed ideals ever a canker in the soul, was a wholly different thing to this living death, sitting quite still to watch one's self die by inches. All these problems he had thrashed out, and determined his course of action. An idea had surged up in a moment of rebellious resentment of rushing home to London and having a "hellfire time" before the end, of blowing the flickering rushlight of life into a fierce flame by the forced draught of artificial pleasures. That was the stirring of the old Laurie. But the tentacles of the octopus ever tightening about him had crushed out the quondam spirit. The temptation soon died; the contemplated robbing of the orchard of pleasure seemed to lose savor. Anyhow, it was not worth the trouble. Nothing mattered. Only by an effort of will could he maintain his determination to carry out his former decision.

Towards Maude Laurie discovered a negative attitude, because with the growth of the poisonous weed of disease the flower of passion was choked out of existence – a sure symptom of the atrophy. This obviously applied to Sula as well; hence his callous indifference towards her only awakened by the paternal instinct, an abstract or passive, rather than a physical or active emotion. The occasion of his arrival at Mbale, to have all the old love and passion for Maude aroused, the first torturing days of his convalescence after blackwater, when the two women squabbled and fought over him, seemed a long, long time ago. He knew that he had lost the correct perspective of time. There was more than one instance of *lapsus memoriae* to help blind his chronological sense. He had no idea how many weeks or months it was since his return to consciousness from delirium. And he dared not inquire, for he harbored a morbid dread of any one sharing his secret. This very fact was undoubtedly a symptom of a partial unbalancing of the mind. He constantly endeavored to command himself not to display any symptoms which he observed in Natts. He would covertly watch the other men, suffering agonies of mind under the hallucination that they were in whispering conclave, commiserating with him.

Sometimes he would find his brain finishing a thought-sentence begun some time ago; he was only conscious that in the middle of the thought a blank had intervened, lasting seconds, minutes, hours – he did not know. His mind simply ceased to work, and, like a machine when restarted, commenced exactly where it had left off. At other times the cogwheels of memory or thought flew round at an amazing pace, and the horror descended upon him like a suffocating blanket, making him irritable with a feverish desire to move, race away from everything – anywhere to freedom from the incubus; or they worked slowly and jerkily, as if the power was running low, then the sodden cloud of indifferent resignation enveloped his soul.

As Laurie sat alone, his mental teeth set with the wish to accomplish his purpose, Fedden emerged from the office. Laurie watched him, observing his despondent moustaches, the cadaverous face, eyes deep sunken, and skin like yellow parchment.

"Fedden!" called Laurie, as he stepped out of the sunlight. "Er – just a moment!"

Fedden, preoccupied as usual, halted and looked across.

Laurie repeated his request, at which Fedden walked over to him reluctantly, as if unwilling to appear to obey the other man's will. During his sickness he had subdued his aversion to Laurie, and, accepting his voluntary offer of help in station work, treated him in a distant, noncommittal manner. He stared at him, coldly interrogative.

"Sit down!" said Laurie, gesturing; but as Fedden made no movement, continued abruptly: "You are empowered, I believe, to marry people?"

"Yes," replied Fedden, slightly surprised by the unexpected.

"Legally?"

"Yes, of course. A civil contract."

"I mean, recognized by the English Courts of Law?"

"Yes, naturally," said Fedden, somewhat testily. "My office is an English Court of Law."

"Then you can grant a license and perform the ceremony at any time?"

"Yes, yes; but why the inquiry?"

"I am going to be married this afternoon," said Laurie slowly.

A suggestion that Laurie proposed to marry Maude flitted through Fedden's mind. The impossibility and absurdity of the idea did not even raise a smile. He simply stared, at a loss. Laurie continued:

"I will come to the office after lunch then, and we can go through the formalities."

"But who are you going to marry?" inquired Fedden bluntly.

"Sula," said Laurie, gazing at the blue of the sky.

Fedden moved uneasily and said:

"But – but you can't."

"Why?" queried Laurie, looking at him coldly.

Fedden paused, as if in doubt how to express himself.

"But – she's – she's –" Laurie cut him short.

"I know what you mean. Is there any law against it?"

"No – but –"

"Well, I wish it. I am the party chiefly concerned. I will thank you to do your official side of the business. I have my own reasons, and am perfectly sound in mind – and body." He finished with a bitter twist of his lips. "We will come to the office this afternoon. Here comes Father Anthony. I shall be obliged if you will keep this matter to yourself."

"Certainly," said Fedden, slowly tugging at his moustache, "if you wish it."

"I do," said Laurie

"Come along," came Father Anthony's voice from the door. "Lunch ready –"

After lunch Laurie went down to the camp and discovered Sula lying upon her bed in disconsolate apathy. At the sight of him her eyes filled with delight; she leapt to her feet with a joyous: "Sula glad! Oh, Sula velly glad! Her starved heart bounded with the insane idea that the old times were about to be renewed; but the first glance at his face turned the flutter of the blue bird's wings into a passing shadow, a mirage born of hope.

"Hullo, Sula!" he said, and the tone was as different to the voice of yore as water to wine.

Nevertheless she seized his arm. But her kisses were frozen; his frigidity burned her lips like ice. She said nothing, sitting back upon the bed without attempting to climb to his lips. His glance swept her figure, scorching her soul. She winced, and attempted to hide herself.

"Sula!" he said, stroking her hair, which made her suddenly long to strike him, "I want you to come up to the office with me. Come along!"

Without a word she arose and followed him, wondering, fearful that something terrible was about to happen.

The Goanese clerk stared at her insolently. Fedden gave her a deliberate, inquiring glance, which made her flame a dull red with anger, raised his eyebrows, and proceeded with the formalities. Sula stared inquisitively at the books and papers in which entries were being made, said "Yes, and signed her name – which Laurie had taught her in the dear old days – at his prompting, and the ceremony was over.

When they had arrived back at Sula's tent Laurie took her on his knee and kissed her with the manner of a father saluting his daughter. Sula gazed up at him wondering, pleading.

"You are my wife now, Sula," he said in the vernacular, quietly.

Sula opened wide her eyes in surprise.

"Have I not always been thy wife?"

Laurie frowned, and remained silent for a moment. The phrase hurt him in some way.

"Yes," he answered at length; "but now you are my wife according to the Serkali" (Government).

"But what has the Serkali to do with us?" she queried in amazement.

Laurie felt suddenly irritable and humiliated at the necessity of explanation.

"It is a matter of adabu" (custom), he said; "now you are the same as – as Bwana and Bibi Fedden."

Sula's eyes flashed angrily at the reference to Maude. She got off his knees and sat on the bed, threatening tears. Laurie felt uncomfortable, and wanted to leave her.

"Now do you understand?"

She shook her head violently, rippling her black mane of hair, jingling her ivory bangles. An irritable, restless phase was creeping over him. He spoke rapidly, impatiently, endeavoring to explain to her by the analogy of adabu. Sula grasped the point, but could not understand the necessity. Either a woman was a man's wife or she was not. She failed to perceive the subtleties of civilization, and retorted by asking why a man did not register all his wives; to which Laurie could find no satisfactory answer, save "adabu" – from her point of view. He left her sorely disturbed at these strange views – never expressed by Laurie before – and the reason for these unnecessary rites, particularly as he no longer cared for her.

CHAPTER XXII

The temperature mounted during the night until the rain clouds sailed up from the lake. The downpour excited the frogs to a universal paean of thanksgiving, the mosquitoes a soprano accompaniment. The dawn struggled through a dense, greasy drizzle. About seven o'clock Maude awoke. Since the episode which had broken her nerve she had suffered miserably from neurasthenia; racking headaches became chronic, increasing at times until she felt that she would become insane. The slightest sudden noise would set her nerves jangling like a broomstick drawn roughly across harp strings. She had not had time to think or brood over matters, developing a violent distaste for the sight of either Laurie or her husband. She felt so weak and miserable that nothing seemed to matter.

This morning, for the first time, she felt a little more normal, and, lying still with closed eyes, dully reviewed the past events. The bare suggestion of the Malima or even the Kichui incident sent her eyes wide open and her body trembling as if with ague. Great long black arms seemed hovering over her, or huge iridescent green eyes glaring balefully from the shadows. She wondered feebly why neither Laurie nor her husband had been near her, forgetting that she had hysterically implored Father Anthony to keep both men from her. She heard Fedden's voice in the next room replying to Father Anthony, who had installed himself as the brewer of morning tea. She felt a sudden desire to see her husband, and called out to him. Father Anthony heard her, and drew the other man's attention.

"Coming, my dear!" she heard him answer, and, somewhat to her surprise, discovered a pleasure in the endearment.

It was not until after he had spoken that she realized that she had been quite anxiously speculating upon the manner of his reply. As he came into the room she noticed the yellow pallor of his drawn features. She did not know that he had had a severe bout of malaria.

"Herbert," she whispered faintly, "open the curtains."

"Yes, Maude," he said.

Advancing to the bedside, he threw back the mosquito netting and stood looking at her. He observed, with a sense of shock, the bloodless peeked face and the great dark hollows of her eyes.

"Sit down," she continued, "and talk to me. I feel better, but so miserable."

The last words were in a tired, pouting voice, like a small child wanting to be cosseted. He sat down awkwardly, wondering and half suspicious, because he did not understand.

She lay quiet and looked at him, and then smiled faintly, as if at some thought prompted by his appearance.

"Is there any tea, Herbert?" she asked suddenly, assuming a normal voice. "I'm so thirsty."

"Yes," he said, a half-disappointed expression flitting across his sad eyes as he got up to fetch it.

"Thank you!" she said, when he had returned. "What's been happening? I've been ill, haven't I?"

"Yes," he said gravely, and the conclusions which had been forced upon him by his interview with Malima leaping to his mind, added: "It was all my fault, dear. I should – er – it could never have happened if –"

"Don't!" she whispered.

He ceased abruptly, dismayed at the effect that his clumsy reference had had upon her.

"I'm sorry!" he said awkwardly.

"Tell me what you are doing now?" she said hurriedly, after a pause.

"Now?" he echoed.

"Yes – well, yesterday. Oh, can't you see? Talk to me!"

"Well – yesterday I married Burke," heedlessly mentioning the first thing that came to his mind.

"What!"

With a smothered scream Maude raised herself on her elbow, slopping the tea in her excitement.

"Married Burke," he repeated falteringly.

"Married Laurie!" she echoed. "To whom – quick?"

"Why to that woman, Su –"

Maude gasped and fell back on her pillow, dropping the cup of tea on the bed, from whence it rolled with a crash on to the floor. Fedden suddenly became conscious that he had been indiscreet, and gazed helplessly at his wife, who was staring at the ceiling, muttering: "Married! Married! Good God! "

"Maude?" said Fedden.

"Why did he marry her?" she demanded, suddenly glaring at him.

"I – I don't know," stammered Fedden, and added: "But I suppose because there's going to be a child."

"A child! My God!" and subsiding, she commenced to laugh and to cry at the same time, murmuring, "Laurie – oh, Laurie – Laurie!"

"Maude," said Fedden, again reproachfully.

"Go away – do go away," she sobbed from the depths of her pillow.

At length, troubled and hurt anew, he went out of the room.

***

Just before midday three soaked white men, marching at the head of a company of Sikhs, fine stalwart men in high turbans, appeared through the greasy drizzle. Fedden came out of the office to receive them. Harvey, of the tobacco-stained teeth, in civil charge, with young Bralett in command of the Sikhs, and Mac the doctor man, all soaked to the skin and lathered in mud.

Fedden, with his too acute sense of the gravity of his position, was inclined to keep them in the office until prosy reports had been exchanged. Not so Harvey, who jibbed at the office door.

"I'm dry inside, and damned wet outside, eh?" he announced in his breezy way. "Got anything to drink, Fedden?"

Fedden reluctantly followed them to the bungalow. Whilst they were awaiting refreshment Laurie and Father Anthony walked in. Harvey, who knew Laurie well, glanced at him in surprise.

"Hello, Burke, eh, you're looking damned rotten. What's the matter, eh?"

"Oh, nothing," said Laurie, frowning; "fever, you know. You look well, but wet."

MacMahon, who possessed an inquisitive soul, had wandered into the dining room, to discover Natts and Blackber. He came back, making grimaces, and swallowed a drink at a gulp.

"You've got a bally[36] hospital here," said he, wiping his moustaches. "What's the matter?"

Bralett, after peeping into the next room and looking at the group of residents, thought that he had never seen such a lot of crocks[37] in his life.

"Well, what's the matter?" resumed MacMahon. "Where's the wife, Fedden? You're the glummest set of beggars I ever clapped eyes on."

"Yes, eh?" said Harvey. "All asleep, eh? No" – to Fedden – "I want a change first, eh? Have another drink, eh? Come!" and he persisted in refusing to discuss official matters, or to allow anybody else to do so, until they were changed and comfortable.

---

[36] Bally (British slang): a euphemism for *bloody*.

[37] Crocks: one that is broken-down, disabled, or impaired. However, when used as a slang term, "crocks" refers to a complaining medical patient whose illness is largely imaginary or psychosomatic.

They, it appeared, had arrived at Kibwezi, to find the old chief hiding amongst his wives in a pitiable state of terror; the only other male was Yama Yama, too far gone to understand or care what had happened. Matalisi and his followers had fled at the approach of the punitive force. After a two days' march in skirmishing order Matalisi had been rounded up in an outlying village and dispatched to Entebbe. The rising had died almost before it was born. The rest of the population, other than those poor wretches already in the grip of the sickness, were too demoralized to entertain any idea of rebellion, at which Bralett, who, in the enthusiasm of youth and the dreary days of military routine, had prayed for trouble, was inconsolable.

MacMahon reported that the trypanosomiasis had made far greater strides than the authorities had for a moment supposed. From inquiries elicited by Harvey – who had an extraordinary influence among the natives – he estimated that the whole of the northern shore of the lake, to about twenty miles inland, was rapidly being depopulated; and added that the latest news at headquarters was that the disease had broken out in equally virulent form in the northwestern shore among the Kavirondo; several more cases were reported from Fajao, up the Nile, at Lake Albert, and as far south as Nyassaland.

It was altogether a gloomy prospect for the country. There were no preventive measures that were of any practical utility save destroying the bush which harbored the fly in the vicinity of the settlements; but such methods were obviously impractical, in consideration of the vast tracts of country with which they had to deal.

After lunch, which had arrived in the middle of the discussion, MacMahon prepared to exercise his profession. His first patient was Maude, whom he pronounced, with knowledge of recent events, to be suffering from nervous breakdown, and unhesitatingly bade her leave for Europe at as early a date as possible.

Blackber's wounds were soon washed and rebandaged. He next turned to Natts, who, with heavy-eyed indifference, allowed him to extract a drop of the cerebrospinal fluid from the lumbar region of the vertebrae by means of a hollow needle, without demur. In the next room he had prepared his instruments, and, with the smear of liquid upon a glass slide, proceeded to examination. He grimaced, and beckoned Fedden to apply his eye to the microscope. Laurie, standing by, an interested spectator, asked permission to look, He saw, amid the round, disclike corpuscles, several minute wriggly creatures, like tadpoles. He gazed at them long and earnestly.

"Accursed of hell!" he exclaimed viciously, and pushed the instrument from him.

MacMahon raised his eyebrows, and looked at Laurie keenly.

"Quite right," he said grimly; "very apt name for them."

"How long has he got?" said Father Anthony.

"God knows," replied the doctor, shaking his head. "Weeks – months. Sure case: that's all I know. Poor devil! And by the way," he added, "I don't want to scare you fellows, but I should like to examine the lot of you – in case."

Fedden nodded gravely. "Certainly, if you wish it."

"Will you do so now, doctor?" inquired Father Anthony.

"Later this afternoon, if you don't mind waiting," replied MacMahon. "You don't look a likely subject, Father," smiling; "in fact, you're the only man who looks at all fit. What d'you do for it?"

"It's the odor of sanctity," returned the Father, with a return of the old twinkle.

"H'm!" laughed the doctor, "quite a new antiseptic, what? I'm afraid we can't get everybody to adopt such preventive measures. Here's Harvey, f'instance. Rather an odor of whiskey, what?"

"Anyway," retorted Harvey, exhibiting his yellow stumps, "whiskey kept me fit for twenty years, eh? Have a drink, eh?"

"No; I think you're quite near enough to a pickled human as it is. I should think the trypanosomes must take you for the local pub. Come along, Fedden, I want to go over the police camp."

As the two men went off together Harvey drew Laurie aside.

"I hear," he said, "that you were married yesterday to Sula Veddes, eh? I congratulate you; but I don't know what people will say, eh?"

"Thank you," said Laurie stiffly, "but I really don't know what concern it is of anybody else. It's purely my private affair."

"Yes, your affair eh? Quite right," returned Harvey; "but extraordinary Fedden tying you up, eh?"

"I don't see anything extraordinary in it. I shall be glad if you will keep your own counsel."

"All right, all right! don't get huffy, eh? But does he know, eh?"

"Does who know – what?" exclaimed Laurie testily, turning away.

"Does Fedden know you've married his sister-in-law, Sula Veddes?"

"Sister-in-law! Sula what? What *are* you talking about, man!"

Harvey looked at him and whistled. "Why, don't *you* know, eh?"

"Know *what*? I wish you'd explain."

Again Harvey whistled and chuckled wheezily.

"Why, your Sula is the daughter of old man Veddes. Mrs. Fedden is his daughter too – by his English wife. She died out here, eh? and then he married a mulatto woman, Sula's mother."

"Married Sula's mother!" said Laurie slowly. "Why – rubbish!"

"No, no, not rubbish, eh?" affirmed Harvey. "I was present when he married her at Kampala – eighteen years ago. Mwanga gave him two young girls as a present. One was a mulatto –

awfully beautiful, eh? – and Veddes married her. I was best man. Ah, the good old days, eh?"

"Then Sula is Maude's half sister?" said Laurie, aloud to himself.

"Yes, ha-ha! thought you knew, eh?"

"But Sula doesn't know, and her mother knew, but said nothing about it?"

"Nothing, eh? These women – hot blood of the south, eh? Don't set store by official regulations. Come and have a drink to celebrate, eh?"

Laurie shook his head.

"Do many people know?" inquired Laurie.

"No; only a few old-timers and missionaries," said Harvey, shrugging his shoulders.

"Will you oblige me by not informing Fedden and his wife? There is no good in doing so."

"If you so wish, eh? Good; come and have a drink?"

Laurie refused and turned away thoughtfully, whilst Harvey departed to the verandah, where, with a whiskey and sparklet and Bralett with cigarettes, lie settled himself for the afternoon.

The rain clouds had drawn away towards Elgon, and the sun blazed down with enervating force once more. Father Anthony, who had gone to inquire after Maude, sought Laurie, whom he found seated at the table contemplating the trypanosomes through the microscope with morbid fascination. The Father told him that Maude was inquiring for him. Laurie rose with a weary sigh. She looked up reproachfully from her long chair as he entered.

"Is it true, Laurie?" she asked quietly.

"Is what true?" he said listlessly, standing by the door.

"Your marriage?"

"Yes, of course it's true."

He frowned irritably at Fedden's abuse of his confidence. For a while Maude did not speak, veiling her eyes.

"Won't you sit down, Laurie? I want to talk to you."

He pulled a chair from the wall and sat down despondently. Maude examined his face intently.

"You look very ill, Laurie," she said. "What is the matter?"

"Nothing."

The single word was sulkily defiant.

"There is something. Tell me, Laurie, why have you done this? For my sake?"

"Your sake?"

He glanced up in listless surprise.

"Yes, Laurie, for my sake. It seems to me that perhaps you have done this to break finally with me. To make me wish to end things between us. Isn't that so?"

"No."

"What is the matter?" she persisted. "Before – some time ago – it seems ages – you spoke queerly of things, and said that everything must end, although you loved me. You see I can speak calmly of these things now, because something seems to have snapped in my brain. Do you understand? Nothing seems to matter."

"Yes, nothing seems to matter," he repeated.

"But you need not have done *this*, Laurie. I – I'm not so terrible as all that." She laughed pitifully. "You had no need to adopt such drastic measures for your protection. I – oh, I don't know. I feel too tired – too weary to care much. It seems – oh, Laurie, Laurie, you have ruined yourself!"

"Yes," he said with a bitter laugh, "I have ruined – or I *am* ruined. I agree with you."

"You know you will repent it. It's all very well to talk of the equality of love, but you know it's impossible for a man to *marry* such people: he pays bitterly in the end. Besides, you never could have loved her – only passion. I understand, but –"

"Please don't," said Laurie wearily. "What is the use of arguing about it?"

"Because I feel for you, Laurie. It all seems different now. I – I feel impersonal towards you. I want to help you. Something has snapped – you killed it yourself. Everything seems in a different light. It is as though I am far above myself, and am reviewing things placidly from an altitude. Once we have chosen a path in life we had best stick to it. At first it would seem quite easy to leave it. But only after battering our wings to pieces against the transparent walls we realize the futility. It's like a moth climbing down a lamp glass – it can see other attractive lights, but cannot escape; and there's always the devouring flame at the bottom. We perish in the end. – You, too, are different, Laurie. I can't say exactly how, but something seems to have gone out of you. Has that something snapped within you too?"

"Yes," he said moodily, "something has snapped within me, too."

"But, Laurie, you've chosen an awful lamp glass to crawl down, and you've such a long way to climb yet."

Laurie smiled grimly and shook his head.

"I am going home – away from you, Laurie. I'll never hunt you again – as you used to accuse me. The new environment will make all the difference to us both."

She paused, conscious that Laurie was searching her face with unusual intentness.

"Why do you look at me like that?" she demanded.

"Nothing," said Laurie, and sighed, wondering why he had never before noticed a curious likeness in the profile and set of the eyes markedly apparent in Maude and Sula. For a moment he was moved to tell her, but bit down the words and said instead: "There is no use in discussing things now, Maude. Our paths lie apart – perhaps for the best. Anyway, it's no use repining." He paused to clasp his forehead wearily. "There was something else I wanted to say, but it doesn't matter. Perhaps the gods amuse themselves by creating these impossible tangles

– anyhow, it's unraveled now. God knows how grieved I am for all the trouble I've brought upon you, but –"

He shrugged his shoulders despondently, and stood up.

"The parting of the ways, Maude. There were many things I felt I wanted to say. Well, I never could preach, so I'll practice the higher art of leaving things unsaid." There was a feeble note of the old breezy cynicism, which soon died. He held out his hand. "Well, goodbye!"

"Why goodbye, Laurie?" she said in surprise. "Can't you bear the sight of me any longer? Are you still afraid of poor me? We shall be fellow travelers as far as Entebbe at any rate, so you can't escape from me until then. Aren't you coming with us tomorrow?"

"No," he said, "I'm afraid not."

"Why, where are you going?"

He smiled grimly.

"I'm afraid I don't quite know, Maude. Won't you shake hands – to please me?"

"Yes, of course," she said, taking his hand; "but I don't understand. You're not the old Laurie. There's something so different. Why do you look at me so strangely?"

"Because I, too, don't understand – many things. Goodbye, dear! May your future be as bright as – oh damn it!"

He shrugged his shoulders as he bent to kiss her hand.

"Goodbye, Maude – God bless you!"

Then wheeling about he stalked out of the room.

CHAPTER XXIII

About four o'clock MacMahon and Fedden returned from inspecting the police and bazaar. Laurie, who was seated at the end of the verandah writing, closed up his dispatch case and joined the group of men for tea, which the servants had brought outside. Harvey, who disdained such a woman's beverage, found a suitable excuse for another whiskey and sparklet. Laurie carefully maneuvered to sit next to MacMahon, and gradually drew him into conversation upon mutual home acquaintances.

MacMahon, of a sociable disposition, responded readily. By slow degrees the talk worked back to the impending horror and the case in their midst.

Laurie gave the doctor a sketch of Natts as he had known him a couple of years ago, and of the man's private circumstances.

"I saw him only a few months ago," he concluded. "He was queer then, but I put it down to alcohol; yet he was always a hard drinker. Do you think there is no hope for him?"

MacMahon pursed his lips and shook his head.

"Have you ever known a case of recovery?" pursued Laurie.

"Humph! no; none that we are sure of," said the doctor. "Several have lived three to six years after diagnosis, and were apparently quite well; but all save one have died since. Those are out of about fifty cases of whites."

"Is there no cure at all?"

"None. In the few cases which are looked upon as cured, it is very doubtful whether the result is due to drugs, to constitution, weak infection, or Heaven knows what."

"Are the symptoms all the same?" inquired Bralett.

"'M-no. They vary enormously. You see we really know comparatively little about it. Sometimes, apparently, the symptoms develop a few days or weeks after the subject is infected; in other cases they may not show for years – at any rate for a long time."

"Good Lord!" exclaimed Bralett uncomfortably. "Then half the able-bodied population we came through may be already infected?"

The doctor nodded.

"Is the tsetse fly the only host of the germ?" inquired Laurie.

"Well, yes, as far as we know at present, and only one species – Glossina palpalis.[38] You see," explained MacMahon, "the sleeping sickness is only one form of trypanosomiasis: a tsetse-fly disease in cattle and horses. Nagana, as the natives call it – and surra – the Indian form – are all varieties of it. But man and wild cattle are immune from them. Trypanosoma gambiense is the only form fatal to man and the monkeys. Our particular friend palpalis can also carry the other animal disease, so he is a particularly mischievous brute."

"How does it work, eh?" put in Harvey, reaching for the whiskey.

"Well, first of all you have the diseased subject which Mr. Glossina palpalis bites – sticks his proboscis into you and draws away some blood infected with Trypanosoma gambiense; these breed in the gut of the fly, and after about thirty-four days are ready for work. Then, at any time the fly shoves his long nose into you he leaves some of those protozoa – waiting in the tip of the proboscis ready for a new home – into your blood, and you are infected. So the game goes on, and the fly bites you and conveys part of the clamoring multitude to someone else. You can comfort yourself with the reflection that almost only one in twenty of flies which bite an infected person breed sufficient to do any harm."

"I thought that it was only two percent," suggested Father Anthony.

---

[38] Glossina palpalis: One of twenty-three known species of tsetse flies.

"Well, take into consideration the percentage of flies not biting a man at all, and that's about right."

"Cheerful subject," commented Bralett. "I vote we make a change."

"But," persisted Laurie, "is there no cure? What drugs do they use?"

"Oh, various preparations of arsenic, bichloride of mercury and atoxyl; but none have been *proved* to be any use save holding the disease in abeyance for a while. It's – to my mind – a case of arsenical poison or the disease?"

"Are these two remedies used at home?"

"Yes."

"But don't they experiment with other drugs as well?"

"Well, I suppose so," evasively.

"Freezing the spine is one, isn't it?" MacMahon looked at Laurie curiously.

"Yes; but it hasn't met with success," he said. "Where did you hear that?"

"What happens?" pursued Laurie, ignoring the question.

"Well, you can't spend your life with your back frozen, and as soon as it is thawed the germs go merrily on again.

"Why the spine?" from Bralett.

"Because the trypanosomes travel from the blood to the spinal marrow and the brain."

"And when they arrive there?"

Significantly MacMahon turned his thumb down.

"Meningitis, epileptiform convulsions."

"Ugh!"

There was a pause.

"Where did this curse originate, doctor?" inquired Father Anthony.

"Well, it's been known as an endemic in the Congo; but –"

"There was no sign of it when I came here twenty years ago," remarked Harvey. "I reckon it must have been brought by Emin Pasha's men coming over here, eh?"[39]

"Probably. If all the infected people could be compelled to remain in their infected zone, the disease could not gain any; but that's impossible," said MacMahon. "The greater the travelling facilities, the quicker the disease spreads. Most of those who flee in a panic immediately infect a fresh area of the fly belt."

"Is the particular species – the Glossina palpalis – to be found in most parts of Africa?" inquired Fedden slowly, after a pause.

"Yes, I believe so; at any rate, another species – Glossina morsitans, which conveys the horse and cattle disease – is, as you know."

"But the morsitans does not carry the sleeping sickness germs as well?"

"'M-no; that is," added MacMahon cautiously, "we have no evidence to that effect – yet."

"Then it might do?" persisted Laurie.

"It might, but there is no evidence."[40]

"Is there no other creature that can carry the germs?"

"Well, trypanosomes, a different species – Lewisi[41] – were discovered in 1888 in the blood of rats in India; and as a matter of fact rats all over the world are known to carry these particular protozoal parasites, but apparently without any harm to themselves."

---

[39] It was theorized that the tsetse fly was brought into Uganda by Emin Pasha and his followers from the Congo.

[40] [Author's note in original text:] Whilst going to Press, news has been received that Trypanosoma gambiense has been located in the Glossina morsitans. This species of tsetse fly is found nearly all over the continent of Africa.

[41] Trypanosoma Lewisi, transmitted by tsetse flies and by congenital infection.

"Then," said Bralett emphatically, leaning forward, "if they can harbor them, why not the sleeping sickness germs?"

"Well, there is no evidence of it."

"Evidence – evidence!" snorted Bralett. "You medicos have no imagination. You don't positively know that they *cannot*, do you?"

"N-no but –"

"But they *might*; if one, why not the other?"

"Well, there is no evid –"

"Damn your evidence!" exclaimed Bralett excitedly. "If they *can*, it means that this accursed disease could spread all over the world; think of it, all over the world! Ain't I right?"

"'M-yes," assented MacMahon reluctantly.

"God forbid!"came Father Anthony's voice.

The hideous idea seemed to envelop the company in a gloomy silence. The gruff barks of the drill sergeant over in the police camp floated distinct on the hot still air. A single mosquito hummed distantly, and a huge flying beetle came whirring across the verandah to crash against the wall, fall, and whirr away again.

"Come, I'm off! "exclaimed MacMahon, breaking the spell as he put down his teacup with the tinkle of crockery. "I'm going over to the dispensary. If you fellows will come when I shout, I'll fix you all up."

He scrambled out of his hammock chair and stalked off. Bralett swore gently to himself and Harvey poured out another whiskey. Laurie, whose heavy eyes wore a look of dull pain, grim set lines about his mouth, got up and followed MacMahon into the glare of the sun.

"Doc," said Laurie, walking into the rough dispensary, where MacMahon was commencing to wipe glass slides, "I want you to examine me *now. I've* got the damned disease."

"What?" MacMahon wheeled about in surprise.

Laurie repeated his statement, adding:

"I merely want your medical corroboration."

MacMahon glanced at him sharply. "Rubbish! You've got nerves, man. You're all right. A little bit run down perhaps, but –"

"Don't, doc. I'm only too sure. Just examine me now, and –"

"How long since your imaginative diagnosis?" inquired MacMahon sarcastically.

"Not imagination, doc. Wish it were."

"Well?"

"About a month."

"Rubbish!"

"You see I've experimented with arsenical injection –"

"Damn your impudence! Very likely poisoned yourself!"

"Don't get jealous, doc," said Laurie, with a sad, tired smile. "A man has just as much right to poison himself as his doctor has!"

MacMahon laughed.

"Come along, then," he said, turning towards his instruments. "I'll soon settle your fears. You're too damn cheerful for a sleeping sickness subject."

"My God, am I!" exclaimed Laurie harshly. "If you damned lucky fools knew the agony and exertion to keep my brain going at all – God!"

MacMahon kept his eye glued to the microscope for an unconscionable time, it seemed to Laurie. At last he raised his head reluctantly. Laurie had no need to put a question; one glance at the doctor's brown eyes and an ominous contraction of the lips under the dark moustaches, sufficed. MacMahon, keenly watching, saw the stiffening of the muscles of the jaw as Laurie braced himself to receive the shock of absolute certainty.

"Say it, doc! Don't lie to me. I can see it, but I want it in words."

MacMahon nodded slowly,

"Say it, damn you!" exclaimed Laurie savagely.

MacMahon raised his eyebrows.

"Steady, Burke! I'm afraid! –"

"Don't be afraid," muttered Laurie irritably; "I'm not."

"By God, I believe you!" exclaimed MacMahon. "Well" – slowly – "the trypanosomes are there – active."

Laurie bit his lip and paused for a moment.

"Thanks, doc.," said he in a normal voice. "Sorry I was rude."

"I understand," replied MacMahon.

"Wait!" as Laurie turned to leave. "Don't be rash now. Best take it quietly, and go home. Nothing's ever quite certain, y'know. They –"

He paused, cursing himself for his indiscreet admissions during the afternoon. Laurie glanced at him.

"All, right, doc. Don't you worry," he said, and walked out into the sun.

"H'm," said MacMahon to himself, gazing meditatively at Laurie's sluggish stride. "Damned shame! H'm, I wonder – Still, I couldn't blame him."

The sun set prematurely in a vast mass of indigo clouds. The heat grew more intense, and thunder rumbled ominously in the distance.

MacMahon had told Fedden and the others. Although they endeavored to conceal their pity, the sense of the horror sprite in their very midst, coupled with the electrical atmosphere, depressed every one. Each man found an excuse in the preparation for departure upon the morrow to absent himself from dinner, necessarily a dismal gathering in such circumstances. Natts, a pitiable threat to them all, continued to lie upon his bed indifferent to all things. Maude, in her room, was a prey to depression and violent headaches, aching for sympathy. Fedden, coming into the room, discovered her seated in her hammock chair, sobbing quietly.

"My dear!" he exclaimed, embarrassed by the sight of her tears.

"Herbert! "she said softly, looking up at him.

He went over and stood by her.

She took one of his hands and held it.

"What is the matter, Maude?" he said, bending over her distressed.

"N-nothing," she gasped. "I – I shall be alright in a minute."

As he stood silently waiting he noticed the stray locks of her copper hair aflame in the mellow light of the lamp. A clamorous fear clutched at his heart, almost awaking him from his official hypnosis. If this hydra-headed horror of sleeping sickness were to claim her, too? A suddenly awakened sense of the injustice in ever bringing her to this land of curses appalled him. The blinding scales of the enthusiast dropped from his eyes, and for the first time he began to perceive things from her point of view.

"Herbert," came her voice plaintively, "I'm so lonely. I – I want somebody near me."

"Maude" – he spoke in the slow, nervous manner of one tackling a new emotion – "Maude, I'm so sorry. I ought not to have brought you to this accursed land. I didn't see things – as I see them now. I've been a long time learning. Will you forgive me?"

"Don't, Herbert, there's nothing to forgive, and I can't stand it now. I'm too weak. I want somebody. Oh, how I want somebody near me! This awful loneliness – solitude is killing me!"

"Yes, dear, I know," he said, and unconsciously he resumed his long-forgotten knack of stroking her hair. "I – you never shall have any more of it."

"Will you come home with me?"

She turned her face up to him with an unexpected note of eagerness in her voice. His face grew troubled. Ever the unceasing war between love and his idolized duty.

"I – I can't, Maude. Don't ask me. I –"

Quite suddenly he was on his knees beside her – an incongruous position for him – holding her hand. He began to speak in a thick, stumbling voice.

"Maude, don't ask me! Can't you see? The service is dear to me. I gave my life to it, and I want to give – I wronged you in bringing you out to it. But I didn't realize nor understand – only my work. I would do anything for you but desert my work. I can't. You torment me now, because I'm just awakening. You know what I mean – I can't explain. I fear for you – and I want to make you happy, but I don't know how to do it."

For a while she did not speak. The high treble of a mosquito was submerged in a wave of approaching thunder. She sighed, weary and hot.

"Your leave will be due soon: will you come home then?"

"Yes, Maude, I will," he answered slowly. "I do want –"

"Don't, Herbert," she said, and sighed resignedly. "Listen!" she continued, in a normal, quiet voice. "I think I can understand you – at last. I will try to help you. I'll try to understand you always. It is difficult, Herbert. Oh, so difficult for us two! I wonder why the Fates ever threw us together? I don't think – no, I'm sure that I don't want you – wouldn't let you give up your work for me – but oh, it is so lonely! We'll try the future – together – somehow."

"Thank you, dear," he said, his voice lapsing into the formal note.

There was a blinding, sizzling flash of light, simultaneously with a deafening volley of tremendous thunder overhead.

Maude screamed in affright. The next flare of lightning discovered Maude in her husband's arms. She clung to him, burying her face in his shoulder. Then, in the resulting blackness after the vivid glare, he stooped and kissed her.

***

About half an hour later the lightning revealed a tall figure leaving the shelter of the back verandah and commence to make his way through the torrential downpour. With head held down Laurie walked slowly, heavily, towards the tents, heedless of the driving rain. Above the souse of water came the bass chorus of the myriad frogs in the swamps below. Dimly he made out the dark of a tent against the sky, and oozing from the closed flaps the yellow flicker of candlelight. When within a couple of yards he halted, arrested by a sound. He turned his head, to hear the voice of Sula crooning softly. The musical murmur ended in a joyous chuckle, subdued; then a thin, plaintive, piping cry, answered by Sula's glad chirruping. For a full minute Laurie strained his ears to listen, all the muscles of his face working the while.

Suddenly, with a deep intake of breath and a broken oath, he staggered away a dozen paces, to fall forward upon the sobbing earth, in which he sought to bury the bitterness of his soul.

CHAPTER XXIV

Dawn. The glittering brilliance of the rain-laved heavens fainted into the pale rose flush heralding the approach of day. A gorgeous pageant of orange, amber, and violet preceded oceans of burning gold and russet red, ere the sun arose in brazen glory.

About the bungalow seethed, like busy ants, a mass of native porters, waiting to be allotted their respective loads. In the brilliant glare walked Father Anthony, distress written in the shadows of his rubicund face. He looked up inquiringly as the doctor joined him.

MacMahon nodded slowly and gravely. The Father bowed his head, and made the sign of the Cross.

Getting Into Their Heads:
Charles Beadle's African Portraits

An Afterword by Rob Couteau

As a long-term expat at the turn of the century, Charles Beadle suffered a sort of double-alienation. Between 1898 and 1909[42] he wandered through various parts of Africa – including those hit hardest by the sleeping sickness – but he would always remain an outsider, as if assuming the role of a freelance ethnologist: absorbing the flora and fauna of various cultures, collecting vivid details that would later propel his chronicles, yet never fully integrating into any of these host nations.

Beadle's more fundamental alienation concerns his own native soil – the place where he felt least "at home." One might say that he was British by parentage but not by inclination. And his birth at sea – in a slewing, watery no-man's-land – is a fitting symbol for a man destined for world travel but who will remain forever in exile.

Utilizing various narrational voices, Beadle often regards his compatriots with a cynical, sardonic eye. His righteous battle against the constricting shackles of Victorianism forms an overarching theme that emerges in his earliest work and crests in the late masterpiece known as *Dark Refuge* (1938).

As an authentic outlier, he detests the rear-garde mentality exhibited by so many of his countrymen in Africa, and he

---

[42] On 6 November 1898, he enlisted as Charles "Marmaduke" Beadle in the British South African Police, Matabeleland Division. (Matabeleland is in southwest Zimbabwe.) Beadle was discharged on 18 July 1901 but remained in Africa until 1909.

remains a vocal critic of all forms of imperialism.[43] He's also dismayed by how the European colonialists humiliate and control Black natives. Though his chief literary protagonists often fail to regard Blacks as intellectual equals, his narrational voice is always sympathetic to them as human beings, never expressing the vitriolic disparagement or racist hatred that other white authors from this period were inclined to. For example, in Beadle's adventure novel, *The Lost Cure* (1922), which also deals with the sleeping sickness,[44] Birskett, the chief

---

[43] In Beadle's story "NQO," published in the *International* in 1917, the narrator describes the protagonist "Bob Byron" as "One of the thousands turned out yearly by the British educational machine, grandiosely ignorant save of the verb 'to rule.'" Another striking passage from Beadle's novel *Witch-Doctors* is remarkable for its lambasting of all forms of Empire. While analyzing the motivations of the character "Zu Pfeiffer" – a wicked German imperialist who attempts to conquer various African tribes in the most sadistic manner – the protagonist "Bernier" remarks: "the driving power in his caste and tribe was love of power to an excess masked with portentous solemnity under the cloak of benefiting this people and the peoples of the world; forcing them to have broad streets and sanitary arrangements, compelling them to laugh, to sing, and to be happy whether they would or no: an urge which is the curse of the world, the impulse to interfere in other folk's affairs, to teach them, to make them to know the true God, the right way of living, the right way of doing everything from the rising of the first sun of consciousness to that happy crack of doom when our planet tries to enforce its orbit upon some other planet." *Witch-Doctors* (London: Jonathan Cape, 1922), p. 178.

[44] "From a biomedical standpoint, sleeping sickness, known today as human African trypanosomiasis, is an infection caused by two different trypanosome parasites (Trypanosoma brucei rhodesiense and T. b. gambiense). It is transmitted exclusively by several species of a biting fly (Glossina spp.) known widely as tsetse. Human African trypanosomiasis caused by either subspecies of parasite is generally fatal when untreated. It is, importantly, a disease of two stages; a person may not know that they have been infected for weeks, if not months, after being bitten by a fly. The first stage of illness, following transmission of the parasite by an infected fly, involves fever, malaise, local swelling of the eyelids and face, headache, and gland inflammation as the parasite becomes established in the blood,

protagonist, sides with the natives in their conflict with the murderous Belgian conquistadores of King Leopold II, who inflict unspeakable hardship and devastation upon the Congolese.

Yet, from today's perspective, we can see that Beadle was not immune to certain prejudices, though it's not always easy to parse his views on the subject. In particular, one must avoid conflating the racism expressed by certain fictional characters with the author's own beliefs. Such hazards are exemplified in this excerpt from Michael Diamond's *'Lesser Breeds'*, published in 2006:

> Ignoring the black man's sexuality could also cause problems. In *A Whiteman's Burden* by Charles Beadle, a white woman in a state of undress thoughtlessly asks a black

---

lymph, and other tissues. Inflammation of the cervical lymph glands on the back of the neck, known as Winterbottom's sign, has been considered a telltale sign of the disease for centuries. As the parasite moves into the central nervous system and causes inflammation, 'progressive neurological disturbances' appear, manifesting in changes in behavior and mood, tremors in the fingers and tongue, difficulty walking, wasting and weakness, and deeply disrupted sleep patterns. Disrupted nighttime sleep and excessive daytime sleepiness, culminating in a coma-like inability to be awakened, characterize late stages of infection and give the disease its colloquial name. The parasites causing human disease, T. b. gambiense and T. b. rhodesiense, cannot be differentiated by appearance during microscopic examination, but cause radically different clinical manifestations of disease. Clinicians distinguish them by the speed of their progress to second-stage illness and death. T. b. rhodesiense causes the acute form of disease, moving swiftly, with outward signs of advanced disease appearing as early as two months after infection, and an average duration absent treatment of around six months until death. T. b. gambiense presents, by contrast, as a chronic illness, with a slow progress and an average of around two years absent treatment before coma and death." Mari Kathryn Webel, *The Politics of Disease Control: Sleeping Sickness in Eastern Africa, 1890–1920* (Athens, Ohio: Ohio University Press, 2019), pp. 3-4.

servant to help her on with her dressing gown, and he assaults her. He must suffer the death penalty because the blacks would treat mercy "only as evidence of weakness in their rulers and as a direct incentive to crime." In his heart the husband, a government official, feels that "he and all Europeans who persisted in treating a native as a thing of wood or brass, an automaton, anything but a human being, were really to blame." This is humane and perceptive, but he goes on, "a savage, nearer to the animal, has stronger passions and control weaker than the civilized races, yet the fact was ignored – because they were natives, a conquered people." The "savage" has been in domestic service for ten years.[45]

What Diamond doesn't make sufficiently clear is that, while this is the view of the character "Fedden" (expressed through narrational third-person omniscience), it doesn't necessarily represent the author's own perspective. This becomes apparent when we compare Diamond's comments to the original text, which reads as follows:

Fedden remained silent. The plea of the man that the temptation had been greater than he could bear appealed irresistibly to his sense of equity. In his heart he felt that he, and all Europeans who persisted in treating a native as a thing of wood or brass, an automaton, anything but as a human being, were really to blame. A savage, nearer to the animal, has stronger passions and control weaker than civilized races, yet the fact was ignored – because they were natives, a conquered people.

Nevertheless he knew that Malima must pay the full penalty of his crime [...]

---

[45] Michael Diamond, *'Lesser Breeds': Racial Attitudes in Popular British Culture, 1890-1940* (New York: Wimbledon, 2006), p. 180 (quoting from Beadle's *A Whiteman's Burden*, 1912 edition, pp. 264-265).

Clearly, Fedden is portrayed from an interior viewpoint and presented as "just so." Indeed, an author may create such a character in order to highlight the shortcomings of such prejudices. Obviously, this is what Beadle is doing with various figures throughout the tale, including Fedden's wife, Maude, who expresses far less sympathy than her husband and who often regards natives with hostility and contempt – much to the chagrin of the protagonist, Laurie Burke. By presenting this in the form of a "just so" story, Beadle leaves it up to the reader to drawn his own conclusion.

To get a better idea of Beadle's actual notions on race – both his biases and his progressive insights – we must examine how Blacks are portrayed via dialogue and interior monologue. What "voice" are they allowed, and what "voices" fail to enter the narrational register?

One should bear in mind that the narrator's use of a term such as "savage," which was universally employed by white authors a century ago when discussing Black Africans, tells us little as regards a particular writer's sensibility. Rather than creating a concordance of politically incorrect terms (such as describing a native's hair as "wooly": again, standard operating procedure in 1912), a more revealing question concerns whether Beadle is capable of portraying Black characters with the same richness and interior depth as white characters. Are the only well-rounded figures Caucasian? Are the portraits of Blacks predictably drawn from "flat," cardboard cutouts, lacking intellectual profundity and nuance of feeling tone? A good place to search for such answers is in Beadle's treatment of interracial romance.

The love triangle in *A Whiteman's Burden* foreshadows a similar situation in *A Passionate Pilgrimage*, Beadle's third novel (published three years later, in 1915). The chief protagonist of that pilgrimage, Jim (who's closely modeled on Beadle himself), is intimately involved with a beautiful bronze-skinned native, Haiwani: an alluring young woman who's presumed to be of partial "Arab extraction."[46]

Haiwani's love for Jim is marked by an extraordinary degree of empathy and tender compassion ("At times her devotion overwhelmed him"). Their playful rapport is endearing (to the contemporary reader), as well as transgressive (to the Victorian of 1915). When Haiwani fears that she's losing Jim to a British woman from his past, in an ultimate act of self-sacrifice she commits suicide – for she knows that only her disappearance will provide him with the freedom to return to his civilization.

The shock of Haiwani's death propels Jim into an awareness of just how precious and irreplaceable Haiwani really was – despite being unable to meet his so-called intellectual standards. But now, it's too late. He eulogizes her as "the finest and best of all. If she were not dead he would return straight to her."

In *A Whiteman's Burden* Sula is also portrayed as a native "mulatto" whose thinking is depicted as primitive as compared to the white man. Reminiscent of Haiwani, she's primarily a creature of intuition, instinct, and primal passion. Yet, despite their differences, both Laurie and Sula establish an intimacy that does not lack for tenderness, empathy, and devotion.[47] (Just like Jim and Haiwani.) And this despite strict taboos – societal

---

[46] As Jim tells his friend and fellow-traveller Miêville: "She's of Arab extraction sure enough — probably from Madagascar. Look at the straight hair, hawk nose and the eyes — hardly a trace of Negro in her. Probably her father settled amongst these people, and by wealth, or superior cunning, or both, became Chief." Charles Beadle, *A Passionate Pilgrimage. Edited with an Introduction and Afterword by Rob Couteau* (New York: Dominantstar, 2024), p. 171.

[47] When Sula is shunned by Laurie after he, too, is lured by a British woman from his past, she dashes off to inflict self-harm but Laurie manages to stop her. One wonders if these passages were based on an actual incident from the author's life.

and literary – against interracial romance, especially when publicly flaunted.

Perhaps without realizing it, Beadle has created a far more interesting, infinitely more likable character with Sula than he has with her white rival, Maude. In fact, one wonders why Laurie would regard the nagging, narcissistic, ever-domineering Maude as a more ideal match than kind-hearted Sula, whose love for Laurie forces her to expose the most vulnerable reaches of her saintly, magical soul. In addition, there's nothing particularly unique about Maude: she's merely a "type": a shallow British colonialist who regards Blacks as subhuman trash.

In one of Beadle's most engaging attempts to enter into Sula's psyche and plumb the depths of her vibrant character, he portrays a scene in which Sula hopes to inflict harm upon Maude by unleashing her pet leopard, Kichui, into Maude's house. Sula's rapport with Kichui is so palpable that she assumes it can read her every intention. (One might say that Kichui is more finely attuned to Sula than Laurie is!) In many ways, this passage is a masterstroke – as well as being highly ambitious. For, how many literary authors attempt to penetrate the mind of a leopard?

> Suddenly he stiffened and snarled at the scent of dog. Then for a moment he was puzzled, for amid the various scents there was one which he knew, faint and old. He heard a movement outside and sniffed at the door, recognizing his mistress, who was whispering in a soft, persuasive tone. He turned and snuffed the air again. The dog scent was near [...] Why had he been put here? [...] The strangeness of his surroundings began to wear off. Curiosity began to stir. He returned to the door, from whence came the scent of his mistress, and, reassured, commenced a voyage of discovery. The first thing which attracted him was the human occupant. All humans were well-disposed towards him except when

they shouted, and that meant trouble with a hard stick. He did not mind until they hurt him, and then he knew he would kill if he could reach them. But this was a female human smell, like, and yet quite distinct from, his mistress.

Kichui felt in quite an amiable frame of mind after he had got over his first vague misgivings. This was something new, and interested him, in contrast to the monotony of his usual life. The human was sleeping, he knew. He wanted to awaken her, hoping that she would pet him. He loved to be caressed and stroked when in that humor. He reached the bed and sniffed inquiringly at it. The human did not move. He could hear the regular breathing. [...]

The regular breathing ceased. Turning his head he saw that the human was sitting up in bed staring at him.

The next instant a piercing scream so startled him that he knocked over the basin, which fell with a crash upon the floor, soaking him with water. Scared and angered by the continuous shrieks, he crouched against the wall as the sound of men's voices and the sharp barks of dogs reached his ears. The screams suddenly ceased as the door was burst open by a man holding a lantern in one hand; behind him were others, and between his legs darted two terriers, their hair bristling, barking shrilly, straight towards him.

Since Kichui thinks with its nose, Beadle positions the animal to follow a meandering trail of scents. There's a twofold purpose to this. Besides authentically rendering the importance of the olfactory function in the hunting beast, it's also through its sense of smell that we become privy to a major new development. For Kichui becomes confused when the fragrance it detects, which resembles Sula's scent, is inexplicably emitted by a different woman: "a female human smell, like, and yet quite distinct from, his mistress."

When the woman is suddenly "sitting up in bed staring at him," Kichui sees that it isn't Sula – it's Maude. We later learn that Maude's scent is strikingly similar to Sula's because Sula is Maude's half sister: a product of Maude's white father and his Black mistress. But Laurie prevents Maude from learning about this, out of fear it will produce a deleterious effect upon her now-fragile mental health. After Maude's shocking confrontation with the beast, she succumbs to a nervous breakdown; and now, she's teetering on the brink.

Here Beadle is playing with the relativity of the question of race, and the irony is priceless. It's also reminiscent of an observation made by John Locke: that in works such as "The White Frog," Beadle loved to blur distinctions "between 'white rationality' and 'Black superstition.'"[48] In a similar fashion, in several of Beadle's novels, a "mulatto" figure personifies a blurred boundary line of race, thus calling into question the absolutism of black-and-white, dichotomous thinking – racial or otherwise.[49]

I might add that I've met "Maude" at least a thousand times, but I've yet to meet a woman who lives with a chained leopard that "snarled menacingly, and flashed luminous green eyes at her when she whispered sharply to him." If trapped for hours on an elevator, I'm sure that Sula or Haiwani would provide more interesting and trustworthy companionship than either Maude or Joan, to whom Jim is drawn as a so-called intellectual equal. Just as pushy and selfish as Maude, and just as lacking in a unique, individuated personality, one wonders what Jim sees

---

[48] John Locke, "Introduction" in Charles Beadle, *The City of Baal* (Elkhorn, CA: Off-Trail Publication, 2007), p. 11. This blurring of distinction is further developed in *Witch-Doctors*.

[49] Although a more cynical reading might posit that a romance with such "mixed race" figures would be more palatable to Victorian publishers than one between a white colonialist and an ebony skinned Black African. Also recall that, with her golden-bronze hue, Haiwani is assumed to be of "Arab" descent.

in Joan that can so easily eclipse the more sympathetic character of Haiwani.

Though Beadle credibly renders Sula's emotional intelligence (if not the subtler gradations of her more sophisticated feeling tones), we're left largely in the dark regarding the deeper thought process that drives her action. Indeed, "Sula glad!" is repeated one time too many. Other Black natives portrayed in *A Whiteman's Burden* and *The Lost Cure* (including the chiefs and witch doctors that comprise the leading figures of their society) also fall short as regards cognitive complexity. It seems that Beadle was unable to conceive of Black Africans as possessing the same level of profundity as their white counterparts.

In this regard, though we have many reasons to be entranced by Sula, one wonders if she's been endowed with an authentic voice. She possesses an acumen that enables her to deftly navigate a world rife with complexity, yet the author fails to provide us with a proper mechanism with which to plumb that acumen with any degree of accuracy or distinction. Her presence is powerful, her empathy profound, but her voice is muffled or silenced.

From this one might conclude that, again unwittingly, the "white man's burden"[50] is the burden of racial prejudice, which blinds him to a more objective vision of his fellow man. Unfortunately, at times Beadle's novels fail to relieve themselves of such limitations. Yet, in many other ways, his narrational voice is more progressive and enlightened than that

---

[50] In February 1899, Rudyard Kipling composed "The White Man's Burden: The United States and the Philippine Islands," a poem in which he urged America to assume the "burden" of Empire à la Great Britain. After Vice President Teddy Roosevelt read the poem in *McClure*'s magazine, he deemed it "rather poor poetry, but good sense from the expansion point of view," the latter phrase referring to the imperialist philosophy of "Manifest Destiny."

of his contemporaries, as can easily be seen by perusing Anglo-Saxon novels published during this same period.

Also recall that the protagonists of *A Passionate Pilgrimage* and *A Whiteman's Burden* transgress strict taboos by openly engaging in romantic relationships with "women of color." As the narrator informs us about Laurie:

> Convention to a man of deep emotions is as the curb rein to a mettlesome horse; and when a savage spur prick of a blighted love idyll is added either animal, if he can get the bit between his teeth, will surely bolt. Laurie had bolted and shown his teeth at his late rider. Convention. Fortunately he had shown some consideration for others in clearing out of England. In South Africa, and later in Uganda, he had flung his own will and pleasure in the face of convention, making a god unto himself, doing whatever seemed good to him, adopting the principle that if others did not approve they could do the other thing, as he cared for no man's opinion and little for his own. He had met Sula living with her mulatto mother upon a shamba bequeathed her by her father, a whiteman [...]
>
> Naturally, after this unorthodox mésalliance, Laurie was ostracized, to which he replied that their room was preferable to their company, adding, with a cynical laugh, that light o' love[51] was better than light love. He became notorious as an abandoned character from one end of the Protectorate to the other and even beyond. A few of the kindly disposed matrons shook their heads sadly, whilst one bold virgin, soured by broken ideals, shocked official tea circles by observing with a sneer that "at all events he was in very good company!" which caused not a few young married women to look extremely uncomfortable, mindful of facts which everybody knew. Still, one open sin is quite

---

[51] A person who is inconstant or fickle in love. Also, a prostitute or a sexually promiscuous woman.

unforgivable, whilst many unostentatious indiscretions are – well, quite another matter.

With a final slap in the face to convention, Laurie marries Sula in order to provide for her, through inheritance.

Rest assured, such blatantly provocative passages would not have sat well with the Anglo-Saxon censors of 1912. But when we read them today, it's Laurie's pique and carefree disregard for such small-mindedness that endear us to him and that lend the spine of the novel its strength.

When Maude learns of Laurie's marriage to Sula, after suffering a fit of hysteria she confronts him and says: "You know you will repent it. It's all very well to talk of the equality of love, but you know it's impossible for a man to *marry* such people: he pays bitterly in the end. Besides, you never could have loved her – only passion. I understand, but –"

But Laurie doesn't bother to argue. Death is approaching; he's burnt out; and besides, her racism is fixed, an irredeemable part of that small-minded character.

> "Please don't," said Laurie wearily. "What is the use of arguing about it?"

Such literary innovation would have been regarded as highly provocative by Beadle's contemporaries. It may also explain why *A Passionate Pilgrimage* was banned by Britain's Circulating Libraries Association and why *A Whiteman's Burden* failed to receive much attention in the press.[52] Add to this the fact that *A*

---

[52] I've uncovered only three reviews, the longest of which appeared in *The Scotsman* (Midlothian, Scotland), on 4 November 1912: "Life in an unhealthy region of Africa, where British representatives carry on their work amid dangers and difficulties, is interestingly described by Charles Beadle in a *Whiteman's Burden*. Going out as an administrator, 'to wait, in heavy harness, on fluttered folks and wild' [quoting from Kipling], Herbert Fedden

Passionate Pilgrimage is largely a confessional novel. Its publication may have provided Beadle with an additional reason to sever himself from his relatives in England (with the exception of his two young nieces, Barbara and Isabel, whom he hoped might represent a more open-minded generation).

Beadle was thirty-one years old when *A Whiteman's Burden* was first published. *Adventure* magazine's serialization of *Witch-Doctors* appeared six years later, beginning in March 1919. In *Witch-Doctors*, Haiwani's thoughts and feelings are rendered with more complexity and nuance than Sula's, as is her dialogue, but many of the same problems remain. Ultimately, Beadle does not succeed in getting fully into the heads of some of his Black characters. Particularly in the case of *Witch-Doctors*, he often exaggerates their "passion" while underrating their rationality, thus shortchanging us when imagining their true intellectual life. The latter is often rendered as more of a deficit trait, rather than a holistic ingredient. On the other hand, as John Locke has pointed out, when portraying characters such as Yama Yama, Matalisi, and Samwili in *A Whiteman's Burden*, Beadle "got well into the native perspective. We understand

---

soon finds that the most difficult problems that confront him are not those created by the natives. He is accompanied by his wife, to whom the dull life is by no means agreeable, and this and other circumstances render possible the complications and misunderstandings that follow the arrival of an old lover whom she had jilted. Many people of widely different characters assist in the development of the somewhat slender plot, and all are convincingly portrayed." London's *Athenaeum* published a two-sentence summary on 26 October 1912: "A tale of the Tropics. The author deals with some of the problems which confront the European in Africa — the tsetse fly, the relations between black men and white women, and the effect of missionaries." And a third, single-sentence blurb was featured in *The Review of Reviews* (London; 1912): "A cleverly put but terribly realistic story of life in Uganda with rivalry and love, and the horror of the sleeping sickness as a background."

their conviction that whites brought the sleeping sickness, and their desire for a murderous rebellion that will exact revenge (and perhaps set the world right again). As outsiders to white culture and knowledge, their view seems rational. They just hadn't yet accepted their powerlessness to deal with the disease."[53] And also to his credit, in *Witch-Doctors* Beadle juxtaposes the fetish-worshipping African tribes with the Anglo-Saxon's fetishizing of religious icons and the "goddess" of romantic love, slyly informing us that everything is indeed relative.

On the positive side of the ledger, the creative power of *A Whiteman's Burden* resides in its tightly woven, superbly controlled literary flair, which the author utilizes to paint vivid details of a collective tragedy: the catastrophic sleeping sickness epidemic. At the turn of the century, African trypanosomiasis killed 250,000 in Uganda alone.[54] The symptoms manifest as a

---

[53] Private communication with John Locke, 25 April 2025.

[54] There are several different estimates of the death toll. "In the five years between the close of 1900 and the end of 1905, sleeping sickness killed over a quarter of a million Africans in the British Protectorate of Uganda. This tragedy sparked off one of the most dramatic chapters in the history of medicine.... Southern Busoga was soon considered the chief focus of the disease, and by the spring of 1902, local African chiefs reported that nearly 14,000 people had died." As noted below, Laurie and Sula pass through Busoga on their way to meet Laurie's friend Natts. "From Busoga the disease spread rapidly east and west, and by the end of 1903 there were over 90,000 deaths. By November 1904, it was epidemic as far west as the shores of Lake Albert, which bordered the Congo Free State. Official calculations of mortality rates varied, but [David] Bruce, a reliable witness, claimed that in Busoga, with a population of 300,000, as many as 200,000 had died! In 1905, one member of the Royal Society's commission estimated that in the past three years sleeping sickness had caused an annual mortality of 100,000 in Uganda. Another reliable source, Brian Langlands, later asserted that in Uganda between 1900 and 1920, deaths from the disease numbered between 250,000 and 300,000. All the colonial powers in Africa took note of events in Uganda. We will never know the

steady, gradual decline in body and mind. Vitality is blotted out by lethargy. The allure of life is eclipsed by an overwhelming desire ... to sleep.

Beadle uses an ingenious device to portray this devastation: Laurie's physiological degeneration progresses at the same incremental pace as his collapsing romantic interest in Sula and Maude. This further intensifies the discord between Maude and Fedden – a heartless functionary who's so overidentified with his role that there's little left over for his wife. The epidemic's harvest of horror even compels the two clergymen (the rubicund-faced Father Anthony and the unctuous Reverend Blackber) to question their own complacent religious convictions, with Father Anthony declaring that it's "More terrible than any plague of the Old Testament!" Thus, decline begets decline. The only faint glimmer of hope that appears at the conclusion concerns Maude's attempt to repair her

---

total mortality for certain, but it is obvious why administrators of all African territories were alarmed." Maryinez Lyons, *The Colonial Disease: A Social History of Sleeping Sickness in Northern Zaire, 1900-1940* (Cambridge, UK: Cambridge University Press, 2002), pp. 70-71.

"From 1900 to 1920, the Busoga region of Uganda experienced a large-scale epidemic of the disease, during which an estimated 250,000 people, a third of the population of the region, died." E. Fèvre, P. Coleman, S. Welburn, and I. Maudlin, "Reanalyzing the 1900 – 1920 Sleeping Sickness Epidemic in Uganda," *Emerging Infectious Diseases*, April 2004, p. 567.

"We now understand that epidemic sleeping sickness exploded in communities around Lake Victoria and Lake Tanganyika at the turn of the twentieth century, concomitant with apparently unprecedented mortality – an estimated 250,000 people purportedly died around Lake Victoria alone – before 1920. Parallel epidemics in the Congo River basin killed hundreds of thousands of people. The epidemic followed several difficult decades for the region's populations, during which internal political conflict, drought, famine, cattle disease, sand fleas (Tunga penetrans) and other epidemics struck in succession, preceding and alongside European colonial incursion." Mari Kathryn Webel, *The Politics of Disease Control*, p. 5.

marriage. But so much damage has been done that one wonders if this is truly feasible.

From such stuff is tragedy woven. While *Dark Refuge* and *A Passionate Pilgrimage* contain an admixture of tragicomedy, *A Whiteman's Burden* maintains a more singular focus: homing in on a fate that remains crushing, wretched, calamitous. Rather than the hallucinatory tragic-comedic ending of *Dark Refuge* or the hopeful, upbeat, euphoric conclusion of *A Passionate Pilgrimage*, the characters in *A Whiteman's Burden* are overwhelmed by the pitfalls of the human condition. At the end they're left to conclude that "something seems to have snapped in my brain," and "nothing seems to matter."

With its abundant depictions of absurdity, alienation, and isolation as the characters anxiously confront the dreadful vicissitudes of life and the indifference of the glittering cosmos swirling above the vast African firmament, we're left to wonder: Is *A Whiteman's Burden* one of Europe's first existential novels … or at least its precursor?

In sum, Beadle has created a well-paced, carefully controlled, tightly composed narrative, with plenty of deftly crafted foreshadowing, twists, and subplots. All of which makes the glinting scythe of the dramatic arc that much more piercing.

***

Circa 1904 – 1906 is a likely time frame for the setting of both *A Whiteman's Burden* and *The Lost Cure*. As we can see in Beadle's personal "Timeline" (below), in August 1904 he conducted an expedition along the Zambezi River in Chikoti, Zambia, near the southeast border of what is now known as the Democratic Republic of the Congo. Working his way north, in December 1905 he was at Government House in Fort Portal, Uganda, near the Congo's northeastern border. "Engaged in recruiting and registering fresh porters," he was organizing another expedition. On 5 January 1906 he embarked from Fort Portal and entered the Congo, heading toward the Semliki River. After the river crossing, his caravan was attacked by a buffalo and nearly killed by a herd of stampeding elephants. These events are chronicled in an essay, "Two Close Calls – A Huntsman's Tale of the Red Rubber Country" (1910) and later portrayed in *The Lost Cure*.

But what Beadle doesn't mention is that he was wandering through Uganda during the most dangerous years of the epidemic; and his travels through Zambia and the neighboring Congo also occurred during a terribly hazardous time. Indeed, it's frightening to imagine that he was embarking upon such Odysseys while the epidemic was raging – and even peaking:

> In 1904, sleeping sickness was declared to be epidemic in some parts of the Congo Free State … The "sleepy sickness" had been noted in the region in the early 1880s, and fresh outbreaks were confirmed by missionaries and travelers. But, by 1901, a terrible epidemic had spread around the northern shores of Lake Victoria and neighboring islands in the region of Busoga, in the neighboring Uganda protectorate.[55]

As the reader may recall, at the beginning of chapter six Laurie and Sula travel through Busoga "upon the borders of the Victoria Nyanza." They pass "reed encircled," "diminutive islands," and round a bay where "strips of blue water seeming like long fingers" are "studded with emerald rings." But how beauty may deceive! For the reedy, marshy shores of the Lake

---

[55] Maryinez Lyons, "Sleeping sickness, colonial medicine and imperialism: some connections in the Belgian Congo," in *Disease, Medicine, and Empire: Perspectives on Western Medicine and the Experience of European Expansion*, ed. Roy M. MacLeod and Milton Lewis (Oxford: Routledge, 1988), chapter 12, e-book version.

Victoria littoral were the most fertile breeding ground of the plague-ridden tsetse fly.[56] Perhaps it's no coincidence that Laurie's pal Natts is living nearby, for he's already become infected.

Although the epidemic is often placed in a broader, 1890 – 1920 time frame, the most deadly period in Uganda occurred between 1900 and 1905 – precisely when Beadle was gallivanting around there.

> In the five years between the close of 1900 and the end of 1905, sleeping sickness killed over a quarter of a million Africans in the British Protectorate of Uganda. This tragedy sparked off one of the most dramatic chapters in the history of medicine…. by 1902, sleeping sickness had become the most important administrative question in Uganda.[57]

And by 1910, the number of infected Congolese had reached "several hundred thousand." Despite his extensive travel through these blighted zones, Beadle not only eluded the illness but also lived to tell the tale: first as a work of literary fiction in *A Whiteman's Burden*, then as a mass-market adventure story in *The Lost Cure*.

---

[56] In 1904, missionary John Moffat (1835 – 1918) traveled in a steamer across Lake Victoria, embarking from Mombasa and heading toward Entebbe, Uganda. In a letter penned to his sister on 18 March 1904, he described the watery landscape as being "as beautiful as fairyland. Everything looks so green and English in the distance, but of course close at hand the palms and bananas disillusion you. Yet there is a dark shadow over it – mosquitoes (and fever) by night, tsetse fly (and sleeping sickness) by day." Moffat's son Robert, who assembled and edited the memoir, adds in a note: "At this time the epidemic of sleeping sickness was at its height and lay like a paralyzing blight upon this goodly, though at its best none too healthy, land." See Robert Moffat, ed., *John Smith Moffat, C.M.G. Missionary: A Memoir* (New York, Negro Universities Press, 1969), pp. 349-350. John Moffat was the brother-in-law of David Livingstone.

[57] Maryinez Lyons, "Sleeping sickness," chapter 12.

At the end of the latter novel, we find the chief protagonist, Birskett, rooting for the natives in their ensuing conflict with King Leopold's merciless legions. But Birskett is chagrined because he knows there's nothing he can do to help them. The Belgians have guns; the natives have spears: defeat is inevitable. Although Beadle can't rewrite history, at least he can chronicle its darkest hours. And he must have been painfully aware of Leopold's despicable machinations:

> Leopold [1835 – 1909] established a precedent for later colonial administrations by insisting upon the importance of the new field of tropical medicine, medical provision, and public health policy as essential features in the justification, sometimes rationalization, of colonialization. His decision to invite British scientists to investigate sleeping sickness in his state becomes explicable in this context. So, while diseased and dead Africans were an economic loss to all involved in the Congo adventure, Leopold had a second powerful motive for his quick response to the discovery of sleeping sickness. He intended to make the most of this opportunity to combat the increasingly effective anti-Congo Free State propaganda campaign being waged in England. In March 1900, E. D. Morel, an Englishman who had worked for Jones's shipping lines since 1891, wrote a series of articles exposing the scandal of "Red Rubber" in the Congo Free State. He publicized the shocking mistreatment by the state's agents of Congolese men, women, and children, who were driven without mercy to collect rubber.... His book, *Affairs of West Africa*, held Leopold personally responsible for these atrocities. On 20 May 1903, a debate in the British House of Commons on the "Congo question" resulted in a resolution indicting the Congo Free State government.[58]

---

[58] Ibid.

Despite Beadle's deeply ingrained cynicism, perhaps even he was dismayed to discover that Leopold regarded the epidemic not as a human tragedy but as an opportunity to drum up positive publicity and whitewash his crimes against humanity.

African Milestones:
Excerpts from Beadle's Timeline

[Age 17] 6 November 1898. Enlists in the British South African Police (BSAP) as Charles "Marmaduke" Beadle, Regimental No. 1019, Matabeleland Division. (Stationed in southwestern Zimbabwe.) According to Beadle's great-niece Patricia, "Charles and his brother joined the South African Police to fight in the Boer War. London was rife with recruiting posters back then. Henry later went missing. He was possibly killed in the war, although there's no military record of his death. I also heard that Henry may have died in a bicycle accident." Source: Conversation with Beadle's great-niece Patricia on 6 October 2022.

[Age 18-21] Abt. 1899 – 1901. Transvaal, South Africa. Serves in the Second Boer War (BSAP), in Morley's Scouts, Stock and Recovery Department. (Source: autobiographical sketch in "The Camp-Fire" column, *Adventure* magazine, 3 July 1918.) During this period Beadle receives various service awards.

[Age 18] Fall 1900. Mashonaland, South Africa. Guest of an Englishman named Mason, who owns a large farm. Beadle is nearly killed by a lioness during a hunt organized there on his behalf. (Source: "My Narrow Escape From a Lioness." *The Brooklyn Daily Eagle*, 7 August 1910.) Historian Geoffrey Pocock informed me that "the only Mason who is listed as a Founder-member of the Legion of Frontiersmen in London is Charles "Chinese" Mason, whom Beadle would have known and have met at early meetings." Source: email from Geoffrey, 18 August 2022.

[Age 19] 18 July 1901. Discharged from British South African Police.

[Age 21] Abt. 1902. Transvaal, South Africa. Employed by Transvaal Customs as Assistant Compound Manager, Witwatersrand Native Labor Association. Source: *Adventure*, 3 July 1918.

[Age 22] August 1904. Travels along the Zambezi River, Chikoti, Zambia. The expedition is chronicled in Beadle's essay, "Our Trip Down the Zambezi," published in the *Wide World Magazine* in 1907.

[Age 23] 1905. Henry Roger Pocock forms the Legion of Frontiersmen; Beadle is a founding member.

[Age 23] December 1905. Government House, Fort Portal, Uganda. "Engaged in recruiting and registering fresh porters" for an expedition into the Congo. (Fort Portal: aka Kabarole, formerly of the Toro Kingdom.) Source: Beadle's essay "Two Close Calls" in *The Captain: A Magazine for Boys and "old Boys,"* June 1910.

[Age 23] 5 January 1906. Beadle's expedition embarks from Fort Portal and enters the Congo, where he's attacked by a buffalo and almost killed by stampeding elephants.

[Age 24] 19 March 1906. Death of father in Buenos Aires. Charles receives a substantial inheritance, including assets that would normally have gone to his brother Henry, who disappeared in South Africa. This allows Charles to finance future expeditions. Source: conversation with Patricia, 6 November 2022.

[Age 24] Abt. 1906. London. Elected as a Fellow of the Royal Geographical Society (FRGS).

[Age 25] February 1907. Northumberland Avenue, London. Elected to the Royal Colonial Institute. Source: *Journal of the Royal Colonial Institute*, February 1907, p. 138.

[Age 25] May 1907. Publishes photo-essay, "Our Trip Down the Zambezi," in *The Wide World Magazine*. One photo portrays Beadle with his back to the camera, sporting a pith helmet.

[Age 26] Abt. February 1908. Travels to Borneo. (Source: diary of Roger Pocock, housed at the Bruce Peel Collection, University of Alberta.) In his autobiographical "Camp-Fire" sketch from 3 July 1918, Beadle notes: "Went to Dutch Borneo, rubber planting. Afterward returned to go to Morocco."

[Age 26] 23 April 1908. Embarks from the Port of London aboard the SS *Agadir*, heading for Morocco.

[Age 26] 4 May 1908. Arrives in El Jadida (originally known as Mazagan), a port city on the Atlantic coast. There he secures the services of William Redman, a British merchant and mercenary versed in the local language and customs. Together they travel seventeen km (about ten miles) north along the coast, to the nearby town of Azemmour.

[Age 26] 19 May 1908. Beadle and Redman embark on a steamer, the *Gibel Kebir*, heading further north to Tangier, where they will join Andrew Belton.

[Age 26] June 1908. A confidential memo penned at the British Foreign Office notes that, after departing from Tangier for a fortnight, Beadle will return around 17 June, to reside at the Hotel Cavilla. Source: letter from Lord Mountmorres to Hubert White, Chargé d'Affaires, Tangier, archived at the British Foreign Office. (Appended to 21 June 1908 memo, as noted in Timeline below.)

[Age 26] 8 June 1908. Prevented from traveling from Tangier to Fes due to civil war. Beadle then boards the *Quetzil*, a steamer headed south, to the coastal city of Larache.

[Age 26] 9 June 1908. Arrives in Larache, where he's joined by Redman and Bolton, who had arrived earlier on another vessel.

[Age 26] 10 June 1908. Redman, Bolton, and Beadle travel inland to Ksar el-Kebir, about thirty km southeast of Larache.

[Age 26] 14 June 1908. After a "wretched journey" during which Beadle is disguised as a dancing girl, the expedition arrives in Fes. Source: Beadle's interview with Moulay Hafid, published in *Pall Mall Magazine*.

[Age 26] 21 June 1908. Following Beadle's successful interview with the Pretender Sultan, Hafid, a memo from the British Foreign Office expresses concern that Beadle, Redman, and a third man (presumably Andrew Belton) "are being treated as if on [a] mission from His Majesty's Government. Steps taken to counteract this impression." The memo adds that Beadle and Redman "arrived from Gibraltar via Larache."

[Age 26] 19 August 1908. According to a contemporaneous newspaper report, Beadle and Redman remain in Fes during the Battle of Marrakech: a decisive encounter between opposing sultans that results in the forces of Moulay Hafid defeating the army of Sultan Aziz. (Source: "Swindon Doctor in Fez," *Swindon Advertiser and North Wilts Chronicle*, 5 May 1911.) Beadle later portrays this conflict in his novel, *The City of Shadows*.

[Age 26] Early October 1908. Publishes photo-essay, "A Talk with the New Sultan of Morocco," in *Pall Mall Magazine*. It includes a picture of Beadle in disguise, his face obscured by veils.

[Age 27] 17 November 1908. Camping in South Africa with fellow members of the Legion of Frontiersmen. Source: Roger Pocock's diary, which notes: "Beadle to camp."

[Age 27] Circa early 1909 – June 1909. Morocco. Begins to write fiction. Source: Beadle's contribution to the forum "Contemporary

Writers and Their Work," published in *The Editor*, 25 February 1920.

[Age 27] Circa May – June 1909. Repatriates to London from Morocco. Source: "What Has Happened to Muley Hafid," *The Sphere*, 3 July 1909.

[Age 28] 9 December 1909. Henry Roger Pocock's diary notes that Beadle was one of several friends who "visited Pocock the day after an operation on his foot," but their whereabouts are not recorded.

[Age 29] abt. February 1911. Publication of *The City of Shadows: A Romance of Morocco* (London: Everett and Co.). According to historian Geoffrey Pocock, Beadle's novel offers the "best account" of the Battle of Marrakech. Source: private communication with Pocock, 12 September 2022.

Illustrations

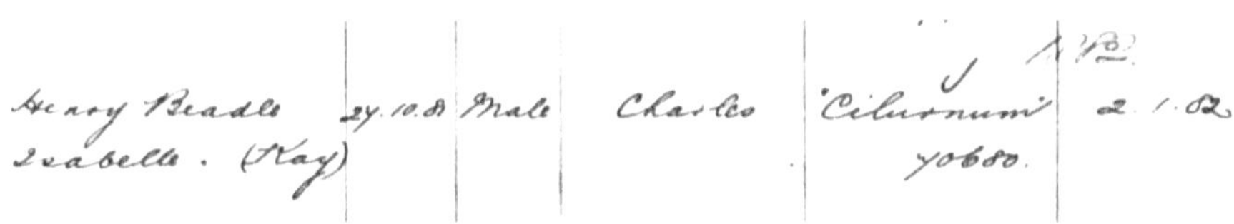

12 July 1873: Marriage of Henry Beadle and Isabella Kay at St. John's, Hackney, London. Both Henry and Isabella's father, Peter Kay, were master mariners. Henry's father, William, is listed as a "gentleman."

27 October 1881: Record of Beadle's birth aboard the SS *Cilurnum*, from "UK Registers of Births, Marriages and Deaths at Sea, 1844-1890." Other documents, such as his draft registration card, indicate he was born the day before, on 26 October 1881.

(Above:) The brothers Henry, Charles, and William Beadle. (Below:) Various portraits of Beadle from a family album. Courtesy of Beadle's great-niece Patricia and her daughter Liz.

Circa fall 1900 or 1901: Beadle in Mashonaland, South Africa. Courtesy archive of Patricia and Liz.

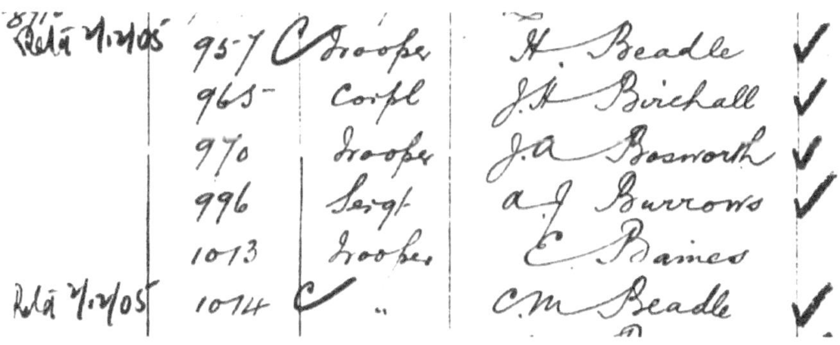

During this period Beadle received various decorations and service awards. The "Roll of individuals entitled to the South Africa Medal and Clasps, April 1901" includes trooper Charles "Marmaduke" Beadle, who served in the National (Waldon's) Scouts and Orange River Colony Volunteers, Nesbitt's Horse, Regiment Number 1014. Beadle may have fictionalized his middle name in order to enlist a second time.

Undated photo of Henry Beadle (1844 – 1906), father of Charles. Courtesy of Patricia and Liz.

Another photo of Henry Beadle, courtesy of Patricia and Liz.

Photo of Charles Beadle featured in *The Wide World Magazine*, May 1907.

Ship's Name.	Official Number.	Steamship Line.	Master's Name.	Registered Tonnage.
S. S. AGADIR.	124092	THE MERSEY STEAMSHIP Co. Lᴰ.	J B Mansfield	1642

I hereby Certify that the Provisions actually laden on board this Ship are sufficient, according to the requirements of the Merchant Shippi

Date 23ʳᵈ April 1908

NAMES AND DESCRIPTIONS OF **BRITISH** PA

Port of Embarkation.	Contract Ticket Number.	NAMES OF PASSENGERS (Passengers holding Contract Tickets as Steerage Passengers should be entered first, and a space left between them and the other Passengers.)	Class. (Whether 1st, 2nd, or 3rd.)	Profession, Occupation, or Calling of Passengers. (In the case of First Class Passengers this column need not be filled up.)
LONDON		Mr Charles Beadle	1ˢᵗ	

Passenger list of the SS *Agadir*, 23 April 1908, with Beadle on his way to Morocco, where he would interview Sultan Mulai-El-Hafid.

Beadle disguised as a dancing girl or, alternately, a holy man, during his June 1908 expedition to Fez, published in the photo essay "A Talk with the New Sultan of Morocco," *The Pall Mall Magazine*, October 1908.

"Your [affectionate] nephew Charlie." Courtesy of Patricia and Liz. "I might have had reason to view some of these encounters with even more miscellaneous feelings, had I known that my guide accounted for my complete disguise by confiding to our assistants that I was a dancing girl bound for the household of a distinguished native official. At other times I was, it seemed, a holy man." ("A Talk with the New Sultan of Morocco.")

(Sideways view:) Rare dust jacket of Beadle's first novel, *The City of Shadows: A Romance of Morocco*, published in the spring of 1911.

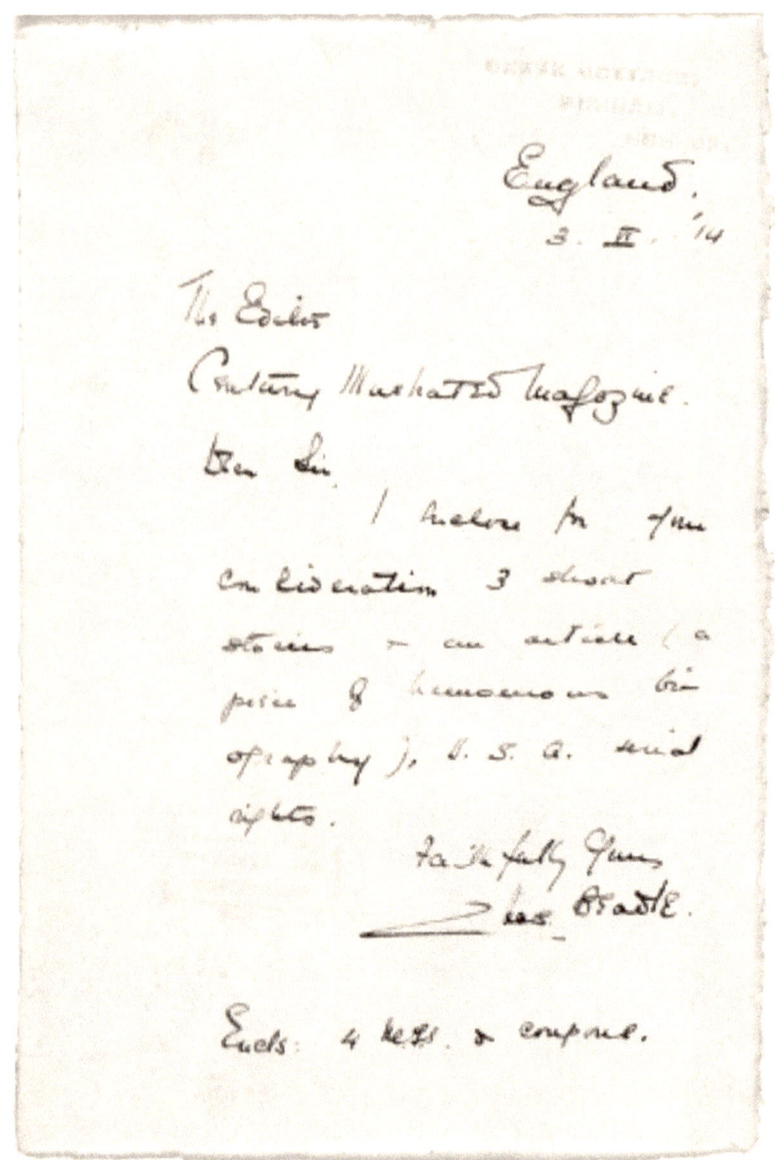

3 June 1914: A letter to the editor of *Century Illustrated*: "England. / 3 VI 1914 / The Editor / Century Magazine / Dear Sir, I enclose for your consideration 3 short stories & an article (a piece of humorous biography) for USA serial rights. Faithfully Yours Charles Beadle Encl. 4 Ms. & coupons." A watermark on top reads: "Creek Cottage, Bosham, Sussex." Courtesy of New York Public Library, Century Company records, Series I.

A PASSIONATE PILGRIMAGE

By CHARLES BEADLE

September 1915: Publication of *A Passionate Pilgrimage*. Hardcover edition, embossed with an image of Beadle's handwriting in red ink.

Early twentieth-century train compartment, South African railway: the setting of Jim's first steamy encounter with Joan in *A Passionate Pilgrimage*. Photo courtesy C. Carlyle-Gall, ed., *Six Thousand Miles Of Sunshine Travel Over The South African Railways* (Johannesburg: South African Railways & Harbours, 1937), p. 13.

Rickshaw driver, Durban, South Africa. Photo courtesy *Six Thousand Miles Of Sunshine Travel Over The South African Railways*, p. 68.

REGISTRATION CARD

SERIAL NUMBER 4661   ORDER NUMBER 13379

1 *Charles* *Beadle*
(First name) (Last name)

2 PERMANENT HOME ADDRESS: 334
King George Hotel Mason St. SAN FRANCISCO CAL
will be 119 Central Av. Sausalito Cal.

Age in Years | Date of Birth
3 *36* | 4 *Oct 26 1881*
Month | (Day) | (Year)

RACE

White | Negro | Oriental | Indian
| | | Citizen | Noncitizen
5 ✓ | 6 | 7 | 8 | 9

U. S. CITIZEN | ALIEN

Native Born | Naturalized | Citizen by Father's Naturalization Before Registrant's Majority | Declarant | Non-declarant
10 | 11 | 12 | 13 | 14 ✓

15 If not a citizen of the U. S., of what nation are you a citizen or subject? *England*

PRESENT OCCUPATION | EMPLOYER'S NAME
16 *Novelist* | 17

18 PLACE OF EMPLOYMENT OR BUSINESS:

(No.) (Street or R. F. D No.) (City or town) (County) (State)

NEAREST RELATIVE 19 *(Miss) Jane Beadle*
Address 20 *22 Gordon Road - Boscomb. England*
(No.) (Street or R. F. D No.) (City or town)

I AFFIRM THAT I HAVE VERIFIED ABOVE ANSWERS AND THAT THEY ARE TRUE
P. M. G. O. *Charles Beadle*
Form No. 1 (ited) (Registrant's signature or mark) (OVER)

ORIGINAL

REGISTRAR'S REPORT 4-1-24. C

DESCRIPTION OF REGISTRANT

HEIGHT			BUILD			COLOR OF EYES	COLOR OF HAIR
Tall	Medium	Short	Slender	Medium	Stout		
21	22 ✓	23	24 ✓	25	26	27 *Blue*	28 *Grey*

29 Has person lost arm, leg, hand, eye, or is he obviously physically disqualified? (Specify.)

12 September 1918: A month short of his thirty-eighth birthday, Beadle registers for the military draft in San Francisco, just before relocating to Sausalito. Under the heading "Description of Registrant" it notes that he's of medium height, with a slender build, blue eyes, and gray hair. His occupation is "Novelist." Under "nearest relative" he lists his daughter (then living in Boscombe, Bournemouth, England).

MAIRIE DE CANNES
Alpes-Maritimes

Acte de décès - Copie Intégrale

N° 83

Hornsby

Sylvia Grace Ellen

Le treize Septembre mil neuf cent quinze à dix neuf heures trente, Sylvia Grace Ellen Hornsby, née à Londres (Angleterre) le vingt huit octobre mil huit cent quatre vingt onze, sans profession, fille de Edmond William et de Teresa Isabelle Hornsby, épouse de Charles Beadle, domiciliée à [...] est décédée à Cannes, Hôtel Beau Rivage _____ Dressé le quatorze Septembre ___, mil neuf cent quinze, à quinze heures du _____, sur la déclaration de Joseph Jallier, cinquante deux ans, comptable _____

et de Antoine Aragon, soixante quatre ans, [...] tous deux domiciliés à Cannes _____

faite, ont signé avec Nous Marcellin Bella, Chevalier de la Légion d'Honneur _____ Adjoint au, Maire de Cannes, Officier de l'État civil par délégation, _____

Copie délivrée selon procédé informatisé.
A Cannes, le 28 juin 2022.

Pour le Maire,
L'officier de l'état civil par délégation

Copy of Sylvia Hornsby's death certificate, retrieved by Céline Cardon on 30 June 2022. The French vital statistics bureau had misspelled her surname (it appears in their index as "Homsby"), making its retrieval a particularly tricky task. From this document we learn that Sylvia died at the Hotel Beau Rivage (now known as the Hotel Majestic). This was during a period in which the villas and hotels of Cannes were used as hospitals, especially for the soldiers of WWI. So she essentially died "in hospital" on 15 September 1915.

FACING PAGE:

Circa 1915: A Modigliani portrait of Charles Beadle, titled *Le Pèlerin* ("The Pilgrim"), pencil on paper, 42.5 x 24.5 cm., featured in a Sotheby's catalog for Sale 6019, held in New York on 17 May 1990. The estimated value was set at $40,000 – $50,000.

The catalog caption quotes a passage from *Artist Quarter* in which the narrator says that Modi represented him with "the head of a hunting dog protruding between my thighs." The catalog adds: "There are three similar drawings of young pilgrims in private collections, but none include the dog…. [Modigliani biographer Pierre Sichel] "ascribes much of the [*Artist Quarter*] biography … to Charles Beadle ... He attributes the anecdote concerning *Le Pèlerin* to Beadle rather than Douglas."

The anecdote in *Artist Quarter* includes Beadle's statement that the drawing was stolen: "Some years after Modi's death the drawing was on show at Zborowski's gallery – just before the latter's death – and was stolen." (*Artist Quarter*, page 227.) Léopold Zborowski died in Paris on 24 March 1932. Therefore, the portrait was still in circulation in 1930, the year that *Expatriates at Large* was released.

Sotheby's dates it from 1916 to 1917, but by November 1916 Beadle was in New York. A more likely time frame is 1914 to 1916, when Beadle's friend and neighbor Beatrice Hastings was involved with Modigliani. (Note how the date corresponds to the 1915 publication of *A Passionate Pilgrimage*.) Regarding the related "Pilgrim" drawings mentioned above, the Sotheby's catalog cites the authoritative J. Lanthemann, *Modigliani, Catalogue Raisonné*, Barcelona, 1970, pp. 345-346, illustration nos. 774, 778, 779. One of these drawings, titled *Le jeune Pèlerin* ("The Young Pilgrim"), was sold at a Christie's auction on 18 June 2007 for $55,636.20. On page 209 of Beadle's novel *The Esquimau of Montparnasse* (1928), the Esquimau protagonist remarks: "I'm merely a pilgrim, I seek and never find."

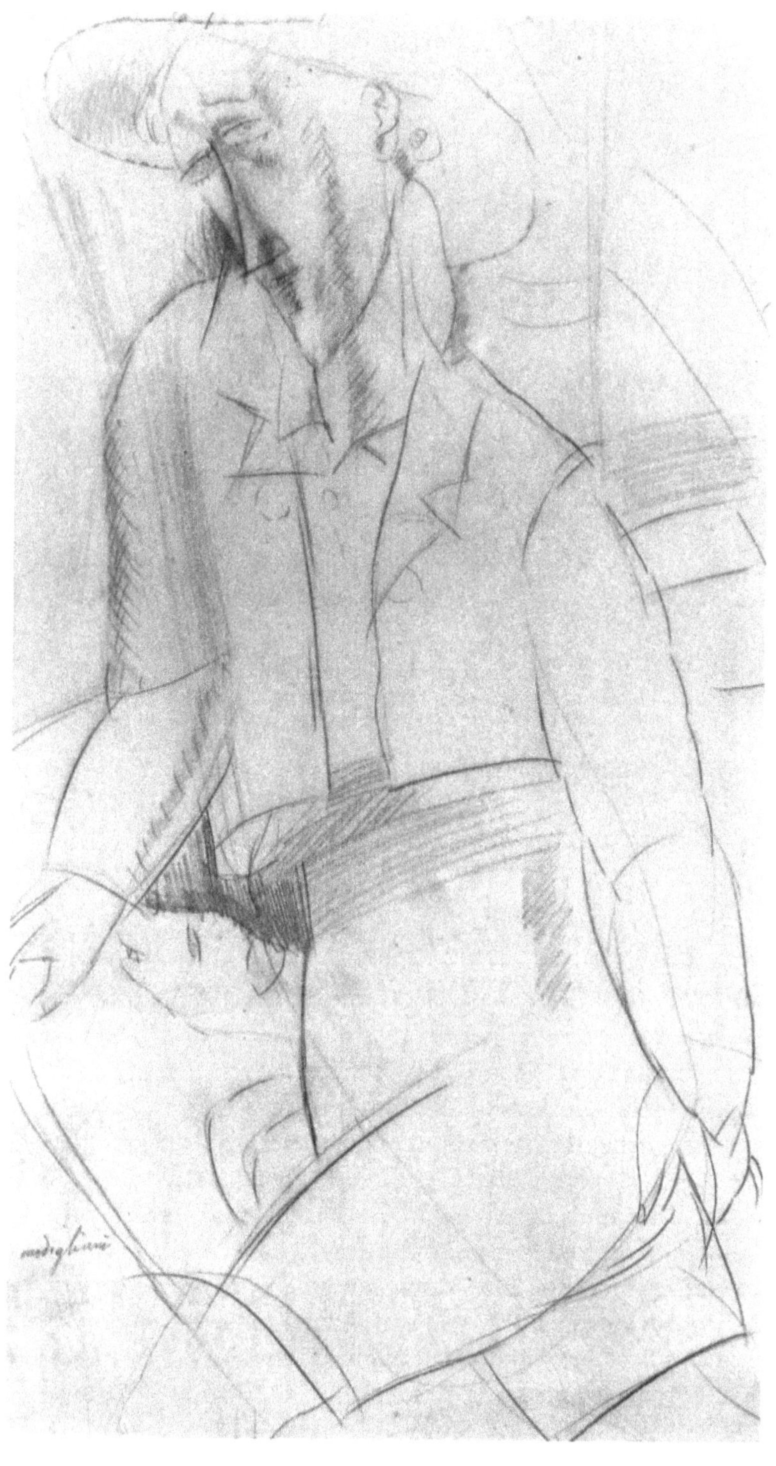

Collectors are searching all over the world for pictures by Modigliani, the artist who died in obscurity, who has now become a sensation in the world of art. A new Modigliani has just come to light, a portrait of the novelist, Charles Beadle (above), whose new book, "Expatriates at Large," is soon to be published by Macaulay.

From the *Omaha World-Herald*, 23 February 1930, p. 57. On 9 November 2024, John Locke discovered a fifth Modigliani "Pilgrim," and one that includes a hunting dog. Note Modigliani's signature at the top left and the words "Le Pèlerin" at bottom left. If this was the portrait that was stolen and never recovered, its disappearance could explain why it doesn't appear in any catalogs and has, until now, been lost to history. As noted above, Lanthemann's *Catalogue Raisonné* includes three other "Pilgrim" portraits "but none include the dog." The newspaper caption unequivocally identifies it as Modigliani's "portrait of the artist Charles Beadle," which we know was still in circulation in 1930, when *Expatriates at Large* was first published. So, it appears that Modigliani made at least *two* portraits of Beadle as the "Pilgrim."

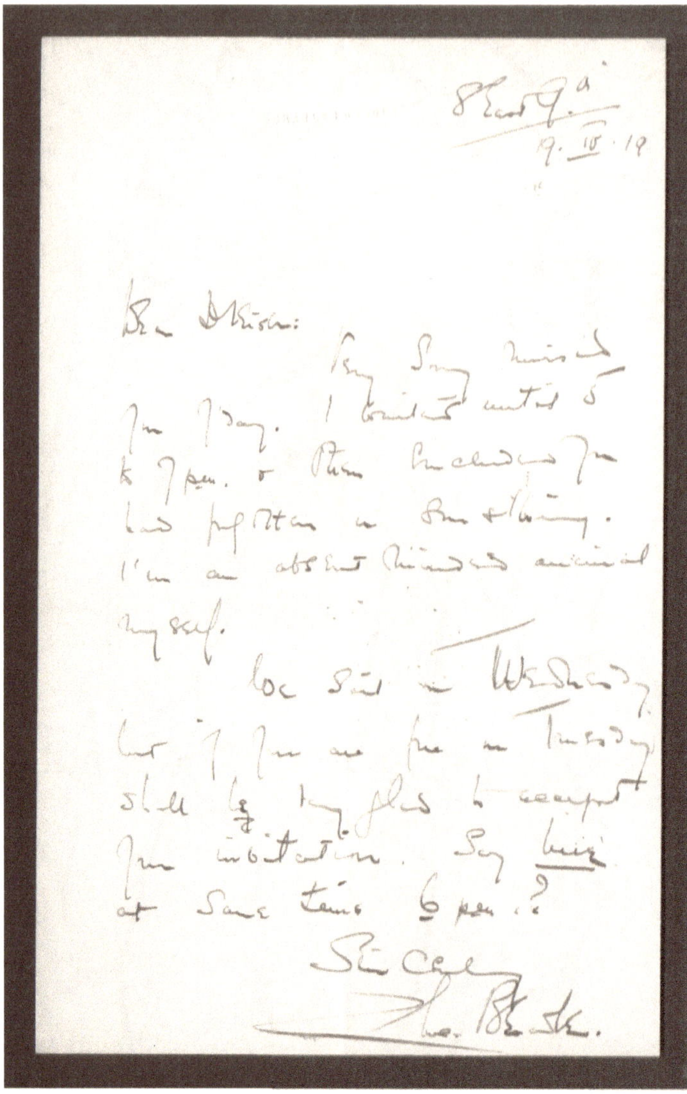

19 October 1919: Letter to author Theodore Dreiser: "8 East 9th / 19.10.19 / Dear Dreiser: Very sorry missed you y'day. I waited until 5 to 7 p.m. and then concluded you had forgotten or something. I'm an absent minded animal myself. We said on Wednesday but if you are free on Tuesday shall be very glad to accept your invitation. Say <u>here</u> at same time <u>6</u> p.m.? Sincerely Chas. Beadle." Beadle's flat was located between University Place and Broadway, three blocks north of Washington Square Park. Dreiser lived at 165 West 10th, a half mile west of Beadle. (Courtesy of the University of Pennsylvania, Kislak Center for Special Collections.)

Autographed copy of *Witch-Doctors*, inscribed "To Frank Harris from Charles Beadle." (Obtained in February 2025.) After Harris self-published his banned multivolume memoir (*My Life and Loves*; 1922 – 1927) it was republished by Jack Kahane's Obelisk Press in 1931: the same publisher who later issued Beadle's *Dark Refuge* (1938). Following the outbreak of WWI, both Harris and Beadle expatriated to New York. Harris became editor of the American edition of *Pearson's*, while Beadle published his stories in *Adventure* and occasionally served in an editorial role. They also traveled to London, Paris, and the South of France at roughly the same time and moved in many of the same circles. Harris settled in Nice in 1922, the same year that *Witch-Doctors* and *My Life and Loves* were published; and he died there in 1931, while Beadle was also residing in the Côte d'Azur. It's possible that Harris introduced Beadle to Kahane or suggested that he approach the innovative publisher with his *Dark Refuge* manuscript. *My Life and Loves* was banned in the United States until 1963, when it was republished by Grove Press.

An artistically enhanced photo of Beadle from the 6 April 1930 edition of the *Buffalo Times*, featured in their "Important Books of the Week in Review" column. Reviewer Kate Burr writes: "'Expatriates at Large' is a novel of genuine power. But the power is impaired by a splurge at brilliancy. Too often the cynicism is forced. The dialogue oscillates too sharply between wit and vapidity. Why ignore the intervening gamut?" Thanks to John Locke for uncovering this rare image.

On 18 May 1930 the *Sioux City Journal* published a copy of the same publicity photo but without any enhancement. Writing about *Expatriates at Large*, reviewer Vera Edwards opens her piece ("Paris Quartier Latin Sans Romantic Gloss") with the sentence: "A portrait of Charles Beadle has just come to light, by Modigliani, the artist who died practically unknown and has now become a sensation in the world of art."

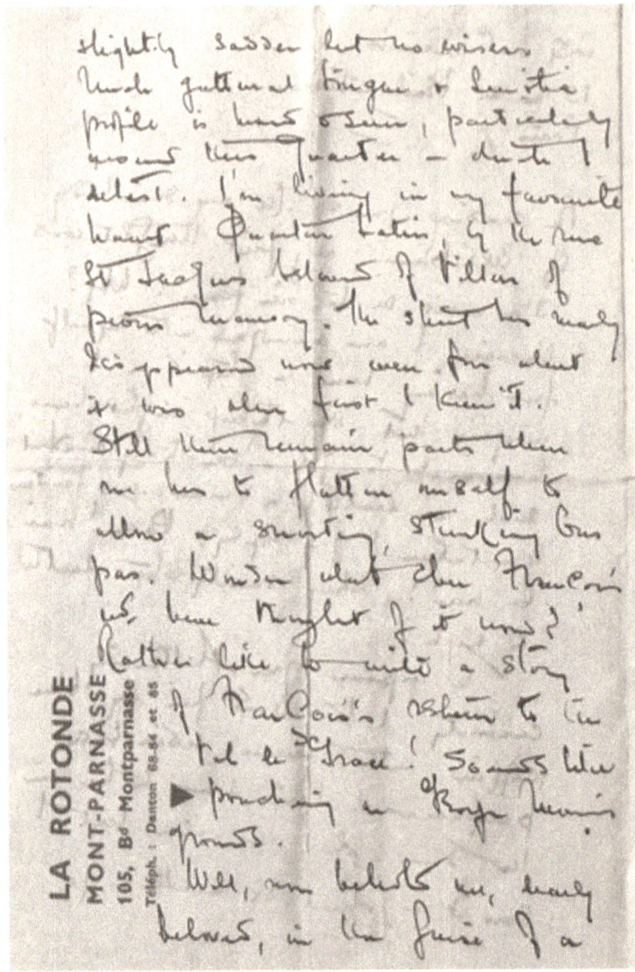

Circa spring 1933: Second page of a letter composed by Beadle and sent to his niece Isabel, with the return address of "Hôtel des Capucines, 13, rue des Feuillantines, Paris." The letter is written on stationery from the Café de la Rotonde, which was located just a few blocks from the Hôtel des Capucines. Courtesy of Patricia and Liz.

Passport-sized snapshot of Isabel Hettie Beadle (1904 – 1999), daughter of Charles' older brother William. If Isabel is thirty years old here, the photo would date from 1934, when she was corresponding with her uncle. Charles severed contact with the rest of his family, but he conducted a lengthy correspondence with his niece, writing from various locations in France. Courtesy of Patricia and Liz.

When and where born	Name, if any	Sex	Name and surname of father	Name, surname and maiden surname of mother	Occupation of father	Signature, description and residence of informant
Seventh August 1946. 9 Saxonbury Road. U.D.	Elizabeth Owen	Girl	Igor Bely	Jane Owen Bely formerly Beadle at 14 Dean Park Road. Bournemouth. U.D.	Chemical Engineer of 29 Rue Assalit. Nice. France.	Jane Owen Bely mother 14 Dean Park Road. Bournemouth.

7 August 1946: Birth of Elizabeth Owen Bely, daughter of Jane Beadle and Igor Bely, at 9 Saxonbury Road (about four miles east of Jane's residence at 14 Dean Park Road, Bournemouth, England). Igor is identified as a "Chemical engineer of 29, rue Assalit, Nice, France."

le _vingt trois août_ mil neuf cent soixante deux, _trois_ heures _trente minute_ est décédé _en son domicile 79 avenue_ _Borriglione Bedat_ _Elizabeth Owen BELY_ née à _Bournemouth Grande Bretagne_ le _sept août mil neuf cent_ _soixante six_ _sans profession_ fille de _Igor Bely quarante six ans traducteur et de_ _Jane BEADLE son épouse_ _interprète domiciliés en cette_ _20 rue Parmentier_ _célibataire_ Dressé le _vingt cinq août_ mil neuf cent soixante deux _dix_ heures, sur la déclaration d _ed Bel de la_ _défunte_

qui, lecture faite a été invité à prendre directement connaissance de l'acte et à le signer avec Nous ____

Adjoint au Maire de Nice, Officier de l'État Civil par délégation

Elizabeth Bely died at the age of sixteen on 23 August 1962 at her home at 99, Avenue Cyrille Besset, Nice. Her death certificate identifies her as the daughter of Igor Bely, "translator," and his wife Jane Beadle, "interpreter." Jane's address is listed as 20, rue Parmentier, Nice.

VILLE DE NICE

ACTE DE DECES
COPIE INTEGRALE

N° 005012 / 2002 Jane BEADLE

Le vingt six novembre deux mil deux à une heure treize minutes, est*****
décédée avenue des Roses "Rimiez", Jane BEADLE, née à Saint-Tropez (Var)
le 8 juillet 1915, en retraite, domiciliée à Nice (Alpes-Maritimes) 8,**
avenue Georges Clémenceau, fille de Charles BEADLE, et de Sylvia Grace**
Ellen HOMSBY, décédés ; veuve de Igor BELY.****************************
Dressé le 28 novembre 2002 à 9 heures 28 minutes sur la déclaration de**
COPPOLANI Tony, 39 ans, Chef de Bureau à Nice (06), 3 rue Alexandre*****
Mari, qui, lecture faite et invité à lire l'acte, a signé avec Nous,****
Andrée GUILLAUMIN, fonctionnaire de la Mairie de Nice, Officier de******
l'Etat Civil par délégation du Maire.**********************************

Nice,
le 7 juin 2022,
Pour copie conforme,
L'Officier de l'Etat Civil délégué,

Aurélie FAREY

Jane Beadle's death record, retrieved by Céline Cardon on 13 June 2022. (The surname of Jane's mother is misspelled, and it appears as "Homsby" instead of Hornsby.) Jane lived at 8, Avenue George Clémenceau, but at the time of her death on 26 November 2002 she was at the Avenue des Roses, in the Rimiez quarter of Nice. This quarter also hosts the Hôpital Les Sources, a geriatric institution. The record also includes the name of Jane's husband, Igor Bely (1916 – 1978).

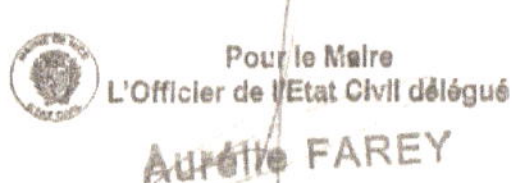

EB 83322

Le *vingt sept janvier* mil neuf cent cinquante-sept, *onze* heures est décédé *20 avenue de la voie Romaine* Charles Beadle domicilié *Nice 4 avenue Victoria* né à *Londres (Angleterre) le vingt six octobre mil huit cent quatre vingt un, sans profession, fils de Jean Beadle et de Isabelle Kay époux décédé, veuf de Sylvia Honsby*

Dressé le *trente janvier* mil neuf cent cinquante-sept, *à dix* heures, sur la déclaration de *Pierre Béritier, 44 ans, employé de commerce domicilié à Nice* qui, lecture faite a signé avec Nous **Paulin GASTAUD** Officier Légion d'Honneur, Médaille Militaire

Adjoint au Maire de Nice, Officier de l'Etat Civil par délégation.

CERTIFIÉ
Conforme à l'acte original

Nice, le **1 4 MAI 2025**

Pour le Maire
L'Officier de l'Etat Civil délégué

Aurélie FAREY

Thanks to her dogged determination while navigating labyrinthian French bureaucracy, my research assistant Céline Cardon finally unearthed the elusive death certificate of Charles Beadle. Though it doesn't reveal where he's buried, it says that he lived at 4, avenue Victoria, in Nice; and that he died on 27 January 1957, at 20, avenue de la voie Romaine, Nice. It also includes the names of his parents and of his wife Sylvia. The Pasteur Hospital is located at 2, avenue de la voie Romaine; so perhaps #20 was part of the Hopital Pasteur Urgences complex. The cert states: "Born London 26 October 1886. Without profession. Son of Henri Beadle and Isabel Kay. Only spouse deceased, widower of Sylvia Honsby." (Note the misspelling of *Hornsby*.)

Timeline

2 January 1844. Birth of Charles' father, Henry Beadle, in Barking, Essex, England.

23 May 1849. Birth of Charles' mother, Isabella Kay, in Liverpool.

12 July 1873. Marriage of Henry Beadle to Isabella Kay at St. John's, the parish church in West Hackney, London. According to the marriage certificate, Henry Beadle and Isabella's father, Peter Kay, were both master mariners. Henry's father, William, was a "gentleman." The newlyweds live on Dunlace Road.

12 July 1876. Birth of poet Max Jacob in Quimper, France. Max will later play a major role in Beadle's novel, *Dark Refuge* (1938), portrayed as the character "Isidore 'Izzy' Ginsberg."

27 January 1879. Birth of Beatrice Hastings (née Emily Haigh) in Hackney. Hastings was romantically involved with Amedeo Modigliani while she was Beadle's neighbor in Montmartre and is portrayed in both Beadle's fiction and nonfiction. She also produced the first English translations of Max Jacob's poetry.

25 October 1881. Birth of Pablo Picasso in Malaga, Spain. Born just days apart, Beadle and Picasso will move in similar circles in both Montmartre and Montparnasse.

26 or 27 October 1881. Birth of Charles Beadle at sea, aboard a Merchant Marine vessel, the SS *Cilurnum*, to Isabella and Henry, the ship's captain. Charles is the youngest of four children. (Henry junior, born in 1874, is the oldest, followed by William, and then Catherine, who died after less than nine months.) The family resides in West Hackney, where Charles is raised.

[Age 2] 2 July 1884. Death of mother from "consumption" (i.e., tuberculosis) at sea, while aboard the SS *Cilurnum*.

[Age 2] 12 July 1884. Birth of Modigliani in Livorno, Italy. In *Dark Refuge*, Modi is portrayed as "Ceccilini" (or "Cecci"), and his biography forms a major part of Beadle's *Artist Quarter* (1941). Modigliani composed a pencil sketch of Beadle circa 1915, a reproduction of which was recently rediscovered by John Locke and included in our new edition of *A Passionate Pilgrimage* (Dominantstar, 2025).

[Age 3] 22 October 1885. Sixteen months after the death of Beadle's mother on the SS *Cilurnum*, the ship is destroyed by fire. A court rules "the explosion and the subsequent loss of the said ship was due to the fire generated by spontaneous combustion in the coal which she had on board, and that the master, officers, and crew used all proper measures ... to save the vessel." Source: Merchant Shipping Acts, 1854 to 1876.

[Age 9] 5 April 1891. English census records that the Beadle family is still residing at 80 Benthal Road, West Hackney.

[Age 9] July 1890. Death of maternal grandmother Catherine Owens, who raised Charles while his father was at sea. Perhaps as a tribute of his enduring affection for her, he will later give his daughter, Jane, the middle name of "Owen." (And Jane will give her daughter, Elizabeth, the same middle name.) On 8 March 2009, Beadle's great-niece Patricia wrote to biographer Neil Pearson and said that Charles "had an odd upbringing." When I spoke with Patricia on 6 October 2022 and asked what she meant by this, she said Beadle's father Henry and his second wife, Sarah Killick, "were frequently away at sea on long voyages, so we think the children were cared for by Henry's sister Sarah Beadle, and by Catherine Owens, Charles' grandmother, who lived with them. Catherine was wealthy and blind."

[Age 17] 6 November 1898. Enlists in the British South African Police (BSAP) as Charles "Marmaduke" Beadle, Regimental No. 1019, Matabeleland Division. (Stationed in southwestern Zimbabwe.) According to Beadle's great-niece Patricia, "Charles and his brother joined the South African Police to fight in the Boer War. London was rife with recruiting posters back then. Henry later went missing. He was possibly killed in the war, although there's no military record of his death. I also heard that Henry may have died in a bicycle accident." Source: Conversation with Beadle's great-niece Patricia on 6 October 2022.

[Age 18-21] Abt. 1899 – 1901. Transvaal, South Africa. Serves in the Second Boer War (BSAP), in Morley's Scouts, Stock and Recovery Department. (Source: autobiographical sketch in "The Camp-Fire" column, *Adventure* magazine, 3 July 1918.) During this period Beadle receives various service awards.

[Age 18] September 1900. At age sixteen, Modigliani contracts pleurisy, which develops into tuberculosis.

[Age 18] Fall 1900. Mashonaland, South Africa. Guest of an Englishman named Mason, who owns a large farm. Beadle is nearly killed by a lioness during a hunt organized there on his behalf. (Source: "My Narrow Escape From a Lioness." *The Brooklyn Daily Eagle*, 7 August 1910.) Historian Geoffrey Pocock informed me that "the only Mason who is listed as a Founder-member of the Legion of Frontiersmen in London is Charles "Chinese" Mason, whom Beadle would have known and have met at early meetings." Source: email from Geoffrey, 18 August 2022.

[Age 19] 18 July 1901. Discharged from British South African Police.

[Age 21] Abt. 1902. Transvaal, South Africa. Employed by Transvaal Customs as Assistant Compound Manager, Witwatersrand Native Labor Association. Source: *Adventure*, 3 July 1918.

[Age 22] August 1904. Travels along the Zambezi River, Chikoti, Zambia. The expedition is chronicled in Beadle's essay, "Our Trip Down the Zambezi," published in the *Wide World Magazine* in 1907.

[Age 23] 1905. Henry Roger Pocock forms the Legion of Frontiersmen; Beadle is a founding member.

[Age 23] December 1905. Government House, Fort Portal, Uganda. "Engaged in recruiting and registering fresh porters" for an expedition into the Congo. (Fort Portal: aka Kabarole, formerly of the Toro Kingdom.) Source: Beadle's essay "Two Close Calls" in *The Captain: A Magazine for Boys and "old Boys,"* June 1910.

[Age 23] 5 January 1906. Beadle's expedition embarks from Fort Portal and enters the Congo, where he's attacked by a buffalo and almost killed by stampeding elephants.

[Age 24] Abt. January 1906. Modigliani expatriates from Italy to Paris.

[Age 24] 19 March 1906. Death of father in Buenos Aires. Charles receives a substantial inheritance, including assets that would normally have gone to his brother Henry, who disappeared in South Africa. This allows Charles to finance future expeditions. Source: conversation with Patricia, 6 November 2022.

[Age 24] Abt. 1906. London. Elected as a Fellow of the Royal Geographical Society (FRGS).

[Age 25] January 1907. Residing at 98 Cazenove Road, Stoke Newington, near the street where he grew up. Source: Masonic registry, listed below.

[Age 25] 11 January 1907. London. Initiated into the Masonic Commemoration Lodge No. 2663. Source: United Grand Lodge of England Freemason Membership Registers, 1751-1921; Folio Number 153.

[Age 25] February 1907. Northumberland Avenue, London. Elected to the Royal Colonial Institute. Source: *Journal of the Royal Colonial Institute*, February 1907, p. 138.

[Age 25] May 1907. Publishes photo-essay, "Our Trip Down the Zambezi," in *The Wide World Magazine*. One photo portrays Beadle with his back to the camera, sporting a pith helmet.

[Age 26] June – July 1907. Picasso paints *Les Demoiselles d'Avignon*. Modigliani visits his studio and sees the painting. In the first volume of *A Life of Picasso* (1991), John Richardson calls it a work that "established a new pictorial syntax" and "the first unequivocally twentieth-century masterpiece, a principal detonator of the modern movement, the cornerstone of twentieth-century art."

[Age 26] September 1907. Resigns from the Masonic Commemoration Lodge.

[Age 26] Abt. February 1908. Travels to Borneo. (Source: diary of Roger Pocock, housed at the Bruce Peel Collection, University of Alberta.) In his autobiographical "Camp-Fire" sketch from 3 July 1918, Beadle notes: "Went to Dutch Borneo, rubber planting. Afterward returned to go to Morocco."

[Age 26] 23 April 1908. Embarks from the Port of London aboard the SS *Agadir*, heading for Morocco.

[Age 26] 4 May 1908. Arrives in El Jadida (originally known as Mazagan), a port city on the Atlantic coast. There he secures the services of William Redman, a British merchant and mercenary versed in the local language and customs. Together they travel seventeen km (about ten miles) north along the coast, to the nearby town of Azemmour.

[Age 26] 19 May 1908. Beadle and Redman embark on a steamer, the *Gibel Kebir*, heading further north to Tangier, where they will join Andrew Belton.

[Age 26] June 1908. A confidential memo penned at the British Foreign Office notes that, after departing from Tangier for a fortnight, Beadle will return around 17 June, to reside at the Hotel Cavilla. Source: letter from Lord Mountmorres to Hubert White, Chargé d'Affaires, Tangier, archived at the British Foreign Office. (Appended to 21 June 1908 memo, as noted in Timeline below.)

[Age 26] 8 June 1908. Prevented from traveling from Tangier to Fes due to civil war. Beadle then boards the *Quetzil*, a steamer headed south, to the coastal city of Larache.

[Age 26] 9 June 1908. Arrives in Larache, where he's joined by Redman and Bolton, who had arrived earlier on another vessel.

[Age 26] 10 June 1908. Redman, Bolton, and Beadle travel inland to Ksar el-Kebir, about thirty km southeast of Larache.

[Age 26] 14 June 1908. After a "wretched journey" during which Beadle is disguised as a dancing girl, the expedition arrives in Fes. Source: Beadle's interview with Moulay Hafid, published in *Pall Mall Magazine*.

[Age 26] 21 June 1908. Following Beadle's successful interview with the Pretender Sultan, Hafid, a memo from the British Foreign Office expresses concern that Beadle, Redman, and a third man (presumably Andrew Belton) "are being treated as if on [a] mission from His Majesty's Government. Steps taken to counteract this impression." The memo adds that Beadle and Redman "arrived from Gibraltar via Larache."

[Age 26] 19 August 1908. According to a contemporaneous newspaper report, Beadle and Redman remain in Fes during the Battle of Marrakech: a decisive encounter between opposing sultans that results in the forces of Moulay Hafid defeating the army of Sultan Aziz. (Source: "Swindon Doctor in Fez," *Swindon Advertiser and North Wilts Chronicle*, 5 May 1911.) Beadle later portrays this conflict in his novel, *The City of Shadows*.

[Age 26] Early October 1908. Publishes photo-essay, "A Talk with the New Sultan of Morocco," in *Pall Mall Magazine*. It includes a picture of Beadle in disguise, his face obscured by veils.

[Age 27] 17 November 1908. Camping in South Africa with fellow members of the Legion of Frontiersmen. Source: Roger Pocock's diary, which notes: "Beadle to camp."

[Age 27] January 1909. Socialite Natalie Barney moves from Neuilly to 20, rue Jacob, Paris, where she hosts a famous salon for the next sixty years. Beadle uses her as the model for his character, "Theodosia" (a wealthy sybarite, poetess, and self-identified "androgyne") in the novel *Dark Refuge*.

[Age 27] Circa early 1909 – June 1909. Morocco. Begins to write fiction. Source: Beadle's contribution to the forum "Contemporary Writers and Their Work," published in *The Editor*, 25 February 1920.

[Age 27] Circa May – June 1909. Repatriates to London from Morocco. Source: "What Has Happened to Muley Hafid," *The Sphere*, 3 July 1909.

[Age 28] 9 December 1909. Henry Roger Pocock's diary notes that Beadle was one of several friends who "visited Pocock the day after an operation on his foot," but their whereabouts are not recorded.

[Age 29] October 1910. The first issue of *Adventure* (dated November 1910) appears on newsstands. Beadle will become one of its major contributors.

[Age 29] abt. February 1911. Publication of *The City of Shadows: A Romance of Morocco* (London: Everett and Co.). According to historian Geoffrey Pocock, Beadle's novel offers the "best account" of the Battle of Marrakech. Source: private communication with Pocock, 12 September 2022.

[Age 29] 2 April 1911. Resides at 69 Antrim Mansions, Hampstead, London. Source: 1911 English census, which identifies Beadle as "author."

[Age 29] July 1911. Café La Rotonde opens at 105, Boulevard Montparnasse. (Source: Luc Bihl-Willette, *Des tavernes aux bistrots: Une histoire des cafés*, Paris: L'Age d'Homme, 1997, p. 174.) The Rotonde is prominently featured in Beadle's novels, *The Esquimau of Montparnasse* and *Dark Refuge*.

[Age 30] 23 September 1912. Picasso leaves Montmartre to rent a flat in Montparnasse, at 242, Boulevard Raspail. His studio is a ten-minute walk from La Rotonde, which he patronizes along with Modigliani, Max Jacob, André Salmon, and many other artists and writers, including Beadle.

[Age 31] October 1912. Publication of Beadle's second novel, *A Whiteman's Burden* (London: Stephen Swift and Co.).

[Age 32] 1914. London. Elected as Fellow of the Royal Geographical Society.

[Age 32] 14 March 1914. British Consulate General, Paris. Marries Sylvia Hornsby (1891 – 1915), daughter of Edmund Hornsby (1861 – 1908) and Teresa Ashwell (1866 – 1940). The couple resides at 4, rue de la Grande Chaumière, a few doors away from the famous Académie de la Grande Chaumière (located at 14, rue de la Grande Chaumière), where Modigliani, Gauguin, and many other artists drew from the model. Source: certified copy of marriage certificate, in possession of Beadle's great-niece Patricia, who recalls having a Picasso print in the house, "for which Sylvia probably modeled."

[Age 32] 3 June 1914. Posts a letter from Sussex to New York's *Century Illustrated* magazine, submitting "3 short stories & an article (a piece of humorous biography)." A watermark at the top-right corner of the stationery reads: "Creek Cottage, Bosham, Sussex." Source: New York Public Library, Century Company records, Series I.

[Age 32] 28 July 1914. Austria-Hungary declares war on Serbia.

[Age 32] 1 August 1914. Germany declares war on Russia. The French General Staff issues the Order for Mobilization.

[Age 32] August 3, 1914. Germany declares war on France. The following day, Britain declares war on Germany.

[Age 33] c. 1915. Modigliani creates a pencil drawing of Beadle, composed in Beadle's flat at Place du Tertre. Titled *The Pilgrim*, the portrait is described in detail in Beadle's Modigliani biography, *Artist Quarter*. (See Illustrations, above.)

[Age 33] January 1915. The hallucinatory drink absinthe is banned in France by presidential decree.

[Age 33] 8 Jul 1915. Birth of daughter, Jane Owen Beadle (1915 – 2002), in Saint-Tropez.

[Age 33] 20 August 1915. Letter from former U.S. President Theodore Roosevelt to Charles Beadle, addressed to Beadle's residence at Villa Robinson in St. Tropez, thanking him for sending his book (probably the forthcoming *A Passionate Pilgrimage*).

[Age 33] September 1915. Publication of Beadle's third novel, *A Passionate Pilgrimage* (London: Heath, Cranton, and Ouseley), while Beadle resides at Villa Robinson, St. Tropez. Source: Last Will and Testament of Sylvia Beadle.

[Age 33] 13 September 1915. Death of Sylvia Beadle, in Cannes. According to her death certificate, she died at the Hotel Beau Rivage (now known as the Hotel Majestic) during a period in which the villas and hotels of Cannes were requisitioned as hospitals, especially for the soldiers of WWI.

[Age 34] 13 November 1915. D. H. Lawrence's novel, *The Rainbow*, is banned in Britain. Censors burn over 1,000 copies.

[Age 35] 30 October 1916. Embarks from Cadiz, Spain aboard the SS *Montserrat*, heading to New York. On the ship's manifest Beadle lists Beatrice Hastings as his "closest friend living in country of departure," noting her address at 13, rue Norvins, Paris (Montmartre). His contact information in Manhattan is Paul Tausig, 104 East 14th Street. An ad for the company Paul Tausig & Son appears in the 28 July 1910 issue of New York's *The Call* newspaper, advertising "Steamship tickets to all parts of the world. Railroad tickets to all parts of the United States and Canada. Money orders and drafts sent to all parts of the world. Foreign money bought and sold. Located in the German Savings Bank Building." The manifest indicates that it's Beadle's first trip to America.

[Age 35] 14 November 1916. Arrives in New York City.

[Age 36] March 1918. Outbreak of the Great Influenza Pandemic, with the first documented case occurring in Kansas. By the end of the pandemic in 1920 about 500 million will be infected worldwide, resulting in fifty million to one-hundred million deaths, with 675,000 fatalities occurring in the United States.

[Age 36] 3 April 1918; 3 May 1918. *Adventure* lists Beadle as a travel expert in its "Ask *Adventure*" column. ("A Free Question and Answer Service Bureau on Information on Outdoor Life and

Activities Everywhere and Upon the Various Commodities Required Therein." His area of expertise is Africa: "Transvaal, N. W. and Southern Rhodesia, British East Africa, Uganda and the Upper Congo … Covering geography, hunting, equipment, trading, climate, mining, transport, customs, living conditions, witchcraft, opportunities for adventure and sport." Beadle's contact info is still c/o Paul Tausig & Son. This is the first of many mail-drop locations that the peripatetic author will provide to *Adventure*: a useful resource for tracking his whereabouts.

[Age 36] 18 May 1918. Publishes "The Christman," the first of twenty-six stories that Beadle will publish in *Adventure*. His contact info is still c/o Paul Tausig & Son.

[Age 36] August 1918. Residing in, or traveling through, Grand Isle, Jefferson, Louisiana. (Source: announcement in *Adventure*, 18 August 1918.) Around this same time Beadle may have visited nearby Mexico.

[Age 36] 12 September 1918. A draft registration card in San Francisco notes that Beadle was living at the King George Hotel on 334 Mason Street, and that he would soon be moving to 119 Central Avenue, in nearby Sausalito. Under "Description of Registrant" it says that he's of medium height with a slender build, blue eyes, and gray hair. His occupation is "Novelist."

[Age 36] 3 October 1918. Contact info in *Adventure* is still Authors' League of America, New York. (Repeated in issues 3 January – 3 February 1919.)

[Age 37] 11 November 1918. Armistice. End of World War I.

[Age 37] 23 April 1919. Departs from New York aboard the SS *Rotterdam*, traveling second class, headed for Paris. His address is registered as 7, Place de Tertre, Paris. Source: Rotterdam, Netherlands, Passenger Lists of the Holland-America Line, 1900-1969.

[Age 37] Late April or early May 1919. Arrives in Paris and resides at the Grand Hotel. Source: Rotterdam, Netherlands, Passenger Lists, etc.

[Age 37] 15 March 1919. *Adventure* publishes the first installment of Beadle's *Witch-Doctors* (a four-part serial appearing between March 15 and May 1, 1919). Published in book form in 1922 by Jonathan Cape (UK) and Houghton Mifflin (U.S.).

[Age 37] 3 April – 3 May 1919. Contact info in *Adventure* is still Authors' League of America, New York.

[Age 37] 18 August – 18 September 1919. Contact info in *Adventure* changes to 7, Place de Tertre, Paris. Repeated in the 3 December 1919 and 3 March 1920 issues.

[Age 37] 19 October 1919. Corresponds with novelist Theodore Dreiser while residing at 8 East 9th Street in Manhattan. Source: University of Pennsylvania, Kislak Center for Special Collections, Rare Books and Manuscripts.

[Age 38] 8 January 1920. Spotted in Paris by occultist Aleister Crowley: "I ran around Paris, and walked into Lapérouse for lunch to find Beadle and Willy!" (The latter was the Pulitzer Prize-winning journalist Walter Duranty.) Source: Aleister Crowley, *The Magical Record of the Beast 666. The Diaries of Aleister Crowley, 1914 – 1920* (London: Duckworth, 1972), p. 90.

[Age 38] 17 January 1920. Volstead Act goes into effect in the United States, prohibiting manufacture and sale of alcohol. Prohibition Era continues until 1933.

[Age 38] 18 January 1920. *Adventure*'s "Camp-Fire" column publishes a letter from Beadle postmarked from Paris.

[Age 38] 24 January 1920. Death of Modigliani.

[Age 38] 25 January 1920. Death of Modigliani's companion, Jeanne Hébuterne, by suicide.

[Age 38] 3 August 1920. Residing in Westminster. Source: announcement in *Adventure*, August 3, 1920: "Care Society of Authors and Composers, Central Buildings, Tothill St., Westminster, London." This same info is repeated in the 18 October 1920 and 16 March 1921 issues.

[Age 38] 3 October 1920. The "Camp-Fire" column publishes a letter from Beadle, postmarked from Paris.

[Age 39] 6 October 1920. Hôpital Cochin, Paris. Death of Modigliani's lover, Simone Thiroux, from tuberculosis.

[Age 39] 18 January 1921. *Adventure*'s "Camp-Fire" column publishes a letter from Beadle, postmarked from Paris.

[Age 39] 21 February 1921. After *The Little Review* publishes excerpts from James Joyce's *Ulysses* in its 1920 issue, the magazine is successfully prosecuted for obscenity, effectively banning *Ulysses* from publication in the U.S.

[Age 39] 3 May 1921. "Camp-Fire" column publishes a letter from Beadle, postmarked from Paris.

[Age 39] 1921. Max Jacob is portrayed by Picasso as a monk in his two large paintings of the *Three Musicians*.

[Age 40] 2 Feb 1922. Sylvia Beach publishes Joyce's *Ulysses* in Paris.

[Age 40] June 1922. After serialization in *Adventure* in 1919, *Witch-Doctors* is issued as a book by Jonathan Cape in London and by Houghton Mifflin in Boston.

[Age 40] 20 June 1922. Beadle's contact information in *Adventure* is now "Île de Lerne," a small island off the northwest coast of France, in the Gulf of Morbihan.

[Age 41] 1923. The Dingo Bar opens at 10, rue Delambre in Montparnasse: the site where Hemingway will meet Fitzgerald, two years later. One of the only all-night pubs in Paris, it will eventually become one of Beadle's favorites. Frequented by artists and writers during the 1920s and Thirties, the clientele includes Pablo Picasso, Aleister Crowley, Nancy Cunard, and Isadora Duncan, who lived in a flat across the street.

[Age 45] April 1927. Publication of Beadle's fifth novel, *The Blue Rib: A Romance of the Riviera* (London: Philip Allan and Co.).

[Age 45] August 1927. Residing in the vicinity of Nice. Source: Beadle's letter to his niece Isabel.

[Age 46] July 1928. An unexpurgated edition of D. H. Lawrence's *Lady Chatterley's Lover* is privately published in Florence. The novel is subsequently declared "obscene" and banned in Britain until 2 November 1960; and in the States until 21 July 1959.

[Age 47] Fall 1928. Publication of Beadle's sixth novel, *The Esquimau of Montparnasse* (London: John Hamilton). A quasi-autobiographical satire about Parisian expatriates, it includes characters based on Modigliani, Beatrice Hastings, Simone Thiroux, and Beadle (as the "Esquimau").

[Age 48] 29 October 1929. A stock market crash ushers in the Great Depression.

[Age 48] February or March 1930. *The Esquimau of Montparnasse* is republished as *Expatriates at Large* (New York: Macauley).

[Age 48] 18 May 1930. The *Sioux City Journal* features a fuzzy image of Beadle, standing in profile, which accompanies a review of *The*

Esquimau of Montparnasse, "Paris Quartier Latin Sans Romantic Gloss."

[Age 49] Circa 1930. Teaching English as a second language at the International School, located at 1, Avenue St-Hilaire, Grasse, Côte d'Azur, France. Source: letter to Isabel.

[Age 49] 19 February 1931. Residing in the vicinity of Nice. Source: letter to Isabel.

[Age 50] Circa October 1931. Visits Paris but doesn't return again until circa May 1933. Source: letter to Isabel, circa spring 1933.

[Age 50] 1 January 1932. Breaks his ankle. After recovering, works as "a cabin boy on a yacht." Source: letter to Isabel, circa spring 1933.

[Age 51] Circa May 1933. Returns to Paris after an absence of "about 18 months." Source: letter to Isabel, circa spring 1933.

[Age 51] May 1933. Paris. The Palais-Royal Press publishes Beadle's seventh novel, *The White Gambit*.

[Age 52] 5 December 1933. End of Prohibition in America.

[Age 52] May 1934. The Dingo's charismatic barman, James "Jimmie" Charters, publishes *This Must Be the Place; Memoirs of Montparnasse*, edited by Morrill Cody, with an Introduction by Ernest Hemingway. Beadle is included in a list of notable patrons mentioned at the back of the book; his favorite drink is said to be a glass of white wine.

[Age 52] 1 September 1934. Jack Kahane's Obelisk Press publishes Henry Miller's novel, *Tropic of Cancer*, which is banned in the U.S. until 1964.

[Age 53] October 1934. Beadle writes a letter to Isabel addressed from the Promenade des Anglais, Nice, which includes the remark:

"The few friends I have are as broke almost as I am. Others don't know me ..."

[Age 56] June 1938. Jack Kahane publishes Beadle's eighth and final novel, *Dark Refuge*. It features thinly disguised portraits of Modigliani, the art dealer Léopold Zborowski, Max Jacob, Beatrice Hastings, and others from the Parisian demimonde.

[Age 57] 6 June 1939. Beadle visits Aleister Crowley at Crowley's home in Chiswick, England: the first of five dinner engagements there, lasting through 23 October (see below).

[Age 57] 1 September 1939. Germany invades Poland.

[Age 57] 2 September 1939. Publisher Jack Kahane dies from heart failure, possibly induced by a suicidal consumption of alcohol.

[Age 57] 3 September 1939. Two days after Germany invades Poland, both France and England declare war on Germany.

[Age 57] 29 September 1939. Beadle is residing at 331 Homewood Road, St. Albans, Hertfordshire. Source: 1939 England and Wales Register. The National Archives; Kew, London; 1939 Register; Reference: RG 101/1668I.

[Age 57] 23 October 1939. Chiswick, England. After Beadle's fifth dinner engagement chez Crowley, the occultist notes in his dairy: "Here to pick my brains regarding Montparno" (Montparnasse). Beadle is gathering material for his only nonfiction book, later published as *Artist Quarter*.

[Age 58] 14 June 1940. German troops enter Paris and march on the Champs-Élysées as Nazi tanks rumble around the Arc de Triomphe.

[Age 58] 20 June 1940. Death of Beadle's mother-in-law, Teresa Ashwell, at La Maison Jaune, Chemin de St. Claude, Antibes. She leaves behind an estate worth £113, 17s, 1d. Source: England and Wales, National Probate Calendar (Index of Wills and Administrations), 1858-1995.

[Age 59] June 1941. Faber and Faber publishes *Artist Quarter: Reminiscences of Montmartre and Montparnasse in the First Two Decades of the Twentieth Century*. Coauthored by Charles Beadle and Douglas Goldring under the portmanteau pseudonym "Charles Douglas," the chronicle will eventually be recognized as a seminal work on the life of Modigliani.

[Age 62] October 30 or 31, 1943. Convinced that she's suffering from a terminal illness, Beatrice Hastings commits suicide in Worthing, Sussex. Shortly afterward, Beadle and Goldring receive a manuscript from her estate: a surrealist novella titled "Minnie Pinnikin," written by Hastings in French, which dramatizes her relationship with Modigliani. According to Modigliani scholar Kenneth Wayne, the curator of the Museum of Modern Art, William Lieberman, was preparing for a 1951 exhibit of Modigliani's work "when he was put into contact with Goldring and Charles Beadle by the art historian Douglas Cooper," and "through them he obtained a copy of Minnie Pinnikin." Source: Kenneth Wayne, *Modigliani and the Artists of Montparnasse*, New York: Harry S. Abrams, 2002, p. 205; and private communication with Wayne.

[Age 62] 24 February 1944. The Gestapo arrest Max Jacob in France.

[Age 62] 5 March 1944. Two days before being shipped to Auschwitz, Jacob dies at the Drancy internment camp.

[Age 63] 2 September 1945. End of World War II.

[Age 64] 7 August 1946. Birth of Beadle's granddaughter, Elizabeth Owen Bely, daughter of Jane Owen Beadle and Igor Bely, in Bournemouth, England.

[Age 65] 10 June 1947. *Short Stories* magazine publishes "Nameless Spy," Beadle's last known original publication.

[Age 70] February 1952. *Short Stories* republishes Beadle's "The Idol," a tale that first appeared in their 10 October 1933 issue.

[Age 75] 27 January 1957. Beadle's death certificate states that he passed away at 20, avenue de la voie Romaine, Nice (which was probably part of the Hôpital Pasteur Urgences complex). It also notes that he was residing at 4, avenue Victoria, Nice. Neither the cause of death nor his burial place are mentioned. The date and location of Beadle's death remained a mystery until 14 May 2025, when Céline Cardon located his death certificate in France. A reproduction of the document appeared for the first time in our newly revised edition of *A Whiteman's Burden*, in August 2025.

Charles Beadle Publications

<u>Literary and genre fiction novels:</u>

— *The City of Shadows: A Romance of Morocco*. London: Everett and Co., 1911.

— *A Whiteman's Burden*. London: Stephen Swift and Co., 1912.

— *A Passionate Pilgrimage*. London: Heath, Cranton and Ouseley: 1915.

— *Witch-Doctors*. London: Jonathan Cape, 1922. Boston: Houghton Mifflin, 1922.

— *The Blue Rib: A Romance of the Riviera*. London: Philip Allan and Co., 1927.

— *The Esquimau of Montparnasse*. London: John Hamilton, 1928. Later republished as *Expatriates at Large*. New York: Macauley Company, 1930.

— *The White Gambit*. Paris: Palais-Royal Press, 1933.

— *Dark Refuge*. Paris, Obelisk Press, 1938.

<u>Nonfiction:</u>

— *Artist Quarter: Reminiscences of Montmartre and Montparnasse in the First Two Decades of the Twentieth Century* (with Douglas Goldring). London: Faber and Faber, 1941. Published under the pseudonym "Charles Douglas." Later republished as *Artist Quarter: Modigliani, Montmartre and Montparnasse*. London: Pallas Athene Arts, 2018.

<u>Short works of fiction and nonfiction in journals and periodicals:</u>

— "Our Trip Down the Zambezi" (nonfiction). *The Wide World Magazine: An Illustrated Monthly of True Narrative, Adventure, Travel, Customs and Sport*, May 1907.

— "A Talk with the New Sultan of Morocco" (nonfiction). *Pall Mall Magazine*, October 1908.

— "What Has Happened to Muley Hafid" (nonfiction). *The Sphere*, 3 July 1909.

— "Two Close Calls" (nonfiction). *The Captain: A Magazine for Boys and "old Boys,"* June 1910.

— "My Narrow Escape From a Lioness." *The Brooklyn Daily Eagle*, "Junior Eagle" section (nonfiction), 7 August 1910.

— "In the Heart of the Kopje. A Story of the Mashonaland Rebellion." *The Wide World Magazine* (nonfiction), June 1912.

— "The Triumph of Tony." *Windsor Magazine*, July 1912.

— "The Better Man." *The London Magazine*, March 1913.

— "Romance for Sylvia." *Cassell's Magazine of Fiction*, March 1913.

— "A Decade of Christmas Dinners." *The Badminton Magazine of Sports and Pastimes* (nonfiction), December 1914.

— "A Pinch of Fever." *The Badminton Magazine*, June 1915.

— "An African Love Song." *The International*, October 1917. This piece appears to be a translation into English of a traditional African poem. (The same issue of the *International* features a lead story by Aleister Crowley titled "Cocaine.")

— "NQO," *The International*. December 1917.

— "The Palm Tree and the Window." Originally slated to appear in the March 1918 *International*. (In the February issue, under the feature "Jugging the March Hare," Aleister Crowley remarked: "Mr. Charles Beadle brought out his Eastern comedy, "The Palm Tree and the Window.") However the story never made it into print.

— "A Doctor of Men. *The International*. April 1918. (In the March issue, under the title "April Showers of Amusement," Crowley writes: "Charles Beadle contributes a delightful sketch of life in the Latin Quarter of Paris with its curious mixture of religious fervor and debauchery."

— "The Christman." *Adventure*, 18 May 1918.

— "The Autocrat." *Everybody's*, June 1918.

— "The Idol of 'It.'" *Adventure*, 3 July 1918.

— "John O'Damn." *Adventure*, 3 August 1918.

— "The Double Scoop." *Adventure*, 18 August 1918.

— "The Cave." *Adventure*, 3 October 1918.

— "The Winged Avenger." *Adventure*, 18 October 1918.

— "The Black Lure." *Adventure*, 18 November 1918.

— A story in *The International*. December 1918. (In the November issue, in a feature titled "The Editor Boosts the Next Number, Aleister Crowley writes: "A story of African magic by Charles Beadle is really better than any of Kipling's African tales. That's going some, but it is true."

— "Rabbit: Philosopher" (novelette). *Adventure*, 18 January 1919.

— "Witch-Doctors" (novella). *Adventure*, 18 March 1919 (part one); 3 April 1919 (part two); 18 April 1919 (part three); 3 May 1919 (part four).

— "Uncle." *Ainslee's*, April 1919.

— "The Breaker of Idols." *Ainslee's*, May 1919.

— "Red Infidel" (novelette). *Adventure*, 18 May 1919.

— "Through Rabat's Eyes." *Argosy*, 2, 16, 19 August 1919.

— "The Tree of Life" (novella). *Adventure*, 3 August 1919.

— "The White Frog." *Adventure*, 18 August 1919.

— "Through Rabat's Eyes" (3-part serial). *Argosy*, 2, 9, 16 August 1919.

— "Captain Tristtam's Miracle." *Adventure*, 18 October 1919.

— "The Inner Hero." *Romance*, November 1919.

— "The Brothers." *Romance*, December 1919.

— "The Woman Courageous." *Ainslee's*, January 1920.

— "The Alabaster Goddess." *Adventure*, 3 January 1920.

— "Technique." *The Blue Magazine*), February 1920.

— "The Spell." *Adventure*, 18 February 1920.

— Untitled. *The Editor: The Journal of Information for Literary Workers* (nonfiction contribution to the forum "Contemporary Writers and Their Work." A discussion of Beadle's writing process), 25 February 1920.

— "An African Love Song." *Coterie* No. 4, 1920. (Reprinted from *The International*, October 1917.) The *Coterie* journal, a quarterly of art, prose, and poetry, boasted an impressive editorial board, including Conrad Aiken, T. S. Eliot, Richard Aldington, and Aldous Huxley. This particular issue features a poem by Douglas Goldring, who would later coauthor the book *Artist Quarter* with Beadle. It also hosts work by several of these contributing editors, poetry by Amy Lowell, and drawings by Zadkine and André Derain.

— "The Singing Monkey" (novella). *Adventure*, 3 March 1920.

— "The Picture." *The Blue Magazine*, June 1920.

— "The King's Sword." *Adventure*, 3 August 1920.

— "The McIntosh" (novella). *Adventure*, 3 October 1920.

— "The Bowl of Alabaster." *Adventure*, 18 September 1920. (A sequel to "Alabaster Goddess.")

— "The City of Baal." *Adventure*, 18 January 1921.

— "Buried Gods," (novella). *Adventure*, 3 September 1921.

— "The Land of Ophir" (3-part serial). *Adventure*, 10, 20, 30 March 1922.

— "Gifts of Diamonds." *Adventure*, 20 June 1922.

— "The Lost Cure" (novella). *Adventure*, 30 January 1923.

— "Sparklers and the Rascals" (novella). *Top-Notch Magazine*, 1 March 1923.

— "The Ghost of Fat Lung." *Argosy Allstory Weekly*, 4 August 1923.

— "Toll of the Jungle." *Tip Top Stories of Adventure and Mystery*, January 1924.

— "The Alabaster Goddess." *The Regent Magazine*, June 1924. (Reprinted from *Adventure*, 3 January 1920 or 1921.)

— "The Philanthropist" (novella). *Short Stories*. 10 June 1924.

— "White Medicine." *Short Stories*, 10 August 1924.

— "The Blond Spiders" (novella). *Adventure*, 20 December 1924.

— "The Wild Man." *Short Stories*, 25 February 1925.

— "White Magic." *The Frontier*, March 1925.

— "Romance," *Adventure*, 20 April 1925.

— "The Mark of the Leopard." *Short Stories*, 10 May 1926.

— "Hashish," "Voyage," and "Small Body." Bob Brown. *Readies for Bob Brown's Machine.* (Cagnes-sur-Mer: Roving Eye Press, 1931), p. 105.

— "Black Velvet." *This Quarter*. March 1932.

— "The Idol." *Short Stories*, 10 October 1933.

— "Mr. Burnjack's Crime." *The 20-Story Magazine*, January 1935.

— "Magic Head." *Short Stories*, 25 October 1938.

— "The King of Many Voices." *Short Stories*, 10 November 1939.

— "The Explorer's Graveyard." *Short Stories*, 25 April 1941.

— "The Baboon's Paw." *Short Stories*, 10 December 1945.

— "Ant Island." *Short Stories*, 10 October 1946.

— "Lost Heritage." *Short Stories*, 25 December 1946.

— "Nameless Spy." *Short Stories*, 10 June 1947.

<u>Posthumously reprinted stories and collections:</u>

— *The City of Baal*. Introduction by John Locke. Castroville, CA: Off-Trail Publications, 2007.

— *The Land of Ophir*. Introduction by John Locke. Castroville, CA: Off-Trail Publications, 2012.

— *The Blond Spiders* (e-book). Good Press, 2020.

— *The Double Scoop* (e-book). DigiCat, 2022.

<u>Commentary in *Adventure*'s "The Camp-Fire" column:</u>

— 3 July 1918. A detailed five-paragraph autobiographical sketch, from which we can draw various threads from Beadle's early life, including childhood trips into Asia and various titles of employment later in Africa. (The letter was composed circa May 1918. See John Locke's "Introduction" to *The City of Baal*, p. 13.)

— 18 January 1920: A commentary on the walled cities of Zululand (with a passing reference to Sir Richard Burton).

— 3 October 1920. Describes the events that inspired "The McIntosh."

— 18 January 1921. Some remarks about "The City of Baal."

— 20 June 1922. Provides biographical background to "Gifts of Diamonds."

Commentary in *Adventure*'s "Ask Adventure" column:

— "Diseases of East Central Africa." 18 September 1918.

— "The Rhodesian Mounted Police." 18 September 1919.

Letter to *Romance* magazine's "Meeting-Place" forum:

— January 1920. Beadle remarks that "Personally I have a theory that a writer should only use material which he has' more or less actually lived. Anyway, I work on that principle." And he adds: "That is all writing is (to me); a mania to tell other folk what I see in my walks abroad."

Reviews of Beadle's Novels

<u>*The City of Shadows* (1911)</u>:

— *The Times* (London).

— *Manchester Courier*.

— *Daily Mirror* (London), 7 April 1911, p. 7.

— "Moorish Revolution." *The Guardian Journal* (Nottingham), 7 March 1911, p. 15.

— *Westminster Gazette* (London), 11 March 1911, p. 1.

— *Croydon Chronicle and East Surrey Advertiser* (London), 18 March 1911, p. 20.

— *The Globe* (London), 7 April 1911, p. 6.

— *The Bookseller* (London), 14 April 1911, p. 11.

— "A Story of Morocco." *Evening Express* (Liverpool), 20 April 1911, p. 3. (Copied verbatim from the *London Globe*.)

— *The Academy and Literature* (London), 6 May 1911, pp. 555-556.

— "A Moorish Romance." *Sheffield Daily Telegraph* (Yorkshire, England), 25 May 1911, p. 3.

— *The Queenslander* (Brisbane, Australia), 3 June 1911, p. 20.

— "New Books," *The Age* (Melbourne, Australia), 10 June 1911, p. 3.

— *The Australian Town and Country Journal* (Sydney), 14 June 1911, p. 55.

— "Morocco Bound," by Charles Lowe. *London Daily Chronicle*, 21 July 1911, p. 6.

A Whiteman's Burden (1912):

— *The Athenaeum: Journal of Literature, Science, the Fine Arts, Music and the Drama* (London), 26 October 1912, p. 477.

— *The Scotsman* (Midlothian, Scotland), 4 November 1912, p. 2.

— *The Review of Reviews* (London), 1912, vol. 46, p. 696.

A Passionate Pilgrimage (1915):

— *Freeman's Journal* (Dublin), 2 October 1915, p. 8.

— *The Devon and Exeter Gazette*, 2 November 1915, p. 6.

— "Echoes from Everywhere: What Men and Women are Talking of." *Liverpool Echo*, 11 November 1915, p. 4. (A list of quotations from various books, including three from *A Passionate Pilgrimage*.)

Witch-Doctors (1922):

— *The Scotsman* (Midlothian, Scotland), 13 July 1922, p. 2.

— *The Times* (London), 28 July 1922, p. 13.

— *Punch* (London), 16 August, 1922, p. 168.

— "An American God." *Westminster Gazette* (London), 29 August 1922, p. 12.

— *The Province* (Vancouver), 30 August 1922, p. 6.

— *The Kingston Whig-Standard* (Kingston, Ontario), 2 September 1922, p. 4.

— *Calgary Herald* (Calgary, Alberta), 2 September 1922, p. 2.

— *The Topeka State Journal* (Topeka, Kansas), 9 September 1922, p. 8.

— *The News Journal* (Wilmington, Delaware), 9 September 1922, p. 8.

— *The Kansas City Star* (Kansas City, Missouri), 9 September 1922, p. 6.

— *Evening Public Ledger* (Philadelphia), 12 September 1922, p. 18.

— *Liverpool Post and Mercury*, 13 September 1922, p. 9.

— *New York Herald*, 17 September 1922, p. 19.

— *Buffalo Morning Express and Illustrated Buffalo Express* (Buffalo, New York), 17 September 1922, section 7, p. 4.

— "Fiction Snapshots," *New York Times Book Review and Magazine*, 17 September 1922, p. 7.

— *Buffalo Courier* (Buffalo, New York), 24 September 1922, p. 15.

— *New York Tribune*, 24 September 1922, section 5, p. 7.

— "Charles Beadle Tells Something about Himself." *Deseret News* (Salt Lake City), 30 September 1922, section 5, p. 3.

— *Detroit Free Press*, 15 October 1922, p. 12.

— *Daily Arkansas Gazette* (Little Rock, Arkansas), 15 October 1922, p. 4.

— *Hartford Courant*, 15 October 1922, p. 13.

— *Democrat and Chronicle Rochester* (Rochester, New York), 15 October 1922, unpaginated, section B.

— "The Witch Doctors." *Oakland Tribune* 15 October 1922, section S, p. 8.

— *The Chattanooga News*, 28 October 1922, p. 8.

— *Omaha Daily Bee*, 5 November 1922, p. 8.

— *The Buffalo Times*, 26 November 1922, p. 45.

The Blue Rib: A Romance of the Riviera (1927):

— *Aberdeen Press and Journal*, 21 April 1927, p. 3.

— *Montrose Standard* (Angus, Scotland), 22 April 1927, p. 6.

— *Birmingham Post* (West Midlands, England).

— *The Observer* (London), 15 May 1927, p. 8.

— *Sheffield Daily Telegraph* (Yorkshire, England), 11 June 1927, p. 10.

The Esquimau of Montparnasse (1928):

— *Sheffield Independent* (Yorkshire, England), 12 November 1928, p. 3.

— *Birmingham Daily Gazette* (Warwickshire), 22 November 1928, p. 3.

— *Northern Whig* (Antrim, Northern Ireland), 24 November 1928, p. 11.

Expatriates at Large (1930):

— *Argus-Leader* (Sioux Falls, South Dakota), 9 March 1930, p. 14.

— *Saturday Review of Literature*, April 1930).

— *Buffalo Times* (Buffalo, New York), 6 April 1930, p. 6-B.

— *Buffalo Evening News* (Buffalo, New York), 19 April 1930, p. 4.

— *Kansas City Star*, 19 April 1930, p. 8.

— *San Francisco Examiner*, 20 April 1930, p. 10 E.

— *Boston Globe*, 26 April 1930, p. 13.

— *Sioux City Journal* (Sioux City, Iowa), 18 May 1930, unpaginated. Features a photo of Beadle standing in profile.

— *The Minneapolis Star*, 3 June 1930, p. 15.

— *Birmingham News*, 8 June 1930, p. 4.

— *The Gazette* (Cedar Rapids, Iowa), 22 June 1930, p. 5 A.

— *New York Times Saturday Review of Books and Art*, 22 June 1930, p. 9.

— *St. Louis Post-Dispatch* (St. Louis, Missouri), 2 July 1930, p. 3 C.

— *Atlanta Constitution*, 3 August 1930, p. 8.

— *Detroit Free Press*, 17 August 1930, part four, p. 4.

— *Los Angeles Evening Post-Record*, 19 August 1930, p. 2.

— *Brooklyn Daily Eagle*, 10 September 1930, p. 18.

— *Book Review Digest*, 1931, volume 26, p. 62.

<u>The White Gambit (1933)</u>:

— *The Daily Times-News* (Burlington, North Carolina), 10 June 1933, p. 2.

<u>*Artist Quarter: Reminiscences of Montmartre and Montparnasse in the First Two Decades of the Twentieth Century* (1941)</u>:

— *The Observer* (London), 13 July 1941, p. 3.

— *Birmingham Post* (Birmingham, West Midlands, England), 22 July 1941, p. 2.

— *News Chronicle* (London), 1941.

— *Western Mail* (Cardiff, South Glamorgan, Wales), 5 August 1941, p. 2.

— *Time and Tide* magazine (London), 1941.

— *The Gazette* (Montreal), 29 November 1941, p. 21.

Posthumous Reviews and Commentaries

"*A Passionate Pilgrimage* was first published in 1915, when it earned the acclaim of being one of ten books blacklisted for years by Britain's Circulating Libraries Association. Modern readers may be puzzled by this fact when they read this novel; but its descriptions of free-ranging sensual encounters between the protagonist and a host of consenting women made it a scandalous piece at the turn of the century. Why reissue *A Passionate Pilgrimage* now? The introductory notes (which are extensive and vital to understanding the novel's continuing importance) state that the novel: 'provides a variety of clues about Beadle's early life.' In so doing, it reveals the essence of social and psychological transformation, toeing the line between autobiography and a fictional discourse containing many topics vital to understanding not just these times, but modern morals and values. Its subjects and considerations make for thoroughly engrossing reading, presented in a way that builds the character's focus, emphasizes his differences, and ultimately creates a captivating tale of transformation and insight. Libraries that choose *A Passionate Pilgrimage* will find it highly recommendable to students of literature; teachers seeking novels that hold lively debates about not just banned literature, but banned ideas; and book clubs that will find *A Passionate Pilgrimage* thoroughly thought provoking." – Diane Donovan, Senior editor, *Midwest Book Review*, March 2025.

"This new publication of *Dark Refuge* is a helpful addition for all those interested in the adventurous life of bohemian author Charles Beadle … His book *Artist Quarter* is the source of both fictional and nonfictional stories about Modigliani still prevalent today. In this book expertly edited, annotated, and commented upon by Couteau and Sawyer-Lauçanno, we gain greater insight into Beadle's life and the origins of his novel, *Dark Refuge*, that thankfully is once more available to the public." – Dr. Henri Colt, Emeritus Professor of Medicine at the University of California and author of *Becoming Modigliani*, January 2024.

"There is no doubt in my mind that *Dark Refuge* deserved to be reprinted, especially in its present form which reinforces the text with numerous annotations, a long Afterword which charts Beadle's life and activities, photographs, a bibliography, and additional material. Rob Couteau, who is largely responsible for discovering so much about Beadle and his publications, deserves our thanks for all his hard work." – Jim Burns, "Three Curious Interwar Novels," *The Penniless Press Online*, October 2023.

"*Dark Refuge* appears in print for the first time since its original publication in 1938, presenting a world traveler's experiences with bohemian life in Paris in a novel that also serves (thanks to Rob Couteau) as a biography of Beadle's life. Extensive annotated references link Beadle's experiences to his fictional representations, offering a literary backdrop for understanding both the atmosphere and progression of his fiction and its roots in reality. Readers should be prepared for a sexual romp that is ribald, explicit, and thoroughly steeped in Beadle's personal experiences of the times....Whether exploring drug experiments and the revelations that follow them or descending into the sordid and colorful world of bohemian Paris, Beadle flavors all of his impressions with the same attention to flowery detail that makes his writing so timeless.... Pair this with the extensive notes and annotated references Couteau injects to not just explain but expand the story, for a sense of the unique literary and historical importance of this reappearance of Beadle's rare classic, which has been out of print for far too long. Libraries seeking literary representations of the marriage between fiction and nonfiction will find *Dark Refuge* a fine example. The 200+ annotated notes come from previously unpublished letters and documents, combining with photos and historical reviews to represent a hallmark of not only literary fiction, but biographical research. *Dark Refuge* deserves a place in any library strong in works of literature that represent the intersection between fictional devices and biographical inspection, whether or not there is prior knowledge of or interest in Beadle's works and importance." – Diane Donovan, Senior editor, *Midwest Book Review*, November 2022.

ALSO BY ROB COUTEAU

Fiction:

Doctor Pluss
Afterword by Jim Feast

Essays and Interviews:

Collected Couteau

More Collection Couteau
Introduction by James Dempsey

*Portraits from the Revolution: Interviews with the
Protestors from Occupy Wall Street*

Biography:

*Picasso, Modigliani, and a Blind Man Crazy for Color. Illustrated by
Picasso's Model and Muse, Sylvette David*

Poetry:

The Sleeping Mermaid
Introduction by Christopher Sawyer-Lauçanno

Selected Poems
Introduction by Ed Foster

Memoir:

Intimate Souvenirs
Introduction by Robert Roper

"Here we have a new, possibly classic memoir of New York. It begins in Gravesend, Brooklyn, and moves outward, to Manhattan and Paris ... That there still exists a path to a writer's life that is not a dutiful march through creative writing academies, with perhaps the apotheosis of becoming a teacher of yet more academy-shaped writers, is heartening to learn. Couteau does not make fun of that approach nor of any other, but he does model something much different, and to see him continuing to write books like this one, which well deserves a place on his already considerable shelf of valued books, is excellent news." – Robert Roper, author of *Nabokov in America: On the Road to Lolita* and *Now the Drum of War*.

"*Intimate Souvenirs* is a memoir with a message that embraces a coming-of-age story with a background in!970s Brooklyn. This influenced Rob Couteau's progressive work as an adult with the homeless and impoverished, from America to Venezuela ... Couteau brings to vivid life his impressions of the world from an early age, and his evolving place in it ... As Couteau moves through different worlds (including France), encountering literary, artistic, and social figures, he finds a new sense of home, place, and purpose which translates to social and philosophical revelations about life, religion, and the world. Ultimately, his very method of engaging with other worlds is what links readers to his life and the exuberant march of its encounters and revelations.

Five hundred pages go by in the blink of an eye as readers absorb an intriguing memoir that deserves a place in any library strong in memoirs that embrace literary, artistic, and social transformation The book features an Introduction by acclaimed novelist Robert Roper and an Afterword by literary biographer Christopher Sawyer-Lauçanno." – Diane Donovan, Senior editor, *Midwest Book Review*.

"In the lanes and alleys of Paris, at the turn of the!9th century, a nearly sightless art collector wandered on the arm of a young girl. The collector, aided by his guide, amassed a treasure trove of work by the greatest artists of the day: Modigliani, Picasso, Utrillo, and more. Yet he died poor, forced to sell the work for a fraction of its value during the dark days of World War I. Little is known about the life – or the fate – of the girl who led the blind collector through the City of Light. This is the story of Léon Angély, the myopic lover of art, and Joséphine, the 'eyes' of Angély, the girl who enabled him to visit artists and 'see' their art. The story is told with a rare grace by author Rob Couteau in his new book, *A Blind Man Crazy for Color*. Couteau has mined the literature for gems, and displays them with abandon, through the generous quotations and anecdotes set within his own lustrous prose. The fine text is accompanied by enchanting illustrations by Sylvette David. In David, the book finds both painter and participant in the milieu Angély so loved: in!954, David began modeling for Picasso, becoming the 'girl with the ponytail' in hundreds of works, including the artist's monumental sculpture, *Sylvette*, in Rotterdam ... We found the friendship of Léon and Joséphine a balm for our souls, so bruised in these difficult days of violence and disease. We hope the story is healing for you, too."
– *Witty Partition*

"In his strange, fascinating new book, writer-painter Rob Couteau assembles and unearths what little can be known about the mysterious collector Léon Angély ... Adding another layer of resonance to Couteau's slim volume are the charming illustrations by Lydia Corbett, also known as Sylvette David, the ponytailed model and muse who inspired Picasso's 'Sylvette' period."
– Scott Sublett, *New Art Examiner*.

"Sylvette David's sketches accent this colorful portrait of Léon's life, motivations, involvement in the art world, and the pieces he collected. Previously unpublished information about the blind man's passion and his influence on the art world enhances a survey that should be required reading and acquisition for any serious art history student and the libraries catering to them ... Readers also receive revealing inspections of the process of interviewing artists and capturing their historical impact, adding to *A Blind Man Crazy for Color*'s importance as a survey that goes beyond a singular biography of an art enthusiast to delve into the world of artists, art appreciation, and muses ... Serious art libraries should consider this extraordinary recreation of artistic ambitions against all odds a mainstay that stands out in many different ways." – Diane Donovan, *Midwest Book Review*.

SELECTED POEMS

"There is a deep tenderness in these words, mingled with the sadness of age. If one goes back to the early poems addressed to Edda Maria Sangrígoli, one can find the tenderness there, too, as it is in his work as a case manager for the poor and homeless. There is much to admire in Couteau's oeuvre, but this tenderness stands out among so many things that make reading his work clearly an important experience."
– Ed Foster, founder of Talisman House Publishers, and editor
of *Talisman: A Journal of Contemporary Poetry and Poetics*.

"*Selected Poems* features 101 poems, 40 of which have been printed in numerous print and online journals since 1985. The rest are new to this collection and represent a satisfying blend of old and new works designed to appeal to newcomers and prior fans alike. Rob Couteau's works are diverse. They follow no set poetic structure, even defying some of them when the muse strikes and special needs indicate that the subject is more important than poetic form ... His inspections of artistic, literary, and social issues are astute and compelling. Don't anticipate set structures, uniform poetic approaches, or singular subjects. *Selected Poems* offers a freewheeling approach to poems and life alike and is a thought-provoking, evocative gathering of works recommended for literary readers not bound by convention or rules."
– Diane Donovan, *Midwest Book Review*.

Couteau provides that familiarity by the structure of his interview questions, which probe the foundation beliefs of each figure … From the possibility that Nabokov suffered unconscious doubts about his own value that led him to insist that the world acknowledge him as a genius to the underlying patriotism of counterculture icons who were commonly seen as rebels ('Ginsberg continually affirmed that, essentially, Jack had always been a sort of patriotic American,' says Sawyer-Lauçanno. 'This had never not been part of who he was. It was patriotic to get into an automobile made in Detroit and drive across the country'), both essays and interviews are designed to make readers think about underlying psychology, social perceptions, and cultural change.

Readers seeking not just a literary presentation but a lively analysis of selected wordsmiths and their lives and influences must add *More Collected Couteau* to their reading lists. It's a powerful presentation that offers much insight … and which should find its way into many a college classroom as well." – Diane Donovan, *Midwest Book Review*.

"Good luck trying to pin down Rob Couteau. Name the genre, and Couteau has almost certainly been there and done that. Poet, novelist, essayist, critic, journalist, memoirist, and travel writer, Couteau is not one to be hampered by constraints. He passes easily from one form of literature to another as if the borders between them did not exist for him. Perhaps they don't.

Couteau has been called a 'literary enthusiast,' and although he certainly is enthusiastic about literature (and indeed all art), the phrase carries the smack of the amateur about it, and Couteau is anything but. He is, in fact, an undeniably consummate professional. He is an independent scholar in every meaning of the word – unaligned with any institution except for the literary and artistic canon he so loves, and a thinker who comes to his own conclusions …

This collection gives the reader a good sampling of Couteau's literary and scholarly talents, not the least of which are his interviews with writers he admires. Having spent many years as a journalist, I believe I have some ability to recognize and admire an artful interviewer, and Couteau is a master. His preparation is comprehensive, meticulous, and profound. His understanding of the process of writing in so many genres allows him insights into the particular problems faced by the writers he interviews. His style is conversational and relaxed, but deceptively so; he is always in control of the interview. This said, however, when a sudden fact or insight takes the interview down unexpected pathways, Couteau has the aesthetic nimbleness to recognize the opening and to follow it.

The collection features interviews with biographers, memoirists, historians, an inner-city antiviolence activist, and the creator of LSD. You'll also find herein Couteau's writings on literature, which I hesitate to call criticism since they lack the worst features of much literary criticism, which can be clogged with so much pretentiousness, cant, and philosophical obfuscation that it would take a plunger of Brobdingnagian proportions to restore a healthy flow. Couteau's essays are often rhapsodic appreciations and evocations of the work under study, and are stuffed with both insights and joy.
– James Dempsey, author of *The Tortured Life of Scofield Thayer*.

THE SLEEPING MERMAID

"Novelist and literary enthusiast Rob Couteau brings readers part of his love with *The Sleeping Mermaid*, a book of flowing poetry and thought that asks plenty of questions and offers plenty of answers. *The Sleeping Mermaid* is a poetry collection well-worth considering."
– Willis M. Buhle, *Midwest Book Review*.

"In Couteau's work there is no phoniness, no artifice for the sake of artifice – though in the great French tradition this poet knows so well, there is some art for the sake of art. Couteau does not venture into realms of obscurity where meaning is confined to the interior of a Klein bottle; his poems all have direct force, subjects, even verbs. He is intent on having his readers share in his observations, whether it be his artful retelling and reinterpretations of Native American story and song, or his appraisal of how a woman parades across the avenue. He does not ever sacrifice ordinary sense for an extra-ordinary significance. Instead, he speaks with fervor, with something to say, with something he wants us to hang onto and, in the process, come to an understanding of why it matters not just to him but should matter to us.

I think it was William Carlos Williams who said that poetry is belief. Couteau believes in belief, believes that poetic worth is measured in faithfulness to what is, what has been, and what could be. These are his talismans; these are the points where he begins and ends. His poetic excursions take us to many places: to the Paris of Rimbaud and Picasso, to the Native North Americans, to mythology and history and how the woman he is encountering is seducing him as he seduces her (and us), and finally, how alone, the cosmos plays itself out at 3 a.m. when the only lap dog is memory." – Christopher Sawyer-Lauçanno.

PORTRAITS FROM THE REVOLUTION: INTERVIEWS WITH THE PROTESTORS FROM OCCUPY WALL STREET

"Most American readers will harbor a prior, casual familiarity with the Occupy Wall Street movement of 2011 based on newspaper headlines and events of the times; but for a more in-depth survey of the philosophies, approaches, and concerns of the protests, *Portraits from the* Revolution is the item of choice, offering unprecedented depth and detail on the history and lasting impact of the Occupy Wall Street movement.

Chapters explore not just each individual's actions but their backgrounds, reasons for participating in Occupy Wall Street, and their experiences. And it offers criticism of media reporting of the movement's history, intentions, and approaches.

From how participants decided to react to violent antagonism against the Occupy movement to the social and political ramifications of not just Occupy but the elements it opposed, these interviews capture participants from all walks of life, from teens to full-time workers, and turn the newspaper reports into a series of personal vignettes about Occupy's deeper meaning.

– Diane Donovan, *Midwest Book Review*

"Intellectual freshness, richness, and potency … Couteau is an impressively creative writer, whom Barney Rosset urged me to review." – Jim Feast, *Evergreen Review*.

"Rob Couteau describes *Doctor Pluss* as 'fiction based on actual dialogues with schizophrenic patients, diabolically "sane" psycho-therapists, and well-meaning yet unerringly destructive social workers. It chronicles the descent of an eccentric, sardonic, and witty psychiatrist into what appears to be a state of complete madness.'

His intention to metaphorically and realistically portray and contrast the madness of psychiatric process as well as its patients is powerfully wrought in a story about patients 'surviving this holocaust of forgetfulness.' During this process, their identities and personalities are lost in the institutional morass of a center purported to excel in rehabilitation, but which actually contains many ethical and personal challenges to the new psychiatric resident at the Walt Whitman Asylum for Adults, Dr. Pluss.

It's a place of rage and despair, of ambiguity where hope and horror run close together, and daily gives Dr. Pluss pause for thought about his patients and his role in their lives: 'In her own unwitting way,' Pluss mused, Evelyn personified the dual aspects of the godhead: horror and joy; awe and fascination.'

Novellas typically are hard-hitting but often artificially succinct in their brevity. Often, one is left wanting for more. The best of them (of which *Doctor Pluss* is one) excels in taking this succinctness to its most logical conclusion, creating slices of life which are narrow enough to receive full-bodied flavor as the plot and characters develop.

One does not wish for more in *Doctor Pluss*. It's complete unto itself, exceptionally well developed, and emotionally compelling, connect-ing metaphorical traditional roles of doctor and patient, linking them in unexpected ways.

Couteau is not afraid to push the literary boundaries of convention in pursuit of a different form of descriptive truth, bringing readers along in a rollicking ride through schizophrenic experience that ultimately questions the foundations of reality and perception from both sides of the therapist's couch. His interpretations and descriptions of the schizophrenic experience are particularly astute, astonishing, and evocatively described …

Readers who choose *Doctor Pluss* are in for a treat. It's like *One Flew Over the Cuckoo's Nest* on steroids: a thought-provoking examination of sanity, insanity, and the crossover process that leaves readers thinking long after this therapeutic slice of life is consumed.
– Diane Donovan, *Midwest Book Review*